BENEATH A KILLER'S MOON

He watches her pass his house, his eyes boring into her back.

She's found him. Followed him to his own street, to his house. Of course, she knows the way.

"Hello," he says, approaching her by the streetlight. "Hello, Danni."

"I . . . I beg your pardon?"

She's staring at him, eyes wide.

"I see you found me," he continues. "But you were always clever, weren't you?"

She takes a step back. "I don't know what in the hell you're talking about."

"It's me," he says. "You know me. And I have something for you. This," he says softly. And he shows her.

He thinks she'll scream, and he's moving toward her as he speaks, but she surprises him. She spins away and sprints down the street.

He races after her, a fierce joy tearing at him. She remembers! He loves this game. *They* love it. If only she doesn't scream . . .

SILVERCAT

• • •

Kristopher Franklin

BANTAM BOOKS
NEW YORK • TORONTO • LONDON • SYDNEY • AUCKLAND

SILVERCAT

A Bantam Book / February 1990

ISBN 0-553-28333-2

Published simultaneously in the United States and Canada

*Bantam Books are published by Bantam Books, a division of
Bantam Doubleday Dell Publishing Group, Inc. Its trademark,
consisting of the words "Bantam Books" and the portrayal of a
rooster, is Registered in U.S. Patent and Trademark Office and in
other countries. Marca Registrada. Bantam Books, 666 Fifth
Avenue, New York, New York 10103*

PRINTED IN THE UNITED STATES OF AMERICA

KRI   0 9 8 7 6 5 4 3 2 1

Silvercat is dedicated to my mother:
Pat Franklin Fletcher
1914 - 1988

She always knew, and maybe she still does

PROLOGUE

Monday–Tuesday, October 14 and 15

The fire in the trash barrel billows orange in the twilight as he burns his clothes. He steps closer, partly for warmth from a cold wind sliding down the piñon-covered foothills across the interstate, and partly from curiosity. He's never before smelled fresh blood burning and the odor is sweet, nearly exotic.

He stands naked at a spot where a thousand miles of the Great Plains butts abruptly against the Rockies. Cars are passing on the highway, using their headlights now, and one could turn in at any moment. But he knows it won't.

He goes to the open trunk of the vintage Buick Roadmaster where he's laid out fresh clothes, reluctant to lose the feeling of the night air on his bare flesh, and he glances uneasily at the squat tile building at the center of the rest area because . . .

Come on, Danni . . .

. . . because she's teasing him again, even now. Because it never ends. Not even when he's so sure.

Dressed and sitting behind the wheel of the big car, he turns on the dome light to study a torn photograph lying beside him on the seat. As always, the uncertainty is returning, but much faster now than it once did. He stares at the photo and then notices the folded map next to it. "Rocky Mountain National Park," its cover reads. "Estes Park, Colorado."

Before he drives away, pulling past a dusty green compact with Texas plates, he tosses the map into the fire.

In full darkness, the animals return to the rest stop. Rock squirrels pick through discarded plastic wrappers and quarrel loudly over bits of potato chips and bologna sandwich. Then they retreat to safety in holes next to the cement picnic tables when the coyotes arrive, darting under the interstate through a weed-choked culvert. The big scavengers cross the dying brown grass, quartering against the wind toward the smell of food. They flinch away from the fire in the trash barrel and follow a fresher scent toward the tile building, but the smell of men is too strong there, and their fear overpowers their appetites. They whine and snap at each other outside a metal door, and occasionally howl, but go no closer. And in the dawn they slink away.

Inside the building, brown mice with hairless tails and no such fear of men continue to feed.

A work truck comes by and stops just long enough to empty the trash barrel, its contents burned down to cooling ash, into the back. It has four more stops to make on its way to the county dump.

After sunrise a station wagon pulls in and parks near the green compact. A short, plump young woman with dark hair emerges and runs her hand along her lower back, groaning slightly as she stretches. Then she goes around to the passenger side and helps a little girl work the release on her seat belt. Together they hurry up a cracked sidewalk toward the tile building. The young woman hesitates, sniffing the air in unconscious mimicry of the animals from the night before. As she goes to the metal door, paint peeling from the word LADIES stenciled on it and the bottom slightly sprung, her steps have slowed and she holds the child's hand tightly. She pushes on the handle.

Across the interstate one of the coyotes has denned up for the day in a sandstone and earth burrow beneath a ragged piñon. When the young woman's screams reach it, echoing in the ravines, it growls softly and crouches lower, hackles stiff along its back.

The First Week
October 15–21

MURDER IN PARADISE

"They came from everywhere
To the Great Divide,
Seeking a place to stand
Or a place to hide."
—The Eagles, "The Last Resort"

"Correct me if I'm wrong, but
hasn't the fine line between
sanity and madness grown finer?"
—George Price

1

Thursday, October 17

No pain, no gain.

That was what he'd always been told. First by a collection of high-school teachers and college coaches who'd diagramed plays on the chalkboard instead of explaining logarithms, then by the others who looked at him and saw a piece of meat, then by the physical therapists. And now by Doug Hutchins.

"Push it, Murph! Push it! Another rep! Push!"

I am pushing, numbnuts, he thought. But he got another rep.

"All right!" Doug Hutchins, a new generation of coach—Murphy's generation—guided the bar back onto the rack. "All right! No pain, no gain!"

"Your ass," Murphy Davis gasped, leaning back against the bench support. "God, I hate incline presses."

"Good therapy," said Hutchins cheerfully. "They keep that joint mobile so the scar tissue doesn't build adhesions."

"Yeah, yeah." Murphy moved aside to let Hutchins get a set, first stripping a twenty-five-pound Olympic plate from each end of the bar. The knifelike pain in his shoulder diminished to a steady ache. "No wonder you're so damned enthusiastic," he grumbled. "Let me take fifty pounds off, and I might enjoy the bastards, too."

"That's 'cause I'm a normal-size human, pal," said Hutchins. "As opposed to someone who frequently shows up on satellite photos. Besides," he lisped, "you're my in-spi-ration, you silly pussy, you. Just watching you gets my ol' round brown twitching."

5

"Hey, goddammit!" Leo shouted from his office. "You can that crap, Doug!"

Murphy waved in that direction and stepped behind the incline bench to spot Hutchins, who was blowing the gym owner a kiss. With the influx of newcomers into his fitness center, Leo was getting touchier every day.

After twenty years in various weight rooms, Murphy approached the process pragmatically, and when a workout was over, he preferred to forget it until the next one. But that was never the case with Doug Hutchins, who was still rehashing when they stepped into the late-afternoon sunshine.

". . . if maybe I add ten pounds on those push-downs? And then drop the reps back—"

"Jeez, Doug. Give it a rest, okay?" Murphy hung the strap of the Sam Browne over his shoulder. "Listen, I'll buy you a beer at the Dutchman if you'll promise to talk about something else."

"Gotta get home. And you know I never touch that stuff. Neither should you."

"I guess I'm just a wastrel at heart." Murphy grinned. "And what's the menu at your place tonight? Brussels sprouts and papaya juice?"

"Spaghetti," said Hutchins. "Come on over if you want. It wouldn't hurt you to get some complex carbs in you instead of all that red meat and fat. You have the diet of an average puma, my friend. And with your potential—"

"Potential's ass." Murphy climbed into a scarred, durable-looking Land Cruiser with a Granite County Sheriff's Department logo on the door. "I left my potential with the orthopedic surgeon. I heard he built a yacht with the money. Named it *Murphy's Potential*."

The car radio had been left on. ". . . those were good ways for an older time. . . ." The campaign ad for Neddie Cameron was playing again. "But these are different times. . . ." Murphy cut it off.

With a wave at Hutchins, he pulled away, turning off First toward the Dutchman. The streets were getting more crowded every day as ski season approached, with no more than one car out of three bearing Colorado license plates. Jeez, he thought. Silvercat's turning into fucking Vail.

Murphy Davis filled the seat of the Land Cruiser. An extremely large man in his late thirties, he would have appeared to a passerby to be the picture of rugged good health. Unless the passerby knew about Murphy's right shoulder, which was bad, or his right knee, which was worse.

Some kids were jaywalking up ahead, wearing commando cuts, which were only old-style crew cuts with a pigtail. Murphy glanced at his own shaggy, dark blond hair in the mirror and thought of his father. Goddamn surfer's hair, Alva Davis had always called it. The old man believed, and said so, that if you had a crew cut, you could get any job in America. Murphy wondered what he'd think of those jaywalking kids, and of the changes in his town.

Silvercat had been a mining and logging town before the tourists had discovered it, and many of the old Victorian buildings were still preserved. They sat along the streets, value inflated by fifteen times, surrounded now by plastic and neon. The downtown had become a hybrid—part traditional, part tourist trap—but, oddly enough, it still looked pretty damned good, Murphy thought. The water of Cat Creek was still turquoise clear where it roared through the town to join the San Juan River downstream. And above the tops of the buildings, the alternating bands of green and gold—evergreens mixing with the last of the autumn aspen—still climbed toward the gray granite of the Continental Divide and Silvercat Peak, towering over the town.

Murphy decided, not for the first time, that it was like a postcard. If you didn't look too closely at the Lady, that is.

To the left of Silvercat Peak, its consort lay broad and open. The Gray Lady, less jagged and forbidding, with rounded slopes of spruce and fir below a domelike summit.

At first glance the Lady appeared bisected and girded by a series of brown lines, but closer inspection revealed them to be ski trails waiting for winter snow. Sunlight glittered off lift towers parading up the side to a new excavation at the top.

"Thirty-six runs and eight lifts," Murphy Davis muttered

aloud. "And still less than half-finished. Jeez, Lady, you're going to look like a Christmas tree."

The Dutchman was loud at night when the regulars were there, and even louder during ski season when the flatlanders came down from Silvercat Village, trying to act outrageous and pass themselves off as locals. But on an October afternoon, it was dark and peaceful with the smells of tobacco and beer.

Murphy headed for the bar, making a wide half circle around Merrill the Feral, who sat at a table staring at A. J. Delaney. He waved at Schuyler Van den Ler, who was hopping by on one foot. Schuyler only wore his plastic and aluminum prosthesis when he was serving designer enchiladas to the tourists. A.J. flashed Murphy a pirate's grin as he slid onto a stool.

"Murphy Davis, the man with two last names." She pouted, laying her soft southern drawl on thick. "My mama always told me to fight shy of a man with two last names. How come I don't get no action from you, Murphy Davis?"

" 'Cause I'm scared shitless of Merrill the Feral." Murphy grinned. "And also because you're a child. How's about a beer?"

A. J. Delaney had been a sorority superstar at the University of Alabama before quitting school to hang out in Silvercat the previous winter. When the melt came, she'd stayed on, tending bar for a healthy salary from Schuyler Van den Ler, and for tips that bordered on the unbelievable.

Murphy had once asked her what A.J. stood for.

"Awesome Jugs," she'd replied with a wink, and he'd seen no cause for disagreement.

"A.J.," he said, taking out a plastic bottle of Tylenol when she placed a pitcher of beer and a glass next to him. "You know I've thanked the Lord many nights running for bringing you to Silvercat, but did you have to invite half the south along? There are so many tourists out there I'm beginning to feel like I'm in Tijuana."

"I know." She nodded. "Ain't it a bite in the shorts how

lower forms always multiply? I read somewhere that it's a rule. And just wait till the lifts open. Y'know, Murph, I came here to ski in the first place 'cause I heard it wasn't like Aspen or Steamboat—''

"It wasn't, up until the last couple of years."

"Yeah, well, I guess I got here too late." The girl shook her blond head. "Come next spring, I'll be haulin' ass for Idaho or Montana. Unless you pass a hunting season on tourists, that is."

"Me?" Murphy wiped foam from his upper lip. "Did someone die and leave me in charge?"

"You're gonna be county sheriff."

"Whoa!" Murphy glanced around quickly. "Watch that kind of talk, okay? It takes more than a primary to get elected."

"Bullshit," A.J. replied placidly. "Everyone tells me it's been forty years since a Democrat won anything in this county. Hobie's been sheriff for five terms, right? Come next month, you'll just fall in line."

"Maybe," said Murphy. "But don't count Neddie out. Lots of the new people in town are from the cities, and they don't give a damn who's always won around here. And a lot of them don't know the job's mostly for show anymore, or that DeVane really runs the town."

"Silvercat Ski Corporation's outside the town limits," A.J. pointed out. "So's the Village. That's county; and the police chief's got no jurisdiction up there."

"Don't remind me."

Two men came to the bar, and A.J. sidled over to serve them. They wore double-knit slacks and tassled loafers, and one had on a baseball-style cap with "Ridglea Country Club, Fort Worth, Texas," on the front. Murphy was turning back to his beer when his attention was caught by a tall, slender woman who came in and crossed the room toward a booth.

Look for changes at *The Sentinel*, everyone was saying. Sara Nichols isn't the type to let Marv sit still anymore.

Across the cool darkness of the tavern, she was talking to Marvin Lanier, who had followed in quietly behind her. She'd put on a pair of square-framed glasses as she referred to some notes. Marv was nodding a lot.

Perhaps she felt his stare, because she looked up and returned his gaze for a long moment with no trace of a smile. Then she turned back to her notes.

"You like that one?"

A.J. had returned to lean over the bar, carefully giving Murphy a reminder of the significance of her initials.

"Who, the newspaper lady?" He was surprised the question made him blush. "I don't really know her yet. I was just thinking about all the hell she's going to give old Marv, that's all."

"Uh-huh." A.J. sniffed. "Sure, Murph. I guess she's not bad, if you go for the older type. I bet she's at least thirty."

"Practically senile," Murphy agreed. "Kind of like me."

"That's different. A guy in his thirties is just right. All hard and hungry . . ."

"Which reminds me, A.J. If you don't quit hanging out all over the bar, I'm going to be forced to take a bite."

"Promises, promises." She grinned.

When he left the Dutchman carrying A.J.'s usual gift for his dog, Glorified Jock—a sack of steak bones—Murphy glanced back at the booth where Sara Nichols was sitting. She didn't look up.

She averted her eyes when Murphy Davis paused at the door before leaving. She felt the same unreasonable irritation as before.

". . . to Neddie Cameron sometime in the next week." She was pleased that her line of conversation didn't miss a beat. "We need more in-depth statements from both him and Davis."

Marvin Lanier smiled indulgently. "Sara, we always get fresh quotes from the candidates before the general," he said. He lit another cigarette from the butt of the old one. "Standard procedure."

She leaned back a little as he politely blew smoke away from her. The sheriff's campaign had pushed itself back into her thoughts at the sight of Murphy Davis sweet-talking the young bartender with the cleavage.

"You think it's going to be a walkover, don't you, Marv?" she challenged. She wasn't certain why the idea made her angry.

Lanier sipped his coffee. "Hard to predict this year," he said. "In the past, probably so. Murph's well-known and well-liked. He was the first boy from the county high school to play at C.U. since Daniel Post back in the forties."

"Which has what, exactly, to do with being a good sheriff?"

"Probably nothing. But it could have a lot to do with getting elected in the first place. People around here admire the way Murph hung in the pros after all that surgery. He never had much talent to begin with, too small for a lineman and too slow for a back, but he had guts. And he's a hard worker. People relate to that."

"I've mostly observed him working hard at the nightlife," Sara said. "But that doesn't answer my question. Do you think he'll win?"

"I'm trying to answer it. Have a little patience, girl." Lanier rubbed at a discolored blotch on his forehead. Skin cancer, thought Sara.

"Like I said, a few years ago he would have." He winced a little and withdrew his fingers. "Hobie could get reelected if he wanted, and Murph works for Hobie. But Manning and his bunch up at the Village are a factor, too. They're pushing like heck for Cameron. And with all these new voters in town . . ."

"Like me?"

"Exactly like you." Lanier flashed a nicotine-stained smile. "The new voters are the key, especially the professional people. Yuppie types who're accustomed to getting involved in local government."

"Again, like me," said Sara. "Marv, it's people like us who help a town grow. We take part in elections, serve on committees—"

"And generally try to take over." Lanier's smile took the

bite from his words. "Silvercat needs that, I guess. But we're booming too fast, Sara. It took Aspen twenty years to reach the sorry state it's in. We seem to be trying to get there overnight."

Sara held back a reply and sipped her tea. Marv would be sixty-six his birthday, and he was a mossback, though a lovable one. Personally, she found the town exciting. New faces, new fashions. Movie and TV stars up at Silvercat Village, and sometimes here in the Dutchman at night. And when Ski Silvercat reopened in November... well, the potential was limitless for a smart young professional. . . .

When they left the Dutchman, sidestepping a crowd that was piling into the drugstore next door, she insisted on picking up the tab.

At Fadiman Drugs, the gypsies were working the room. They'd timed their arrival perfectly and caught Sally Fadiman, age sixteen, behind the main counter.

"How much is this?" asked an elderly lady in heavy blue eye shadow and false lashes. "I can't find a price."

"It's right there." Sally reached for the can of hairspray. "Right on the—"

"You got any flashlight batteries?" A small boy, black hair and eyes, tugged at her sleeve.

"Aisle four, over there by—"

"Pack a' gum, please. Doublemint," said a teenage girl about Sally's own age. The girl smiled at her. You know, don't you? the grin said. Oh, yeah, you know all right. But there's not a damned thing you can do.

And Sally answered questions and rang up cheap items and pushed the bell connected to the family apartment upstairs while the gypsies, at least a dozen in number, spread out through the drugstore and stole her blind. When her father hurried past the cursing pharmacist up to the cash register, he found his daughter alone and in tears, and his inventory down by about four hundred dollars.

"Thieving bastards! Trash!" Harry Fadiman pulled Sally into his arms. "Every fall it's the same goddamned thing.

Goddammit, DeVane's got to do something before one of 'em murders somebody!''

Jesse knew the feeling that moved him. It was a restless twitch in his arms and legs, the kind that caused him to drum blackened fingernails in cadence on the arm of his chair. For several days he'd felt it, and he didn't bother to analyze the feeling because that wasn't his way. He went with it, as his grandson would have said. He let it take him as it would.

He walked up into the trees on the shoulder of the Watcher, which the white people called Silvercat. Past open basins that held flowers and young deer on summer evenings, climbing into forests of Douglas fir near the timberline. Then past threadlike waterfalls and onto the tundra, where the last marmots of autumn whistled angrily at his approach. Finally, he came to the Place of Power, rising a sheer thousand feet of gray rock above his head.

Jesse DePriest was seventy-eight years old that autumn, and the walk had been hard. He sat for a while, drinking occasionally from a small K-Mart canteen and rolling a cigarette with steady fingers. Above him an eagle pushed out from the cliff, riding the thermals, and the marmots ducked for cover.

He was a short man, though ramrod-straight and thickly built. His hair, cut square across the bottom and ear length, was more black than gray, and his eyes were sharp as he studied the broad dome of the Gray Lady, below and to his right. An elk herd was entering the trees near a fresh excavation at the summit, raw and brown.

"So, here I am," he said conversationally. "I've come up. But you already know why I'm here."

He spoke English. That and Spanish had gotten easier for him in recent years than the old tongues. His words echoed faintly against the Place of Power.

"Sky's blue today," he continued, "but it's pretty damned cold up here. If I had some decent boots instead of these tennis shoes, it would've been easier."

He smiled a little, which he rarely did anymore because

most of his teeth were gone. "But you're not interested in hearing me complain, are you? I apologize."

He drank from the canteen and began again. But first he removed a pouch hanging from a leather thong around his neck. He took a dried piece of peyote cactus from the pouch.

"There's something in the town," he said. "Something wrong. I've been feeling it for days. Can I know what it is?" He bit into the peyote bud.

He sat for a long time, occasionally spitting out a chewed piece before taking another bite. He didn't notice the bees picking over the autumn pollen and landing on his hands, or the marmots that had returned to sit like overfed emperors at the edge of the talus. A jet passed by far overhead, bound for Salt Lake City, and left silvery twin contrails against the blue sky, and still he sat. Sometimes his mouth moved for minutes at a time, but the sounds were only a muted drone.

Finally, coldness crept up from the granite and into his hips and thighs, and the pain forced him to rise and move around. He took another drink of water and replaced the pouch, then started walking down toward the trees. It was late afternoon, and he had a long way to go. He'd probably miss "Cosby."

He knew only a little more than when he'd gone up, and that knowledge itself was hazy and poorly formed. Couched in vague symbolism he knew was mostly the mescaline. It was a damned good thing he wasn't just a superstitious old redskin, he reflected, because the only consistent image he'd identified during the long afternoon had been the Beast.

She's here. She's followed him home, and that's never happened before. For years—fifteen? twenty?—he's been safe here.

In the street near the post office, he's caught a glimpse of her. The others he ignores, wearing their tight T-shirts with suggestive words and pictures and their satin jogging shorts that expose first one cheek of a rounded buttock as they walk, then the other. As always, his eyes are only for her. Tunnel vision.

Only this time, she's here. After all the years, here again in

Silvercat. But it's not the same, of course. She's changed, and that's something he must never forget. That, and the way she tried to kill him . . .

But didn't he leave her down on the plains in that rest stop where someone was surely going to get a surprise going into the bathroom? He can't remember, but he must be wrong. Because she's here.

He enters the quiet of his house and sits for a minute at the piano bench, rubbing Alistair Three's curly head. He looks at the nineteenth-century daguerreotypes that are arranged above the old upright. His grandfather is there, staring in eight-year-old wonder at the camera. And the great-grandfather, sitting in an overstuffed chair with the wife behind him, docile hand on his shoulder.

He goes into the kitchen and washes his hands again, wincing when the Lava Soap rubs against the bite marks on his right palm and remembering how a human bite is more septic than that of a cat or dog. He dabs hydrogen peroxide onto the scabbed flesh and watches it bubble up.

Later, after a light but excellent meal, he plays the piano. It usually soothes him, but tonight it isn't working. He botches the simple ones—"Ticket to Ride" and "Please, Please Me"—and has to restrain himself from slamming his hands down on the keys. Because this time she's followed him home.

He goes upstairs, past *that* room and its staring eyes, to his own bedroom and takes a handmade wooden box from under a pieced quilt in the back of an antique armoire. He removes a pair of black corduroy jeans, faded and softened from repeated washings, and high-top black boots with rubber soles. Then an old black sweatshirt, its logo barely readable with age. They're all clean since he wasn't wearing them at the rest stop. And he wasn't wearing them because . . . He frowns. He can't remember that, so it must be unimportant.

He puts on the clothes, his fingers beginning to quiver as tension builds. Finally, from the bottom of the box, he brings the razor.

His throat tightens as it lies in his hand, reflecting the

overhead light. Four inches of double-edge blade with both cutting surfaces so sharp he has to handle it with the greatest care. A thumbnail inserted, a pull, and it slides out of its ornately patterned silver handle. He sits looking at it for a few minutes, lost in thoughts of rose-colored water and humming an old song. Then he closes it gingerly and fits it into his left boot behind the anklebone.

Come on, Danni . . .

2

Friday, October 18

Toya's mother had always told her, "If you really like something, keep on doing it till ya get it right."

She stifled a giggle at the thought before the pain hit her again. Sharp, digging in like the knuckle of a fist someone had pressed against her breastbone. She held to the railing of the apartment-house balcony and fumbled in her jacket pocket for antacid tablets.

She chewed two at a time, their chalkiness drying her mouth, then two more. She squeezed the railing, waiting for the nausea to pass.

Better. By the time she'd descended the stairs to the parking lot, the pain was nearly gone.

She wondered if that guy in the apartment upstairs (Darrell? Darnell?) was still sitting in bed with his mouth hanging open. She smiled again, remembering the shocked look on his face when she'd emerged from his bathroom fully clothed.

"What the hell?" He'd sat up with his Tony-face, the sheet around a waist going to love handles. "You're leaving?"

"Yep," she'd said, zipping the fly of her tight jeans. "Gotta get going, baby. I got a big day tomorrow. Last day in town."

"Yeah, but I thought . . ."

"Hey, practice makes perfect, baby. If I were you, I'd practice some more."

That usually held them. She hurried through the hallway to the small living room. And apparently it had again, since total silence followed her out the door.

17

If you really like something . . .

But what if I don't, Mama?

. . . keep on doing it till ya get it right.

Outside the apartment the night was cold, and from the feel of the air, the long Indian summer was almost over.

Toya Jalecka had been in Silvercat for a week. On the advice of a friend from the office, she'd passed up Aspen to try the place.

"It's really hot," her friend had said. "In a few years it'll be where everybody's going. You should check it out."

She had, and found that her friend was right. The town was just starting to cook. Lots of nightlife, easy drugs, and the men . . . Dark-haired, dark-eyed types. Tony all over again. And that jerk upstairs hadn't been the first who'd lie awake wondering what the hell had hit him.

In and out. One quick bang and then gone, leaving the bastards to chew on her parting shot. Practice makes perfect. . . . She felt tears burning at the back of her eyes. Bastards.

She glanced at her watch. It was getting close to two, which meant everything would be shutting down.

"Damn," she muttered, surprised at how the sound carried in the quiet parking lot. It had been a mistake to let him drive her to his apartment. Two A.M. and she'd have to walk back to her car. Good thing it's still a small town. It couldn't be more that seven or eight blocks.

The apartment house had been built in a residential area, probably on land some enterprising local had sold for ten times its original value. All along the street were the gingerbread-trimmed Victorians that photography buffs loved to shoot, with small porches and steep metal roofs an indicator of the winter's heavy snowfall. Aspen, evergreens, and a few hardy cottonwoods grew in postage-stamp-size front yards.

She heard a screen door close quietly behind her and glanced back. The only streetlights were at the corners, and she barely made out a dark figure descending the steep porch steps of one of the old houses.

That character's out late, she thought, and hurried on, her

spike heels clicking on the sidewalk. Her mind flashed back to the apartment for a moment, which reminded her of Tony. But then everything reminded her of Tony.

She wondered what he was doing right at that moment. Nearly three A.M. in Kansas City, which probably meant he was humping one of his backup singers.

Bastard, she thought, and felt her eyes burning again. She wiped at them brusquely and decided she'd been balling Darrell-Darnell at about the same time as Tony had his bimbo. That made her feel a little better, but not much.

"Do it till ya get it right," she whispered.

He watches her pass his house even as his hand hesitates at the doorknob. He'd been within seconds of going back upstairs. Instead, he glides down the stairs to his gate, his eyes boring into her back.

She's found him. Followed him to his own street, to his house. Of course, she knows the way.

And now she's walking past, pretending not to see him in her high heels and tight jeans. Teasing him again.

He closes the gate behind him and steps out onto the sidewalk. The rubber soles of his boots make almost no sound as he walks, humming softly, under the cottonwoods his father planted so many years ago.

Toya first realized she was being followed when she heard the faint sound of leaves crunching underfoot. She thought of the figure she'd seen back up the block.

For an instant her pulse quickened, then she relaxed. This is stupid, she thought. Some of these old Victorians are going for two hundred thou, and she certainly had nothing to fear from someone who lived in one of them. Maybe some old dude the age of her father. All crow's-feet and stern lines at the corners of his mouth (You're no good. Your mother was a slut and you're a slut. You'll come to a bad end just like she did. . . .) like Leonard McNamara, gentleman farmer from Missouri.

She stopped and waited.

* * *

"Hello," he says, approaching her by the streetlight. "Hello, Danni."

"I . . . I beg your pardon?"

She's staring at him, eyes wide. Shocked at first, then . . .

"I see you found me," he continues. "But you were always clever, weren't you?"

She takes a step back, but he sees she isn't afraid. The corners of her mouth curl with the laughter he senses building inside her.

"I don't know what in the hell you're talking about."

"It's me," he says. "You know me. And I have something for you."

Her face changes then, in the faint overhead light. The amusement is gone, and something harder takes its place. Her eyes go bright with malice, and she puts her hands on her lips. "Oh, really?" The sound is like a sneer. "So tell me. What do you have for me?"

"This," he says softly. And he shows her.

He thinks she'll scream, and he's moving toward her as he speaks, but she surprises him. With a quickness he hadn't expected, she spins away and sprints down the street.

He races after her, a fierce joy tearing at him. She remembers! He loves this game. *They* love it. If only she doesn't scream.

Toya didn't scream. She was tough, raised on the back of the hand and matured in disappointment. Besides, it never occurred to her that the occupants of the little gingerbread houses would open their doors to her if she did. At home she'd carried Mace in her purse and never used it once. Now, she had only her keys and her wallet.

The spike heels were useless for running, but her pursuer was either slow or not trying very hard. Once, passing under a streetlight, she thought she heard laughter behind her, but she wasn't sure.

After another block, the combination of the altitude and her own living habits began to drive the thin air from her lungs.

A tight band settled around her forehead, shooting darts of pain into her temples. She crossed a street and found a small park on her left. Dead brown grass lay under a single streetlight, and she saw playground equipment in the distance. Trees grew irregularly across to a low bluff at the back edge.

There were no sounds behind her, and she stopped to look back. Just a dark, empty street with intermittent pools of light.

She turned and, half-walking, half-running, started along the edge of the park. It couldn't be more than another block or two back to the main streets. She held her side against the sharp stabs that came with each breath. Her stomach was burning again.

Ahead, at the end of the park, was another streetlight. And a figure leaning against it, watching her.

She cried out, but it was a short, choked sound that didn't carry far. She heard a dog beginning to bark as she dashed to her left toward the trees.

By turning into an alley at the first intersection, he reaches Fuller Park well ahead of her. It feels good to run again, even in the heavy boots.

He leans casually on the lamppost, striking a pose, and waits for her to see him, or to run right up. Either way's okay, though he hopes she'll see him. And she does.

He waits for her to pass the swings in the park before he moves again, vaguely aware that Reggie, Ben Dubose's dog, is barking in its backyard. He's known this spot since he was big enough to walk. He remembers when his father pushed him in these swings and held him tight, tight against the cold.

At the back of the park, a section of Cat Creek runs along beneath the bluff. If she thinks there's a way out back there, she's in for a surprise.

When Toya reached the World War II artillery gun that was the centerpiece of the park, she looked back at the lamppost beyond a clump of aspen. She wasn't surprised to see it deserted.

Stay calm, dammit! Stay calm, and you can still get out of this.

She thought for a moment of her father, and his big hands, and how she'd thought more than once it was the end for her. But it hadn't been then, either. Just stay calm.

Behind her, lined by trees, was a stream. She heard it rushing over stones and filling the silence that surrounded her labored breathing. The dog had stopped barking.

Her eyes were adjusting to the darkness, and with a three-quarter moon and a starry sky, she could see clearly. The bluff across the creek was perhaps ten feet high and not completely vertical. As a last resort . . .

She removed her shoes, feeling the shock of the cold brown grass beneath stockinged feet. Better to move along this side of the creek, then reach the street at the end of the park and run for it.

Go slow and listen. Don't walk into a trap.

Leaving the shoes, she crept toward the edge of the water. Grass gave way to hard, cold dirt and protruding rocks that hurt her feet. She stopped to listen. Except for the rushing water, there was silence.

No, wait. Not total silence. Something moved next to a large tree ahead. Faint starlight reflected in small, red eyes.

With a gasp she spun away and tripped, falling headlong across the low bank of the creek. A rock slammed against her mouth and white sparks exploded behind her closed eyes.

"Oh, God!" she cried out. Then, more softly, "Oh, sweet Jesus . . ."

She sat up to see a small shape scurrying away. Her jeans were ripped at the knee, and she was sure she'd chipped some teeth. The pain from her stomach punched nausea up into her throat.

God, it's so cold! So cold! she thought as a wave of shivering broke over her. Her hand brushed a dainty lace of ice that was forming along the edge of the water.

You can't stay here. You've got to get out.

But it's so cold. . . .

She had taken a step back into the trees when she heard the low chuckle, almost right beside her.

"Danni . . ." A hand touched her. "You're It."

With a low moan vibrating in her throat, Toya plunged into the icy water of the creek.

You'll come to a bad end. . . .

She stumbled toward the far side and the bluff.

She's just like he remembers. Tough. No scream at the sight of the raccoon or at the touch of his hand.

Now he watches her, falling and rising, fighting the current across to a section of rock she won't be able to climb. Her soft moaning, steady as a metronome, comes back to him.

She'll start screaming soon, he decides with real regret. No matter how tough she is. It's the first time they've played the game in so long, and now the game is over. She's It.

He sees her reach the far bank and stumble into the chokecherry bushes that grow next to the bluff, then he crosses after her.

She's managed to climb several feet up the side when he reaches for her. . . .

"Daddy. . . ?" she whispers. Her eyes are flat and glazed in the moonlight. She looks through him without seeing him.

"Danni!" Tears fill his eyes, blinding him. "Oh, Danni! Oh, my love!"

And he cries. Dark and bitter tears.

3

Friday, October 18

In the dream Murphy was wedge busting on the kickoff. Meat-wagon work for expendable, borderline bodies. Only he was too slow, and the blocker nailed him blindside. The helmet smashed into his back, shoulder into his kidneys, and his right side went numb. In a floating, slow-motion sequence, he was facedown with dirt in his mouth and a steady ringing in his ears. The odor of his own body rose up to his nostrils, and for a moment, it was like the odor of blood. . . .

Then he was awake, gagging on the foul taste in his mouth, with the telephone ringing beside his bed.

"Yeah, yeah, dammit!" He jerked the receiver toward him, sending a stab of pain through his shoulder. "What the hell . . .''

"Murph. Wake up, kid. It's Hobie."

"Hobie?" Murphy turned the clock toward him and tried to focus. "What's going on, Hobie? It's not even—"

"No rest for the wicked" came the older man's dry answer, and Murphy pictured his boss striking a kitchen match to start his pipe. "We got trouble."

Murphy stretched his neck, reaching automatically for the Tylenol bottle on the night table. "What's going on?" he asked again. He dry-swallowed two of the caplets.

"Tourist got herself killed in Fuller Park during the night. I'm headed there now."

"Fuller Park? Is DeVane—"

"Yeah. He just called me. I know it's his jurisdiction, but he says he wants us both. I figure it can't hurt, right?"

24

"Yeah. Yeah, I see what you mean. I'll meet you there."

Murphy slid to the side of the bed, stopping to wash down two more caplets with stale, warm beer from a can on the bedside table. As always, his knee had stiffened up during the night, and he put weight on it carefully. He pulled the blanket up over his pillow, which caused the German shepherd at the end of the bed to raise a massive head and look his way.

"Excuse me," Murphy muttered. "I didn't mean to inconvenience you. Please remember that I'm the human and you're the dog around here."

Glorified Jock yawned widely, exposing a pink tongue and canine teeth fully an inch long. He was accustomed to this byplay, though usually not so early in the morning. He closed his eyes and went back to sleep.

Winter's going to be early this year, Murphy thought, climbing from the Land Cruiser. There were ice crystals in the park's dead grass, and the aspen leaves were nearly all gone. Harv (of the "Little Buddy and Big Harv Show" on KCAT) had just followed another Neddie Cameron campaign ad by giving the temperature as twenty-four degrees. Murphy's headache rolled over him in waves.

Hobie's Blazer was parked next to a police car, and despite the early morning chill, the people who lived across the street were out on their porches.

"Hey, Murph! What the hell's going on?"

"Morning, Mr. Dubose. I don't know the details yet. Did you hear anything last night?"

"Nope. Well . . . maybe. Reggie started raising hell around two. Told Janice, when they cut that dog's nuts, they shoulda got his goddamn vocal cords, too."

Murphy laughed politely. "I might be back to talk a little, Mr. Dubose. Gotta go now."

"You come ahead on, Murph. We'll have the coffee going. You got our vote, y'know."

"Thanks, Mr. Dubose." Murphy trotted, limping slightly with his holster slapping against his thigh, across the park to a stand of trees by the creek. Hobie Jameison was waiting for

him on the other side of a rope barricade, sucking patiently
on his old pipe.

"Took your time, kid," said Jameison. He was a large
man, nearly as tall as Murphy and heavily built, with a snow
white thatch of crewcut hair under his Los Angeles Dodgers
baseball cap. "You must've been hustling some votes. I've
noticed your limp gets worse at times like that."

"It's a cold morning." Murphy grinned. Across the creek,
he saw police chief DeVane Belleau and Arthur Morse, who
served Granite County as coroner. "What's it look like?"

"Looks bad," said Jameison. "I mean, *real* bad. I had to
come over here for a breath of air."

Murphy studied his old friend in the brightening light.
Hobie Jameison's ruddy face was pale, and the wrinkled flesh
near one eye was twitching slightly. He felt a wave of sick
apprehension slide through him.

"Let's go," Jameison was saying. "You better get this
over with. You look like shit, by the way."

They crossed the stream, ice-clogged along the edges,
stepping from rock to rock, then climbed through dead
chokecherry bushes on the far side. Henry Light and two
other policemen were methodically combing the muddy bank.
Their faces were tight.

Belleau and Morse were standing with their backs to what
lay in the brush next to a zippered plastic bag. They were
talking about it, but they weren't looking at it.

"Je-zus!" whispered Murphy.

The woman had been tall and slim. He could tell that. And
without the expression of pure madness on her face, she may
have also been attractive. Her clothes had been ripped, the
shirt lying partly beneath her back and the pants shredded
around her ankles. There was a slight odor in the cold air.
Faint, like pennies in a coin purse.

Her legs were bowed at the knees in a parody of the sexual
position, and through his need to vomit Murphy felt a
sickening sense of arousal. He averted his eyes.

"Knife?" he managed to get out. Blood had partially
frozen in the brush and on the rock face of the bluff.

"Hi, Murph." DeVane Belleau's thin features were strained. "You aren't going to puke, are you? Take some deep breaths."

"No . . . I'm okay."

"It was a sharp instrument of some type." Dr. Morse was older than Hobie Jameison and, in the morning light, his face looked as gray as the rocks. "Right now I couldn't say more. The damage is so damned . . . extensive." He changed location and took another photograph from that angle.

"Art?" Jameison said, bending near the woman's face. "Art, did you see this?"

"Yeah. First thing, once I got past the shock."

Murphy pushed in closer. "What is it, Hobie?"

"Her eyelids, Murph. Take a look. Top and bottom. They're gone."

Murphy often thought the office Hobie Jameison had inhabited for twenty years was a lot like its occupant. A little scuffed up, not too attractive unless you looked closely, and comfortable with its smells of wood smoke, coffee, and pipe tobacco.

The Fisher wood stove in the corner was radiating warmth off the log walls of the room, and Murphy removed the jacket he'd been wearing over his standard-issue khaki shirt, hanging it near the huge painting of the four dogs playing poker. He was still replaying the scene at the park in his mind. He wanted a drink very badly.

"Remember when your uncle Evan had that woodcutting accident?" Jameison was saying. "I was right there, along with your dad, and I watched that goddamned chain saw go through his leg. I always said that was worse than anything I'd ever seen in twenty years of law enforcement, but this . . ."

"Jeez, Hobie. Cut me some slack, okay?"

"But nothing like this," Jameison continued. "You better get some coffee, kid. And some breakfast."

"You must be kidding."

"Yeah. Sorry. Anyway, at times like this, I'm real grateful that Belleau's police chief and I'm just county sheriff. He's the one gets to talk to the press."

"To *The Sentinel?* That shouldn't be so tough."

"Don't kid yourself. Wait'll it hits the wire services, starting with the Denver AP office. As I recall it, you had some dealings with those media types when you were playing ball, Murph, so you should know what they're like when they smell trouble. They'll pick you cleaner than buzzards on a dead possum in the road."

"Yeah." A muscle tightened in Murphy's jaw. "Yeah, I hear that."

"Silvercat's getting a reputation, anyway. Pretty soon it'll be all jet-setters, drugs, and sex. Another Aspen, I hear people say. Remember all the flap when that woman shot that pro skier over there a few years back?"

"They were both celebrities, Hobie. This . . . Toya Jalecka was a data processor from Kansas City."

"Doesn't matter. Hawaii or the Rockies, it's murder in paradise. That's how the public'll see it. We'll be up to our ying-yangs in reporters before long. You just hide and watch."

He sat up. "Speaking of which, here comes trouble right now. Straighten up and try to look alert, kid."

The door opened and Sara Nichols entered. Her long, dark hair was pulled back in a single braid, and she was wearing her glasses.

"Sheriff Jameison. Deputy." She nodded curtly in Murphy's general direction. "I wonder if I could talk to you."

"Sure," said Jameison, rising to offer her his chair near the wood stove. "Coffee?"

"Never touch it, thanks." She remained standing and took a small cassette player from her bag. "What can you tell me about the killing last night in Fuller Park?"

Jameison reclaimed his chair and looked up at her. "Not a lot as yet." He smiled. "I expect you've already been to Chief Belleau's office."

Murphy thought she blushed a little. "Yes, I have," she replied. "But I hoped you might have a different perspective. All your years of experience . . ."

"Don't mean much. We're all green as gourds on one like this," the sheriff answered. "But I can tell you what you

probably already know." He picked up a typed sheet of paper.
"Name was Toya Jalecka. Age twenty-two. Home address,
Kansas City. That's Kansas, not Missouri. Twice divorced,
the most recently five months ago . . ."

"Has anyone checked on the whereabouts of her ex-
husbands?"

Jameison smiled again. "DeVane's got someone on it now.
Figured he'd have told you that. Let's see, occupation, data
processor. Lived alone. Mother deceased. Father's been
notified."

"Cause of death?"

"Dr. Morse'd have to comment on that."

"And your impression, Deputy Davis?"

She said it so smoothly, without a glance in his direction,
that Murphy was caught completely off guard studying the
shape of her cheekbones and nose.

"Huh?" He felt his face redden. "Well . . . I guess I'd
agree with Sheriff Jameison."

"You guess you'd agree with the sheriff." Her dark eyebrows rose in frank amusement. "I see. May I quote you on
that?"

She'd set him up perfectly.

"If you like." He tried to recover, feigning indifference.
"We'll know more when we hear from—"

"And how would you handle the investigation? If you were
already sheriff, that is?"

But he was ready by then. "Well, as you probably know,
it's Chief Belleau's jurisdiction and therefore his case. I'd do
just what Hobie . . . Sheriff Jameison's going to do. Provide
full support and all our resources to aid Chief Belleau." He
gave her a bland smile.

"Uh-huh," she said, green eyes appraising him. Then to
Jameison, "When do you expect to hear from Dr. Morse?"

"Soon, at least with the preliminary. If he turns up something exotic, our facilities may be inadequate for a complete
report. As you know, we have no crime lab in Silvercat, not
even at the new police station."

She nodded. "In that case, I'll be on my way. I'll be

talking to the doctor, and I'll check with you again later.''
She smiled at Jameison and, ignoring Murphy, left the office.

"Damn pretty woman," said the sheriff. "Outstanding, in
fact. What's she got against you, kid?''

"Beats me." Murphy watched Sara Nichols cross the
street. "I wish I knew.''

When he came back from breakfast at the Elkhorn Café,
Murphy saw Jesse DePriest outside the sheriff's office. The
old man was leaning against the building's rough-hewn log
wall with closed eyes, absorbing the sun's warmth like a
flower. In one hand he held a half-eaten beef chimichanga.

"Morning, Murph." Jesse pushed himself erect. Despite
the morning's chill, he wore only a pair of tan corduroy jeans
above his discount-store sneakers and a red T-shirt with a
logo on the chest that read: "Happiness Is a Texan Headed
South with a Democrat Under Each Arm.''

"Like your shirt." Murphy grinned. "But you'd better
start wearing a jacket, unless you want to freeze your ancient
ass off. Summer's gone, Jesse.''

Jesse snorted and began to roll a cigarette. "Murph, I was
wintering in these mountains before your grandpa was weaned,''
he said. "Just stay in the sun. That's the secret." He pushed
the last of the chimichanga into his mouth with an old man's
reluctance to leave any food uneaten.

"If you say so.''

"Got a minute to talk?" Jesse's voice was casual, but there
was intensity in his expression, and Murphy stopped with one
hand on the doorknob.

"Always got time for a visit with you, Jesse. You wanta
sit?''

They walked along the outside of the office to a bench, cut
from the same logs as the building and facing the street, and
sat down. Jesse positioned himself so sunlight poured across
him from the side, then struck a kitchen match on a horny
thumbnail.

"I went down to New Mexico last week, Murph," he said,
drawing on the homemade cigarette.

"Yeah? Did Estrella take you?"

"Uh-huh. Don't know why. She drives worse than I do."

Murphy leaned back with a smile. He'd known Jesse for practically his entire life. The old man would get to the point in his own time.

"We went to a tent revival, Murph. Some silly bastard from Albuquerque was preaching. He had a band there, guitars and drums and everything."

"What was his name?"

"The preacher? Who knows? He was just a damn Navajo, anyway. Wasn't too long before all those people started yelling hallelujah and shaking on the floor. You should have seen it, Murph. Scared the hell out of me."

Murphy laughed. "Sounds like they had that old-time religion, Jesse."

"Maybe." Jesse sniffed. "But you know churches aren't the Indian way. You white people know how you got churches and how to use 'em, but I can't see the point." His eyes were faded and milky at the edges, nearly disappearing into the wrinkles when he smiled.

"That damn Navajo, he said to throw away our eagle feathers and corn pollen. Stop the singings and the fire dances. He wanted me to get baptized, Murph. You believe that? I told him I was a Mormon."

"What? No, you didn't!"

"Did, too. And it worked, 'cause he went away and laid hands on some old lady, and she gave him a dollar."

Jesse rubbed the end of the cigarette across a callused palm and flicked his fingers to spread the ash and tobacco on the ground. Then he rolled the remaining paper into a tight ball and put it in his pants pocket. "I went up yesterday," he said.

Murphy followed the line of his friend's sight up and beyond the mercantile across the street, recently bought out by a company from Phoenix and renovated as an indoor mall, to the twin towers of Silvercat Peak and the Gray Lady, hanging above the town.

"Up Silver . . . the Watcher?"

"Yep. That killing last night? I knew it was going to happen."

"You knew..." Murphy's eyes narrowed. "What do you mean?"

"I'm not sure. But I'd had a feeling, so I went up and I asked to know. It wasn't real clear, but there was something. *Something.* Murph, I believe it was the Beast."

Across the street, Muzak was coming from mounted speakers outside the entrance to the mall. "Do You Know The Way To San Jose?" played with a bouncy, almost Latin beat. Murphy tried unsuccessfully to ignore the subtle prickling of his scalp. He was thirty-eight years old, for God's sake. No longer some wide-eyed kid who believed that owls call the names of the dead.

"C'mon, Jesse," he growled. "Talk plain, okay? This is just your paleface pal, not some tourist. What beast? That girl was murdered with a sharp blade of some kind."

"Maybe." Jesse nodded. "The Beast takes different forms, Murph. Like I said, I knew it was going to happen. And it's going to happen again."

4

Friday, October 18

Damn that poker-faced old bastard, Murphy thought, opening the office door. Drop a statement like that, matter-of-fact as saying hello, then head off down the street.

Arthur Morse looked like hell. Smelled like it, too, with that particular odor Murphy always associated with dead things. A painfully thin, almost frail-looking man, he was sitting in Hobie Jameison's big chair, holding a coffee cup in one quivering hand and a nearly smoked cigarette in the other. Camels, Murphy observed. The original lung-thumpers.

"Simmer down, Art," Jameison was saying. "Old fart like you gets all fired up, only means more work for the next coroner."

"That's real funny, Hobie," Morse snarled. "I'll tell you one thing. The day I croak, you'll have already been mole meat for years."

"Probably so." Jameison nodded. "You high-pressure types who rant and rave and live on caffeine and tobacco generally outlast the rest of us every time. C'mon in, Murph. What's the funny look you've got on your face? I know the Elkhorn's breakfasts aren't *that* bad."

"Never mind." Murphy pulled a straight-backed chair across from the two and sat down. "So, what's the story, doc?"

"He was just about to tell us, weren't you, Art? After another cup of coffee and a coffin nail. That's *his* breakfast."

Morse shot the grinning sheriff the finger and turned partly toward Murphy. "It was a sharp instrument. I can't tell more than that. Double-edged. Maybe a knife that's been whetted down or a straight razor. One of those kind you're afraid to even handle 'cause it's so damned sharp."

"Beautiful," murmured Jameison.

"Oh, it gets better," Morse replied, rising to refill his cup. He handed another to Murphy. "The girl was messed up some incidentally. Cut kneecap, scrapes on her arms and shoulders, a broken tooth. But the major trauma was caused when the knife, if that's what it was, was introduced into the vagina—"

"Shit!" Murphy felt hot coffee hit his pants.

"—and forced upward toward the sternum. That goddamned blade tore right through the pubic bone and literally bisected the abdominal organs, as well as lacerating the stomach, liver, and spleen."

"Someone strong," said Jameison. "Strong as hell, or crazy. Right through the pubic bone. Damn! Was she raped?"

"I really couldn't tell." Morse shook his head. "I took fluid samples best I could, which should help when they're analyzed. But with all the trauma, all the blood in the cavity. . . Off the record, I'd say possibly so. There was mild tissue damage to the posterior wall, which was uncut, but vigorous enough intercourse could do that."

"What about the eyelids?"

The doctor lit another cigarette. "Now, that's weird. They were slit away, top and bottom, with only the barest damage to the eyeballs themselves. Somebody knew what he was doing. Then it looks like the area was wiped repeatedly until the blood flow had completely stopped. That's why none of us noticed it at first."

Jameison scowled. "You're saying the killer sat there mopping the girl's eyes until they quit bleeding? Instead of running off?"

"I doubt it took that long. I'm almost certain she was already dead by then. With that, and all the other blood loss, I imagine it took very little time."

Morse looked up from his coffee cup. "How about you, Hobie? Anything from your end?"

"That's where I'd have to pull it from." Jameison laughed mirthlessly. "And even then it wouldn't smell any worse than what we've got. The Farley sisters claim they heard sounds about two."

"Miss Ellen and Miss Arlene." Morse smiled.

"Yeah. And old Dubose told Murph his dog was barking about that time."

"Well, that's close to my own estimate, working backward at the rate of body-temperature loss, though it's harder to tell when the ground's so cold. I wonder why she didn't scream?"

"Me too." Murphy nodded. "I was thinking about that. Someone she knew, maybe?"

"Maybe." Jameison shrugged. "It's an angle we'd explore anyway. One thing's for sure. Our man was pretty quiet. That neighborhood has lots of old folks, and they sleep light."

"What about the scene itself?"

"Nada. Practically nada, other than the blood. Some dislodged rock and dirt where she may have fallen on one side of the creek. Torn bushes on the other. No footprints going in except hers. She took off her shoes, by the way."

"Trying to move faster?" asked Morse. "Or quieter?"

"Maybe. They're those spike heels women seem to wear with jeans anymore. Maybe she just wanted to take a barefoot walk."

"At two in the morning?" Murphy snorted. "With the temperature below freezing?"

Jameison grinned. "Not too likely, huh? We did get one partial print besides hers. Just the heel. Someone stepped on a rock and let the heel down on dirt. Don't know if it means anything. It could have already been there."

"Also no skin or hair under her fingernails," said Morse. "Whoever killed her seems to have taken his mess with him."

"Transient?" asked Murphy.

"Hell, yes, transient!" Jameison's square jaw clamped down hard. "Had to be. Gypsies, maybe. Some of them blow through here every fall, stealing everything that's not nailed down. Or some goddamned newcomer. Nobody who's—"

He was interrupted by the telephone.

"Get that, would ya, Murph? Like I said, nobody who's lived in this town over the years would . . ." He looked over at Murphy, whose face had gone pale. He was writing rapidly. "What's up, Murph?"

Murphy held up his hand, then kept writing. He put down the phone.

"That was DeVane. Tuesday morning a lady stopped at a rest area south of Denver on I-25. She found two Texas women dead in the bathroom."

"I heard about it. Hell, it was all over the news. So?"

"Well, DeVane's been on the phone with the police at Castle Rock. One of the women . . . she'd been butchered like a hog. That's how they said it. And her eyelids were sliced off clean."

The Sentinel was an afternoon newspaper, which gave Sara some time to think.

Until a few months before, she'd have had even more time, because the paper had been published only twice weekly. One of the factors in her decision to accept Charlotte Post and Marvin Lanier's offer to become assistant editor had been its changeover to a daily.

Even her office, if one could call it that, was new. Plywood partitions separated an area from the rest of the newsroom, and the scent of fresh paint was still strong. She had a desk with her P.C. and its video display terminal linked to another terminal in the typesetting room, and they were as new as the paint. *The Sentinel* had never needed an assistant editor before.

Sara had gone straight from UCLA's School of Journalism and a brief marriage into a job with a small daily in the San Joaquin Valley. She'd been Sara Bowlin in those days, before a feminist friend had persuaded her to legally reclaim her maiden name. Larry Bowlin hadn't minded. He'd been too busy being seen in the right places and calling his agent twice a day to worry about his ex-wife. She still saw him occasionally in commercials—usually in the background, though he did have a speaking part in a new Michelob piece—and generally flicked her remote-control channel changer. A big, macho bastard, that was Larry. Maybe that was why . . .

She'd worked hard at covering the social fluff her paper kept foisting upon her, waiting for a real chance. And then, purely by accident, it had come.

She'd been driving home one afternoon and had cut down a back road to avoid traffic, which was how she happened onto a rescue in progress.

There were a number of irrigation canals in the area, usually running high in spring, and a four-year-old boy had fallen in. Apparently he'd managed to hang on to some brush at the edge briefly, because his mother, a huge woman probably weighing two hundred pounds, had climbed down the muddy bank and almost reached him when his grip failed.

Sara drove by just as a small, wiry black man dived into the dirty water. The woman, wet cotton dress plastered to her body, was screaming by the road.

"Roy Neil!" she screeched. "Roy, you get outta that water, goddammit! I tol' you not to play near that ditch!"

Sara had run to the roadside with her little Kodak Instamatic and gotten several shots of the man's head emerging, then disappearing under the water. She had only been there a few minutes when he came up the last time, holding the limp child in his arms, then struggled to the side.

"Roy!" the woman screamed, sliding along the bank. "I'm gonna whip your butt, Roy Neil!"

She yanked the little boy from the man's arms.

"Gimme my baby, nigger!" she snarled. "I can take care of my own son!"

Nevertheless, the man had helped her back up the muddy

slope. The child lay motionless, eyes half-open, a trickle of
water sliding from his nose.

"That baby's drownded, lady!" said the man. "We gotta
give it air, or it's gonna die!"

He tilted the boy's head back and opened the mouth,
clearing the tongue. The mother stood in slack-jawed wonder
as he pinched the nostrils and began mouth-to-mouth
resuscitation.

Sara was standing so near that she could smell the stale
beer odor coming from the woman's mouth and sweat glands
in a palpable wave. She had taken one picture and was
moving into position for another when the woman emerged
from her stupor with a roar.

"Nigger!" she bellowed. "You get your goddamn black
nigger mouth off my baby!"

She swung a doughy arm like a club, hitting the small man
in the side of his head and knocking him across the child to
the ground. He staggered upright, eyes dazed, as the woman
dropped to her knees beside the boy and began to shake
him.

"Roy! Goddamn you, Roy! Get up!"

"Lady," said the man. "That baby's drownded. We
gotta—"

"Shut up, nigger!" she rasped. Then, turning toward Sara,
"You! What the hell are you doin' with that camera?" And
Sara saw, with fascination, that there were small black hairs
growing in the center of the woman's tongue. "You get the
hell outta here!"

And with a backhand swipe, she sent the Instamatic flying
across the asphalt.

She was still holding her child, alternately cursing him and
the two others, when the paramedics arrived. Surprisingly,
Roy Neil was briefly revived with oxygen, though he never
regained consciousness and died the next day.

Sara's grainy 110s were edited to serviceability and went
in the paper along with her taut account of the tragedy, and
suddenly she found herself handling "real" news. From
there, it had been a series of steps over an eight-year

period that had culminated, at age thirty-two, with her sitting in a jerry-built cubicle in the San Juan Mountains of Colorado as the assistant editor of a newspaper. In a town headed for stardom, right up there with Aspen and Steamboat Springs.

Only now, Toya Jalecka may have brought it a little sooner than any of them had expected.

"Knock, knock. Anyone home in here?"

Sara came back with a jolt, looking up to see Charlotte Post leaning in the doorway.

"God, you scared me, Char! Don't lean on that thing too hard, by the way. You could find yourself on the floor."

"Thanks a lot." Charlotte entered and slid gracefully into a high-backed chair. "I'm not certain if that's an insult to my staff's handiwork or a stab at my weight."

"Neither." Sara grinned. "But it would be nice to have the permanent office you promised when you lured me away to the wilderness."

Charlotte returned the smile and glanced around the cubicle. The owner and publisher of *The Silvercat Sentinel* was a tall woman in her midforties, though her neatly styled and frosted hair and slim figure gave the impression of someone a decade younger. Sara had noted the unusual similarity of their height and frame when she'd first met Charlotte Post and had thought, That's what I'll like to look like when I grow up.

"It is a bit cramped in here now that you mention it." Charlotte completed her inspection. "Especially compared to Marv's office. But I thought—"

"That I'd tough it out a year or two until he retires and you make me editor," finished Sara. "Pretty close?"

"Close enough." Charlotte leaned back and studied Sara with her pale blue eyes. "You've got to stop reading my mind, girl. Anyway, we could dress this place up some with paneling and curtains, maybe one of those male-model calendars. You know, 'Best Buns Under the Sun.' It'd look pretty sharp in here if you don't lean on the walls."

"Right, Char." Sara laughed. "At least the calendar sounds interesting."

Charlotte's expression became serious. "So, anyway. What's the word on the Fuller Park business?"

Sara also frowned. "It's trickling in slowly. We've got the pertinent stuff on Jalecka, except for the whereabouts of her two ex-husbands. And it doesn't look like that's as important now."

"Really? How so?"

"I just found out that some of the characteristics match that double murder down on the Front Range Monday."

"You're kidding! The women at the rest stop? But that's at least three hundred miles away." Charlotte leaned forward. "What kinds of characteristics?"

"You know Arthur Morse a lot better than I do, Char," said Sara. "He's really sitting on the details, almost like I'm too much of a lady to be exposed."

"He's from the old school, Sara. He's been practicing medicine here since I was a kid."

"That long?" Sara kidded. "Seriously, I wouldn't know much of anything except for a guy in DeVane Belleau's office."

"Henry Light."

"Aren't we observant? I suppose Hank does fancy me a little. Anyway, turns out Jalecka was sexually mutilated. Eviscerated. She died from shock and massive blood loss."

"My God!" breathed Charlotte. "And the women at the rest area were the same?"

"It seems one was killed with a single wound. But the other, her death sounds like a match. This is a big story, Char. Thirty inches, main bar."

Charlotte didn't reply at first, her eyes slitted in thought. "Does this sound like one of those serial things to you?" she finally asked.

"Like the ones around Seattle, you mean?"

"Yes. Or that guy on death row in Florida. He killed a woman here in Colorado, they believe."

"I don't know," said Sara. "They certainly don't sound

like unrelated events, do they? But wouldn't you need more than two? Coincidences do—''

"How do we know there are only two? Did you talk to Hobie?"

"Early this morning. But he's as bad as Dr. Morse, and his deputy's no better."

"Speaking of 'Best Buns Under the Sun.' " Charlotte smiled. "How is Murph?"

"Like anyone you'd see in a cage playing with a rubber tire, I imagine. Who knows?" Sara felt a surge of exasperation. "Also, who cares? Why are people always asking me about Murphy Davis? I hardly know the guy."

"Why, indeed? Of course, it is DeVane's case, but I'm sure Hobie and Murph will be assisting."

"Actually, I guess I should take note of how Davis deals with this," mused Sara. "After all, he'll be in an election a few weeks from now."

"No contest."

"You too? Don't be so sure, Char. There are a lot of new voters here, and Neddie Cameron's more their type. They're too sophisticated to elect someone just because he once made a bunch of touchdowns."

"Murph was a linebacker, Sara."

"Whatever. As I see it, he's just another glorified jock."

"No." Charlotte chuckled aloud. "That's his dog."

"What? I don't follow."

"Never mind. The point is he's a good, solid—"

"I've also heard he drinks. A lot."

Charlotte shook her head. "Sara, Sara." She sighed. "Okay, back to business. Why don't I give Art Morse a call? He and I are on the school board together. Maybe I can persuade him to part with some real facts, or at least confirm what Hank told you, if it doesn't hinder the investigation. I hate that damned 'reliable source' business."

Sara rebelled inwardly at the idea of the owner pulling strings to get her information she'd obtain eventually anyway.

But Silvercat was, in most ways, still a small town, and she was still an outsider to the locals.

"Okay, boss," she finally said. "I should have time to run over there, then bang this out before the press run. And besides," she added with a smile, "I'll bet you could charm Dr. Morse right out of his stethoscope. I've seen how he looks at you."

Charlotte dropped her a wicked wink. "Art's a bit old for me, dear," she said. "But I'll still take that as a compliment."

5

Friday, October 18

The football stadium lay in a natural bowl near the main
branch of Cat Creek. A hillside had been cleared of brush,
with grass planted and wooden seats built into the sloping
ground. On the other side, a row of metal bleachers surmounted
by a press box rose next to an aspen grove and the stream
itself. Patrons parked in a lot behind the south end zone that
held cars from the nearby high school during the day. The
playing surface had been lined off for the Mountaineers' game
that night, and the smell of mown grass, turning autumn
brown, was in the air.

Murphy was on his third lap around the composition track
when he noticed Sara Nichols sitting on the grassy hillside.
She was wearing a long skirt of some brownish color tucked
around her and a jacket over her blouse. Her hair was still in
a braid, and she wore mirror-surfaced sunglasses. She was
petting Glorified Jock, who lay by her side.

He pretended not to see her and picked up the pace,
consciously pulling together his running form, which had
slipped some with the pain in the last lap. He went past his
start point next to the press box and kicked into the final
four-forty. When he passed her again, near the southwest
corner of the end zone, he was fighting it hard, lungs and
knee protesting.

He finished by the press box, gasping for air, then limped
into the curve, grateful he was so far from Sara Nichols that
she couldn't possibly hear him.

By the time he'd walked the three hundred yards around

the track to the far corner, his breathing had nearly returned to normal. He looked at Sara, sitting halfway up the hill, and nodded a greeting.

"Hi," he said. "I didn't see you there." He trotted up the stands in her direction.

"Really." Her voice was amused. "I thought perhaps you'd spotted me on your next-to-last lap. I guess I was wrong."

He didn't reply, but his trot slowed to a walk. Damn. Nailed him again.

"Is this your dog?" she went on. "He's magnificent. But I thought German shepherds didn't like strangers."

"Not Jock." Murphy walked across the end of the stands and onto the grass. "He likes anyone who'll pet him. Or feed him peanut butter."

"Jock?" There was a note of surprise in her voice, then she appeared to fight with a grin. "That's his name?"

"Actually, it's Glorified Jock. Sort of a private joke . . . Hey, I didn't know it was *that* funny."

She was trying unsuccessfully to stifle a giggle. "No, no, it's just something . . ." She bit down on her lip and forced a serious expression. "It's just something I heard today. This is a nice track."

"New money. Lots of fitness buffs coming into town. They commissioned this all-weather surface back in May, mostly for themselves, I think. But the school benefits from it, too."

"How far do you run?"

"Usually about three, four miles," he lied. "Today I just went two."

"Really," she said again. "The reason I came looking for you, Deputy, is to confirm some information I received this afternoon. Regarding the Jalecka matter."

"Oh . . . what information is that?" Murphy sat down on the hillside, just within the scent of her perfume. He was fairly sure he'd masked his disappointment. Glorified Jock remained by Sara's side, his big head resting on her knee while she rubbed his ears and the sides of his muzzle.

"For one thing," said Sara, "I was told that another

killing, identical in nature, occurred near Denver on Monday. Is that true?''

Where had she heard that? Murphy mentally pulled up his guard. "Well, there was a double murder on I-25. It's been in the news."

"Under identical circumstances?"

"Maybe you'd better ask—"

"I'm asking you, Deputy." The lenses of the sunglasses reflected back his own image. "You're planning to be sheriff. Dealing with the press is something you'd better get used to."

"I've talked to the press before, *Ms*. Nichols." He felt a hot flush creep up his neck.

"I'm sure you have, but I'm not referring to locker-room interviews, Deputy." Her expression was unsmiling. "As I asked, were the circumstances of the killings identical?"

"Yeah, they were," he replied angrily. "Mutilation, ripped clothing, even the eyelids."

"Eyelids?" She sat suddenly erect. "What about the eyelids?"

Jesus, he'd done it. She hadn't known. She'd purposely gotten him mad, then played him like a cheap jukebox.

"I'm afraid all this is evidence in an ongoing investigation." He rose to his feet. "Any information to the press would have to be cleared by both Chief Belleau and Sheriff Jameison." He knew how pompous he sounded.

He started down the hillside, feeling a tightness in his right hamstring. Oh, great. Goddamn outstanding, in fact. "C'mon, dog," he said. "See ya, Ms. Nichols."

"Sure." She'd leaned back on her elbows in the grass and removed the sunglasses. Her eyes were green, clear, and mocking. "See ya, Glorified Jock."

She was talking to the dog, but she was looking straight at him.

It wasn't as much fun as it should have been.

Sara squinted in the late-afternoon sun, cleaning her glasses on her skirt, then rose to her feet. Murphy Davis was already going through the gate to the parking lot, his back stiff with wounded pride. She knew he was mentally kicking himself every step of the way.

Even with Charlotte Post's phone call, Dr. Arthur Morse had remained noncommittal. Yes, the murder had been a particularly gruesome one, and yes, he'd heard of the I-25 killings on Monday. Similarities? He couldn't comment on that yet. Details on Jalecka? He was still running tests.

She knew she'd get the same song and dance from Jameison. Not that she blamed them. They were just beginning a murder investigation, and it was their job to hold back pertinent details that might jeopardize it. Just as it was her job to ferret out those details. It was often an adversary relationship.

That was when she'd thought of Murphy Davis.

He hadn't been hard to locate. She'd checked Leo's Gym, then the Dutchman, then she'd driven to the stadium. The fact that she knew a lot of Murphy's habits wasn't something she cared to dwell on.

He'd seen her on the backstretch of his next-to-last lap and had immediately kicked it into overdrive, which both amused and flattered her. Not that he'd looked so bad before, loping along with the fluid stride of a natural athlete, albeit a damaged one. She didn't care to dwell on *that,* either.

It had been easy enough. She'd learned years before how to play off someone's anger to get extra information, things that person never intended to say. And with Murphy Davis, she'd guessed instinctively which buttons to push because he liked her, and she knew it.

Eyelids. What in hell was that? Another similarity to the Monday killing, obviously, but what? She knew for certain she'd get no more from Belleau's or Jameison's office before the weekend. Besides, there was Ray Manning's party at Silvercat Village, beginning in about three hours. She had to get home.

Maybe she'd give the Castle Rock police a call Saturday morning. Mention eyelids as if she already knew...

"Glorified Jock," Sara said aloud, walking past the end zone of her way to the gate. She remembered Charlotte's remark.

"No, that's his dog," she said, and began to laugh again. But it wasn't as much fun as it should have been.

It's dark in the upstairs bedroom, and its musty smell is in his nostrils. The only light, from the hallway near the head of the stairs, cuts diagonally across the foot of the bed. The shape, lying still under the covers, is in shadow.

And they watch his every move. The eyes.

He stands rigid, hands shaking, just inside the door. The razor is already out of its holder in the boot, already in his grasp.

Come on, Danni . . .

He knows every floorboard, every creak, and his steps are silent. One, two, three—past the old cedar chest—four, five, six, seven. He's in shadow, too. A dark figure, quivering slightly, above the bundled shape in the bed.

He feels the tears begin again and makes no effort to stop them.

"Hello, love," he whispers, because he knows she's found him again.

The tears slide down his cheeks, discolored and bitter tasting on his lips. The sounds of his crying have become audible in the room, but the shape in the bed doesn't move.

"I loved you," he sobs, snuffling down saliva and snot and the dark, bitter tears. "I loved you. But you couldn't let it be, could you?"

His voice rises, shaking in its intensity. For the first time he wipes angrily at his eyes with the back of his hand. The shape in the bed doesn't move.

"Oh, no! Oh, no, no, no. You couldn't. You changed. I didn't change. You did."

He raises the blade to waist level. Its tip just catches the edge of the light lying across the foot of the bed and reflects a thin streak across his face.

"Teasing me." He shifts the razor, the shape of the silver handle familiar against his palm. "Teasing . . ."

He raises the blade in a glittering arc, catching the light from the hallway, then slashes it across the shape on the bed.

"Oh, Danni!" he cries, ripping again and again. "Oh, my love!"

Later, he sits at the side of the bed, the blade still embedded in the old blanket, and hides his face with his hands. Then he pulls the handle free from the pillow. Feathers fly from gaping tears and settle on his black corduroy pants.

After a time he rises and turns on the bedroom light, avoiding their unblinking stare. The eyes. He takes the blanket, shredded from countless slashes, and folds it before putting it back in the cedar chest. The pillow is ruined, so he dumps it in a plastic trash bag, along with the feathers he picks up from the bed and the floor. He inspects the mattress to be sure there's no damage, then pulls the covers neatly into place. He turns off the light, and in the dark, he can look up again. He goes into the hall, pulling the door of *that* room closed behind him.

Later he plays the piano. John Lennon's music, over and over. His hands no longer shake.

6

Friday, October 18

The north highway out of the town was a cambered blacktop, newly paved as far as Silvercat Village. It had originally been a logging road of gravel and dirt, extending twenty miles in serpentine coils up through the San Juan National Forest. The remainder of that road now detoured into the town along the east fork of Cat Creek. Silvercat Village didn't want the logging trucks coming through.

The Village, as it was known by the residents who owned condominiums there, sat on a sloping plateau of the Gray Lady, about two miles away and five hundred feet above the town. Its main street connected intricate loops of circle drives and cul-de-sacs winding through aspen and evergreens. The condominiums followed a dozen different architectural forms from redwood and glass and stone to tongue-and-groove and brick, and from one-bedroom lofts to monstrosities with four-car garages. Some were occupied year round, but the majority sat vacant most of the time, groomed by cleaning crews from Ray Manning's Village Management, waiting for their owners' visits. Many, smaller and less grand, were time-shares, used by a number of owners who arrived on a regular, rotating schedule.

The main lodge of Ski Silvercat lay on a rise above the condos. In a basin behind it the lower lifts, including the new gondola, spread in different directions up the side of the mountain. The ski trails, carved from forest, were brown with a covering of straw to ensure a smooth snow base. A giant

redwood deck on two levels, partly enclosed by glass, overlooked
the basin.

On the upper level, behind a second glass wall, was a
large, lighted room. The private banquet facility of the Ski
Silvercat Corporation, it was reached only by a staircase and
the second-level deck, both also private.

Sara kept reminding herself not to let her jaw drop. She
was from Southern California, after all, had been seeing
celebrities in the flesh for most of her life.

"Your mouth is open." Ray Manning leaned over her
shoulder to kiss her on the cheek, not an easy task since she
was taller than he. "Impressed?"

"Bullshit," she answered automatically. "I'm from California, remember? I used to pick up my dry cleaning from the
same shop as Peter Marshall. We were on a first-name
basis."

"Your mouth was still open." He slipped an empty glass
from her hand. "Refill?"

"Thanks." She took a sip. "I have to admit you've
rounded up a lot of talent, Ray. The culture vultures are all
about to pee their pants."

He shrugged and wiped his nose with a pale blue mono-
grammed handkerchief. "Piece of cake. Colorado's very *in*
these days. Most of these characters jet to Durango, then limo
up for free lodging and eats and to look for the photogra-
phers. They're outta here tomorrow or Sunday."

"Not all. I see some in town—"

"The town's funky. Do people still say that? Funky?"
Manning waved across the room to the co-star of a network
comedy series. "Look at her." He grinned. "Queen of the
nose-packers. You think she'll remember any of this tomorrow? Anyway, some of them, mainly the younger ones, like
the town. They put on their jeans and flannels, from L. L.
Bean, of course, and hang out in the bars waiting for
someone to recognize them."

"At the Dutchman."

"Especially at the Dutchman." Manning grinned. "Digging
the atmosphere, you see. You've heard of Derek Westphal?"

"The undercover cop on 'Mean Streets.' Very macho."

"That's him. He went into town one night last summer to engage the rough trade. He was in the Dutchman, really laying it on until he ran into an unemployed logger who didn't give a damn about Neilsen ratings. The guy offered to feed Derek's balls to a wolf, at which point he hauled his tight ass back up here."

Sara applauded lightly. "Imaginative story," she said. "Is it the sort you usually tell to impress the townsfolk?"

Manning was deeply tanned, and if he blushed, it didn't show. "True story," he insisted. "Besides, you're not townsfolk, Sara, and you never will be. And the story illustrates a point, true or not. It's safer for our kind of people up here. Use the town, but don't get to be a part of it. The town's too real. Especially now."

"Speaking of—"

"Don't." He put a finger against her lips. "Speak of it, that is. We're pretending it didn't happen—until it gets solved, of course. Not that anyone up here would ever admit . . ."

"Admit what?"

Sara looked up from her drink at the sound of a deep, baritone voice. An extremely tall man, made even larger standing next to Manning's five feet seven inches, was resting one fleshy hand on her host's shoulder. In the other he held a homemade cigarette. She smelled the familiar odor of expensive marijuana.

"Oh, hi, Lon." Manning nodded. "To you I wouldn't admit anything. Do you know Sara Nichols?"

"Not until now." The man was at least six feet five and heavyset, with a round face and receding hair that reminded Sara of a Brillo pad. "I'm Lon Everell. And you're the new editor of our little city's journalistic arm."

"Assistant, actually." Sara stared in wonder at Everell's purple-and-red sweater with a cable-stitched reindeer on the chest.

"Whatever." He took a deep drag from the joint and held

it a few seconds. "I'm in the writing trade myself. I'm Priscilla Ravenspur."

"You're . . . excuse me?"

"Also Honor Delacroix. Not to mention—"

"Lon writes romance novels," said Manning, wiping his nose again. "Those are his pen names."

"Romance novels?" Sara looked up doubtfully at the huge man. "I suppose there's money in it. I see entire racks of them at the supermarket."

"It's not bad." Everell shrugged heavy, soft-looking shoulders. "Nothing like it was ten years ago, of course. That's when the romances first discovered graphic sex, you see. Publishers suddenly realized that housewives were bored with those cheesy gothic virgins. What they really wanted were hot, steamy fuck scenes . . ."

Sara choked on a sip of her drink.

". . . all nicely cloaked in romantic euphemisms, of course. God, there was money in those days! I was turning out a book a month under four different pen names. Didn't make a damn bit of difference if the plots were all alike as long as I worked in the juicy stuff. I tell you, Mrs. America was eating it up."

"Fascinating," Sara murmured, trying to catch her breath.

"The trick's always to stay one step away from porn," said Everell, taking on the air of a lecturing professor. "Especially from the waist down. That's where you need a talent for euphemisms. 'His proud, rigid manhood.' Or 'Her warm, trembling core.' Stuff like that."

Sara knew Manning was trying to catch her eye. Oh, God, she thought, her sides beginning to ache with suppressed laughter.

"Come on, Sara." Manning grinned. "There's someone I want you to meet." He took her arm and began guiding her away.

"Just once," Everell was saying behind them, "I'd like to write a scene where the heroine snorts a line of coke and screams, 'Okay, big boy. Give me all your come.' Just once . . ."

"This is my father, Ed Manning," said Ray. Sara, who had

finally given in to laughter, wiped her eyes and smiled at a small, gray-haired man in an expensive-looking three-piece suit. She caught the subtle odor of expensive cologne. "Dad, this is Sara Nichols."

"My pleasure, Sara," said the chairman of Ski Silvercat. "What's the joke?"

"Just Lon," replied his son. "Stoned, as usual, and I think he has writer's block. Sara's Marvin Lanier's new assistant."

"I heard." Edward Manning wore the type of prescription glasses that react to light. In the bright room the lenses had darkened, and Sara could barely make out his eyes. "So, how are you enjoying Ray's little soirée?"

"It's been . . . interesting, so far."

"They often are. Tell me something." The elder Manning touched his glass to his lips. A touch, no more. "What's *The Sentinel*'s position going to be on the election?"

Murphy Davis's face, angry and embarrassed, flashed through her mind. "The sheriff's election?" she stalled.

"That very one. I expect I know how old Lanier'll go, but how about you?"

"I . . . haven't decided. Not yet."

"Better think about it, Sara." Ed Manning took the edge off the statement with a bright smile. False teeth, she thought. "Silvercat's changing fast. With the right kind of city and county government, it could go far. I think you'll agree Neddie Cameron's more our type of—"

"What type is that?" Sara interrupted.

Manning shrugged. "More . . . urban-oriented, I suppose you could say. Less naïve, as a result of all his courtroom experience. And Silvercat's going to need that type of leadership for what I foresee as a very complex future. Sheriff, mayor, police chief, city council . . ." He smiled again. "And editor of the newspaper."

Sara returned his smile automatically.

"Now, this, uh, business in town," he continued. "Do you think Davis and Jameison'll break it soon?"

"Actually, it's DeVane Belleau's jurisdiction," Sara replied, knowing she was echoing Murphy's earlier statement.

"Agreed. But DeVane's not up for election. The city council appoints the police chief." Manning waved across the room. "Neddie! Over here!" He turned back to Sara. "You've met Neddie, haven't you?"

"Yes. Once . . ." She watched the angular, smiling man in a pullover sweater and tie work his way through the crowd toward them, shaking hands and exchanging greetings as he came.

Neddie Cameron was about six feet in height with brown hair, tinged with gray along the sides, and a short, neatly clipped beard, also gray at the chin. His eyes, behind steel-rimmed glasses, were a startling blue. Sara had met him once before, and her first reaction had been that he didn't look like a candidate for sheriff. Maybe a district attorney in an eastern city. Her second reaction had to do with being very impressed. She still was.

"Ed." Cameron grinned again, lines crinkling around the blue eyes. "Ray, how are ya? And Ms. Nichols, isn't it?" His eyes on her were clear and direct, and for a second Sara felt as though they were alone in the room. A blush crept up her throat.

"I'm flattered you remembered, Mr. Cameron," she said.

"Are you kidding? And please call me Neddie. I know it's a silly name for a grown man, but my dad was Ned, also, and it's always stuck."

"What were you so serious about over there?" asked Ray Manning, and Sara realized it was the first time he'd spoken since they'd approached his father. "You can't come to one of these things radiating gloom, Neddie. All the beautiful people'll pick up their toys and go home."

"I know," said Cameron ruefully. "It's just that someone was telling me about KTNN's latest editorial. They've been running it all day."

"KTNN?" asked Sara.

"That Navajo station down in Arizona," said Ed Manning, a look of disgust on his face. "They lobbied the government into doling out God only knows how much cash to build it.

Damned thing can be heard in every state west of the Mississippi on a clear night.''

"What editorial are you talking about?"

"Unfortunately, the same song and dance as always," Cameron replied. Then he winced. "No ethnic pun intended, I promise. They've opposed the development of this ski basin from the beginning, and now the expansion has them in another uproar. It's all tied in with Silvercat Peak and tribal religions.''

"But your expansion is here on the Gray Lady," said Sara. "The terrain on Silvercat's too rugged for skiing, isn't it?"

"Doesn't even concern them!" snapped Manning. "There aren't any goddamned Navajos in these mountains."

"Very few." Cameron nodded. "But they're the militant arm of all the tribes in this area, and they have the government's ear. What distresses me is that they've brought that murder from last night into it. Now they're saying that's the sort of thing that happens if Silvercat gets 'Aspenification.' Their word, by the way. That the killing is only the beginning."

Sara was puzzled. "I don't really understand your concern, other than from a public relations perspective," she said. "You already have the Forest Service permits for the Gray Lady's expansion, don't you? With everything legal and aboveboard. Besides, who listens to this KTNN anyway?"

"You might be surprised." Cameron took her arm. "Could I persuade you to take a walk out on the deck with me?"

Sara knew she was being sidestepped, and years of journalistic experience started to rebel, but only briefly. She stored the thought for future reference, then linked her arm with Cameron's and walked toward the door.

Behind her she heard the elder Manning.

". . . know they'll dig out that '81 Seminole business. I'll guarantee you . . ."

"The moon's nearly full." Cameron slid the door shut behind them. "It's bright as day out here."

The enclosed deck was half the size of the room they'd just left. Perhaps thirty to forty feet each way. Despite the soft, nearly inaudible hum of forced air heat, it wasn't as warm as inside, and Sara felt a chill through her thin dress. It was sheer maroon silk, cut to be worn braless, and she was acutely aware of Cameron's eyes on her rigid nipples pressing against the material.

They walked to one end overlooking the ski basin. Sara looked up at the moon, throwing pale light across the summit of Silvercat Peak. She was trying to recall something the scene triggered in her memory when Cameron kissed her lightly on the neck. She inhaled a clean, masculine smell.

"Whoa." She pulled away, the aftermath of the touch tingling like an electrical shock. "Slow down, Neddie."

"Slow . . . ?" There was honest puzzlement on his face. "I'm sorry, Sara. I didn't think—"

"Then it's time you did. I seem to remember a Mrs. Cameron, don't I?"

He grinned, and she felt her resolve slip. "You do," he said. "But you'll notice she's nowhere in evidence. That's because she's back in Denver. It's over between us."

"I see," she said, although she didn't. "Won't that be a little awkward politically?"

"Politics." Cameron sighed. "You know, I read a book once—"

"That many? I'm impressed."

"—which said politics exists in the functioning of every social organization larger than two people," he finished with a smile. "I've been a politician ever since I ran for student government in high school, Sara. I can handle it."

"Really. By nuzzling the neck of the town newspaper's representative in full view of a roomful of guests?" Sara replied, putting more snap into her words than she was actually feeling.

"Those people?" Cameron laughed aloud. It was a full, rich sound, and she felt her stomach tremble. "They have nothing to do with the town or this county. Just a bunch of bubbleheaded celebs Ray brought in to promote Ski Silvercat, and the Village culture vultures who drifted in to suck up to them. All they're looking for is the nearest photographer. Or dealer."

"But, why me? We've only met once. Surely, you're not going to say that I—"

"Of course not. Marilyn's and my marriage was already in the compactor. It had nothing to do with you. But I was interested, all right, from the first time I saw you, and I've been thinking about you. I got the impression you might feel the same. Was I wrong?"

"No." Sara didn't move toward him, but she didn't move away. "No, you weren't."

Two miles away the town lay under bright moonlight and the reflected glow from the football stadium, where Doug Hutchins's Mountaineers were thumping an undermanned Spruce Canyon team. The Dutchman was rocking, pine-slabbed walls seeming to vibrate from the giant amplifiers mounted on either side of a small, elevated stage as the country-rock band got down. A. J. Delaney was pulling drafts and filling pitchers, sharing the bartending duties with the owner, Schuyler Van den Ler, who moved so smoothly on his artificial leg that only the locals were aware of it. An enormously fat man, Van den Ler had been with the Dutch underground as a teenager during World War II. He'd lost his lower right leg "during de var." Any further questions on the subject only elicited a fierce scowl.

A.J. was perspiring from the press and heat of the crowd, with its smell of sweat, tobacco, and booze, and she stopped to towel her cheeks and forehead. She'd pocketed so many tips that she'd begun stuffing the money into an empty milk carton under the bar.

Merrill the Feral was sitting at the far end near the window, which had effectively emptied the immediate vicinity. He was well over six and a half feet tall, with coal black shoulder-length hair and a beard the same color that covered his huge chest. Neither the hair nor the beard, nor the coveralls nor the flannel shirt, nor any other portion of Merrill the Feral had been washed within the recent memory of the Dutchman's patrons. He was presently glaring, eyes as black as his hair, at a small tourist from Chicago who'd been making lame attempts at conversation with A.J. while trying to look down her shirt when she slipped a five-dollar bill into the cleavage.

Nothing down there to see but money, jerkoff, she thought. If you want to stare at Washington and Lincoln in the brief moments you have left before Merrill the Feral examines your gallbladder without surgery, be my guest. She wondered, for perhaps the tenth time that night, where Murphy Davis was.

Away from the streets that made up its tavern area, the town was quieter. Stores, windows and doors shuttered, branched out to houses and apartments and to motel row on the south highway. Some couples who had already connected were there, moving beneath thin sheets and ignoring the motel televisions blaring out MTV or "M*A*S*H" reruns. Few rooms were empty. The summer tourists were gone, but the hunters had arrived from Texas and Oklahoma and Kansas, in blaze orange and pickup trucks, to try for deer and elk. And before their season was over, the skiers would come.

On the porch of a two-story log house his father and uncles had built northeast of the town, Murphy Davis sat in a wooden glider and alternated sips of Coor's with Tylenol. He shifted a thick down pillow under his knee, holding up the leg and then propping his heel on the porch railing. The knee throbbed in steady rhythm with the hamstring he'd strained trying to show off for Sara Nichols at the track. A copy of *The Silvercat Sentinel* lay on the wooden floor beneath the glider.

His house sat on a ridge, with heavy growths of spruce and fir on two sides. Alva Davis and his brothers, Evan and Walt, had clear-cut the northwest side of the ridge, for firewood, they'd claimed, but Murphy had always suspected it was also to provide a clear view of Silvercat Peak and the Gray Lady.

He stared moodily at the stadium lights down the mountainside and wondered if Doug Hutchins's team was winning. Sure, Spruce Canyon was always a piece of cake. His senior year, Murphy had scored . . .

Forget that. That was another time, stupid. There's nothing

worse than some over-the-hill hero dredging up high-school memories. Springsteen said it best. Glory Days.

Good times, though. Just worry about being a high-school hero and trying to impress Charlotte Post, that "older woman" at the newspaper who'd filled his fantasies. Let the coaches sweat the rest of it. The decision making.

Of course, that was before the pain and the orthopedic surgeons. And the Greenies and Blue Thunder . . .

He could also see, in the distance, faint lights up at the Village. He knew about the party the Mannings were throwing, and he supposed Neddie Cameron was there. Also Sara Nichols.

He'd campaigned up there some, though Hobie insisted it was a waste of time. Some of them, standing in the doorway of their condos, knew about his pro career.

"Hey, I saw you play once," they'd say, and he hadn't pressed them for details. People were always telling him they'd seen him play—very few actually had—and these characters in their LaCoste shirts and Topsiders might jaw with the rustic ex-jock, but they'd vote for Neddie Cameron.

God, he was in a piss-in-your-beer, self-pitying mood tonight.

He offered a sip of Coor's to Glorified Jock, who had the good sense to smell the bottle and turn away, then he downed another Tylenol, wincing as he moved. It wasn't that thirty-eight was so damned old, he decided. Just that two or three parts of his body thought they were sixty-eight.

"You're really a dumbass, aren't you, Davis?" he whispered, thinking of Sara Nichols and that afternoon. Jock whined and shifted his weight on the glider, laying his head on Murphy's thigh.

Murphy drank another beer and stared at the lights.

Jesse DePriest sat on a hard-swept dirt floor in his grandson's garage. The door was raised, and the opening faced east.

In front of him, between his feet and the doorway of the garage, was a crescent-shaped altar of clay about three inches high. It was two feet wide by two feet deep, and its open end faced east, toward the doorway.

Jesse was staring rigidly at the four smooth stones he'd cast down for the fourth time. There was no difference from the previous four casts, or the four that had preceded them.

He chewed on another peyote button from his pouch, working it carefully along the slick, toothless regions of his jaw. His vision, already blurring, began to waver, and he placed one hand on the floor next to his hip to steady himself. He looked out through the garage opening, and as he'd expected, he saw wonders.

The moon was nearly full, and he saw in its ravaged face a canvas of smaller faces. Staring eyes, frozen snarls, stark and lonely lines.

It hung on the right shoulder of the Watcher, and it was no longer the soft, cheerful gold of harvest. Now it was hard and silver and cold.

Jesse saw monsters on the mountain, born in the moon's cold light. He watched them caper there, soulless, while the passing clouds destroyed them and resurrected them, then destroyed them again.

It was a killer's moon. . . .

He tried to fight the dread that rose in him like nausea, but utterly failed. After a while he began to pray.

7

Saturday–Sunday, October 19 and 20

Murphy pulled up outside the sheriff's office at seven A.M. Saturday morning, stiff and seriously hung over. Seeing the log bench reminded him of Jesse DePriest.

But when he opened the door, raised voices from inside changed his focus. Hobie was busy.

". . . have been killed, for all you know! And you're telling me to calm down?"

A plump, sunburned man was pacing back and forth in front of the Fisher stove. He wore double knits and a sweater, with a red windbreaker and a baseball-style golf hat.

Hobie Jameison was sitting in his old swivel rocker, hands across his considerable belly. His face was grave, but his small brown eyes were dancing. He flashed Murphy a quick wink.

"Come on, Mr. Halloran," he said in a soothing tone. "I'm fairly certain you were in no danger. It just wanted those fish, that was all. You really shouldn't leave food near—"

"Right!" Halloran broke in. "I figured it'd turn out to be my fault. Blame the flatlanders, like always." His voice trembled in outrage. "Well, I'll tell you what, Mr. Sheriff. Without the tourist money from people like me, this god-damned burg'd dry up and blow away. And good riddance!"

"That may be true, Mr. Halloran." Jameison nodded in Murphy's direction. "This is my deputy, Murphy Davis. Murph, Mr. Halloran here's camped in his Winnebago at

61

Dripping Springs. He left some trout overnight on a folding table, and—''

"And I heard a noise outside before dawn.'' Halloran interrupted again. ''So I opened the door, and there was a goddamned grizzly bear! Right here inside the city limits!''

"There aren't any grizzlies left in Colorado, Mr. Halloran,'' said Murphy. ''We *do* have some black bears that wander into town in the fall looking for a handout. I'll bet that little guy was more scared than—''

"Right here in town! This place isn't safe, you know that?''

"Speaking of fish.'' Jameison studied a ragged fingernail. ''You are aware that trout season's over, I guess.''

Halloran stopped in midpace. ''Season?'' His eyes cut back from Murphy to Jameison. ''What season?''

"Your fishing license should have indicated that information,'' the sheriff continued smoothly. ''You do have an out-of-state license, don't you?''

"License?''

"Oh, well, never mind about that, Mr. Halloran.'' Murphy watched his boss struggle to maintain a straight face. ''You did say you were leaving today, didn't you? And the bear did eat the alleged fish. . . .''

"Yeah, well . . .'' Halloran's eyes locked with Hobie Jameison's, and a look of complete understanding passed between them. ''I guess there wasn't any real harm done. It was just a little scary.''

"I'm sure it was. Probably would've scared the hell out of me, too, and I've lived here most of my life.''

Halloran nodded, edging sideways toward the door.

"You have a safe trip home,'' continued Jameison. ''And come again real soon.'' He leaned back with a wide grin as the man hurried out of the office.

"Come again, my ass!'' Murphy snorted. ''That's one pilgrim we've seen the last of. Trout season, Hobie?''

"Ah, well.'' The sheriff chuckled. ''Our loss, Disney World's gain. Actually, someone like Mr. Halloran can be

a welcome spot of relief. Especially on a morning like
this.''

Murphy nodded. "I admit it. You were right about the
press. I saw two news helicopters on the high-school parking
lot as I was driving in.''

"Channels four and nine from Denver. They're on DeVane's
butt right now, but we'll catch 'em before the day's out.''

"Heard from Art?''

"Yeah. Some odds and ends. For one thing, the test for
sperm was positive.''

"So she was raped.''

"Or had sexual relations a short time before. Or maybe
both." Jameison sighed. "Type O, naturally.''

"What else?''

"Mostly just some confirmations. Jalecka was murdered—
hell, butchered—by an extremely sharp cutting instrument,
honed on both sides. Even if someone'd happened by immediately, instead of old Mrs. Tatum at dawn, there'd have been
no saving her.''

"God.''

"I know. The area below the bluff was all trampled out
from the old lady and her dog, wet shoes, wet feet, and the
photos don't show a damned thing that's valuable. We have
that one heel print, some kind of boot, for what it's worth. If
there were more, we could at least measure for length of
stride.''

"What about the house-to-house?''

"Nothing that adds to what we already know. Henry talked
to Ben Dubose, who told him just what he'd told you. One of
the other cops, Howard Dimmitt—''

"Dimwit Dimmitt?''

"Yeah." Jameison flashed a fleeting smile. "Dimwit Dimmitt.
Mrs. Prevost, down by the corner there, told him she was up
around two redigesting some cheese enchiladas from the
Elkhorn. Heard what sounded like a scream, real quick, then
cut off. She thought it was a cat.''

"So the girl did scream. I wonder why Mr. Dubose didn't
hear it.''

"Did you ever listen to Reggie bark? He sounds twice the size of Glorified Jock. Besides, old Ben can't hear shit without his hearing aid. Oh, another thing. The angle seems to indicate the killer's left-handed. Maybe."

"Not much."

"Not so far. Do me a favor, Murph, since you're so fresh looking and bright-eyed this morning. Sum it up for me."

Murphy thought for a minute, ignoring the sarcasm and the pounding of his headache.

"Okay," he said finally. "How's this? He's strong and quick. And he's quiet. Maybe an athlete, or ex-athlete. Probably fairly young, probably wearing boots, probably left-handed. And either very smart or very lucky."

"All right," said the sheriff. "I'll buy that, such as it is. Maybe you're not as hung over as you look."

"Oh, yes I am." Murphy limped over to the coffeepot. "You don't have to be that sharp to know we don't have much."

"We don't have diddly. Bring me a cup of that, wouldya? We better face up to it that if this creep doesn't hit again— please, God—we may never get him. These random things are the toughest kind to figure."

"They're bound to be." Murphy handed Jameison a cup and sat across from him. "Ever had one before?"

"Not a real one, no. I've seen 'em where there didn't seem to be any reason, but it always turned out to be something. Greed, passion, *something*. And the people involved either knew each other or had something the other wanted. There's a standard line of procedure; you know that. The law uses it everywhere. You begin with the question 'Who stands to profit, and how?' and ninety percent of the time that nets the guilty party. Of course, that was before drugs got so big. Now, sometimes, that procedure's not worth a fart in a high wind."

"When there's no sane motive, you mean."

"Exactly. And if there's no sane motive, the killer's nuts. Or if he's doing it for kicks or he's drugged out, then he's also nuts. Either way, how do you figure it? And this is one we need to figure, Murph. Especially you."

"You mean the election."

" 'Fraid so. Cameron's gaining ground, kid. You've seen the ads in *The Sentinel*. And he's got Ed Manning and the Silvercat Ski Corporation right behind him."

"You think that'll make the difference?"

"Not openly. But there's a lot of money up at the Village, Murph. And I've learned to never be surprised at what money can do."

Murphy shrugged. "If I don't win, I'll make out okay, Hobie. Maybe help Doug with some coaching, or go partners with Leo at the gym. He's all set to expand. Nautilus, aerobics, jazzercise . . ."

"Yeah?" Jameison snorted. "Ordered your leotard yet? That's bullshit, Murph. This county needs someone who understands it, who's a part of it, especially with all the changes that're coming. Not some Denver lawyer in a five-hundred-dollar suit. Forget Leo and his goddamned gym and win this election. And start by helping me to help DeVane clear up this mess." He stopped to drink his coffee. There were mottled red spots on his cheeks.

"You're out of breath, Hobie," said Murphy.

"Up yours."

"Up mine." Murphy nodded. "And don't you forget it. Thanks, Hobie."

"Anytime." Hobie's color was improving.

"So . . . Jalecka's father's in town, I hear."

"Yeah. Drove straight through from Missouri. He even brought one of the exes with him. They're getting some sleep over at the Best Western, DeVane said. Said the old man told him he always knew something'd happen to her one day."

A memory stirred at Murphy.

"That reminds me. I talked to Jesse DePriest right outside here yesterday. He said he knew it was going to happen."

"What, the Jalecka murder?" Jameison laughed. "That

old jailbird's always claiming stuff like that. Goes over big with the tourists.''

"You don't know him like I do, Hobie. As far back as I can remember, he's always known things, and I could never figure out how.''

"It's the peyote talking, Murph. That's all it is. You know the Native American Church uses it as a sacrament, which means the law can't touch 'em.''

"Jesse's not in the NAC. He doesn't believe in any kind of church.''

"Maybe not, but that doesn't keep him out of the mescaline. I'll bet his old brain's about two-thirds burned out from that crap by now. So, what'd he say about the killing?''

"Just that he'd had a feeling. So he hiked up Silvercat to the Place of Power to ask about it.''

"Up a fourteen-thousand-foot mountain, just like that.'' The sheriff gave a low whistle. "Crazy or not, that's something. I couldn't do it on a bet, and I'm probably twenty years younger.''

"I guess the peyote hasn't reached his legs yet." Murphy grinned. "Anyway, he said he was told the killer's the Beast, whatever that means. And that it's going to happen again.''

Hobie Jameison began to laugh while lighting his pipe and choked on the smoke. While Murphy pounded him on the back, he looked up from coughing, tears running down his cheeks, and his eyes held an odd, almost frightened look.

Sara Nichols stood by the kitchen window, morning sunlight on her face, trying to smooth a wrinkle from her silk dress. On the rare occasions when she'd gone home with a man without previous planning, the most depressing part was putting the same clothes back on the next morning. No matter how carefully folded or hung up, they always felt dirty.

"Penny for your thoughts.'' Neddie Cameron came up behind her, slipping an arm around her waist. One hand slid up inside the dress to her breast. "Or should I say a buck-fifty, considering inflation?''

"You'd get short-changed." She tried to say it lightly, with a laugh, while moving his hand. "I was just thinking I'd better get home, and then to work." She stepped out of the circle of his arm and toward the kitchen table.

"Nope. No way. You're having breakfast, woman, and I'm just the guy to fix it. Now sit."

"Neddie, I can't," she said, but she sat down anyway. "I have to go."

"Okay." His blue eyes held her. "I'm not going to tie you down and sit on you, Sara. But I really wish you'd stay, at least for a while."

Her eyes strayed around the room looking for traces of Marilyn Cameron. It was a restored kitchen in an old Victorian, all stainless steel, chrome, and light paneling, and there was an antiseptic odor that was like no smell at all. He lived in a condo up at the Village when he'd first returned to Silvercat, until he was able to buy the house, he'd said. Oddly enough, it had belonged to his family once before, years ago. It was politically expedient to live in the town, of course, but he'd wanted the house for personal reasons.

"Does this room make you uncomfortable?" he asked, reaching across the table to take her hand.

"No," she lied. This time she didn't pull away.

"It's just a room, Sara. And this is just a house. Next time we'll go to your place, okay?"

"Next time?" She looked up at him suddenly. "Will there be a next time?"

Without releasing her hand, he rose and came around the table. He pulled her to her feet. "Yes." He pressed with his hand against the small of her back, and his body was against her. "Isn't that what you want, too?"

She could feel him, and the beginnings of his erection, through the thin robe. For some reason, that reminded her of Lon Everell, and she smothered a laugh.

"So, what is that?" asked Cameron, reaching for the zipper of her dress. "Is that giggle a yes?"

She supposed it was.

* * *

After lunch, Toya Jalecka's father and ex-husband came to the sheriff's office, and Murphy was struck by the contrast.

Leonard McNamara was a farmer from the southwestern corner of Missouri, not far from Joplin. He was wiry and tough looking, the deep lines of his face accentuated by fatigue. For a small man he had enormous hands, sinewy and rock hard. When they were introduced, Murphy felt swallowed in the grip of the little farmer at least eight inches shorter than he was.

Terry Francis had been Toya Jalecka's first husband, and now sold home and life insurance in St. Louis. He was a bit over six feet and going to fat.

That old man could mop the floor with this guy, Murphy thought, lightly touching a damp, pudgy hand.

"... going to hell in a hand basket for years," McNamara was saying. "After she dumped this one"—a contemptuous nod toward Francis—"she married Tony Jalecka. Goddamn wop rock-and-roll singer. Or maybe Greek, what the hell. Her mother was to blame. Tall, good-looking. Toya looked like her, more's the pity. Maybe if she hadn't..." His voice trailed off.

"Mrs. McNamara's been dead for ... four years?" Jameison consulted a sheet of paper.

"I guess. We been divorced since Toya was thirteen. Colleen ran off with some kid ten years younger than she was, then later she got sick. I never kept up with her after that. She hung around long enough to ruin my daughter. That's all I needed to know."

"And Toya left home ..."

"When she was sixteen," replied McNamara. "With this one here." He cut a look of black malice toward Terry Francis, who quickly glanced away.

Could mop the floor with him, *and* would enjoy doing it, Murphy silently amended.

"I brought this one with me 'cause I couldn't find the other one." Leonard McNamara smiled thinly. "Don't think he much wanted to come, but he did."

"Now, Len, that's not true," Francis protested. He had a smooth, evenly tanned face going to jowls. Trust me, it said. Let's talk insurance. "When I heard what'd happened to Toya, of course I wanted to come with you." He turned to Murphy with a winning smile. "It's just that this is a real busy time. . . ."

Capped teeth, thought Murphy.

"Bullshit," muttered the farmer.

McNamara and his ex-son-in-law stayed only a little longer. Despite continuing pronouncements on his daughter's worthlessness, the small man had made arrangements for her body to be shipped home after the final postmortem and seemed determined to supervise every detail personally.

"This was hers," he said at one point, and showed Murphy a slender ring with a cameo inset. "I gave it to her mother before Toya was born. She left it on the dresser when she left home."

Murphy wasn't certain how to reply. "It's very nice, Mr. McNamara," he finally said, handing it back. "Kind of . . . delicate."

McNamara put the ring into his shirt pocket, and Murphy saw that his massive fingers were trembling. "They're gone now." The farmer looked toward the back of the room, nodding as if in affirmation. "Both of them."

"He loved that girl," said Hobie Jameison after the pair had left.

"I know. Even when he was talking her down like that."

"Yeah. And the mother, too. Y'know, Kari's only a little older than Toya Jalecka. Praise God, that's where the similarity ends, but I know what it's like to love a daughter. That man's dying inside."

"He's tough, though."

"Like old, knotty juniper wood. That other one . . . whadda they call 'em nowadays?"

Murphy grinned. "A pussy? A wimp?"

"Yeah, that's it. Both. How'd you like to be him driving round-trip from Missouri with that old man? I'll bet his shit's the color of mustard by the time they . . . DeVane, come on in."

"The color of what?" Belleau closed the door behind him. He straightened Jameison's dog picture, then took a chair by the stove, lightly punching Murphy on the arm as he passed. When he was dressed in plainclothes, like now, Murphy thought his physical resemblance to Rod Serling was almost uncanny.

"Mustard," said Jameison, pushing a coffee cup toward the police chief. "That . . . whaddayacallit, wimp with old McNamara."

"Him." Belleau's thin face flashed a grimace that passed for a smile, another Serling mannerism he cultivated. "Yeah. That guy'll be lucky just to make it back home alive."

"Anything new, DeVane?" asked Murphy.

"Something." The grimace again. "It's not evidence, but it's something, and you're not gonna like it. You know that new assistant editor at the paper? Sara Nichols?"

"Murph knows her." Jameison grinned. "He spills his guts to her every chance he gets."

"Fuck you, Hobie," said Murphy tonelessly.

"Yeah? Well, he won't have to worry about that anymore," said Belleau. "I just talked to her on the phone. Seems she called the police down at Castle Rock and laid a major con on them. Gentlemen, our Ms. Nichols now knows as much about the connection between Jalecka and the I-25 murders as we do."

"Shit," muttered the sheriff.

"The color of mustard," Belleau agreed. "I just spent about half an hour trying to convince her that the details could ruin our chances to nail that creep if she prints them. She was pretty noncommittal, but maybe she'll sit on it awhile."

"You could go over her head," said Murphy, his voice harsh. "Talk to Marv or Charlotte."

"Say, you're a little bitter there, Murph," said Belleau. "Stepped on your feathers a little, did she?"

"Murph's not a happy camper today, DeVane." Jameison grinned. "A little too much Coor's and Sara Nichols, I'd bet. *Did* you consider going over her head?"

"Considered it. Rejected it. I think we have a little time before it comes to that. That's why I came by. We've got to get cracking on this thing."

"Like we're not already?"

"I mean all out. Equal jurisdiction. You, me, Murph, Hank, and my other people. Equal credit, and forget the jurisdiction, okay? A united front for this Nichols and for the hairsprays up from Denver in their helicopters, okay?"

"Sure. Why not?" Jameison replied. "That's essentially what we've been doing ever since you invited us in. But it's going to be beside the point, DeVane."

Belleau had risen and started for the door. "How do you figure that?" He stopped and turned back.

"'Cause our murderer is some transient psycho, that's how. Jalecka was killed over twenty-four hours ago, and the girls on the interstate seventy-two hours before that. He's somewhere in Utah or Arizona by now, maybe even California, and he'll do some poor woman out there before long. Then what Sara Nichols prints or doesn't print isn't going to matter."

"I hope you're right, Hobie," said Belleau. "God knows I do."

Murphy nodded, but he was remembering Jesse DePriest's words.

Saturday passed, the afternoon turning colder as a north-west wind blew through. Then Sunday, sullen and gray, colder still. Silvercat had seven ski shops, all competing for sales and rentals after a summer of peddling T-shirts with iron-on transfers ("If God Had Wanted Texans to Ski, He'd Have Made Bullshit White!") to tourists, and all seven opened their tune-up shops, ready to file edges and wax ski bottoms.

The nights, cloudy now, were less cold. Action picked up at the taverns, with patrons stepping outside periodically to check for the first snowflakes. Except for the usual fights and domestic squabbles—Betty Lindner shot her longtime roommate, Eric Doer, in the thigh (she missed) after finding that she was pregnant and he'd lied about a recent vasectomy—things returned to rowdy, turbulent normal. People forgot about Toya Jalecka, three days dead.

8

Monday, October 21

Silvercat awoke to light snow on Monday morning. It was only an inch or so, but the mood was set. People crossing the steets looked upward, even more than normally, toward the giants north of the town. The rumor was that it had snowed five inches at the new construction site near the summit of the Gray Lady. Some said six.

Hobie Jameison and DeVane Belleau were eating chocolate-covered doughnuts, drinking coffee, and rehashing Sunday's Denver Broncos game when Murphy arrived at the police station. A new building, low and modern with synthetic marble floors and acoustic dropped ceilings supporting banks of fluorescent lights, it had a completely different atmosphere than the sheriff's office. Businesslike and hurried, with a faint odor of air freshener. Belleau's private office was glass and paneling enclosed, and insulated for sound. It was nearly as large as Jameison's entire front area.

"Must be nice to drag into work whenever you want." Belleau nudged Jameison. "I wish I'd played in the NFL."

Murphy pulled a plastic Tylenol bottle from his pocket and flipped it onto the desk. "If you had, you could chew these for breakfast along with those doughnuts," he said. "It's only ten after eight, anyway. I can't help it if you old farts don't sleep well."

Jameison studied his deputy carefully. "You're not looking too bad for a Monday morning," he finally decided, sucking chocolate from the end of his thumb. "How's Glorified Jock?"

"Outstanding. Right now he's probably flat on his back out by the porch, airing his oversized balls. What've we got, DeVane? You sounded pretty fired up on the phone."

"Something." Belleau sat behind his desk and flipped open a manila folder. "Actually, two somethings. First, here's a physical description of the two I-25 victims. Came in Saturday, but I didn't think too much of it till today." He slid a sheet toward Murphy.

"Lacey-Ann Lewis," said Murphy, reading from the page. "Age, twenty-seven. Five-four, one hundred and thirty-six pounds. Brown hair and eyes." He looked up. "Which one was this?"

"She was the older one," replied Belleau. "One slash entering about mid-diaphragm and pulled straight up, lacerating the heart. Read the other one."

"Sherry Zebke. Age twenty. Five-eight, one hundred and fourteen pounds, blond hair, gray . . ." He stopped. "Wait a minute."

"Toya Jalecka." Belleau was reading from another sheet. "Age, twenty-two. Five-six, one hundred and ten pounds, blond hair and blue eyes."

"They both had long hair, Murph," said Jameison. "Botn were tall, slender blondes in their early twenties."

"Here's the other something." Belleau pulled a third sheet from the folder. "It's what caused me to take another look at the first one. I'd already contacted VICAP, the Justice Department clearinghouse, after I found out about the similarities with the interstate business. They compare various MOs on crimes against persons through their computer, looking for so-called coincidences. They sent this sheet this morning on the teletype."

He ticked off several items on the paper with a manicured fingernail, counting aloud. "Since 1965, there have been eleven killings that fit the Jalecka-Zebke pattern, including the eye mutilations. These two make thirteen."

"Thirteen?" Murphy's voice rose in disbelief. "No way, DeVane. Someone would've tied them together before now."

"Apparently not. Remember, the computer can't make

correlations unless it's asked to. Listen to this. April 1965 in Albuquerque. September 1969 in Denver. May 1973 in Tucson . . .'' He looked up. "And so on. Long periods of time apart. Different cities. Salt Lake, Phoenix, Boise. The only repeats in all that time were Denver and Dallas, and they were years apart. I called Denver, and they'd noticed and filed the similarities between September '69 and June of 1983, but nothing had happened since then, and—''

"They could've contacted this VICAP bunch," said Murphy.

"—and the detective sergeant who headed up '69 had already retired and died," finished Belleau. "Anyway, they didn't. You take a look at this sheet, Murph. Tell me what you see."

Murphy went down the list of eleven names, mentally adding Sherry Zebke and Toya Jalecka. He noted the physical descriptions, which were as he expected, knowing Belleau wanted him to see more. He tried to ignore the two men and concentrate.

It was the second time through that a realization hit him. He was about to speak when he saw the second thing and felt the hairs stiffen at the base of his neck.

"What?" asked Jameison.

"Three things." Murphy kept his voice neutral. "First, all of them over the years were physically similar. Tall, slim blondes around twenty years old."

"Okay."

"Second, the way the locations radiate out. Look at this map."

On one of the two paneled walls in Belleau's office was a Rand-McNally map of the United States. It was about four feet by five feet and hung next to a plastic-form three-dimensional map of Colorado. There were numerous pinholes in it, mostly in the Rocky Mountain area.

"Okay," said Murphy, pointing as he talked. "North to Laramie. West over here to Arizona, Nevada, Utah, and up into Idaho. South to Albuquerque and down into Texas and Oklahoma. And as far east as Kansas City."

"Yeah. So?"

"So, I figure that whacks Hobie's theory of a transient. I'll bet if you drew connecting lines, you'd see that all these locations radiate out from Colorado."

"We already have." Jameison scowled. "Damn. I thought you'd see that. Makes it unanimous. What else? You said three things."

"This is the worst part," said Murphy. "Check the dates. At first there were these long time spans, sometimes more than four years. Then, in the last few years, they've started getting closer together. Less than a year between the June '83 in Denver and March 1984 in Las Vegas. And now we have Zebke and Jalecka, on a Monday and a Friday."

Belleau nodded. "Not bad. So, sum it up. What're your conclusions?"

"What are yours? You tell me for a change."

Belleau mustered his grimace. "Okay, I figure it like this. Our nut case, for reasons of his own, is killing young girls who, superficially at least, all look alike. And he's been doing it for years. I'm not a psychiatrist, but—"

"Maybe we need one," put in Jameison. "Sorry to interrupt, DeVane, but how about presenting all this theoretically to a shrink? Get a—whaddayacallit?—psychological profile of this animal."

Belleau made a note on a pad. "Maybe. And what'll you bet we hear that he's killing the same girl over and over? In his head I mean."

"Someone from his own life," said Murphy. "From before 1965."

"Good point, unless the first one was the real one. So, we have this character who periodically goes to some western city and kills a young blonde in a particularly gruesome way. . . ."

"Sex as a weapon," said Murphy. "Have you heard that song?"

"Not if it's rock and roll." Jameison sighed. "If Sinatra can't sing it, I don't want to hear it."

"Pat Benatar." Murphy grinned. "But it's the idea. Like the guy's using the knife, or whatever it is, as a sex organ."

"Impotent?" said Jameison. "Remember Toya Jalecka tested positive for semen."

"After she was dead," said Belleau. "Maybe we're dealing with some form of necrophilia. Let's go on. The cities. Why does he go there? Concealment? Anonymity?"

"Probably," said Murphy. "It's for damn sure he'd have been noticed long before now if he'd been operating in places like Silvercat." He paused for a moment, then, "Speaking of being noticed, I thought that's what these crazies wanted. Don't they usually send letters to the newspapers and stuff like that?"

"Jack the Ripper did," said Belleau. "Son of Sam, too. But they didn't wait around for years between killings, either. It's like this guy's more . . . I don't know, controlled, maybe. But that's the kicker. The murders are getting closer in time. And the last ones aren't in cities at all. A highway rest stop where anyone at all could've walked right in on it and where, for the first time, someone else completely unrelated was also killed. A fourteenth victim, who wasn't tall, slim, or blond."

"He wanted Zebke too bad," said Jameison. "For some reason he couldn't pass her up."

"And the other's in a small mountain town. In a residential park surrounded by houses and potential witnesses. Where's the careful planning? The twenty years of eliminating risk?"

"Too dull," said Murphy. "Maybe there's no challenge to the old way anymore. It got boring."

"That's possible," said Jameison doubtfully. "Or maybe he's just losing his handle on the situation. I don't think he's out for kicks, Murph. That's just a feeling I have. I think whatever discipline that's held him all these years is finally coming apart for some reason. I think he's out of control."

"Neddie Cameron." Charlotte Post rolled her eyes in a mock doubletake. "As my old English professor used to say, 'Who'da thunk it?' "

"I don't know what you're talking about, Char." Sara picked at her french fries and looked out the Dutchman's ornately lettered front window. "Think it'll snow again tonight?"

"Horse puckey," was the cheerful reply. "This isn't California, dear. This is a small town with very large ears. So don't try rationing caca to the troops, okay?"

Sara turned back from the window, conscious of the blush staining her cheeks. "Does . . . everyone in town really . . . ?" She looked quickly around the room. There were a large number of lunch patrons in the tavern, two of them engaged in a heated discussion with Schuyler Van den Ler, but no one was looking in her direction.

"Of course not." Charlotte smiled. "Just those of us with access to state secrets, and I doubt we'd talk. The question is, how do *you* feel about it?"

Sara shrugged. "I'm not sure. I don't make a habit of shacking up. Especially not with a married man I barely knew before Friday night."

"You're thinking about Marilyn Cameron." Charlotte gave a gesture of dismissal. "She's gone, I hear. Somewhere . . ."

"Neddie says . . ." Sara felt another blush. "He says to Denver. He says they were already finished before . . ."

"Denver?" Charlotte's soft voice had a cynical edge. "Why not? I just heard she was gone. In any case, Sara, I doubt you did her any damage. As I said earlier, the important thing's how you feel about it. If you're happy, great, though I'll admit I thought you and Murphy Davis—"

"There you go again, Char." Sara forced a laugh. "That's a match made in other people's minds, and I don't even know why."

"Maybe it's like that old song from the sixties. 'Because they thought you fit together walking,' or some such. You would make a handsome couple."

"I kind of think Neddie and I might make a handsome couple," replied Sara. "Besides, Murphy Davis and I have never had any dealings other than purely professional. I'm not really attracted to his type."

"Type? Murph's not a 'type,' Sara."

"You know what I mean. The big, muscle-bound jock type."

"Glorified Jock?"

Sara gave her first genuine laugh of the day. "Right. I'll get you for that one, Char. But you know what I mean. I prefer someone with more intellectual interests. Less physically..."

"Threatening?" Charlotte squeezed lemon into her tea. "Intimidating?"

"Intimidating? Like you said earlier, horse puckey. No man is going to..." She saw Marvin Lanier enter, and waved. "Over here, Marv!" She looked back at Charlotte. "Now we can change the subject, thank God."

"For the time being." Charlotte flashed her a wink, then turned to her editor, who was approaching their booth. "Squeeze in, Marv. Next to me, I'm slimmer."

"Thanks loads." Sara grinned. "Want some lunch, Marv?"

"Already ate," he said. "Bologna and Swiss on sourdough like every day, thanks to Dora Nell's unbridled imagination. I came by with the stuff you asked about." He removed a crumpled sheet of paper from a vest pocket. "The '81 Seminole ruling, wasn't it?"

"That's right." Sara saw Charlotte's inquiring look. "At the party Friday night, I heard Ed Manning say something to his son about it. I was curious."

"I don't blame you," replied Charlotte. "There are a number of things about Edward Manning that make me curious, too." She turned to Lanier, who was lighting a cigarette. "So?"

"Supreme Court decision," he said, blowing a stream of smoke toward the ceiling. "It had to do with gambling. In 1981 the Court upheld some bingo operation run by the Seminole Indian tribe on their reservation in Florida. What it said, in essence, was that Indian tribes hold sovereign-nation status with the federal government, which means they're bound to observe state criminal laws on their own land, but not state civil regulations."

"Big deal." Charlotte had a puzzled expression. "That's certainly not news around here. The tribes all take advantage of their reservation status. They hunt and fish year round without licenses, for whatever animals they choose, and that big bingo parlor down near the state line brings in half a million dollars a year. And I've heard they're looking at jai alai and horse tracks. But why would Manning be interested in that? That jerk has the worst possible relationship with the tribes because of Ski Silvercat. One of their newspapers recently called him—freely translated—the back end of a diseased coyote.''

"I'm trying to remember." Sara frowned in concentration. "My mind was on ... other things by that time."

"No doubt," replied Charlotte dryly.

"We'd been talking about that Navajo radio station in Arizona."

"KTNN," said Lanier. "Down in Window Rock."

"Right. And Manning was pissed ... excuse me, Marv, because of the station's editorializing about the Ski Silvercat expansion on ... damn! Excuse me again, Marv. I just remembered something."

"Remembered what?" Charlotte leaned closer, fanning away Marvin Lanier's cigarette smoke.

"Neddie was saying the station's beef this time had to do with religion and something about Silvercat Peak."

"They're not building on Silvercat," said Charlotte. "The SSC owns land on the Gray Lady they bought from the Forest Service, which originally obtained it from the tribal leaders. But they have a gentleman's agreement not to try acquiring any of the big mountain. The Place of Power's up there."

"That's what I just remembered. I asked Ed Manning about it, and he never really answered me. Just changed the subject. Char, is a gentleman's agreement binding in court?"

"Doesn't matter if it is," said Lanier. "That's National Forest land. It'd have to be bought or leased, and neither's going to happen without a public hearing."

"Which still doesn't explain the Mannings' interest in reservation gambling laws," mused Sara. "Casino gambling's illegal in Colorado, isn't it?"

"At the moment. It keeps coming up in the legislature every year."

"Well, looka here," said Lanier. "Here comes a grim-looking bunch."

They looked up as Hobie Jameison and DeVane Belleau, in his full police blues, entered the door, followed shortly by Murphy Davis. The three men took the only available table, a few feet from the booth. When Murphy saw Sara, he hesitated, frowning, then sat down.

She made herself return his flat stare. He was still angry about the way she'd obtained the Jalecka information from him, she supposed. Plus, Belleau'd probably told him about her call to Castle Rock. There was no way for him to know about Neddie Cameron . . . not that it was any of his business, anyway.

"Afternoon, Char," said Jameison. "Marv. Ms. Nichols."

"Hello, gentlemen," said Charlotte. "How's the investigation coming along?"

Jameison was tamping tobacco into his pipe. He looked up with a faint grin. "Maybe you should ask Ms. Nichols there," he said. "She seems to know more about it than we do."

Sara saw Murphy wince. "Just following leads, Sheriff," she said, avoiding Murphy's glare. "You'll notice it's remained confidential, so far."

"I have, and we appreciate it," said Jameison. "More than you know right now, Ms. Nichols."

"Oh?" said Charlotte. "Something new?"

"Something," said DeVane Belleau. "We can't comment on it at present, other than to say it's become even more important that your information remain confidential awhile longer."

"How about off the record? For now." Sara looked directly at Hobie Jameison. "There are a number of out-of-town media organizations nosing around this thing, Sheriff, and I think you owe me."

He didn't reply for a while, going through the lengthy process of getting his pipe lit. Sara wasn't deterred. She'd had other pipe smokers use the same procedure on her as a stalling tactic. She sat waiting, not allowing her eyes to stray toward Murphy.

"Off the record," Jameison said finally, glancing at Belleau for confirmation. "Come by this afternoon. Maybe after five."

"You can count on it," said Sara.

As dusk approached, the snow returned, beginning with small hard pellets blown before a northwest wind. Longtime residents began to cast around in the crawl space or garage for rock salt and their snow shovels, and those few without four-wheel-drive vehicles made sure their tire chains were available. Tourists wandered in the streets, collars turned up against the cold, and speculated on an early opening for Ski Silvercat.

After dark, the pellets became flakes, getting thicker as the wind built. Snow began to pile up, first on lawns and vacant ground between the trees, then on buildings and roads. By ten P.M. it had reached a depth of five inches and was falling at the rate of an inch an hour.

He puts the letters aside.

He's read and reread them, listening to the pellets of snow hit the metal roof. Especially the earlier letters. Sometimes they soothe him. He doesn't read the later ones at times like that, or look at the photographs. Instead, he reads the ones from when it was good, then he plays the piano, Lennon and McCartney, for her.

It isn't going to work tonight.

Other times, bad times, he reads the last ones and looks at that one picture, then he goes into that room—and the blanket and the bed. And new pillows.

That isn't going to work, either.

He's been in the town, after the snow began, and he's seen her there. Just a glimpse through a window. She's clever like that, giving him glimpses, then pulling away. But he's clever, too, because now he knows where to look.

He pushes Alistair Three out into the hall and closes the

door, then he takes the wooden box from under the quilt in the armoire. Sometimes, when he's dressing to go into that other room, his mind wanders, especially lately, and he finds himself wondering what he's doing. But when he knows he's going out, his concentration becomes complete. Focused, isn't that what they call it?

He puts on the clothes. The black corduroy jeans didn't come completely clean the last time, or the sweatshirt, either, because he waited too long to wash them. He hasn't been remembering very well at times, and there are headaches . . . .

Maybe it's time to replace the clothes. They're very old.

He pulls on the high-topped black boots and slips the silver-handled razor into place, then he rises and walks to the front window. Snow is falling in windblown swirls down across his lawn and his street.

He sees her face, almost as if she's there, outside his window . . . calling him. And he knows where she is.

9

Monday, October 21

Inside the Dutchman, the howl of the wind was drowned out by the sounds of Bearclaw Junction playing "Rocky Top, Tennessee" in accompaniment to a large screen TV showing "Monday Night Football" with the sound turned off, and by close to one hundred voices, some less sober than others, each trying to outsing the next. It was only when the group paused to acknowledge rowdy applause before starting into "Ramblin', Gamblin' Man" that the gusts could be heard, whistling past the corner of the building.

A. J. Delaney thumped her knee against the keg under the bar, practiced ear telling her, even above the din in the place, that another would have to be rolled from the storeroom in back within the hour.

She was tired of Bearclaw Junction and wished they'd take a break. All they played was shitkicker music, and she could really go for a little Springsteen or Madonna. Maybe even one of those English fag groups.

"Say what, Lon?" A.J. leaned across the bar to provide Lon Everell with a good look. She had privately decided he was probably a fag, too, cranking out those soap-opera novels under a woman's name, but he claimed to be basing a character in his latest one upon her, so it couldn't hurt to inspire him a little.

". . . work," he was muttering to himself, unaware she'd spoken. "I can't just say. . ." The last part was lost in a surge of laughter from a nearby table.

"What?" A.J. nudged his chubby shoulder.

"Huh? Oh, hello, A.J." Everell leaned forward for his peek. "My, you're certainly looking . . . bountiful tonight."

"Thanks," A.J. replied dryly. "So are you. What were you saying before?"

"It's the fuck scenes, A.J." Everell's round face was squeezed up in a pout, reminding her of her baby brother, Dennis—the latest of the four Delaneys—just before he began to bawl. "They're driving me nuts. I think I've got"—he paused dramatically for effect—"writer's block."

"You have my sympathy, Lon. Whadda you make off those housewife horrors? A hundred thousand a year?"

"Oh, no!" He looked around quickly, as if to see whether anyone was listening. Down at the end of the bar, Merrill the Feral sat glaring at him, a red gleam in his eyes. "Nowhere near that."

"Right, Lon. So, what were you saying about fuck scenes?" The blond girl reached across to hand a patron his beer. The tourist, middle-aged and drunk, flinched for a second at the words, then began to eye her with predatory interest. A.J. ignored him.

"It's the damned euphemisms," Everell said. "For instance, how many—"

"Euphe-whats?"

"Oh, come on, A.J. You went to college. You know what—"

"Lon, my major during my brief college career was sex. As opposed to my roommate, who majored in begging and fetching."

"Okay, look. How many different ways can you describe a guy's dork, for instance? I've used them all at least twenty times apiece."

"You're asking me?" She grinned. "Well, let's see. How about the German meat whistle? Or the salami of love?" She passed another beer to the tourist, whose breathing had become audible above the sounds from the band.

Everell shook his head vigorously. "No, no. Get serious, A.J. These are romance novels, for God's sake, not Midnight

Readers sold from underneath the counter. Romantic but not graphic, remember?''

"How could I forget?" She sighed. "Okay, how about . . . his rigid missile of manhood? With its potent payload of love."

"Oh, come . . ." Everell stopped in midsentence. "Wait a minute. His rigid—"

"You work on it, Lon." A.J. moved down the bar. The drunk, clearly enthralled, followed behind her, making kissing sounds and walking directly toward Merrill the Feral. "I'd better get busy. Say, you haven't seen Murph tonight, have you?"

"—of manhood. That *does* have a ring, but . . . What? Murphy Davis? Nope."

"Dammit." A.J. took an order from a sweating barmaid with red hair hanging in her eyes. "Where is he?"

The crowd, impacted by late arrivals in town, swelled into the Dutchman, already full past fire-laws standards, and A.J. continued to work, bandying humor with the other regulars after Lon Everell left and adding hefty tips to the milk carton beneath the bar while she watched female tourists work the room. My God, there are some real desperado women in here tonight, she thought.

Occasionally, she glanced at the snow blowing past the windows, swirling and catching the light of the Dutchman's nineteenth-century portico lamps. An hour later, when a figure took up vigil in the darkened doorway of Chelsea's Rock and Mineral Shop across the street, she never noticed.

At a few minutes before eleven, A.J.'d taken it as long as she could. Despite excellent tips and Bearclaw Junction's calling it a night, she gave in to a more pressing need. She informed Schuyler Van den Ler that it was her time of the month and that her cramps were getting worse. And Van den Ler, who knew a valuable employee when he saw one, told her to go home early, even though it was, by his informal count, the girl's third menstrual cycle in the past four weeks.

A.J. put on her fleece-lined sheepskin jacket and traded her Reeboks for the Red Wing hikers she kept behind the bar. She stuffed a zippered inner pocket with her tips for the night and pulled a bright yellow knit cap down over her blond head. Merrill the Feral stood by the heavy wooden door and pushed it open for her as though it were weightless. He ducked his head to avoid hitting it on the top of the doorframe.

"Thanks, Merrill," said A.J., squeezing past him. "G'night."

Merrill the Feral blushed and muttered something unintelligible, glazed eyes following her.

Her old orange Subaru four-by-four was partly buried at the curb, and she spent ten minutes digging out after she'd started the motor and the heater. When she pulled away, engine clattering and cutting out, she saw another car start up behind her, but she quickly dismissed it from her mind. She turned onto Old Cat Creek Road and followed it northeast out of town.

She hadn't seen Murphy Davis since Thursday afternoon. If he'd been in the Dutchman, it hadn't been when she was there. A.J. wasn't sure how he'd react to her showing up at his front door in the middle of the night, but she was going to find out. At worst, there'd be no one home (no, at worst, he'd be there with someone—Sara Nichols?—and she'd be standing on his porch looking like a total cosmic ass). At best . . . she steered to follow a single track in the deepening snow and let her fantasies take over. They weren't new fantasies.

She passed the old Spanish cemetery, unused now, and began to climb the hill past the county high school. At the beginning of the incline, headlights some distance back flickered in her rearview mirror. That was a relief. If she broke down, at least she wasn't alone on the road.

It was still over a mile up through the trees to Murphy's cabin. A.J. had never been inside, but she knew where it was. She'd driven past several times, stopping in the road on the chance he might come out onto his porch.

She shifted from front-wheel drive into four-by-four. The traction improved, but the engine began to miss again. She pulled the smaller knob into low four.

The engine backfired, and the small car bounced forward

and to the left. "Dammit!" she muttered, turning the wheel to follow the skid. "You cut that out! Right now, goddammit!"

The car corrected and found the track again, just as the engine died.

"Fuck!" A.J. swore savagely, turning the key. "Fuck a duck!" The starter cranked and the engine turned over, but it wouldn't catch. "Fuck *Donald* Duck, goddammit!" She hammered the dash with a gloved fist.

The engine sound grew weaker, and she released the key before she ran the battery down. Headlights glared in her rearview mirror.

"All right!" A.J. opened her door and stepped out into the snow. The other car, big—it looked like the old model Buick her grandmother once drove—and snow-covered, pulled in behind the Subaru. The door opened, and she saw a figure emerge.

Glorified Jock ran in circles around the Land Cruiser while Murphy swept off snow with a broom. The big dog's eyes were dancing with excitement, his tail curved above his back and his tongue lolling out the side of his mouth. He began to bark.

"Okay! Okay, dammit!" Murphy opened the passenger-side door, and the dog jumped in. "God, you're such a pain sometimes."

Jock apparently didn't care. He pressed his muzzle against the windshield, leaving nose prints, and licked Murphy in the eye when he climbed behind the wheel.

"Okay, I said." Murphy took Jock's head between gloved hands and shook it back and forth, trying to ignore the insistent ache on the inside of his knee. "We're going already."

A needle of pain hit when he depressed the clutch, then subsided to the dull throb of before. He glanced at his watch.

"Eleven-fifteen, Jock." He slipped the vehicle into reverse. "I hope Cody's running late."

Cody Bailey's Quick-Stop was a seven-until-eleven operation, but he was sometimes there until nearly midnight watching Johnny Carson and then Letterman, waiting for Prissy Bailey to go to sleep before he went home.

Murphy hadn't noticed all the Tylenol bottles were empty until that night. He sometimes thought he was keeping those people in business, declining—so far—Arthur Morse's offer of a prescription for something stronger.

He turned down the tree-shrouded road toward the town, making his own tracks in the snow. Gusts of wind buffeted the Land Cruiser, and he steered to the center of the road.

"Seven or eight inches down," he said. Jock whined in response. "Bet it'll be a foot before morning."

The wipers swept the flakes away, and the heater was a soothing sound, and Murphy found himself thinking about the game when he first injured the knee. It had been his senior year at C.U., playing Iowa State in Ames. He'd been hot stuff then. Well, maybe not that hot. Not All-America or anything, but . . .

It'd been standard coverage for third and long, so he'd picked up the running back swinging wide. Then their flanker had crossed, driving Murphy's own teammate, his own cornerback, right into him. It was a basketball pick, illegal as hell, which hadn't helped any when the corner slipped and his helmet smashed into the inside of Murphy's knee.

He ran his fingers along the scar, unconsciously massaging it as he drove down through the trees.

A.J. walked alongside her car toward the dark figure. The headlights of the Buick partly blinded her, and she could only see a silhouette through the whipping snow.

"God, am I glad to see you!" She laughed, a little nervously. "That damned car . . ."

". . . not important, Danni." The voice was faint, blown away by the wind.

"What?" She stepped closer, and the headlights' glare went past her. "I didn't hear."

". . . my love. I have something. . . ."

Then she could see, and her eyes widened in recognition. "What in hell are you—" Her laughter cut short. "What?

Hey, wait a minute! You just hold it right there!'' She began
to back away.

"Danni. Oh, my . . .''

She leaped to the side as the figure moved, and tumbled off
the road into the deep snow of the ditch. Then she was on her
feet, clawing up the far side. She heard a faint *whump* behind
her, close and somehow terribly intimate, before she reached
the top of the bank and saw the lights of the county high
school across a snow-covered meadow.

A.J. had lied about her age to get her job at the Dutchman,
and Schuyler Van den Ler, glad to get her, had never
checked. She was nineteen years old, tall and strong, and had
always been an excellent athlete. Now she tore free of a hand
on her ankle and dived through a fence, a piece of wire
cutting her cheek. She staggered to her feet and ran, into the
howling teeth of the blizzard, toward the lights and the
school.

He leans on a fence post, gasping for breath, and watches
her go. He slips the razor back into its spot behind his
anklebone and shades his eyes against the blast of the wind.

She's so very quick, so agile. He'd forgotten that. But he
sees where she's going, and he knows the school—like the
back of his hand, one might say.

Jimmy Alber would be in there somewhere, just as James
Ray Alber, Senior, had been before him, as custodian and
night watchman. And like James Ray Alber, Senior, Jimmy
would be asleep, stone drunk, on a Monday night near
midnight.

He looks back at her car and realizes he doesn't remember
it. That's not right, because she can't own . . . But perhaps
he's forgotten again.

After crossing the ditch to the road, he backs the Buick
along for a hundred yards, then turns up into the school's
parking lot. His car plows through the snow toward the lower
west entrance, and his heart beats, strong and steady, in time
with his anticipation.

* * *

A.J. huddled along the wall, out of the wind. She'd tried two doors, found them locked. Her mind had already dismissed the significance of what she'd seen on the road and was functioning on a different level now, dealing only in survival.

This was a school, goddammit! That had to mean a janitor somewhere. Somewhere inside. And a telephone to call for help. Murphy . . .

She straightened up, then hurried along the south side of the building, the front, randomly banging on windows as she ran. The wind was increasing, blowing snow past her in lateral sheets. No one inside would hear her.

The front doors were heavy glass, with small vertical windows on each side. By the glow of the outside security lights, she saw their glass was thinner. She bent her arm, averted her eyes, and smashed one with her elbow. The sound of glass falling into the hallway seemed distant, like a dream she knew would dissolve into morning light.

She removed a glove and reached through, snagging her sleeve, and turned the window latch, then dug her fingernails, breaking one, into the latex sealer and pulled. With a tiny pop of vacuum release, the window slid sideways.

She was squeezing through, one leg dangling outside, when headlights appeared from below the hill. She pulled free and ran down a dark hallway.

Murphy had topped Three Mile Hill and begun to descend when his lights reflected off metal. He gently tapped the clutch, gearing down, and leaned forward, squinting, trying to see through the snow. A car was stopped, squarely in the center of the road, about halfway down. A Subaru wagon, already nearly covered.

He crept forward in low gear, flicking up his high beams, and stopped a few yards away. His lights showed the passenger side of the car, more protected from the wind. The door was bright orange.

"A.J.?" Murphy muttered. "What in hell?"

He turned up the collar of his jacket and climbed out with a flashlight. "No, Jock! Stay . . ." he began, but the dog was already past him.

The road on the passenger side of the Subaru was smooth and untouched, but the snow was trampled on the driver's side, not yet filled in. Murphy opened the door. The inside was still warm, and he caught the familiar scent of her perfume. "A.J.?" He cupped his mouth and yelled, but the scream of the wind carried the sound away. "Dammit, A.J.!"

Trampled snow led behind her car. There were tracks back there, rapidly filling in, from another vehicle. Double-indented, as though the driver had pulled forward, then backed up. His headlight beams were fainter now, partly blocked by the Subaru, so he walked past once before he noticed torn snow at the edge of the ditch. From below, he heard a low, droning noise.

Someone had jumped, taking off the top layer while tumbling down the side.

"A.J.?" Murphy clambered down toward the sound, bright bolts of pain ripping through his knee. "A.J., is that . . ."

The snow in the bottom was gouged and scattered. Glorified Jock was standing there, tail high and eyes looking upward at the far side. The fur along his spine stood bolt upright, and a low, steady growl was coming from his throat.

Next to his feet, the flashlight beam showed a splash of color. Murphy reached down for a yellow knit cap.

"Jock, what is it?" He touched the German shepherd's collar, and the dog flinched. "What is it?"

Someone had climbed the far side of the ditch. When Murphy started up, Jock shot ahead of him.

There was a wire fence and more trampled snow at the top, and in the distance, the security lights of the county high school. Jock bounded in that direction, and Murphy crawled through the fence, nearly slicing himself on a piece of loose wire, and followed.

A.J. left a trail of blood down the hall. Her leather coat had borne the brunt of the window breaking, and she hadn't noticed her torn fingernail at the time. But now the pain was constant, and blood dripped from its tip.

The doors were locked, all of them. She'd tried the administrative offices first, then worked her way down. The only interior lights were at each end of the hallways, and she cast a long, faint shadow between. As she moved farther from the broken window, the wailing of the wind lessened and became a background sound to her footsteps.

Pay phones. Every high school had pay phones. It was just a matter of finding them, and she had a zippered pocket full of change. Maybe the gym . . .

The sound of the wind was getting louder again. That was odd.

She came to a corner and looked to her left. At the far end of the corridor she saw the glow of soft-drink machines. Where there were pop machines, there'd be a pay phone. She hurried toward them.

What's wrong with this picture?

She passed more doors on one side, a blank wall on the other. There was a staircase to the second floor across the hall from the drink machines. One machine was Pepsi, the other had the red-and-white stripes of Coca-Cola. Cola wars. The thought flashed unbidden through her mind. Taste tests . . .

What's wrong with this picture?

And pay phones. Two of them mounted in the wall, each with its own small booth. The wind was blowing in her face as she ran, sweeping back her long, wet hair.

I'll tell you what's wrong with this picture. She staggered to a halt. There's no corridor light. There's broken glass on the floor, but there's no light. And that's not all.

She stood staring at the open door. The wind rocked it back and forth, and snow was spreading across the floor and glistening white in the faint illumination from the soft-drink machines.

There were footprints in the snow. . . .

"Danni. Oh, my love . . ."

The voice was a whisper on the scream of the wind.

* * *

He follows her up the stairs, flowing lightly because there's nowhere for her to go. He sees her fall once, twice, the second time heavily, and crawl into the stairwell.

When he reaches her, she's fallen again and lies facedown. Her legs in the tight, soaked jeans are splayed apart, buttocks taut, as she tries to rise.

He feels a heat that's both sorrow and rage. And . . . something else. Something less pure, because she's teasing him again.

He seizes her by the shoulder and flips her over, his hand snaking into the top of his boot. He rips her coat.

"Wait," she says, her voice almost conversational, her eyes going glassy with shock. "Wait, please."

"Danni." He hears a droning, a roaring sound in his head as he cries, tasting dark tears. "Oh, my love."

He slits her blouse and touches her, the roaring growing louder. He tears through the denim and is ready, ready, when the shape behind him hits the top of the stairs and smashes into his back.

He screams, a shrill, high-pitched sound.

Murphy ran, limping badly, along the hallway. Somewhere ahead, he heard Glorified Jock's roar change to a howl.

Oh, God. Jock. Oh, Jesus.

He ran faster, the thick figure of Jimmy Alber falling behind as he ran faster than he'd ever run, the pain forgotten.

He turned a corner and saw an open door in the distance, with snow blowing in. And a tall, dark figure, silhouetted black against the storm, only for a second before it disappeared. There were footprints in the snow, and there was blood.

He took the stairs two at a time—more blood—toward a sound from above, nearly muffled by the wind. He stopped at the top, flicking on his flashlight. He saw a dark stain on the floor. A pair of feet in Red Wing hikers. He raised the light toward the sound.

A.J. lay against a bank of lockers in the corner. Her shirt was torn, and her jeans had long slashes in them. She was holding Glorified Jock around the neck, fingers taut in his fur. Blood trickled down the dog's chest and pooled on the floor. He was licking the side of her face.

Her eyes were vacant, staring without blinking into the light. When Murphy stepped closer, she raised one hand, blood dripping from a torn fingernail, as if to ward him off. She tried to pull Jock closer.

"Wait," she said. Her voice was flat and monotonous. "Wait, please. Just wait. Just . . ."

The Second Week
October 22–28

THE SILVERCAT SLASHER

"Where the pretty people play,
Hungry for power...
To light their neon way
And give them things to do."
—The Eagles, "The Last Resort"

"Insanity is the ultimate
contradiction of reality."
—Dr. Jordan Adler

10

Tuesday, October 22

"Hold it, Paul. Move a little to the left. No, man. My right, your left. Sorry."

"Jesus, Hack, get it straight, okay? You still stoned?" Paul Killian had taken a half step to one side. He moved back the other way, replacing his dark glasses while the cameraman set a second focus.

"I said I was sorry. Flow me some rhythm, man." Hacker Morlan took a stride backward. "It's the glare off this frigging snow. I'll have to try another filter, Paul. You have time for a run-through, if you want."

Killian nodded and looked over the first page of his copy, typed on computer flimsy. He lifted his microphone to chest level and focused on a church steeple in the mid-distance. "Do you need a reading on this?" He tapped the mike with a glossy fingernail. "No? Okay, then." He cleared his throat and patted his jet black hair, but he didn't remove the shades. It was only a run-through.

"This is Paul Killian in Silvercat, Colorado," he began, his deep voice a surprising contrast to his small stature. "If the name isn't as familiar to you as other mountain resorts like Aspen or Vail, it soon will be. Though perhaps not for the reasons its citizens had intended.

"Until a few years ago this was a quiet place, unknown except to the lumbering and mining industries and the occasional tourist drawn to its scenic beauty..."

He turned to be certain that Silvercat Peak and the Gray Lady were directly behind his position, marking it by scuffing

a line in the snow. When he looked back, he noticed a
light-haired man in a denim jacket near the edge of the park,
leaning against a gnarled tree and staring at him. There were
the expected number of locals standing around, rubbernecking
the videocassette camera, so he wasn't sure why this one
caught his eye. Maybe the man's size, or his grim expression.

". . . to its scenic beauty," he repeated, looking at the copy
sheet. "But that was before Ski Silvercat was completed
three years ago on the slopes of Gray Peak. Damn! That's not
right. The Gray Lady—what the hell kind of name is that for
a mountain?—on the slopes of the Gray Lady behind me."
He made a half turn with his upper body to allow Morlan an
unimpeded shot of the mountain. "Now Silvercat is a boomtown
in the making, its promoters claim. Soon to be another
destination resort for the rich and famous."

He looked over at Morlan. "This is where we'll switch to
voice-over with the file tape on the Jalecka girl. How's it
sound so far?"

Hacker Morlan reached to scratch a beard that wasn't there.
Since he'd gone to the moderate punk look—clean shaven,
with a crew cut that was long and moussed on the sides and
back—he was continually running his index finger along his
chin, searching for the scraggly whiskers he'd worn for years.

"Too much intro, man. At least forty-five seconds. I'd cut
right to the juicy, if it was me." He placidly returned Killian's
stare. "But you please yourself. You generally do."

Killian didn't reply, bringing the microphone back up and
finding his place again. "Unfortunately, Silvercat's first real
brush with national attention has arrived in a tragic and
unexpected way," he said, reading directly from the paper.
"In the early hours of last Friday, October eighteenth, a
twenty-two-year-old tourist from Kansas City, Toya Jalecka,
was brutally murdered in this quiet, residential park. Say,
Hack? That's all wrong. Let's move the clip back to after I
say 'in this quiet, residential park.' It'll have more impact if
that part's on camera."

"Whatever." Morlan shrugged.

"Okay, then roll from . . . here. Both local police and the

Granite County Sheriff's Department have been sketchy with details of the killing, but sources indicate Ms. Jalecka was also sexually assaulted. And last night during the height of an autumn blizzard, a second attack took place."

"We have ninety seconds on the high school, Paul," said Morlan. "It starts outside with a long view, then pans in the open door to the police barricade and the goop on the carpet just inside. But it's that indoor-outdoor stuff, so the blood-stains won't show up much. Not enough contrast."

"Damn. Any word on getting inside? Up the stairs to the landing?"

"Not yet. Y'know, crime scene and all that bullshit. But I did talk to a guy named Alber. He's the night janitor, and I think he'll slip me inside."

"Yeah? What did you do? Threaten to slay his firstborn?"

"Not unless his firstborn's named Jack Daniels." Morlan grinned. There was a faint brown stain on his teeth near the gum line. "One head can always spot another, man. You just gotta know how to talk to them, and what to offer."

"I don't want to hear about it." Killian made a gesture of dismissal. "It sounds good, but I don't care to know the details, thank you." He turned back to his copy. "How long are we getting on this, anyway?"

"They said edit to three minutes, which is why you don't have time to play talking head with all that intro crap. Maybe longer on the next one if this goes over good."

"Hot damn!" Killian flashed a grin, teeth glittering white and perfect. "We're finally going to make it, Hack!"

"You know it."

"Okay, let's see . . . a second attack took place. Alison Jerrard Delaney, age nineteen, is currently in guarded condition in a hospital in Durango, Colorado, where she was transported early this morning by one of the state's Flight for Life helicopters. Ms. Delaney, an Alabama native, is a Silvercat resident employed at a local tavern—"

"Underage," said Morlan. "Some saloon owner's gonna have his balls in the wringer over this."

"Good point. Keep it in mind for a sidebar." Killian wrote

himself a note on his copy, then continued. "She was reportedly pursued and attacked by an unknown assailant—roll the high-school tape here, Hack—after seeking refuge inside this building, Granite County High School, and was subsequently rescued there by Deputy Sheriff Murphy Pless Davis, a former NFL linebacker. Davis, who is the Republican party's candidate for sheriff in an upcoming election, last played professionally..."

"They're going to make you a star, my man." Doug Hutchins had come up behind Murphy. "By the time this circus is over, the election'll be in the bag."

"Who's covering your class?" Murphy's voice was toneless. He was leaning against the shattered crotch of an old juniper watching the two men with the videocassette camera. "They've probably set fire to the building by now."

Above his upturned jacket collar, his face was pale and grim, cheekbones prominent. Mirrored sunglasses hid the dark circles beneath his eyes.

"Study hall," replied Hutchins. "Betty Parnell and I team-teach it. Ol' Sweaty Betty." His smile faded when Murphy didn't reply. "So ... what's the word on A.J.?"

Murphy felt his throat tightening up again, so he shrugged and looked away. "Who knows? She has some cuts and bruises."

"But she's going to be all right? God, that's a relief! Did she say anything?"

Murphy released a pent-up sigh. All right? When they'd finally pulled her loose from Glorified Jock, she'd immediately gone rigid. Arms locked at the elbows, legs at the knees. And all she'd said was "Wait. Wait, please" over and over again, her eyes vacant as an empty house.... "No, she didn't say much."

He was told they'd given her a large stuffed animal at the hospital, and that she'd wrapped her arms around it and turned on her side, away from them. Murphy wondered if it was a stuffed dog.

"Jock?" Hutchins was saying.

"Huh?"

"Glorified Jock. Is he all right?"

"Oh. Yeah, you know Jock. He has a long cut across his chest and down the inside of one leg. Took sixty stitches to close him up, but it wasn't deep and he's already getting around some. He's the one who saved her. I'd never have made. . . . Listen, Doug. I'm sorry, but I gotta get out of here."

"Okay. No problem."

"That hairspray junkie with the cameraman keeps looking this way. Besides, I have to meet someone."

"I said, no problem. Those newsies are all over town this morning. Three times as many as the first time. See ya later, pal."

Murphy tapped Hutchins on the shoulder and backed away behind the juniper. Then he turned and trotted across the park toward a side street. He welcomed the pain in his leg.

"Then the killer's still here." The lights, muted in the paneled room, reflected off Edward Manning's glasses.

"That's it," replied the man sitting across the table.

"No gypsies?"

"Nope. They pulled out in the early hours Monday. Even Hobie's quit kicking that dead horse."

"Still here." Ray Manning touched a tanned finger to the bristling stubble on his upper lip. He pulled it back and stared at the perspiration.

The man nodded. "The computer showed that clearly enough, even before this latest . . . business. The guy's no transient, Ed. In fact, it's beginning to look like he's been here all along."

"And the girl's no help?" The elder Manning took a cigarette from a burnished case inside the vest pocket of his tan, three-piece suit. "You mind?" he asked, already lighting it.

"Not at all. The girl? She was practically catatonic when they took her in. It's hard to say how much she'll improve, if at all. A shame. She was a real beauty, and only—"

"Do you think she recognized him?" Manning interrupted abruptly. "Could that be what freaked her out?"

"Freaked her out?" The man smiled, then nodded. "Possibly. She knew a lot of people in the town. Or maybe it was just being that close to her own death. That's one we may never know."

"So, what happens now?" asked Ray Manning.

"I'll tell you what happens," said his father. "We scrub the whole business, that's what happens. Neddie'll just have to win this one on his own."

"I agree," said the man.

"Ray?" Manning glanced over at his son for confirmation.

The younger Manning wiped another trickle of perspiration. "I suppose," he said. "It's just . . ."

"It was a good idea," said his father. "And the credit's yours. But the whole thing could get out of hand now, and I want . . . Ray?" He watched his son hurry from the office.

"How long has he had that . . . problem?" asked the man.

Manning's eyes were like pieces of flint behind the bifocal glasses. "What problem is that?" he asked.

"Nerves. What else?" For a moment their eyes locked, then the man looked away with a faint smile.

"He'll be fine." Manning flicked an embossed business card across the table. "What do you know about this character?"

The man picked up the card. " 'Clinton Gold,' " he read aloud. " 'Attorney-at-Law, Albuquerque, New Mexico.' Nothing I can recall. Who is he?"

"Some Jew lawyer, I suppose. He's connected with that goddamned Indian station, so he may be ACLU. He wants to see me."

"So?"

"So, all the more reason to get the problem in town wrapped up. I don't need to tell you that the last thing we need is more attention on this thing. Media types and lawyers seem to run in the same packs anymore, and if it gets to the Whispering Man, we've got real trouble. So we get out of the business of county politics right now, and you"—he pointed a

finger at the man across the table—"you take back over the
investigation and conclude it. Fast, and as quietly as possible."

DeVane Belleau's smile was a tight grimace. "Whatever
you say." He nodded.

She watched him shift uncomfortably in the hard-backed
chair, his face pale and drawn, and she almost began to regret
the sharp-edged questions, with their oblique snares, that
she'd prepared for him. Almost.

"Your knee hurts, doesn't it?" asked Sara. "Would you be
more comfortable—"

"This is fine." Murphy Davis smiled for the first time, and
she noticed how it softened the hard angles of his face. He'd
been described to her as handsome, but she'd never really
thought so until this moment, looking at the dark circles like
bruises beneath his eyes and the edge of pain that tightened
his lips. She decided she didn't like where her thoughts were
taking her.

"A football injury, I believe," she said. "Charlotte Post
tells me you were a star player."

She was surprised to see him blush. "Char's thinking of
high school. That was a long time ago. But, yeah, to answer
your question, the knee's from football. Also the neck, the
right shoulder, and other assorted items." He removed a
plastic prescription bottle from the pocket of his denim jacket
and shook out two small yellow caplets. "Art . . . Dr. Morse
gave me these this morning. I finally gave up on fighting it
with Tylenol, though I suppose it's a good thing I went after
some last night." He dry-swallowed the pills with an expression of distaste.

"You don't approve of prescription drugs, then," she said.
"What is it? Did I say something funny?"

"In a way. Have you ever heard of Blue Thunder? Or
greenies?"

"A movie helicopter and Martians." She shrugged. "That's
my first reaction. But I take it they're drugs of some kind?"

"Steroids and amphetamines." He nodded. "Blue Thunder's what we called the ten-milligram size of Dianabol a

long time before that movie, and the greenies . . . they're what
made you feel like running a marathon, even if you had a
broken leg at the time. That's why what you said was kind of
funny. Without prescription drugs I'd have never made it
through my last few years in the league. These things''—he
put the bottle back in his pocket—''are strictly small-time
pain pills.''

"I hope they help. I noticed you favoring that leg the other
day. . . ." She realized suddenly where her statement was
taking them, but it was too late. "At the track, I mean."

"Oh, yeah." His expression changed, and she silently
cursed herself. "The track. Actually, running seems to help
some, even though Art swears I'll have to have an artificial
knee joint eventually. It was trying to chase down the school
corridor after coming through the heavy snow that fu—messed
it up this time."

"Trying to reach Alison Delaney." Sara nodded. "By the
way, let me say that I appreciate your talking to me privately
about it. The information you've provided today is very
valuable."

Murphy shrugged. "Hobie figures we owe you one. You've
been sitting on some stuff the last few days those network
guys'd kill their mothers for. We appreciate *that*."

She felt a blush of her own and pretended to check off an
item on the pad lying on Charlotte Post's desk. There were
some strong currents circulating in the room, just below the
surface, and she realized they were both aware of them. "I
won't be able to do that much longer, Dep—Murphy," she
said. "There's too much competition now, since the . . . Delaney
incident. We can't allow ourselves to be scooped right here in
our own town on a national story."

"Scooped." He grinned at her. "I didn't know they really
said that." He looked around for the first time since they'd
entered the office. "I always thought this was an impressive
room. It's still Char's, isn't it?"

"Of course it is." She wasn't certain why she'd set the
interview for the publisher's office rather than her own
cubicle. Or maybe she was.

"I never really knew him." Murphy was looking up above her head. "Now, Doug—Doug Hutchins, the football coach at the high school—threw the paper for years, but I was always off helping my dad and uncles—"

"Who?" asked Sara. "What on earth are you talking about?"

"Oh, sorry. That picture got me remembering. Haven't you ever noticed it?"

Sara swiveled her chair. "The picture of Char's father? Sure, I've seen it."

The frame was heavy walnut, stained nearly black with age. It was centered on the back wall of Charlotte's office, surrounded by plaques and commendations and city-council membership scrolls. It was about three feet square.

The picture it enclosed was done in oils, a man's head and shoulders down to midchest. The artist had painted the man's face against a dark background that gave the skin, accentuated by a thin mustache, a nearly unnatural sheen. The eyes, deep blue, caught Sara's gaze.

"It is arresting," she admitted. "I've never really looked at it closely before. He was a handsome man, wasn't he? A little like old photos of Errol Flynn. So, anyway"—Sara shuffled her notes—"let's get back to what we have here." She was acutely conscious of changing into her "business" voice. "We have a pattern killer who's been active for at least twenty years, which is nearly unheard of in these cases. He may live in Colorado, maybe even in this part of the state."

"Somewhere close to Silvercat," said Murphy. "Count on it."

"Maybe even in this town," Sara continued, "but he also frequents large cities. Denver, Phoenix, Kansas City . . . Wasn't Toya Jalecka from Kansas City?"

Murphy nodded. "Coincidence, probably. The lone killing in Kansas City was in 1980, just before the World Series was played there. She was just married to her first husband, Terry Francis, then. They lived in St. Louis."

"Okay," said Sara. "Scratch that." She looked back at her pad. "These women. Girls, I should say. They were roughly the same age, same appearance except for the color of eyes, which doesn't seem to matter . . . Or does it? Could that have something to do with the eyelids?"

"I don't know. Maybe."

She'd been waiting for his first "I don't know." It was a part of the strategy, and now she was surprised to hear herself passing over it.

"Okay. What about the changes in pattern? The narrowing down of time and location. Why? Or is there ever a why with someone like this?"

"I think so," said Murphy. "Hobie says every person has reasons for what he does, that the motive hides within his mind is how he put it, and I agree with that. His reasons may not make sense to anyone else, but they do to him, and every part—the selection of victims, the mutilations, the time and place—is perfectly logical from his point of view. What we need to know's what that point of view is. That's why Hobie contacted a psychiatrist in L.A. named Adler. To look over our information and try to establish a psychological profile. In the meantime, it's back to the same ass-busting stuff as right after Jalecka. Go back and question everyone around the park again, everyone we can locate who was in the Dutchman last night, A.J.'s friends, and so on. All the reasons that law enforcement's such a thrilling line of work, Hobie'd say. But I like it."

She watched him, seeing the previous night's pallor leave his face as he talked. It wasn't like it was supposed to be. *He* wasn't like he was supposed to be. Things were strange now between them. And getting stranger.

Their eyes met, and held. She felt her heartbeat accelerate. Cut it out! she thought. Then: "About that day at the track . . ." she said. It just popped out, and she regretted it instantly.

Everything changed in the room. She felt it. "Forget it," he said.

"It . . . it was nothing personal, Murphy. I needed the information, and you—"

"And I was handy, and not real bright." His expression

was mild, rueful. But the warmth was gone. "My loss, your gain."

"I really didn't . . ."

"Sure you did. So, what else do you have there?"

She looked down at the pad and took a deep breath. When her eyes rose again, they were cool and level because everything was back to normal now. Whatever had flowed between them, just at the edge of recognition, was gone.

"That's nearly it, Deputy," she said, her voice flat. "A couple of points more. I understand a local man, Darnell Pollard, came forward with some information on Jalecka."

"Yeah. She was with him the night she was murdered. He said she left his apartment a little before two. The apartment's about four blocks up from Fuller Park."

"Anything, you think?"

"I doubt it. Pollard came in on his own. He said they drove from the Vantage Inn to his place in his car, and that he asked her to stay the night, but she turned him down. We believe she was walking back to her own car when she was attacked. Her father claimed the car from the parking lot of the Vantage Inn before he went home."

"I thought he'd disowned her years before."

"That may be, but he'd also bought her that car. He recognized it right away."

"She and this Pollard. Did they have sex?"

"Several times, according to him," replied Murphy. "Which may or may not account for the semen Art found. Pollard said she went to the bathroom, and he heard water running."

"Did she have a purse? Something she could have carried a disposable douche in?"

"We didn't find one."

"Suppose someone had sex, and then was later raped by someone else," said Sara. "Would an examination show a difference between the semen of the two men?"

"If they were different blood types, I guess it could. If they were the same? I really don't know."

Damn. There he went again. "It might." "I really don't know." The man was a sitting duck.

"And Type O, which Dr. Morse found, is the most common type." She listened to herself giving him another out.

"Afraid so. It's also Darnell Pollard's type. Hobie asked him."

"Okay, one last thing. What are the chances of Delaney . . . A.J. being able to identify her attacker?"

His face hardened into a mask, planes and angles, brutal lines, and Sara involuntarily slid backward in her chair. "Identify him? A.J. may never speak rationally to anyone again," he said softly, his gray eyes shards of ice. "She may never know her parents or her friends again, or even get out of the goddamned bed for the rest of her life, Ms. Nichols."

"I'm sorry . . ."

"Forget it." He rose from the chair, favoring his right leg. He smiled coldly. "I seem to be saying that to you a lot, don't I? I'm going down to Durango as soon as they'll let me see her. I'll take her your warmest regards."

Sara flinched. "You saved her," she said anyway.

"No, I didn't. Jock did. And I'm not sure how much of her he really saved. Now, is there anything else?"

From Charlotte's window she watched him cross the street.

Well, you really went for the old Pulitzer, didn't you? she thought. You really fried him. Oh, yeah, you really raked him over the coals. Tested his mettle. Put him to the test. Shit. She was suddenly miserable, and she wanted Neddie Cameron very badly.

Didn't she?

11

Wednesday, October 23

Ed Manning's office had track lighting. He'd specifically requested it for times like these.

He moved his arm out of the shadows and looked at the diamond-encrusted dial of his Rolex. Ten minutes to one. Clinton Gold kept unusual business hours.

The lights were arranged to fall on a leather-backed chair a few feet in front of his desk. The back half of the desk and his own chair lay in shadow.

It was melodramatic—corny as hell, actually—but effective. A display of power. There were power lunches and power wardrobes, after all. It was the trend. He studied the old banner draped across his trophy case, Japanese letters once red but now faded to beige, next to his black-market collection of Anasazi pottery. He was a firm believer in power, not trends, and had been for a long time . . .

In late November 1945, a group from the Army Corps of Engineers arrived in the ruined city of Hiroshima, debarking at the port of Ujima. Among their number was Edward Raymond Manning, age twenty. Jeeps took them through streets where fine gray ash drifted ahead of a cold wind and past the gutted remains of the three-hundred-and-fifty-year-old Hiroshima Castle. They crossed and recrossed branches of the Ota River, which wound down the delta from the northern hills. Edward Manning noticed bodies floating in the river—mostly animals—and that many of his comrades averted their eyes. He made certain they noticed that he didn't.

His group was garrisoned in the northeastern outskirts near Mt. Futaba, which would have been only a hilltop in the high country around his hometown of Truckee, California. They were several miles from ground zero near the site of the Shima Medical Center, and destruction was less severe.

The rebuilding being done by the Corps of Engineers allowed considerable time for leisure, and it was an evening in early December when Manning and three friends, bored by the cafés and their bitter green tea, wandered into the shop of Azoi Wakaba.

Wakaba was a frail, gray man, not as old as he appeared. He was unusually tall, over six feet, which only made his gauntness seem more fragile. Along the left side of his neck and head was the puckered trail of a burn scar. No hair grew on that side of his head, and the ear itself was slick and seared-looking.

Manning, not a large man, often surrounded himself with them. Wilson and Fitzgerald were well over two hundred pounds, Jennis not far behind. Though all four were corporals—Fitzgerald recently promoted—there was no question who was boss.

"Lookit this shit!" said Jennis. "What is this place, Japan or goddamn Tijuana?"

"Hey, you," said Manning. "You. Scarface. You speak English?"

Azoi Wakaba spoke English, had spoken it for longer than these Americans had been alive. "Yes," he said, and straightened up from his sewing. He held his hands, with a wooden thimble on one thumb, below the counter so they couldn't see them shaking.

"Well, let's see what you've got, then." Manning leaned on the counter, deliberately turning his back on the man. "Anything worth buying?"

"Yeah." Wilson grinned. "Like your daughter, maybe?"

"My . . ." Wakaba pretended not to understand. "Gentlemen, I sell clothes, shoes—"

"Dry goods?" interrupted Jennis. "What the hell's going on, Ed? You hauled us into a goddamned dry-goods store."

"Keep your shirt on." Manning continued to survey the room. "Things aren't always as they appear, pal."

The store's windows were gone, replaced by blankets fastened across the openings, and when the wind gusted through, dirt and ash swirled across the floor. There were shelves along the walls and behind the counter, and the center of the room had three large tables, covered with articles of clothing.

Manning saw a piece of cloth, once white but now the same dingy gray as the ash, partly folded behind a shelf.

"What's this?" he said, reaching for it. It was wedged in, and he tore it pulling it free.

"Nothing," said Wakaba. "Nothing important."

"Nothing important." Manning spread the cloth. It was a banner, perhaps six feet by two feet and inscribed in Japanese. "What's it say?"

The thin man swallowed and considered lying. Then he straightened and looked down into the American's eyes. "It says, 'Forget self! All out for your country!'" Then he looked away.

"What?" Fitzgerald's laugh was a harsh bark. "All out for your country? What country is that?"

"No country," said Manning, smiling faintly. "Not anymore, isn't that right? That sounds like something the kamikazes might've used, doesn't it? I believe I'll have the thing." He folded the banner several times and stuffed it inside his coat.

"Hey, c'mon, Ed!" protested Jennis. "Whadda we get?"

"Don't cry," said Manning. "There's more, if my sources are correct." He stepped through the counter opening. "Let's take a look back here."

Ignoring Azoi Wakaba's faint protests, they pushed him through a curtained doorway and into the back, where water-soaked coke balls smoldering in hibachis provided pockets of warmth.

"Say, this is more like it, Ed!" said Wilson. "Step aside, Pop."

Wakaba watched silently as the young men went through

his private quarters. They took the ceremonial swords his family had possessed for five centuries. They took the tessens, with their delicate landscape paintings on one side, and the bushido blade from a small altar at the back of the room. They argued over a battalion flag that had been presented to him after his son's death on the Yangtze in 1939.

The MPs came before they turned on him personally. A big, grizzled sergeant ran them out the door, studiously overlooking the loot they'd stashed in their jackets and pants.

"Hey, no harm done, right?" he said before going out the door. "Fortunes of war, right?"

Wakaba closed up his shop before he continued his sewing. The soldiers were very young and—except, perhaps, for the small one—they weren't bad men, just full of victory and themselves. A time would come when they would remember this day and be ashamed. If not, as the military policeman had said, it was the fortunes of war.

Edward Manning, promising the others to divide up later, smuggled the articles into the United States wrapped in several pairs of skivvies he'd ruined during a shipboard bout with diarrhea. The foul-smelling underwear proved an adequate deterrent to searches until he reached San Diego, where a grinning lieutenant, obviously forewarned, rummaged them out and took the swords and flags and fans from him.

It all fit, he decided, and merely confirmed what he already knew. Namely, that the big dog shits on the little dog, and the little dog eats it. He'd taken what he wanted from the Jap as though the old man didn't exist, and now the officer had done the same to him. An exercise in power.

"To being the big dog," said Manning, tipping a glass in the direction of the old banner above the trophy case. He touched the glass to his lips. A touch, no more.

He reflected on the call from Belleau that evening. The business down in the town was getting messy now. National press, free-lancers, even the tabloids. Put that many reporters in the same place, each looking for something the others didn't have, and it wouldn't be long before someone branched

off the main story. Started looking for . . . what did they call
them . . . sidebars? Human-interest stuff, like maybe something on that big, new ski resort up the mountain. He thought
of the Whispering Man and shivered slightly. Better check
that thermostat . . .

There was a light rap at the door.

Manning looked at his watch again. Two minutes until one.
"Yeah," he said.

"Clinton Gold," said the man who opened the door. "Mr.
Manning?"

Clinton Gold wasn't a Jewish lawyer, at least not by his
appearance. The man who stepped into the overhead beams of
the track lighting was an Indian.

He glanced up at the lights, then over to the figure sitting
in shadow. He smiled faintly. "Kind of theatrical, don't you
think?" he said.

He was of average height and very slim—narrow shoulders, narrow hips—with a large, square head. He wore an
expensively cut suit, pearl gray with a black pinstripe, over a
white shirt and patterned tie. His tie tack and cuff links were
polished turquoise, as was the wristband of his watch. Beneath wire-rim glasses, his eyes were an odd shade of
greenish yellow. He could have been any age from thirty to
fifty.

"Nice jewelry," Manning muttered to cover his surprise.
"That turquoise stuff's a hot commodity. Ethnic as hell.
What'd you pay for it?"

Again the faint, ironic smile. "I get a discount," said
Gold, and Manning decided he was closer to fifty than thirty.

"Nice office," said the man, walking past the pottery
display to the leather-backed chair. Manning recognized a
deliberate imitation of his own comment. "What does that
say?"

"Some kamikaze crap." Manning didn't look at the banner. " 'Don't give up the ship' or some such nonsense.
I . . . liberated it in combat, along with this knife."

Gold studied the blade without taking it from Manning's
desk. "Impressive," he said. "I imagine its previous owner

fought hard to keep it.'' He looked up, his eyes glittering behind bifocal lenses.

''Yeah.'' Manning returned the stare. ''He did. Your name's . . . Gold?''

The man's teeth flashed against dark skin. ''Golden Sun,'' he said. ''Clinton Golden Sun. It's a Lakota name.''

''Lakota?''

''Sioux. I dropped part of it when I entered law school at Brown. Now, when people see the name and the fact I'm an attorney, they seem to assume for some reason that I'm Jewish.''

''Funny,'' said Manning. He leaned forward into the light, his eyes bright with malice. ''You don't look Jewish.''

''That's quite amusing, Mr. Manning,'' said Gold. ''I'll bet the Japanese also thought you were a riot. But I'm not here to bore you with anecdotes about my name.''

''No? Why are you here then? Isn't''—Manning looked at his watch—''one-oh-five in the morning an odd time for . . . whatever it is you have in mind?''

''Less odd than discreet,'' replied Gold. ''As you must have realized when you agreed to it. And discretion's a valuable commodity, in this case for both of us. I came to discuss your latest venture.''

Manning felt a stab of unease. ''You mean the ski resort.'' He took the burnished cigarette case from an inside pocket. ''You mind?'' he asked, flicking his platinum Dunhill lighter.

''Yes, I do,'' said Gold. ''What you do to your lungs is your affair, but I don't care to share it.''

Manning snapped the lighter closed.

Gold set his briefcase, a dark leather, on his lap. ''Your ski resort is involved, of course,'' he said, opening the briefcase and taking out a slim manila folder. ''But only peripherally. I was referring to your other new venture.''

''I don't follow. I have new projects all over—''

''This,'' said Gold, removing a sheet, ''is a copy of a conversation I had with one Theodore Morrison. Ah, I see you know the name.'' Manning felt the blood drain from his face. ''It was taped. Entirely illegal, naturally, but interesting.''

He slid the sheet across the desk. "Take a look, if you like. Keep it. It's only a copy."

Manning refused to wipe the trickle of perspiration that ran down his temple. He didn't look at the paper.

"No?" said Gold. "I don't blame you. It's pretty boring stuff. In summary, it refers to a transaction involving Mr. Morrison's rather enviable position with the Forest Service."

Manning stared at the lawyer. His insides were heaving, but he saw with pride that his hands lay dead-still on the desk.

"Of course, Mr. Morrison mentioned in there that there's absolutely nothing between you in writing." Gold plucked absently at something on the lapel of his coat. Manning saw it was a Phi Beta Kappa key.

The lawyer removed a second sheet from the folder. "This is a topographical map of the area around Silvercat Peak," he said. "I've penciled in a rectangle showing some rough coordinates Mr. Morrison gave me. See the wavy lines? They're to show elevation gradients of one hundred feet—"

"I know how to read a topo map," Manning snarled.

"I'll bet you do. The closer together the lines, the steeper the grade. There's some pretty rugged terrain here, Mr. Manning. Especially this one spot. A cliff, looks like. Several hundred feet high."

"You think you're pretty smart, don't you?" grated Manning. "Pretty goddamned smart."

"I try." Gold smiled. He removed a third sheet. "This is another copied conversation. It's with an employee of yours working down in New Mexico. Kevin Turley."

"Turley? That bastard! That stupid—"

"Mr. Manning! Take pity. *Prenez-moi en pitié* as the French say. Turley's name was given to me by an old man from the Indian community south of here. Turley had actually said very little to him, awaiting your instructions. I merely made use of what I'd already surmised, much as with Mr. Morrison. Neither is particularly bright."

Manning sat staring at the lawyer. Then he extracted a cigarette from the case and lit it, blowing the smoke toward

Gold. "It occurs to me," he said finally, "that you don't have any legal proof."

"Not a shred," Gold agreed cheerfully. "Everything I have is either conjecture or else illegally obtained."

Manning rose to his feet. "Then I don't believe we have anything further to—"

"Oh, sit down, Ed." Gold laughed. "God, you're a pompous little honky, aren't you? Use that manicured brain for a second."

Manning sat, bristling. Filthy prick. Filthy red nigger prick.

"Don't you see that I don't have to prove anything?" said the lawyer. "Not a thing. All I have to do is point out a few facts, privately, to some people I knew in the tribal councils. They're poor people, Ed, but they're far from stupid. . . . Something funny?"

For the first time Manning smiled. "I just realized something about you," he said. "Here I was, thinking you were some kind of redskin crusader, sent by that goddamned radio station to save your people." He rolled the last part out mockingly. "Bullshit. This is blackmail, isn't it? You don't give a good goddamn about your people. What you want is a piece of the pie."

Gold sat back in the chair with a placid smile. "Let's just call it a limited partnership," he said. "A form of expiation for your sins, you might say. After all, if your god had believed in permissiveness, He'd have named them the Ten Suggestions."

"I'll have to think about this," said Manning. "There are . . . people who'll have to be consulted. Decisions that'll have to be made."

"Oh, I fully understand." Gold rose to his feet. "Much like that other ski venture in the Sierras. Crown Peak, wasn't it?"

"How did . . ." Manning snapped his mouth shut.

"I'll be in touch." Gold started toward the door. "To discuss the details. Oh, by the way." He pointed at the banner. "The actual translation is 'Forget self! All out for your country!' Japanese is one of several languages I'm conversant with. Also, that was a home-front banner, Mr. Manning. Neither it nor that Bushido knife would have been anywhere near combat.'' He glanced at the stolen pottery. "It appears that being a thief is not a newly developed facet of your personality.''

He closed the door softly as he left.

Murphy was being hypnotized by the clock, so he watched it more closely. Maybe, if it made him sleepy enough, he could go to bed and forget the drawing pad.

The clock had belonged to his uncle Evan, a bachelor. He'd given it to Alva Davis when his leg, crippled by a chainsaw accident, could no longer tolerate winter in the San Juans.

"It's no city clock, Alva," he'd said. "It'd look silly in an apartment. You keep it here to remember me by."

None of them had thought he'd last long in California, especially his brother Walter—who made some scathing comments regarding Sodom and Gomorrah—but Uncle Evan was still out there, using a polished, knobby aspen cane to get around, years after Alva Davis had died and left the clock with his son.

It sat on the mantle behind the wood stove, all dark, gnarled oak, coated with a light sheen of dust. It made a soft, belching hum as it ran, second hand always hesitating on the seven, and Murphy—as his father had before him—referred to it as Uncle Evan's clock. It was six minutes before two.

Glorified Jock limped across scattered sports pages on the floor to the Naugahyde couch and climbed up beside Murphy, laying his head on Murphy's thigh and the drawing pad.

"What's wrong, pal?" Murphy rubbed the big dog's ears. "Let some mad slasher put a few dings in your hide, and all you want to do is lie around. Some dog of the wilderness you are."

Jock whined, then rolled awkwardly onto his back. Murphy scratched the dog's chest, checking the bandages again, then pulled the sketch pad free.

Like many athletic people, he tended to operate mostly on instinct and reflexes, as well as intuitive skills. So, when it came to methodical study, Murphy had to induce patience, and he did so with pencil drawings.

On the thin-papered sketch pad, he'd begun with calligraphied numbers along the side, opposite a vista of flat-edged mountain peaks. In the center he'd started the rough outline of a face. Along the bottom were jotted a jumble of words and phrases, his own particular shorthand. It was an attempt to create an image. To see in his mind what he'd glimpsed running through the door of the high school.

He'd written the word *Strong,* and he looked at it as he absently shaded in a hairline.

Strong. To cut through bone with a thin blade, leaving purpled bruises where the fist had slammed against flesh. Bruises that were poorly developed, though. Bruises, after all, required blood beneath the skin.

Overpowered his victims. Probably someone big and young and quick. He'd caught A.J., and she was an athlete.

Was. The word made his eyes blur momentarily. Is, he silently amended. Is an athlete. With a primitive, unreasoning area of his mind, he knew this had ceased to be only a case of murder and attempted murder for him. It had become personal.

Maybe not so young. He turned the pencil on its side along the temples to suggest gray. If he's been killing women for twenty years, he's probably not that young anymore. He marked out the word. Like me, he thought. Not so young anymore. Which caused him to reach, without connecting the thought process, for the prescription bottle on the end table.

"Don't take these things with booze, Murph," Arthur Morse had warned him sternly. Murphy shook two of the caplets from the bottle and washed them down with a mouthful of Cutty Sark. The page swam briefly in front of him. "Here's to you, A.J." He knew how inane it was as he said it.

Strong. Someone who worked out? He wrote a note to check Leo's membership list.

He sketched in a full moon above the serrated peaks.

Somewhere above the snow there'd been a full moon the night A.J. was attacked. He made a note to check the VICAP sheet for dates.

Something clicked in his head. When it happened like that, especially if he was half-drunk, it felt nearly audible. He didn't have the sheet, but he was certain all eleven killings listed had occurred during warm-weather months. Say, April to October.

That fit. Silvercat lay ninety-four hundred feet high in the mountains. In the past, before the ski resort, it'd been difficult to get in and out during many winters. And any longtime resident who did leave would have been missed by the tight-knit, insular winter community.

He began to shape eyebrows. He made them heavy and dark above the eyes.

Eyelids. He wondered if Sara Nichols had hit on something. The victims didn't necessarily have the same color of eyes. Blue, gray, green . . .

His thoughts drifted back toward Sara. Green eyes that looked right through you, only interested in what she wanted. The story's the thing, was that how it went? No, the play. The play's the thing. He shook his head angrily and began to shade in the eyes.

Motive. He'd written it in capital letters and underlined it twice. Everyone has a reason for what he does. . . . Hobie'd contacted someone in Los Angeles. Dr. Jordan Adler. Now, there was a perfect name for a shrink. Maybe this Adler would have a line on the "why."

Rule out a so-called sane motive like greed. Even temporary aberrations like passion or rage. If this person had passion or rage, it wasn't temporary. It lived in him.

Okay, then. Sick motives. Revenge? Murphy wrote it under the capitalized word. If he was trying to kill the same person each time, like DeVane Belleau had said, then he didn't realize the victims were different women. He must think she's immortal.

The tip of an idea, buried deep, nudged him. He sat very

still for several minutes, waiting, but it was gone. Damned
booze . . .

He made the eyes black. There was a face now, staring up
at him. He stared back.

The telephone, which he'd only recently replaced on the
hook, rang, breaking the room's silence. He jumped involuntarily, sending a mild stab of pain through his knee. The pills
are taking hold, he thought. Jock yawned and rolled away, his
head off Murphy's leg, and papers fell to the floor.

Jesus, I'm either going to have to clean this place or burn
it, he thought, reaching for the phone. It looks like a
goddamned landfill.

"Murph? Listen, I'm real sorry to wake—"

"It's okay, Hobie. I wasn't asleep."

"No? God, I'm sorry, kid. Are those people still hanging
around outside?"

Murphy laughed. "I don't think so. I guess I froze them
out for tonight. Just us wounded warriors, Jock and me.
What's up?"

"A couple things. Probably could've waited for morning,
but I was lying in bed tossing 'em around till finally Maribeth
tossed me. I'm in the den."

"She should've done it years ago. What things?"

"First, the police department at Estes Park called me here
at home about nine. Some park rangers up in Rocky Mountain National Park found a woman's body a little before
sundown. From what they said, if fits with the others."

"At Estes Park?" Murphy sat up. "Hobie, that's hundreds
of miles from here. You think—"

"Don't jump to conclusions." Murphy heard a sound he
knew was Jameison drawing on his pipe. "She'd been there
for a while. It was a road crew that actually found her while
they were closing Trail Ridge Road for the winter, putting up
barricades and so forth. The body was partly buried under
new snow, and frozen into the old stuff. They figure at least a
week, Murph."

"Then she was killed around the time—let's see, a week

ago is last Tuesday. The day after the women on Interstate 25.''

"Or earlier. I figure earlier. I-25 goes north to Denver, right? Let's say our man had been there, and let's say he ended up in Rocky Mountain National Park for some reason. So, he finds this girl, then he starts home like always. Only this time he stops at a rest area along the way to take a leak, and there's Sherry Zebke.''

"Yeah.'' Murphy found himself nodding. "Purely by accident. Jesus, Hobie, I just had a thought. Do you think seeing her on the way back, so soon after the other one, is what got him going here in Silvercat?''

"Like she was following him home, or something. It's a thought. Let me write myself a note.''

"You too?'' Murphy grinned. "You said a couple of things. What else?''

"Uh-huh.'' Murphy sensed Jameison's hesitation. "This is the part that's kept me up. The cop who called from Estes Park is Herm Shawcroft. He's a Mason, too, thirty-second degree, and I've known him since Moby Dick was a minnow, which is probably why he called me at home. He said his office got in touch with DeVane right after the rangers called them. Said he asked DeVane if he should call me, too. DeVane said no, he'd get in touch with me.''

"So maybe he tried to call you.''

"I've been home since six, Murph. Herm said he went ahead and called because of a remark Belleau made that he didn't much like. Something about it being his jurisdiction and his case, and he'd handle it.''

"That doesn't sound like DeVane, Hobie. Besides, A.J. was attacked out at the school. That's county, if anyone wanted to get technical. And I'll bet you DeVane comes by first thing in the morning. Your friend just misunderstood him.''

"Probably. I hope so. DeVane and I go back a ways together. Well, I'll let you go, Murph. Just felt like talking.''

"Anytime.''

"That makes fourteen, Murph. Sixteen, if you count A.J. and the Lewis woman."

"I know."

"And that's the ones we know of. There could be that many more that nobody ever found. Twenty years is a long time. Well . . . get some sleep, kid. We've gotta look sharp tomorrow for that psychologist."

"Psychiatrist, isn't it?"

"Six of one, half a dozen of the other. Take care, Murph."

Murphy replaced the phone and looked down at the pad. The face he'd sketched stared back at him.

12

Wednesday, October 23

DeVane Belleau didn't come by the sheriff's office that morning, but Neddie Cameron did.

"Hobie." He nodded toward Jameison, who sat brooding by the wood stove with a cup of coffee. "Hi, Murph. The knee better today?"

"Some." Murphy had never been bothered by strangers or near strangers using his first name, probably because of sports, with its interviews and easy familiarity. He wondered why it bothered him now. "How'd you know about that?"

Cameron was looking around the office, blue eyes intense behind the steel-rim glasses. Memorizing the place, it looked like.

He shrugged. "Oh, I guess Sara must have mentioned it. Sara Nichols, you know."

"Yeah." Murphy kept his expression impassive. "I know."

"She said you hurt it at the school the other night. The old football injury, huh? Hey, Murph, when you get to be our age, you have to be more careful." Cameron chuckled and patted his flat stomach.

He was wearing faded jeans and a matching denim jacket over a western shirt. Machine-faded, Murphy decided. Cowboy chic.

"Incidentally, that was a real solid effort in saving that girl's life," Cameron continued. "Just think, if you'd gotten there a little quicker, you might have caught the killer, too." Behind the smile his eyes were hard.

"That could be," said Murphy. There had been a dull

pulse pounding in his neck since the mention of Sara's name, but his voice was even.

The response seemed to surprise Cameron, and his grin faded slightly. "Yeah . . . well, that's not to say you didn't do a professional job on it, Murph. You saved Alison Delaney, and that's what counts."

"Thank you." Murphy kept a stare locked with Cameron's until it was the other man who finally broke contact. He looked around the office again.

"Taking inventory, Neddie?" Hobie Jameison's voice came from near the wood stove. "I suppose you may have some remodeling plans."

Cameron laughed. "No, not really, Hobie. I expect to be very comfortable here. Actually, I came by to talk to Murphy about the debate."

"What?" Murphy's head snapped up. "What debate?"

Cameron spread his hands in a gesture of innocence. "Hey, don't blame me for this, Murph. It's just that I've been approached by a number of voters who're interested. They'd like to see where you and I stand on the issues, I suppose. Anyway, *The Sentinel*'s willing to sponsor it."

Murphy saw Sara's green eyes again. "Yeah," he said, "I'll bet they are."

"Did you ever stop to think maybe this isn't the best possible time, Cameron?" asked the sheriff. "There are one or two things on Murph's mind right now."

Cameron nodded. "I know the timing's lousy, Hobie. These attacks . . . I know both of you are really busy, and of course, I want to see this lunatic captured just like everyone else in town. But the election's coming up in less than two weeks, and the voters *do* have a right to this type of forum. Don't you agree, Murph?"

Murphy sat looking at Cameron, watching the eyes behind the smile. Either way, they said. Either way.

"Okay." He leaned forward to shake Neddie Cameron's outthrust hand. It was surprisingly large and firm. "You're on, Mr. Cameron."

"Neddie. It's Neddie, Murph. I'll call you later to finalize

the details, but how about a tentative date of next Monday
night? If we can get you out from in front of 'Monday Night
Football,' that is." He laughed, and gave Murphy a broad
wink. "That's the twenty-eighth."

"Fine," said Murphy.

"Then I'll be looking forward to it." Cameron headed for
the door. "Better do your homework, Murph." He nodded to
Jameison as he went out. His face was set in a grin.

"Dammit, Murph!" hissed the sheriff after the door closed.
"What's with you? Have you gone nuts?"

Murphy shook his head. "I had no choice, Hobie. He
knew it, and so did I."

"Bullshit! You have support in this town, kid. You don't
need a debate, but he does. My God, don't you know it's
always the one who's behind who wants to debate? I got
elected to this damned job five times, remember? And every
one of those silly bastards wanted to debate. Except Marlin
Janes, that is, and he's the one who gave me the tightest
race."

"You didn't have to, Hobie. It's different now because this
is a different town, whether we like it or not. You heard what
he said about the newspaper. If I turned him down, you can
bet he'd see that people read about it. And with everything
that's going on right now, they'd be wondering what I was
trying to hide."

"Nonsense. Marvin Lanier'd never be a party to that kind
of crap."

Murphy swung around to face his friend. "I wasn't thinking of Marv, Hobie," he said. "Or Char, either."

"Who, then? Sara Nichols? I thought you and that girl
straightened out your differences. Whatever they were."

"That's the point, Hobie. I've never figured out what they
are. Sometimes, she seems to loosen up and I think we can at
least be civil, then . . . Ah, the hell with it. I guess Cameron's
hit it on the button. I'd better do my homework."

"You got that right." Jameison opened the door of the
wood stove and nudged in a chunk of scrub oak. "I'm afraid
you're going to find you've made a serious mistake this

morning, kid. There's no way that Nichols woman could've done you damage to equal what Neddie Cameron'll do in a debate. Hell, Murph, the guy's been holding one kind of office or another in Denver for years. Public speaking's his specialty."

"I don't know about that," Murphy protested, "but I've had some experience myself."

"Yeah? Which was what, interviews with a bunch of dumb-ass sportswriters?" Jameison held an imaginary microphone. "So tell me, Mur-phy Da-vis, num-ber fifty-four," he said, rendering an abysmal imitation of Howard Cosell. "Were you sur-prised, nay, mys-tified, when Thun-der Thighs Kozanaski ran ov-er you at midfield, leaving his chin strap thrust up your rectal ap-er-ture?"

"Gee, ah don' know, Ha'ard." Murphy grinned, falling in with their old game. "It wuzn't mah fault, y'know? Ah wuz, y'know, surrounded by incompetents. Y'know."

"I see. Then tell me this, num-ber fifty-four. If a group of incom-petents can manage to sur-round you, how smart does that make you?"

They both laughed at the familiar routine, but Murphy saw Jameison's heart wasn't really in it.

"Come on, Hobie," he said. "Why don't you just call DeVane?"

"And say what? That I heard he's holding back information from us, and I was just curious why?"

"Okay, how about this? I need to check the dates on that VICAP sheet for an idea I had last night—"

"We have a copy right here, and you've already checked it."

"—and I misplaced our copy," continued Murphy. "So, I bring him up-to-date on the warm-weather theory, and see what he has to say. I can take off now. There haven't been any reporters lurking around here since breakfast."

"If you want," the sheriff grumbled. "Tell him I said . . . no, never mind. This whole damned thing's beginning to sound just like a couple of pissed-off fifth-graders to me."

                    *   *   *

Murphy looked around outside the door, then decided to take a chance and walk it. The day was bright and a little cold, with dirty snow from Monday night's storm lying unmelted along the curb.

He cut down an alley between Gage's Bakery ("Indian fry bread our specialty!") and a new tavern, the Ceramic Defecatorium, and arrived on Second Street just as a rusty green Ford Pinto careened around the corner and clipped a newspaper dispenser, spinning it into the street.

"Oh, shit! Estrella DePriest!" Murphy leaped for the curb while the vendor at the corner shouted a string of curses. A plump arm snaked out the driver's-side window and shot the man a stiff middle finger.

"Murph! Hey, Murph!" Murphy heard Jesse DePriest's voice. "Stop the car, dammit!"

The Pinto lurched to a halt in a series of bounces, and Jesse emerged from the passenger side. "You go on," he said. "I'll walk. I want to talk to Murph."

"You come home," Estrella declared. "You come home by twelve, and you stay out of the Dutchman." She turned a broad, beautifully unlined face toward Murphy and smiled. "Hi, Murph. Don't let that old fart talk you into a coma." Then she waved and pulled back into traffic in the left lane, sending a Chevy Surburban with Oklahoma plates skidding sideways, its horn blaring.

Despite the morning chill, Jesse was wearing his usual corduroys and sneakers and a black T-shirt with a logo that read "Eat the Rich."

"Murph," he said without preamble, "I was right, wasn't I? When I told you it was gonna happen again, I was right."

"And a good morning to you, too, Jesse. Let's get out of the street, okay?" Murphy took the old man's arm, rock-hard and sinewy beneath sagging skin. "I'm headed for the police station. I'll walk you as far as the corner of Endicott."

"Was I right?" Jesse's eyes, nearly Asian in their configuration, were twinkling. Pleased.

"Yeah, okay, Jesse. You were right." Murphy's smile faded. "God knows I wish you weren't."

"You're grieving for the girl, Murph. I saw it right away."
Jesse studied him keenly. "You're walking like an old man.
Like me. Was she your woman?"

"No. No, she was . . . *is* just a kid. But she's a friend,
Jesse, and I like her a lot. And I didn't get there in time."

"Nothing you could have done." Jesse clicked his teeth
together as he spoke, and Murphy saw he was wearing his
dentures—his "store teeth"—for a change. "It's like I said,
Murph. It's the Beast. And I've seen it."

"You've . . . what?" Murphy wheeled around and grabbed
the old man's shoulder, regretting it instantly when he saw
him wince. "You've seen the killer? Where did you see
him?"

Jesse nodded. "Up there." He pointed toward the peaks.
"On the mountain. And in the moon, too. It's here, Murph."

Murphy sagged back in disappointment. "Dammit, Jesse. I
thought you were serious."

"I am serious. I told you, I saw it. It's here."

"Jesse, that's peyote talking." Murphy steered his friend
across Fremont Street, holding up a hand to stop a car with
Nebraska plates. "When you saw . . . whatever you saw, were
you chewing peyote buttons?"

"Of course."

"I thought so."

"And sitting before an altar with four smooth stones,"
continued Jesse. "The Crescent and the Four Levels of the
Earth. But that doesn't change a damned thing, Murph. I was
right, wasn't I?"

Murphy stopped. They were almost to the corner of Second
and Endicott. "Yeah." He nodded. "You were."

"You think you can defeat the Beast by staring at a
computer, Murph? Or by going around looking for clues, like
on 'Murder, She Wrote'? You can't. It doesn't care about your
computer or your clues. When it's fed, it goes away. When it
gets hungry, it comes back."

Murphy felt a chill. He looked up from Jesse's eyes for the
cloud overhead, but there was none. Only bright sunshine.

"Then how will I find it?" he finally asked. There was no sarcasm in his voice. "I really want to, Jesse."

"Come with me" was the reply. "Come up with me, and you'll find out the truth."

"To the Place of Power, you mean."

"And past it."

Murphy shook his head to clear it. Reality slid back in, accompanied by car horns and the other sounds of the town. "Wait a minute," he said. "You're talking about drugs, aren't you? Mescaline."

Jesse shrugged. "That's your word. You open a pathway. To the Four Levels."

"Uh-uh. No way, Jesse. I've heard about peyote."

"And you already know about booze, don't you?" Jesse's black eyes were flat. "It's not a hard step, Murph. You just step up, that's all."

Murphy's jaw tightened. He turned away, embarrassed and angry, without a reply.

Jesse's voice came from behind him. "You'll come with me, Murph. You have to. It's the only way."

Murphy crossed the street without looking back.

When he reached the police station, Murphy saw where the news media had gone. There were cars and panel trucks parked everywhere, many with station logos and numbers painted on the sides. As he approached, the glass doors opened and a group of people began to emerge. Blazers and suits, expensive hairstyles and expensive suntans. Dressed for success. They were followed by a less splendid entourage, mostly in jeans, carrying cameras and sound equipment.

He saw them before they saw him, and ducked around the corner of the building. There was a back door opening to the squad-room lockers, and he went in that way.

DeVane Belleau was talking to Henry Light, both men standing outside Belleau's private office. When he saw Murphy approaching, Belleau fell silent. His grimace-smile looked strained.

"DeVane. Hank." Murphy nodded at Light, a thick, red-haired man with a matching brush-style mustache. "What's going on, DeVane?" He dismissed the nonsense of using the VICAP sheet as an excuse.

"Oh, you know, Murph. Just trying to get the newsies off my back. Same as you, I hear."

"With a press conference?"

"No, no. Nothing like that." Belleau nodded at Light, who hurried off toward an arrangement of desks under the fluorescent panels that illuminated the outer office. "Come on in, Murph. Where's Hobie?"

Murphy followed him into his private office. "If it wasn't a news conference," he said, ignoring Belleau's question, "then why were they all here at once?"

"Well, you know. I'd had so many of those damned characters asking me the same questions over and over, I figured I'd talk to them all at the same time. Save time and energy."

"So you made an announcement for them to meet—"

"Nothing like that, Murph. Just passed the word, that's all."

Murphy took a deep breath. He could feel his anger rising at the obvious runaround, and he wanted to control it. Belleau was an old friend of Hobie's. "Okay." He nodded. "That makes sense, I guess. But why weren't Hobie and I here? No one . . . passed the word to us."

Belleau had begun to drum his fingers on his oak-topped desk, a well-known sign of his developing irritation. "Murph, there was nothing new for you to add," he said. "All we have on A.J. is the slashes in her clothing and the blood on the stairs where Jock ventilated the creep. Type O again. Hell, after Jimmy Alber closed that door, the snow melted down before we could even photograph the footprints. Stupid bastard. Besides, I figured you'd had enough newsies chasing you around the last couple of days. Maybe I was wrong."

"No. No, you weren't—"

"Camped outside your driveway, I heard. Calling you on the phone at all hours. Shit, Murph, I thought I was doing you a favor. But maybe you'd like a little free publicity, with the élection coming up.''

''That's not—''

''Maybe you'd prefer I just step aside and let you conduct the next 'press conference.' '' He put scornful emphasis on the words.

''No, thanks.'' Murphy thought of the debate. ''I guess you did do *me* a favor, DeVane. But shouldn't Hobie have been here?''

''Well, maybe. But I'm keeping you guys up-to-date on all the new developments.''

''Then I guess you were planning to call and tell him about the body in Rocky Mountain National Park.''

''Yeah, when I got the time.'' Belleau's expression showed mounting irritation, but no surprise. ''Though I figured Herm Shawcroft'd give him the word. They're old buddies in the Masons, aren't they? Not that there's anything new or revolutionary about the''—he glanced at a notepad—''the Pamela Stone killing, at least not until we get the ME's report from there. Over the phone it sounds like a match for all the others. A tall, young blonde, age nineteen, and a student at Colorado State. Last seen leaving Fort Collins for Granby on the morning of the fourteenth. A lot of people go by way of Estes Park and Trail Ridge Road until it closes for the winter. The girl's family lives in Granby, by the way. There was a missing persons on her since the fifteenth, but nobody tied it to our problem up here.''

''And that's what you want me to tell Hobie?''

''You tell him what you damned well please!'' Belleau snapped. ''I'm not real sure I like your attitude this morning, Davis. I know that was some rough business at the school, and I know you're under pressure with the election getting close. But if I'm reading your insinuations right...'' He stopped and wiped a shiny forehead with the navy blue sleeve of his tunic. ''Listen, you just tell Hobie I'll call him before noon.''

He stood up. It was clear the conversation was over. ''One more thing.''

Murphy had started out of the office. He turned back at Belleau's voice. The police chief was looking above his head, at the door.

"Hobie Jameison's been my friend for twenty years," said Belleau. "I would never do anything, whatever the reason, to hurt him personally."

"DeVane, I never said—"

"That's all, Deputy. You know the way out."

"Yes, sir," said Murphy. "I do."

"Murphy Davis! You're Davis, aren't you?"

Murphy stopped, staring at the stocky, well-dressed man who had stepped into his path from behind a stand of cottonwoods along the street. He recognized the man from Fuller Park the day before.

"Yeah, I am." Murphy started to push past. "And I'm in a hurry."

"Killian," said the man. "Paul Killian. I've gotta tell you, Murphy, it's a real kick to finally meet you. I saw a lot of your games in the pros."

"Sure you did." Murphy looked around warily. Paul Killian appeared to be alone, but he was patting down the sides of his carefully coiffed black hair and establishing a profile. Murphy remembered that look. "Okay," he said. "Where's the camera?"

"What cam—" Killian stopped in midsentence, a faint blush on his pink skin. "Okay, Hack," he called. "This one's too smart for us."

A taller man walked out of an open garage on the other side of the trees. He had a spiky haircut and an earring in one ear, and he was carrying a videocassette camera.

Murphy was ready to lash out at Killian, but he was surprised to find himself grinning instead. The man was like a saggy, overaged puppy. A dyed-black beagle, Murphy decided. That hair had to come from a can of shoe polish.

"That's trespassing," he said mildly. "Mrs. Opal Ingram owns that garage. She also owns a shotgun. Twenty-gauge."

"Ouch!" The man Killian had called Hack winced.

"How'd you spot me?" asked Murphy.

Paul Killian looked pleased. "I saw you when I came out of the police station. Hack and I . . . this is Hacker Morlan, by the way. Don't let that 'I'll ravage your grandmother' look fool you. He's as good as they come with a camera and tape. Anyway, we followed you around to the back door and waited."

"I see." Murphy couldn't keep from returning the grin. Maybe it was just the human's reflex response to another smile, he thought. We smile at people who smile at us, even if they've just said "fuck you." "So, who are you guys with?"

"We . . . uh, sort of free-lance," said Morlan. "But we've got a big—"

"When you came out," Killian interrupted, with a fierce scowl at his partner, "you looked somewhat pissed."

"Somewhat," Morlan echoed.

"So we were hesitant at first. I mean, you're what? Six foot three? Two twenty or two thirty?"

"Six-four," said Murphy.

"Then I decided, what the hell. You're a tough guy to get hold of, Murphy. I've called you—"

"You and everyone else this side of Bumfuck, Egypt," said Murphy. "I took the phone off the hook. Now, if you'll excuse me, Mr. . . ."

"Killian. Paul Killian. Wait, hold it a minute. Murphy's an Irish name, right? It means 'sea warrior.' I looked it up."

"So?" Murphy stopped again, mystified.

"So, I'm Irish, too. Killian. You know, 'Killian red'?"

"Or, in his case, Killian black." Morlan grinned.

"Big deal. What is this, the St. Patrick's Day Parade? Like I told you—"

"Wait, wait. Do you know Irish tradition, Murphy? How if you catch a leprechaun, you get a wish?"

"What in hell . . ."

Killian held up a chubby hand. "Everyone's been chasing you around for two days now," he said. "And we caught you, sort of. So how about one wish? I mean, one question."

Murphy looked from one of them to the other. Definitely

the Three Stooges, minus one. "You two are nuts," he finally said. "Especially you, Killian. You know that, don't you? Okay, one question, but you're wasting your time and mine. Someone or other has asked me everything I could possibly answer."

"Not this one." Killian turned to Morlan. "Are we rolling?"

Morlan's grin widened. "Never stopped," he said.

"Okay." Killian adjusted his shoulder-pack microphone. "Please give me an opinion on something, Deputy," he said, his voice dropping an octave. "Regarding the assault upon Alison Delaney Monday night: how did the assailant get inside Granite County High School in the first place?"

Shit, thought Murphy.

"Probably through the same window that A.J. . . . Ms. Delaney broke," he said aloud. "And you were wrong, Killian. I have been asked that question."

"But when you reached her at the other end of the building, Jimmy Alber told us—"

"That's your one question, Killian. This leprechaun's outta here." Murphy started away, then thought of something. He turned back. "Hey, Killian. Did you really see me play?"

Paul Killian shrugged, holding up both hands innocently. "It's a possibility," he replied. "They tell me you were with a lot of different teams."

"Thanks a lot," said Murphy, walking away. "See ya around, Killian Black."

"Oh, I think you can count on that, Sea Warrior," Killian called after him.

13

Wednesday, October 23

In Silvercat, like any small town, rumors maintained a life of their own. During the morning, DeVane Belleau's statements to the press circulated and became distorted, and following the same geometric progression, paranoia increased. Ornal Kelly Fletcher's sporting goods sold small-caliber rifles to four local women, and there was vigilante talk at the Dutchman. Predictably, the tourists were less worried and more enthralled by the entire situation. Innkeepers, noting their accommodations filling *before* the Ski Silvercat opening, could only conclude that the lunatic the press was now calling the Silvercat Slasher was good for business.

Both the police and sheriff's offices had begun receiving telephone tips Tuesday morning. Most were anonymous, but some specifically named the caller's own relatives and especially in-laws. These continued on Wednesday and each had to be checked.

Shortly after the press conference, a small man in his early twenties named Gary Calvert appeared at the police station and confessed to murdering Toya Jalecka and attacking A. J. Delaney. His motive, he said, was that both women had pursued him sexually, trying—in ways he described in graphic detail to DeVane Belleau—to force him to renounce a vow of celibacy he'd taken at age fourteen. Calvert was five feet four inches tall and had no wounds or abrasions anywhere on his body. He was placed temporarily in a holding cell and later released in the custody of his parents, a Baptist minister and his wife who had stopped off overnight on a trip from

Arkansas. By the time the news media found out about him,
Gary Calvert and his parents were on their way home.

Hospitals in Durango, Cortez, and Farmington—as well as
private practitioners in those towns—reported no one receiving treatment for wounds that could be dog bites.

The morning passed, and rumors ran the town.

"You're certainly quiet today, Char," said Sara. "For you,
I mean."

Charlotte Post swiveled her chair forward. "Implying what?"
she asked with mock severity. "That I'm normally a blabber-
mouth? Show some respect for your elders, child."

She was wearing a pink wool overblouse with a turtleneck,
a lighter shade of the same color, beneath. Perfect for her
eyes and hair, Sara decided. They were sitting in Charlotte's
office, going over the afternoon's lead story, and while *The
Sentinel*'s publisher had listened carefully, she'd remained
mostly silent.

She looks pale, Sara thought. Worried.

"Char," she said finally. "Seriously, is something wrong?"

Charlotte shrugged. "A feeling I can't shake," she said.
Her long fingers worried at a pencil. Tapped one end on the
desk blotter, sliding it through, then let it flip over to tap the
other end. "Probably just the last clutches of menopause."

"No, really."

"Really?" Charlotte shook her head. "I don't know, really.
An uneasy feeling, I suppose. First, the Jalecka girl and then
A.J., and now this story."

"We have no choice, Char." It was at least the third time
during their meeting she'd used those exact words. "When
Howard Dimmit told everything he knew to that free-lancer—"

"Dimwit Dimmit," muttered Charlotte. "That idiot!"

"He thought he was going to be on national television, not
lose his job," said Sara. "He couldn't help himself. If he had
any sense, people wouldn't call him Dimwit. Besides, I've
heard that Killian guy's pretty smooth."

"He's a sleazebag!" Charlotte snapped, and Sara hid a
smile at such a word coming from her boss. "He doesn't

even have a network connection. Or he didn't. Now, with what he got from poor, stupid Howard, he'll probably be co-anchoring with Dan Rather.''

"It gets worse.'' Sara sighed. "Did I tell you about Killian's suggestion at Belleau's little gathering? He wanted the police to put out a decoy on the street in tight pants and a blond wig. He seems to think the whole thing is a TV detective show.''

"What?'' Charlotte's eyes widened in indignation. "In Silvercat? Surely DeVane didn't—''

"No, of course not. He told Killian this is Colorado, not 'Mean Streets,' and that if he *did* try something like that, he sure as hell wouldn't announce it to the press. That really cracked the place up.''

"I can imagine.''

"But it doesn't change the fact that Paul Killian has everything we have, and on videocassette besides. We have to run the story, Char, and get it in today, even if it means a chaser to the main edition. It can't hurt the investigation any more than Killian will. The whole damned town's afloat in rumors, anyway.''

"You're right,'' said Charlotte. "I see that you're right. It's just that . . . Oh, hell, if DeVane and Hobie scream about it, I'll just fill them in on Killian.'' She swiveled around to look up at the framed picture behind her desk. "I wonder what he'd do in a case like this,'' she murmured.

"Your father? The same thing we're doing, I'd bet.''

"Maybe. His journalistic codes were very strict.''

"Well, why don't you call him up and ask? He lives in Arizona, doesn't he?''

"Mostly,'' replied Charlotte. "He travels a lot. Actually, Sara, he and I haven't seen much of each other since my mother died.'' She swiveled the chair back forward. Her eyes were moist and unnaturally bright. "Besides,'' she said, smiling, "your choice is the right one. We run the story.''

"Okay.'' Sara gathered up her notes. "I'd better get on it, then. It's crying for a rewrite, and the press run's already set up.''

"Yes, you had. Oh, I just thought of something I was going to ask you. It has nothing to do with business."

"What's that?" Sara turned back at the door.

"The Halloween party next week. What are you and Neddie going as?"

"What?"

"Oh, you know. Up at the Village. It's a costume party, a masked ball, they're calling it, and—"

"Oh, that." Sara laughed to cover the blush creeping up her throat. "We . . . we haven't decided yet," she lied.

"Better decide," said Charlotte. "Costumes aren't that plentiful around here, you know. Unless you design your own. I'm considering either Elizabeth the First or a cat burglar. What do you think?"

"Oh, the cat burglar, Char." Sara beat a hasty retreat through the door. "It's definitely you."

Outside, carrying the copy back to her own office, Sara shook her head in confusion. What in hell . . . ?

"The difference between a psychiatrist and a psychologist," said Dr. Jordan Adler, "is that a licensed psychiatrist has a medical degree." She shifted her weight, denim tightening across a shapely leg, and glanced over at Murphy from under long, mascaraed eyelashes. "I've always had a fascination for medicine. Especially anatomy."

"I see." Hobie Jameison nodded. "Thanks for explaining it to me."

Murphy hid a grin. Jameison was giving Jordan Adler the hayseed bit, laying it on with a trowel. He was the one who had pointed out the difference to Murphy, in almost identical terms, that morning. The act was nothing new. He often employed it at first while sizing up strangers, especially when one surprised him.

Dr. Jordan Adler was a surprise. Murphy had half expected a stuffy, pipe-smoking old man in a tweed suit. He hadn't expected a small slim redhead with long permed hair and a pair of Pre 1200s in the ski rack of her rented Camaro Z-28.

"Outrageous!" she'd declared, by way of a greeting,

staring up over his head at the Gray Lady. "Who ever said psychiatry was a dull line of work?"

Now, after having checked into her room at the Silvercat Best Western, courtesy of Granite County, she was sitting in Hobie Jameison's favorite chair in a buff-colored leather shirt—half-unbuttoned—and skintight jeans, booted feet propped against the wood stove, while Jameison thanked her for explaining the difference between a psychiatrist and a psychologist.

"No problem," she replied. "Six of one . . . You know."

Jameison choked on the smoke from his pipe.

She removed xeroxed papers from a folder she'd brought. "Incidentally, thanks for the information you sent," she said. "Just so you don't think I came strictly for a free ski trip, you'll notice I've made a few preliminary notes." She flipped open a yellow legal pad. "This whole thing is extremely intriguing." She turned to Murphy. "So, on the night at the high school, you had only a glimpse of this person?"

"Just an outline, really, Dr. Adler. All I saw—"

"Oh, come on. Call me Jordan, okay? Or Adler, if you can't deal with that. I've seen you play ball, by the way."

Murphy grinned. "That's the second time today I've heard that one."

"S'truth, I promise. It was several years ago when I was still in med school. You were with New Orleans and you guys played—if you want to call it that—the Rams at the Coliseum. Number fifty-four, right?"

"I'll be damned," said Murphy.

"Which has nothing to do with this." Jordan Adler glanced at a scowling Jameison. "Sorry, Sheriff," she said. Then to Murphy, "You were saying you only saw . . . what?"

"Very little that's turned out to be useful," replied Murphy. "Let's see. An open door with snow blowing in. Glass from a broken light fixture. The shadow of a figure running out. Some footprints and some blood in the snow."

"The footprints. Did they match the heel print you had from"—she consulted a sheet—"from Cat Creek?"

"I didn't stop to look. I ran up the stairs to where A.J. was. In the meantime, Jimmy Alber had closed the door."

"He's the custodian?"

"Yeah. I guess it was force of habit. Jimmy's not too sharp, and he drinks some. The heat was turned on, of course, and it only takes a few seconds of melt to distort a footprint."

She nodded. "Then what?"

"I left Jimmy with A.J. and went outside. There were the remains of some tire tracks near the west side of the building, but that was the direction of the blizzard and they were already partly filled in. We took a cast, anyway. A big, heavy vehicle of some kind, it looks like, without snow tires. I never heard a car engine, but maybe the wind covered it."

Jordan Adler studied another sheet, her pale, lightly freckled forehead furrowed in concentration.

"Did you find any fingerprints in the school?" she asked.

Jameison snorted. "Are you kidding? Hundreds. It's a school."

Murphy tried to soften the sheriff's retort. "In a situation like this, Chief Belleau's men always dust for latents. But all they found were smudges everywhere."

"Plus, they're harder to get in cold weather, right?" said Jordan Adler. "I remember reading that somewhere. The pores close up, and there's less oil." She looked up at Jameison. "One thing I've wondered about. You've established that Alison Delaney got in the school by breaking a front window, and Deputy Davis—"

"Murphy. Or just Murph, if you can't deal with that."

She smiled, showing a deep dimple. "And Murphy was let in by Alber. How did the attacker get inside?"

Hobie Jameison released a long breath. "We've discussed that, Dr. Adler," he said with exaggerated patience. "And the plain fact is, we don't know for sure. Either Jimmy didn't lock the door—and he swears he locks every door every night—or there was a window left open somewhere. Or there was a key. The location of the car, along with the amount of snow Murph saw in the doorway, lets out the idea he came through the same window as A.J.''

"Who has keys?"

"The superintendent of schools and his assistant." Jameison ticked off on his fingers. "The principal and her assistant. All the teachers. Both of the secretaries. Members of the school board. The other custodians and cooks . . ."

Jordan Adler held up a hand in surrender. "I get the picture," she said. "A small town and a rural school. Half the county could get in there if they wanted."

"Not to mention the Unitarian Free Church of the Rockies," added the sheriff dryly, "which meets in the cafeteria twice a week." He tapped old tobacco out of his pipe. "Now, if this was a big-budget office, like in Los Angeles, with a lot of personnel, I'd say make a complete list and then run it down for alibis, which we're doing, by the way. So why don't we get down to cases on the reason the county paid your way out here?"

"Touché." She grinned. "Okay, I'll stop playing detective— poorly, I might add—and start earning my free trip."

When Jameison failed to return her smile, Jordan ducked her head and began rummaging through her papers. He doesn't like her, thought Murphy, and that's going to be bad for the whole business. Sometimes Hobie was like that, for his own reasons, and he rarely changed his mind once it was made up.

I hope you're good, girl.

"Here." She took out two sheets and handed one to Murphy and one to Jameison. "These are copies I made, so write on them if you like. The way that's always worked best for me is to go fact, supposition, fact, supposition, and so on. When studying a subject without his presence or even his identity, a psychiatrist can only make educated guesses based on the information available, plus one's own experience, training, and opinions." She smiled again. "Now, I could couch those opinions in jargonese bullshit, but I won't if you promise not to quote Freud at me."

"That's a deal," said the sheriff, still unsmiling. "Now, can we get started?"

"Fair enough." She put a check by the first item on her copy. "Fact: All the victims except Lacey-Ann Lewis at the highway stop were similar physically. That's over a period of twenty years minimum. My supposition is that the murderer is trying to kill someone from his own past. Maybe he did kill the original but doesn't remember it, or maybe she got away from him. Ran off. Or maybe even died from some other cause."

Murphy saw Jameison shifting impatiently. "That's what DeVane thinks," he said before the sheriff could speak. "That he's killing the same girl over and over. Would he stop by himself?"

She shook her head. "Doubtful, unless he found the original girl. He may see himself as the agent of her retribution, for instance, and see her death as some type of mission. Under those circumstances, if he did actually find her, then he might stop. Of course, if she's still alive, she wouldn't look the same after twenty years. I wonder if he'd recognize her, since he's apparently obsessed with destroying the person he remembers."

"He hates her that much?" Jameison asked.

"Or loves her, and was hurt by her that much," Jordan replied. "It's the old cliché about love and hate, would be my guess. And in this case, a frightening kind of . . . rage that's lasted for twenty years."

She made another check. "Fact: The method of killing. He slashes the victims, literally disemboweling them with an extremely sharp weapon. Maybe a knife or a razor. The supposition appears to be a violent, twisted version of rape. Which would fit the pattern of the sexual rage I just mentioned."

"With the knife as a phallic symbol?" asked Murphy.

"Possibly. But don't be too quick to attach labels. Remember the old song from the sixties? 'A thing's a phallic symbol if it's longer than it's wide'?"

Murphy grinned. " 'And the id goes marching on,' " he said. "Melanie Safka."

"You remembered. But, yeah, in this case I think you may be right. Out of thirteen pattern murders, not including the one from Estes Park, some reference is made to a test for semen in ten of them. It's routine in such cases. But only three, including Toya Jalecka, tested positive."

"With all the blood loss and the release of other fluids, like bile and urine, into the cavity," said Jameison, "isn't there the possibility the semen wasn't detected?"

Jordan Adler winked at Murphy. "This is the rustic who was asking me to explain what a psychiatrist is?" she said. "Yeah, that's a real possibility, especially in the older cases. But you're paying for my opinion, and here it is: I believe those three women had prior sexual relations, and I believe our man does *not* rape his victims, other than what I feel is symbolic rape with the weapon."

"Impotent, then?" asked Murphy.

"Maybe, though it could also be that he's only impotent in what he perceives as the presence of this particular woman. With other women he may perform quite normally."

"What if being potent or impotent has nothing to do with it?" asked Jameison. "Maybe he hates this girl so much, his only interest is in killing her."

"Not likely. If there was no sexual connection, he'd probably just stab her, strangle her, something like that." Jordan Adler looked back at her list. "Okay, fact: At some time, probably after the victim's death, the killer removes her eyelids, top and bottom, with surgical precision. I gotta tell you, guys, this is the part that's been messing with my sleep."

"Mine too," said Murphy. "Any theories?"

"Other than the guy being a doctor?" She frowned. "I'm not certain. There's always the reverse of putting the eyes out. Instead of saying, 'You can't see me now,' he could be saying, 'Look at me.' Or maybe it causes the women to more nearly resemble his original model."

"The original didn't have eyelids?" Jameison snorted. "Come on, Dr. Adler. That's about as asinine as—"

"I know. I'm only speculating, remember. I'm more in-

clined toward some scenario involving making them see him.
Or see something. Maybe the original *wouldn't* see. *Couldn't*
see. Not literally, perhaps. I don't know. The eyelids are the
hardest part to figure. And the creepiest.

"Fact," she continued. "Both the locations and the time
spans have moved radically inward. I tend to agree with your
note in the margin, Sheriff. It appears his control's slipping
away. One sign of relative sanity's a healthy sense of self-
preservation, and what he's done here in this small a town—
possibly his own town—has put him at risk."

She looked over at Jameison. "Is there any way to see if
some longtime resident has been out of town on the dates
from that sheet? Just a thought."

"Playing detective again?" His smile was thin. "No way.
That's something I discussed with DeVane Belleau. There are
about four thousand permanent residents here, and you're
talking about roughly once every two or three years over a
period of—"

"Okay, forget it." She turned to Murphy. "What about the
old Indian you mentioned in the notes? Jesse DePriest. Is
there a chance he really knows something?"

Murphy hesitated, aware of the sheriff's glowering expression. One thing about Jordan Adler, he decided. She wasn't
going to be intimidated by Hobie Jameison's notions of what
her role should be.

"I don't know," he said finally. "If you mean factual
knowledge, I'd say no. Unless the killer's from the Indian
community. If you mean spiritual knowledge, or something
like that—"

"Horseshit," said Jameison.

"—then maybe so," Murphy continued. "Jesse has a kind
of sixth sense about things sometimes. He said there'd be
another attack, and he was right."

"You shouldn't encourage my deputy," said Jameison
dryly. "When it comes to that old button chewer, he's not
real objective."

"I love Jesse." Murphy nodded. "I admit it. I've known
him all my life."

"Button chewer?" asked Jordan. "He uses peyote?"

"Uses it?" the sheriff snorted. "Listen, doctor. I have this cousin and she weighs maybe two fifty. We used to say the woman eats like she's going to the chair. That's the way Jesse DePriest *uses* peyote."

"Peyote." Jordan smiled faintly. "During my formative years, I had a nodding acquaintance—pardon the pun—with some mind-altering substances myself. Can I be arrested for admitting that in a sheriff's office?"

"Not by Murph," said Jameison, with a cynical glance at his deputy. "No wonder you two get along so well. What's your point?"

"Only that sometimes things like that can sharpen perspectives, at least temporarily." She returned Jameison's hard stare for a second. "Let's go on to Alison Delaney. As far as we know, she's the only person to survive an attack by our subject. If she could tell us something, anything . . ."

"Not much chance of that," said Murphy bleakly. "I called the hospital this morning, and she's still unresponsive. Also, her parents have arrived from Alabama and are pushing to take her home."

"Which is exactly where she should go," said the sheriff. "Oh, I know she could be the key to the whole thing *if* she came out of it and *if* she'd recognized her attacker. But if Kari—that's my daughter, doctor—if Kari was like that, I'd—"

"You'd want to find out who did it to her, Hobie," said Murphy. "I'm going down there to see A.J. this evening. I have an idea I want to try."

"Can I ride with you?" Jordan asked. "I'd like a chance to see her, too."

"Take her along, Murph," said Jameison. "Can't hurt."

And it gets her away from you, right? Murphy thought. "Okay," he said. "I could use the company."

They turned back to the list.

He cries out when he pours hydrogen peroxide onto the bites along his left forearm, and it makes him ashamed. So he grits his teeth and does it again. This time he doesn't make a sound. Better.

The scabs are still soft in places, and the liquid works its way beneath them, bubbling up. It hurts worse than when he tended them the first time.

And as always in that room, the eyes watch him. Judge him in their expressionless way. Which is why he was ashamed.

His sweatshirt had been ruined by the dog's attack, a sleeve ripped past the elbow and his own blood on the front, so it was necessary to destroy it that same night in the wood stove. The odor, as the bloody cloth burned, had triggered a memory he's still unable to summon up.

He soaks a new strip of cotton with the peroxide and smears a layer of Vaseline along its edges, then covers the bites again. He winds gauze around the cotton, not too tightly, then splits the ends to tie it off, pushing away Alistair Three's curious nose. He knows Murphy Davis and Glorified Jock well enough not to worry about rabies.

When he's done, medical supplies put away, he comes back to that room and the pink-and-white dresser. He sits there and looks at the photographs, unaware that he's begun to hum softly. Lennon's "In My Life." Not the early photos, because they always make him gentle, and that's not how he wants to feel. He looks at the last one.

The picture is half of a larger photograph that's been torn to eliminate the person who was once on the other side. It shows a slim face, oval-shaped beneath blue eyes and high cheekbones. A full lower lip, nearly in a pout, with long blond hair cascading around the pale throat and shoulders. Beautiful, of course. Perfect. Once again, for the uncounted thousandth of times, he memorizes the face.

He wonders where she is. He's looked for her, knowing she'll be drawn to the television cameras and the media people from New York and California. Once or twice, he'd thought he'd seen her, but he was wrong.

He even considers the possibility she's gone from Silvercat, back to the cities, like the other times. But he doesn't really believe that, because the town has changed now. Like she's changed—innocence into corruption. She's still here.

Everything changes. Everyone too, except her. Even him. It had disturbed him at first that, for hours at a time, he'd begun to confuse his memories. It makes things complicated, dangerous, and he feels his very concealment from the other one beginning to fray at the edges. But he accepts it now because he understands what it means.

Under the ever-present, unblinking gaze of the eyes, he lifts the photograph from the dresser and kisses the lips gently, gently.

14

"He doesn't much like me, does he?" Jordan Adler looked out the window at the banks of snow alongside the road.

In places where the trees created a permanent shade, snow had melted across the road and then refroze. Murphy geared the Land Cruiser down, barely tapping the clutch. In the back Glorified Jock sat up and whined softly.

"Black ice," said Murphy, not answering her question. "You can be on it before you know it's there."

She nodded. "It's called glare ice in the Sierras. Same stuff." She reached back to rub Jock's head. "I was with this guy once, coming back from skiing at Mammoth, and he geared down right on top of some. He never touched the brake and we weren't going more than twenty, but we swapped ends before you could say Hail Mary. Luckily, we ended up in a snowbank and not off a cliff."

"You're Catholic?" Murphy shifted back into fourth on dry pavement. "I . . . noticed your cross."

She glanced down into the V of her shirt at a small gold crucifix lying against the lightly freckled skin between her breasts.

"You were supposed to." She smiled, eyes unreadable. "Lapsed Catholic, actually. I suppose my primary religion these days is skiing. The Church of the Immaculate Mogul."

He had no answer for that, so he watched the road. They were dropping almost continuously in a long series of switchbacks, with banks of partly melted snow under the evergreens that bordered the highway and the jagged profile of the

Needles Range towering in the distance to their left. The late-afternoon sun poured diagonally across the cliffs above them, striking an occasional waterfall silver, then turquoise, as they passed.

"Murphy." She turned sideways to face him, and the shirt gapped even more. "You never answered my question about Sheriff Jameison. Does he really dislike me that much, or does he treat all strangers that way?"

Murphy framed an answer. He remembered the sheriff's words after Jordan Adler had gone outside ahead of him.

"Did you ever hear such bullshit, Murph?" Jamieson had said in a cutting whisper. "Talk about a waste of the taxpayers' money! She didn't tell us a thing we didn't already know."

"That's not entirely true, Hobie," he'd said, trying to defend her.

"What, all that blue sky conjecture? She's just a damned kid, Murph. Out here trying to shine us on for a free ski trip. And the only reason you're taking up for her is 'cause she came in here with her boobs hanging out and got you with a hard-on."

"That's crap, Hobie. What've you got against her, anyway?"

"There's something about her. Can't put my finger on it now, but I will."

And that was all he'd say. So Murphy was left in the middle again.

"He's a little gruff sometimes, Jordan," he said. "And things are kind of weird right now. There's that business with the police chief I told you about, and there's all the media types around."

"Then it's not me?" she said. "That's a relief."

"It's things in general," Murphy lied. "It's like a zoo. The killer's even started getting fan mail. Joyce Lopes, over at the post office, called just before you got in today. She said they have nearly two dozen letters addressed to the 'Silvercat Slasher.' "

Jordan nodded. "There'll be more, at least as long as it

stays in the news." She took a small plastic squeeze bottle of 4-Way Nasal Spray from her bag and pushed it into each nostril. "Damned sinuses," she muttered. "High altitude gets me every time. About the letters, there'll be propositions, requests for an autograph or a lock of hair, even proposals of marriage."

"That's crazy."

"People are crazy sometimes, Murphy. And they've always been fascinated by evil."

"That's what he is." He banked into a turn. Half a dozen mule deer were feeding on the slope above the curve, so he slowed even further. "Evil, I mean." He remembered A.J.'s face in the twilight of the school hallway.

"In the standard sense, certainly," she replied. "But there's all kinds of evil, Murphy. Let me give you an example. I had a referral about four years ago. A welfare family out in the valley, not far from Bakersfield. The guy I was working with, Pat Calder, had been to their apartment a couple of times, and he was getting the word from the neighbors that there was a kid missing."

"How many did they have?"

"Pat had seen four, ranging from a baby to a girl seven years old. He asked them, and they both swore there weren't any more. But the neighbor in the next apartment insisted there was a fifth."

"Couldn't he check on it?"

"He could, and did. Since the family was receiving government aid, there were files. Food stamps, welfare receipts, and so on. Pat checked and, sure enough, five kids.

"The husband was away a lot—looking for work, he said—and Pat was uncomfortable around the wife, so he asked me to ride out to the valley with him. Murphy, it was April Fools' Day, I remember, and it was just pouring rain. The gutters had backed up, and everything along that street was sunk in red mud. Pat made this joke. He said, 'April's not coming in like a lamb this year, Jordie. It's coming in like a trout.' And I was still laughing when we pulled up at the apartment."

Murphy glanced at Jordan Adler out of the corner of his eye. She had turned back forward, and her face was still. In the fading light, she was so lovely he felt a quick stab, almost like pain, in his diaphragm.

"By the time we got to the porch, we were both soaked and giggling like teenagers," she said. "We had to stand under this tiny overhang and knock on the door until finally a woman let us in. She couldn't have been any older than I was. Midtwenties.

"I took one look at her, and I knew why Pat didn't want to be alone with her. There was . . . something missing, that's the best way I can describe it. His notes had indicated she was marginally retarded, but it was more than that. She was little, with straw blond hair, and she had these bright blue eyes. China blue. And when you looked into them, there was just nothing there.

"The apartment was clean to have all those kids in it, but I kept smelling something. Lysol, I think, and something else. An under smell. The kids were sitting in the living room watching a new color TV, and they all smiled at us at the same time. I swear to God, even the baby.

"Well, Pat was quizzing the mother, showing her the file and asking about Joseph, and she was saying there was no Joseph, she'd never heard of Joseph, when I finally got up and went into the hall. That woman was up like a shot, following me. There was this staircase to the second floor, and I saw a . . . little door underneath it."

Jordan Adler's face had gone pale, each freckle standing out individually.

"Joseph," said Murphy. "That's where the kid was."

She nodded. "The woman went for me when I touched the door. She was screaming, and her fingers were curled up like claws, and Pat had to hold her back. The smell when I opened it . . . almost made me faint. I pulled a cord hanging down and it clicked on a light bulb.

"There was this naked little kid in there, Murphy." Jordan's voice had dropped into a dull monotone. "We knew from the file he was four years old, but he couldn't have weighed over twenty pounds. He had olive skin and black hair, and the most beautiful eyes I've ever seen.

"'The smell was rotting food lying on the floor, mixed with his own . . . urine and feces. It looked like it'd been tossed in the door, and when he ate, he had to pick it out of his own excrement.

"Over on one side was a trashed-out dollhouse. We found out later the seven-year-old had slipped it in there. After he looked up at me for a moment, the little boy turned—and I could see what looked like cigarette burns all over one side of his back—and he started playing. He was using his fingers as people, and he was playing in the dollhouse. And then he looked up at his mother, who was still screaming and trying to break loose from Pat, and he smiled at her and said 'Hello, Mommy.' "

"Jesus," whispered Murphy.

"That's my horror story," said Jordan Adler. She tried without success to smile. "I'm sure you have worse ones."

"No." Murphy's hands tightened on the wheel. "No, I don't."

"Turns out the father had claimed Joseph wasn't his because all the other kids were blond. So they closed him up under the stairs and pretended he didn't exist. The doctors said he'd have died in another week, two at the outside."

Jordan took a deep breath, then let it out. "That's what I meant about there being all kinds of evil, Murphy," she said. "Evil's not always clever and complex. Sometimes it's just dull and stupid and brutal."

She looked over at him. "The person you're after's in pain, Murphy, or the memory of pain. I'm sure of that much already. He gets no joy from what he does. Sometimes the memories get too large—too big. They consume us then, 'cause they're more than we are, more than reality is. Some people just get strangled by their own memories."

"Not a sociopath, then."

"I don't believe so." She inhaled again from the bottle of

nasal spray. "Since you know the term, you probably know that, by definition, a sociopath feels no pain as a result of his actions. He's essentially lacking emotion where others are concerned, and may even see the whole thing as an intellectual contest to be savored. If that's what you were dealing with, I think there'd have been letters, phone calls, something as a means of seeking recognition during the twenty years that have elapsed. I'm more inclined toward some type of schizophrenic disorder."

"Split personality?"

"Actually, a separation between thought and emotion," she replied. "Insanity is the ultimate contradiction of reality, after all. But in this case, your definition may be better. In order to have lived in that little town, right in the middle of you, and do what he's been doing all these years without his friends and neighbors having any idea, he'd either have to be some type of sociopath—which I doubt—or be two different people, quite possibly with neither aware of the other's existence."

"You keep saying 'he,'" said Murphy. "Any chance it could be a woman?"

Jordan shook her head. "There's nothing physical to absolutely rule out that idea," she said. "But it's my impression that we're dealing with a sexual anger and pain here that's distinctly masculine in its mind-set. And it's like your sheriff said. The key to the whole thing is in Alison Delaney's subconscious. I just hope this plan of yours works, for our sake as well as hers."

They rounded a curve past some condominiums and emerged in a long, flat valley that ran alongside a river. DURANGO—4 MILES, read a roadway sign.

The hospital was on a ridge, cut artificially into the side of a mesa. The vegetation around it, some three thousand feet below Silvercat's elevation, was drier and more desertlike. Low, gnarled cedar and gray sage.

Riley and Carlene Delaney sat sharing a cigarette on a brown vinyl couch in the solarium. They both rose when they saw Dr. Donald Magill enter, accompanied by a red-haired woman, a large man, and a dog.

"You're . . . the deputy from Silvercat," said Riley Delaney, snuffing the cigarette into a metal ashtray. "You have to be. And this is the dog."

He was a slim man, medium height, with just a trace of a paunch where his knit shirt tucked into Sans-A-Belt slacks. His hair was light brown intermingled with gray, thinning on either side of a widow's peak.

He bent forward abruptly and put his hands on both sides of the dog's head. Jock, who was undaunted by strangers, looked up at Delaney and sniffed the wristband of his watch.

"You saved her." The man's voice broke as he continued to rub Jock's head and neck. "Good dog," he whispered. "Good, good dog . . ."

"Mr. Davis, isn't it?" The woman's voice hit Murphy like an electrical jolt. It was A.J.'s voice. Soft, with the trace of an accent at the edges. A hint of laughter even when it was serious. "Alison's spoken of you many times," she said. "I'm Carlene Delaney, and this is my husband, Riley."

"Call me Murphy, please, Mrs. Delaney. This is Dr. Jordan Adler from Los Angeles. She's . . . helping us with some matters related to the case."

"Medical doctor?" asked Mrs. Delaney, automatically sizing Jordan up. Murphy noticed with relief that she'd buttoned the leather shirt.

"Psychiatrist," said Jordan.

"Oh . . . I see." Carlene Delaney was as tall as A.J. but thinner, her dark jersey dress expensively simple. Her beauty, striking in the same way as her daughter's, was diluted by lines of fatigue and grief.

"Riley," said Magill. "I've been bringing Deputy Davis up to date on Alison's . . . progress. He has an idea I think's worth listening to."

Delaney straightened from petting Jock. His eyes were

dazed, as though he were hearing each word on a radio's five-second delay.

"Dr. Magill says A.J. . . . Alison's not responding," said Murphy, unconsciously enunciating each word slowly. "And that she's still holding on to the stuffed animal. I thought maybe if Jock . . ."

"Yes." Delaney's eyes cleared. "Yes, the dog," he said.

"We don't usually allow animals in the building at all," said Magill. "But in this . . ."

"Yes, of course. The dog." Delaney turned toward his wife. "Carlene?"

"I agree," she said without hesitation. "Let's try it right now."

They took an elevator to the third floor, then walked along a lighted corridor as Jock sniffed the faint medicinal odor Murphy always associated with hospitals. There were framed prints on the beige walls between the doors. Mountain views.

Carlene Delaney took Murphy's arm and held him back when they reached Room 324. "You saved my daughter's life," she said. Her eyes, soft brown like A.J.'s, were intense. "You know she's in love with you, don't you?"

He pulled away from her. From her words. "She's a kid, Mrs. Delaney," he fumbled. "I'm exactly twice her age. And besides, Jock was the one who—"

"That doesn't matter. I've read her letters, Murphy Davis. I can read between the lines of my daughter's letters." She stretched up and kissed him, quickly but firmly, on the mouth. Then she walked through the door.

A.J. lay in a bed in a room with bright colors. The walls were a pale yellow with diagonal designs of orange. The window drapes, her bedspread, sheets, and pillowcases were variations of the same shades. It was a light, cheerful room.

The girl in the bed lay on her side, covers pulled up to her chin, body curled like a comma. Her hair looked clean and healthy, freshly washed, and it hid her face from Murphy's view.

"Alison?" Magill went to the side of the bed. "Alison, you have some visitors. Can you sit up?"

The girl didn't move.

"Alison, honey." Carlene Delaney put a hand on A.J.'s shoulder. A.J. raised her head.

Murphy felt his stomach twist. The face was no one he knew. Soft, shapeless, its beauty gone into blankness. Vague, staring eyes, rimmed with dark circles.

A.J. looked up at her mother. "No!" she screamed, recoiling so hard the headboard of the bed slammed against the yellow wall. "No! No! No!"

She held the stuffed toy, a small brown dog, against her chest. She buried her face in its side.

Carlene Delaney staggered back, buffeted by her daughter's screams and the horror in her eyes. "Riley?" she gasped, her voice quivering. "Oh, sweet Jesus, Riley . . ."

"Alison. Alison, it's okay." Delaney reached down for A.J.'s hand. She flinched away from him.

"Wait," she said, her voice low and flat. "Wait, please. Just . . ."

Jordan Adler took Magill's sleeve. "Has she been like this since you brought her in?"

"As a matter of fact, she's improved some," he replied in a hushed tone. "At least she's started to eat on her own now." He motioned them away from the bed. "She was virtually catatonic when she came in. We tried to clean her up, get off the blood and paint, get her out of those torn—"

"Paint?" Murphy interrupted. "What paint?"

"Why . . . it was on the ends of her fingers," said the doctor. "Her right hand, I believe. The one with the torn fingernail. Surely someone mentioned it to you."

"No. No one did. What kind of paint?"

Magill frowned. "That's odd. I thought the resident in Admitting would've included that. It was water-based stuff, I understand. Washed right off. There was only a little of it."

"What color was it?" asked Jordan.

"Color? Brown, I think Ellen said. I'm sorry we didn't get that information to you. I honestly assumed we had. I can see where it might be important."

"Maybe." Murphy nodded. "Is the person who cleaned A.J. up here tonight?"

"Sure. Ellen Bailey. I'll page her later if you like, but shouldn't we . . . ?" He nodded toward the bed.

"Yeah. I'll get him." Murphy went back into the hallway and found Glorified Jock lying against a water cooler, trying to chew the strip of adhesive tape off his chest.

"Oh, great move, Jock. Smart dog. You have stitches under there."

Jock dropped his ears for a second. Then, when he realized that was the extent of the scolding, he began to chew again.

"Leave it alone, dammit," said Murphy. "Come on with me."

They went back into the room. Jock padded over to the side of the bed and sniffed the covers.

"A.J.?" Murphy leaned over the bed, careful not to get too near her head. A. J., it's me. It's Murph, and I brought someone to see you. Up, Jock."

Glorified Jock hopped lightly onto the bed, eyes intent on A.J. He leaned forward, tail starting to wag.

A.J.'s eyes passed over him, then cut back again, muddy brown and unfocused. After a few seconds, they seemed to sharpen. "Please," she whispered, and raised her hand.

Jock whined, then he smelled her hand. He began to lick her fingers.

The girl dropped the stuffed toy and surged forward. She grabbed Jock and held him, wrapping her arms around his neck and shoulders, hiding her face against the bandages on his chest.

She began to cry. Long, wailing sobs that grew in intensity, shaking her body through her orange-and-white flannel nightgown. Jock pulled back at first, front legs stiffening and the whites of his eyes showing as he looked up at Murphy. Then he relaxed and let his big head rest against her.

"Oh, God!" Carlene Delaney burst into tears, turning to her husband. "Oh, God, Riley!"

Murphy realized he was crying, too.

Ellen Bailey was paged from the cafeteria. She was a trim woman in her forties, smile lines etched deep in a sunbather's tan. She remembered cleaning Alison Delaney's hands.

"It wasn't paint," she said. "Not really. Donald Magill, I swear." She rolled her eyes. "That man is so . . . so *literal*."

"What, then?" asked Murphy.

"Stage makeup," was the reply. "We used to call it greasepaint when I was doing summer stock back in Pennsylvania. Of course, it's entirely different stuff now. My daughter—"

"Stage makeup?" asked Jordan. "Are you sure?"

"Honey, I should be. I see enough of it. Besides me, there's my daughter. She had the lead in *Paint Your Wagon* at the college last spring. When I heard they brought that poor girl here from the high school in your little town, I just assumed she'd been at play practice."

"What would someone use that kind of makeup for?" asked Murphy.

"Well, let's see. It was too dark for a skin cover, unless they're doing something . . . you know, ethnic. No one does *Porgy and Bess* anymore. Isn't that a shame? So afraid of offending . . . certain people. Of course, there's still the historical melodramas. Indians and Mexicans, you know."

"If it wasn't face makeup, how else could it have been used?"

Ellen Bailey laughed merrily. "Oh, many ways. They're very clever with it. For instance, to draw on beards and mustaches, if they don't have the stick-on kind, or for eye makeup, to darken eyebrows and eyelids—''

"Eyelids?" Jordan glanced over at Murphy.

The woman nodded. "Also for shading in hollows beneath cheekbones and at the temples. Around the nose. They're so versatile now. My daughter..."

They finally shook loose from Ellen Bailey, who, it turned out, did volunteer work three days a week at the hospital. She continued to go on about her daughter and about her own stage career, and apparently had no conception of the seriousness of A.J.'s condition.

When they opened the door to Room 324, the lights had been dimmed and the Delaneys were sitting next to the bed. A.J. lay asleep. Her face was relaxed, more like the girl Murphy knew, and her breathing was deep and steady. Glorified Jock lay at the foot of the bed. His head was next to her legs, and he looked up when Murphy entered the room.

"Stay, Jock," Murphy whispered and the dog lay back. Magill motioned them into the hallway.

"She's asleep," he said, closing the door softly. "Really asleep, for a change. It was a good idea, Deputy." He offered his hand.

Murphy shook it, feeling the tightness return to his throat. "Did she say anything?"

"No, and I don't think you'd better count on too much happening anytime soon, either. Her parents want to take her home whenever she can travel, and I'm inclined to agree. She still has a long haul ahead, I'm afraid, and it can only he helped by home and familiar surroundings."

"You're optimistic, then," said Jordan.

"I am now, Dr. Adler. It may take a while, which I realize doesn't help your investigation, but I believe she'll eventually make it back. Before you two brought in that dog, I wouldn't have taken any bets."

Sara was watching Neddie Cameron. But whenever he'd look her way and smile, she averted her eyes.

They were at his house, in the same bedroom they'd used before. There was a nineteen-inch Sony TV on a stand at the foot of the bed, and Cameron was using a hand-held remote control to flip channels.

Sara turned on her side toward him, enjoying the feel of the satin, pearl gray sheets against her skin. He lay propped up by two pillows against an antique brass headboard, the sheet around his waist. He was very hairy, she decided, and not distinctly muscular, but rather long and smooth and slim.

Like me, she thought. Give him some tits—very small ones—and a shave, and we could be twins. She contrasted him mentally with Larry Bowlin, who lathered and shaved his torso twice a week with a Bic disposable and would become somewhat prickly between times. To show off the bod, he'd explained. An actor needed every edge.

He *had* been pretty well built, she had to concede. Big and muscular, somewhat like . . .

Forget that. She had no choice but to forget that, and him, didn't she? He'd made that clear enough the day before at the newspaper office. She moved closer to Cameron, who slid an arm around her shoulders. He punched the remote button, cutting off the television.

"Do you remember what I said to you that first morning in the kitchen?" he asked, sliding his fingers down her side. "A penny for your thoughts?"

"That tickles. And I thought we agreed on a buck-fifty."

"I'll have to write you a check. So, what's on your mind?"

She took a deep breath. "I was talking to Charlotte Post today. She told me about your debate next week with Murphy Davis."

"Is that all?" He did Bogie. "Lishen, don't worry about a 'ting, shweetheart. I'll moider da bum."

"She also asked me what costumes we were going to wear to the Halloween party up at the Village." Sara forced a weak smile. "It was a little embarrassing, Neddie. I didn't know what she was talking about."

He rolled over to face her. "The masked ball," he said. "And that's what all this is about? That's why you haven't said a dozen words all evening?"

You're stalling. The thought flashed through her mind, and she dismissed it almost as quickly. "Actually," she said, "I seem to recall saying something like 'fuck me, fuck me, fuck me' a little while ago."

"That's six words," he replied with a grin. Then his face sobered. "I'm sorry about the party, Sara. The plain fact is, I didn't mention it because I can't go myself. I know it's selfish, but I hated to think of you going with someone else."

"Oh." Liar. The word thrust hard against the back of her tongue. What in hell was going on in her head? "Why can't you go?"

"I'll be out of town," he replied. "In Phoenix, for a bar-association get-together."

"Your law practice seems to take very little of your time anymore, Neddie. Why go to something like that?"

He shrugged. "The contacts are still valuable. I try to make one of them at least every year or two, mostly for that reason." He leaned down to kiss the slope of her breast. "I'm really sorry, Sara. I'd already made the commitment before I knew about the party."

He pushed the sheet aside and stood up beside the bed. "Ta-dum!" he said, making a stylish pirouette. "And now, lady and assorted termites, this perfect speciman's off to the kitchen for a drink. Can I bring you anything?"

"Mr. Furry America." She smiled. "Bring me a Diet Coke."

After he'd left the room, Sara picked up the TV remote, then dropped it. Too much Silvercat on television these days. For the first time she could recall, she had no desire to watch a news broadcast. She wondered what Hobie Jameison had thought when he'd read *The Sentinel*. And Murphy Davis. Her byline, though Char'd decided they should gangbang the story—use several different writers—to take pressure off Sara.

Her right contact lens felt dry and itchy, and she popped it out. She rarely wore them, preferring the more businesslike look of her square-framed glasses when she needed to read something, and as a result her eyes didn't always accept the damned things. Her eye felt teary, so she reached into a tissue box on the bedside table. Empty.

She'd opened the top drawer, looking for a handkerchief, when her hand touched something stiff. She drew out a picture.

The woman—girl, really—was slim-faced and blond. Long hair, cut in the fashion of the midsixties, straight to past the shoulders with square bangs low across the forehead. She was smiling.

When Sara looked up, Neddie Cameron was standing in the doorway watching her.

"Oh!" She dropped the picture and, for some reason she didn't analyze, pulled the sheet up over her breasts. "God, Neddie! You scared me."

"Sorry." His voice was odd.

"Is this . . . your wife?"

His smile had a cynical edge to it. "Twenty years ago it was," he said, crossing the room with her soft drink in hand. He'd put on a maroon velour robe. "She always preferred that picture to something more . . . contemporary."

"Have you heard from her?"

"Marilyn?" He shook his head. "I told you. She's gone."

Sara put the picture back in the drawer and slid it shut. "I wonder how she'd feel . . . if she knew. About us, I mean."

"Who can say?" Cameron sat on the side of the bed. "The fact is, Sara"—he turned to face her—"there wouldn't be much she could say. She owes me one."

"What? I don't follow."

"I'm sorry. That was a pretty tasteless way to put it. What I meant was, she had an affair of her own once. Many years ago, right in this town. I forgave her, took her back. That was what I meant."

Sara remained silent, unsure how to reply.

"It was a long time ago," he continued. "I was fresh out of law school. . . . Anyway, it's not important now, Sara. Here's your drink."

Sara took the glass and moved to the center of the bed, and Cameron removed his robe and joined her. For a while they lay there, her head on his chest while he clicked the channel changer, one hand absently stroking the inside of her thigh. After a while his fingers moved higher, pushing her legs apart. They made love.

15

Thursday, October 24

In the fickle moodiness of Rocky Mountain autumn, Thursday brought more snow, but this time without the gale-force winds. The snow fell lightly to the ground.

In the town, tourists packed the ski shops, fueled by the titillation of a killer on the loose and the rumor that Ski Silvercat would open on Saturday, a full two weeks ahead of schedule. They shouldered into the Dutchman, shouting greetings at Schuyler Van den Ler and pretending to know him personally. Van den Ler hopped about, not bothering with his prosthesis, to serve them. He'd temporarily promoted LuGail, the red-haired waitress, to evening bartender, but he hadn't hired anyone yet for table help. His thoughts were still on A.J., and his mood was black and somber, so he didn't play along with any of the greetings. Some of the tourists were offended and, if the Dutchman hadn't been the trendiest night spot in town, would have gone somewhere else.

On the Gray Lady, Lester Nelson and his Snow Gods were moving the product, too valuable to be allowed to rest where it fell from the sky, around the slopes. Huge, multibladed cats rumbled up the mountain, grooming the novice runs first. The Snow Gods were a diverse group, ranging from retirement-age former truckers to twenty-year-old ski bums who handled the big cats like a housewife handled a station wagon. This was that rare time of the year when they worked in daylight. Once the ski resort opened, they'd be on the mountain mostly at night, Walkmans playing Prince or Merle Haggard as they tilled December powder or March slop, and flipped aside

Death Cookies with their blades while breaking up the January boilerplate. Lester Nelson, sixty and bald, with half-frozen snuff glittering in his beard, cut back and forth between trails on his Black Magic snowmobile, making sure the Snow Gods did it right.

Murphy Davis awoke before the alarm and padded to his bedroom window, rubbing a stiff shoulder. He stood for a while, watching snow accumulate on his woodpile of aspen and scrub oak and hang in the branches of the fir trees, then he dry-swallowed a pill from the plastic prescription bottle and eased back into bed. The slender, red-haired woman next to him turned, still mostly asleep, and slid one leg over his. He dropped his head to her freckled breasts and began waking her up.

Higher toward the peaks at another cabin, a giant, black-bearded man sat bareheaded in the snow. He'd been there most of the night, as he had the two previous nights, and the fingers of his ungloved hands were going pasty gray with frostbite. Snow lay across his shoulders and back, and shifted when his body heaved. He hadn't eaten since Tuesday morning, but his enormous strength hadn't waned. It had only grown with his anguish and rage as he sat and cried for his golden girl.

"More coffee, Charlotte?" Arthur Morse was carrying the pot with him. When Charlotte Post joined the breakfast group at the Elkhorn Café, the doctor invariably made himself her personal maître d'.

"No, thank you, Art," she replied with a smile. "I haven't been sleeping too well lately, and the last thing I need is more caffeine."

"I'll have some, Art," said Hobie Jameison, holding up a large white porcelain cup.

Morse set the pot on the table. "You do look pale, Charlotte," he said. He leaned toward her. "What seems to be the problem?"

"Thanks a lot, Art." Hobie reached for the coffeepot himself. Murphy winked at Jordan Adler.

"I'm not sure." Charlotte let Morse take her hand. Murphy suppressed a grin while the doctor pretended to read her pulse. "Premonitions, maybe? I've had an odd feeling for a couple of days now. Like something's about to happen."

"Something else? Bite your tongue, woman," said Jameison. "You're beginning to sound like Jesse DePriest. As if enough hasn't happened already."

"It's settling down, though." Morse still had Charlotte's hand, one finger on her wrist. "Did you notice the network boys are all gone? The Silvercat Slasher's become old news, children."

"Until he does something else." Charlotte made a face. "Erase that," she said. "Change the subject. How is Jesse, by the way?"

"Like Paul Simon says, 'Still crazy after all these years,'" answered the sheriff. "Right, Murph?"

Murphy thought of Jesse's words of the day before. "He goes his own way, Hobie," he said. "Always has."

"Ninety-one," said Morse, finally releasing Charlotte's hand. "That's too high, young lady. Someone your age, slim as you are, should have a resting pulse in the seventies."

"I usually do," she replied. "I imagine it's just another part of this . . . feeling I have." She smiled at Jameison. "At least, it's good to know you're not angry about the story in yesterday's paper. I hope DeVane feels the same." She looked around the small, smoky café. "Where is he this morning?"

"Haven't seen him much lately," replied Jameison, a little stiffly. "I expect he's busy." He rose and went over to a long Formica-topped counter for a toothpick.

"When do you want to see Jock again, Art?" asked Murphy, quickly changing the subject.

"What?" Jordan Adler laughed. "Dr. Morse took those stitches?"

"Of course I did," said Morse. "You don't think Murphy'd take Glorified Jock to a *vet*, do you? Bring him in on Monday, Murph."

"I'm so glad he's all right." Charlotte touched her lips

with a napkin and reached for her purse. "I know how attached you are to him, Murph. My father's always been like that about his dogs, too." She rose to her feet.

Arthur Morse plucked the check from her fingers, as he always did. "My treat, Charlotte. You call me if this... uneasiness persists."

"I will, Art." She smiled and touched his arm. "And thanks for the breakfast."

"My pleasure." Morse rose to his feet and remained standing until Charlotte walked through the door. Outside, the snow continued to fall.

"Wasn't Charlotte's father the publisher of the paper at one time?" Jordan asked, sipping from a glass of orange juice. Under the table her hand moved on Murphy's thigh.

"And editor," answered Hobie Jameison, who had returned to the group as Charlotte was leaving. "The guy was a legend around here. He came back from the Pacific with a chestful of medals, only twenty-five years old, and bought into *The Sentinel* in 1945, when it was about to fold. Turned it right around. He was writer, editor, even typesetter at times. Bought the other owner out in 1951."

"He sounds like quite a man," said Jordan.

Arthur Morse folded his napkin on the table. The sound of disgust he made was so low that Murphy doubted the others heard it.

"He retired to Arizona, didn't he?" Jordan continued. "Is Charlotte's mother there, too?"

"She died." Morse rose from the table. "I'll see you bastions of law and order later. Dr. Adler."

"There goes a man carrying a serious torch," said Jordan, watching him leave. "How long has he been in love with Charlotte Post?"

"Oh, not more than twenty-five years," said Jameison. His expression was lazily hostile. "You ask a lot of questions, don't you, doctor?"

She smiled back at him, unfazed. "It goes with the job, I guess."

"Uh-huh. Well, let's get back to the office. Maybe you can match them with some answers, for a change."

Jordan's hand was moving again, and Murphy felt a sudden erection bulging against his pants.

"I . . . I, uh, think I'll sit a few more minutes, Hobie," he said, a blush burning his face. "Finish this last biscuit."

"Whatever. See you over there."

Beside him, Jordan was biting down on her lower lip, giggling into her orange juice.

Edward Manning gently replaced the telephone in its cradle. Sometimes, when he was angriest, it made him feel better to do a thing like that. A display of power, in a way. He'd always secretly envied big men who never shouted. He tried never to shout.

"What'd he say?" asked DeVane Belleau. He was out of uniform, wearing dark slacks and a heavy sweater and standing by a large window that overlooked the ski basin.

"Just about what I told you he'd say," Manning replied.

"Bastard!" snapped Ray Manning. "Little red-ass son of a bitch." He was sweating again and looking frayed around the edges. Someone missed his morning toot, Belleau guessed idly. He wondered if the old man was weaning his son cold turkey.

"It sounds like you're the one with the red ass, Ray," said Manning mildly. "Shouting won't help." He turned to Belleau. "He wants it up front. He has no interest in a percentage deal."

"That's because he's smart." Belleau watched one of Lester Nelson's Snow Gods maneuver his big cat just above a boarding ramp, narrowly clearing the dangling chairs. "He knows once the deal's finalized, you could invite him to—how did I hear it?—to go perform a sex act possible only to an amoeba." Belleau nodded, almost to himself. "Because it wouldn't matter what he knows then."

"Maybe this is better," said Ray Manning. "What he gets up front's nothing compared to what he'd gouge us for on a percentage. I mean, we're talking millions over the—"

"Ray," said his father. "Are you really that thick? Do you really believe that crooked little bastard's going to settle for just one payoff and then shuffle politely on back to his tepee?"

Stung by his father's sarcasm, the younger Manning's fingers went to his upper lip and the stubbly mustache. "What're our options, then?" he asked. "You. Mr. Serling." He glared at Belleau. "Any suggestions from the Twilight Zone?"

"I'm completely open to suggestions," put in Manning. "Wherever they come from. What about it, DeVane? Do you have anything?"

Belleau turned back from the window. "I've done some checking in Albuquerque," he said. "Friend of mine who works vice down there told me about a hooker named Diaz. Lupita Diaz. Seems she walked right out of a roust once by using Clinton Gold's name."

"So he knows a whore," said Manning. "Most of those do-gooder types do. Social reform, and all that shit."

"It's not that simple," said Belleau. "My friend gave me a number, and I got hold of her last night. Really interesting."

"So? Is it something we can use?"

"Maybe." Belleau's smile was a death's-head grimace. "Maybe something."

Vanessa crossed Second again and passed Hacker Morlan at the corner.

"Ow, ba-by!" he moaned. It had been mildly amusing the first time he'd said it, but this was her fourth trip by.

"Hey, get some therapy, man," she mumbled, and kept walking.

The snow had let up a little past dusk, and Vanessa had pulled back the hood of her red vinyl jacket. Light from the shop windows and passing cars caught in her blond hair.

Her scalp itched. On the bottle, Clairol Loving Care had claimed to contain no peroxide, but Vanessa wouldn't have bet the house money on it. If her hair was damaged by that crap, Paul Killian would owe her more than any damned ten percent off the top.

Of course, if there way anyone who should know all about hair dye, it was old Killian Black.

She glanced at her digital watch. Twelve minutes later than the last time she looked, which made it 9:34. It had gotten colder since the snow stopped. Her legs, despite the Damart thermals under her tight jeans, were getting numb. Likewise her feet.

How in the hell did she let that little dork talk her into this? "It's the break you need, Vannie," he'd said in that deep phony-ass voice. "What've you had in the last few years? A couple of commercials?"

She'd shot a stiff middle finger at the phone. "Three commercials this year," she'd replied. "And two good feature parts—"

"In dinner theater," he'd said. "What do you get for that? Besides free Salisbury steak and pot roast, I mean. That's okay for some kid just starting out, but you're what? Thirty-one?"

"I'm most certainly not!" she'd lied. "I'm twenty-seven, and most people say I look twenty-two."

"That's exactly my point," he'd replied. "I need a tall, slim beauty about twenty, with blond hair. You'll be perfect, Vannie."

He'd always known where to reach her. "But I'm not blond," she'd said, letting the other qualifications pass as givens. "And I'm not very interested in being bait for some nutso, either."

"Blond we can fix, and I already explained about the other. You'll never get off the main drags. Hack and I'll be on you at all times. You'll be a decoy, for God's sake. Not bait."

"Like on 'Mean Streets'?"

"Exactly. Like Derek Westphal's partner on 'Mean Streets.' As soon as we spot someone tailing you, on foot or by car, we'll pull you out. We take it from there."

"I don't know, Paul."

"Vanessa," he'd said, his voice showing a trace of impa-

tience, ''do you have *any idea* of what this'll do for your
career after that creep's caught and the story breaks? Next
season it might be you on 'Mean Streets.' Not to mention
your share of the payoff from the networks. But, hey, if
you're that uncertain, I understand. No problem. I'll just give
Debra Martindale a call over at . . .''

So, eight hours and two flight changes later, here she was.
Because she believed him. He'd do it. It wouldn't be the first
time he'd massaged some useless bullshit into a story.

She turned back off First and onto Hammersmith again.
Paul Killian was ambling along ahead of her, stopping to look
in the window of a Sears catalog outlet, and he barely glanced
up as she passed.

Murphy slowed for the second time in that block to let
jaywalkers cut in front of him. The streets were filling up,
and it was only Thursday night. And none of them seemed to
care about, or even notice, the sheriff's department logo on
the door of the Land Cruiser.

His eyes passed, then automatically locked on to a tall
blonde in a shiny red jacket near the corner of First and
Hammersmith. He'd begun to notice girls like that almost
reflexively. He slowed his vehicle to a crawl, and car horns
started up behind him.

Good figure. Lots of makeup. She was moving along
oddly, though. Furtive, glancing around. Most girls who
looked like she did walked upright and proud. Take a good
look, sucker, at what you're not getting. Unless you're
carrying an American Express Gold Card and maybe driving
a Saab turbo.

The blonde passed on around the corner, and Murphy was
shifting back up to third gear when Glorified Jock exploded
out of the back.

It happened so quickly Murphy nearly veered across the icy
street and into a parked car. One moment, the dog was lying
on a pull-down seat idly looking out. The next, he'd bounded
into the front, hitting the steering wheel and Murphy's win-

dow with a jarring thud, and roaring out a series of barks next to his owner's ear.

"Jesus Christ!" Murphy yelled, trying to free his arm from Jock's weight. "What the hell's wrong with you?"

The Land Cruiser stopped. People on the sidewalk were staring, pointing at the vehicle and the big German shepherd trying to claw its way through the glass. Murphy yanked back on Jock's collar and white foam from the dog's mouth spattered on his jacket. He pushed Jock toward the passenger side.

"What is it, Jock? What's wrong?"

The dog leaped into the back again, barking louder, and began to dig at the flip-up rear door. Murphy pulled into a no-parking zone and killed the engine, letting a stream of angry drivers past. Then he climbed into the back with Jock and grabbed him around the neck. The dog was trembling, his heartbeat pounding through the bandages on his chest, and his mouth was wide open in a snarl. A woman passing the back of the vehicle looked in at the animal, fur standing upright on its back and teeth gleaming. She screamed.

Finally, Jock began to calm, growls changing to long whines. Murphy held him, looking over his head across the crowded street. There were people everywhere, some familiar, others not.

He climbed back behind the wheel and started up, then made a U-turn back up First, moving very slowly. In the back, Glorified Jock pressed his nose against a window and whined.

He moves briefly from shadow into light—the sounds of the barking dog fading—then into shadow again. Up ahead, her blond hair is a beacon that draws him in its wake.

She's following a long rectangle. Up Hammersmith from First to Third, then east one block to Fremont. Down to First and repeat. She's looking into shop windows occasionally, but mostly just moving on.

There are people everywhere, especially on First and Third,

like in the cities. But that isn't a problem. He knows how to cope with people in a city.

He cuts across diagonally, still using the shadows from the west side of Hammersmith, where everything is closed, and walks rapidly toward Fourth. It's mostly residential, partly zoned for business, with a welding shop and an auto supply. Everything is shut down and dark, the street deserted. He races along the block, the rubber soles of his boots crunching almost soundlessly in the new snow, and turns back south onto Fremont. It's the quietest part of her circuit. Between Third and Second is only a J. C. Penney's and High Country Sporting Goods, both closed, and between them an alley leading to Penney's Car Care and a loading ramp.

He reaches the corner of Fremont and Third ahead of her. Looking back, he sees her pass a thin, spike-haired man who glances up and says something. She ignores him and comes on.

He's careful not to hurry, though Fremont is virtually deserted. When he's next to the alley, he turns in and moves along the wall in the darkness. At the back, next to the loading ramp, is a series of tin-roofed garages from when the Alpenview Hotel had stood where Penney's is now. The old wooden doors hang, either open or half-open, in their own pools of black shadow above the snow.

He waits, just along the wall where the streetlights don't reach, and drops his left hand into the top of his boot.

Come on, Danni. . . .

Vanessa saw a figure turn the corner behind her as she passed along the storefront of a J. C. Penney's. The lights on this block of Fremont, with the stores closed down, were less bright, and her eyes weren't adjusting properly. The figure seemed to hesitate, then came on toward her.

Oh, God. Oh, Jesus. She looked around quickly for Morlan or Paul Killian. The bastards had been everywhere, except on this one block. The darkest, most deserted section of the loop.

She could run down to Second. There were people there. Run? Through freezing slush in these goddamned spike heels?

Maybe he hadn't seen her. He was moving slowly, and she was in the shadow of the building. There was an alley a few yards ahead. Duck in there. Let him go past. Then cut back up to Third.

She hugged the wall, sliding toward the alley entrance. Someone down on Second had a boom box, turned up loud. It was playing ... something. She couldn't keep up with the new music anymore. She wasn't twenty; she wasn't even twenty-seven. She was getting old. Old and ... Oh, God, so scared. She felt a hot trickle of urine down the inside of her leg.

Oh, Jesus, he was still coming. It was dark under the storefront awning, but the alley was darker. She put her gloved hand on the rough stone corner and pulled herself around it.

Footsteps, quicker and louder than before, crackling on wet, freezing snow. She began to back up, making small moaning noises in her throat. Down the alley, away from the street. Into the darkness ...

"Vanessa! Dammit, Vanessa!" The figure turned into the alley entrance. "Where the hell do you think you're going?"

"Paul?" She rushed forward, vaguely aware of soft movement just behind her. "Oh, God, Paul! You son of a bitch! You scared me to death!"

He took her by the arm and yanked her out into the light of the street. "I told you we'd be close by, didn't I? Dammit, Vanessa, how's this going to work with you ducking into alleys? We can't cover you if you're going to pull stuff like this."

"Then you forget it!" She jerked free of his grip. "I quit! You go catch your goddamned slasher without me, you conniving little bastard!"

"What?" His tone changed instantly. "Vannie, babe, what are you thinking about here? This is the best opportunity—"

"I said, forget it!" She backed into the street. "Do you know what I did? Do you? I was so scared I peed on myself, you creep! And I went into that ... that dark alley to hide. ..."

Her voice began to break, words tumbling over each other.
"And there was *something back there!* I heard it just as you
yelled at me!"

She saw him grin. "That cat? Down at the end? Look,
Vannie, there the damned thing goes."

She saw a shadowy movement, close to the ground, hurrying past some old sheds with wooden doors.

"I . . . I don't care, Paul. Do you hear me? I don't care if it
was a cat. I'm through. I'm going back to the motel. You can
pay me there, then drive me to the airport in Durango."

"Vanessa . . . oh, hell, okay!" Paul Killian yelled after her.
"Who gives a damn? I'll get someone else!"

"What happened, man?" He turned as Hacker Morlan
trotted up beside him. "What's wrong with Vanessa?"

"Forget Vanessa!" Killian snapped. "Vanessa got scared.
She saw me come around the corner and thought I was the
mad slasher. So she ducked into that alley there."

"Back there?" Morlan looked into the shadows. "Radical,
man. That's twice as spooky as the street. We got to get her a
fucking lobotomy, or something."

"It's my own fault." Killian patted his pockets for a
homemade cigarette. "What more could I expect out of the
lowest IQ this side of Golda, the Dancing Bear? Got a
match?"

Morlan lit the joint, and then one of his own. "What
now?" he asked.

"Now we call Debra Martindale, like I should have in the
first place."

"I don't know, Paul. She won't come as cheap as Vanessa."

"Who cares? Thanks of Officer Dimmit and that advance
from *The Enquirer,* we can afford her. Woops! Stash the
weed."

They curled their hands around the cigarettes as a Land
Cruiser with a sheriff's department logo on the door went
slowly by.

"It's our old pal, the Sea Warrior," said Killian, waving at
Murphy Davis. "Just keep walking." They reached the cor-

ner of Second. "One thing's for sure. Vanessa Burke can go whistle for more money. She'll get her plane fare back, and that's it, brother."

When he can no longer hear their voices, he relaxes his grip on the silver handle. His fingers feel like blocks of wood in the biting cold, and they hurt when he straightens them.

They were clever. They nearly fooled him. It was only when she was standing in the light of the street, shouting at the short man, that he'd realized it wasn't her at all.

He glides to the head of the alley and watches the two men cross Second. The deputy's jeep—with the dog—pulls away from them. In the light he sees, with the shock of realization, that his hands are trembling. That he had been afraid.

He has to get off the streets, get home, because the night has gone all wrong with this stupid, amateurish trick he's nearly fallen for. She'd been walking the same six blocks over and over, obvious to anyone with half a brain it was a trap, and he'd almost . . . Get home and think. Lie down and relax, or play his music, *something*, until the headache goes away and he can think.

He knows that she's still somewhere close by. But now there are obstacles, dangers he's never encountered before. He'll have to be more careful.

Fremont Street is deserted again. He crosses over to its other side and heads north to Fourth. Then he turns east and walks between rows of darkened houses, away from the center of the town. After a while his spirits improve, and he begins to hum "Hey, Jude," very softly and exactly on key.

16

When he shifted in his sleep, Murphy's fingers trailed across Jordan's bare stomach, and she got the shakes again. She tried to lie very still, counting backward from one hundred, but finally gave it up. There was no sleep to be had.

She slid from under his arm and quietly rose from the bed. Glorified Jock, lying on the carpet beneath her, raised his head. She patted him, then tiptoed to the bathroom.

The light, when she cut it on, glared into the mirror and hurt her eyes. After squinting a few seconds, she stepped closer and leaned on the lavatory. She consciously forced the face in the mirror to relax and return her stare.

She examined her eyes, a shifting blue green, and watched the pupils contract from the light.

"You're going to blow it again," she whispered, and nodded to herself. "Aren't you?"

No. The face in the mirror shook its head. Not this time, not with this man. I can't this time.

Try harder. She held the stare, picking out one tiny green fleck in Mirror Jordan's right eye. A minute went by. Two. That's it, Jordie. Breathe in. Pull it down deep and relax. Breathe. Breathe . . .

Then the other face was there, in the green fleck of her eye. All the other faces . . .

"Damn," she whispered, breaking contact. There was no heat in the curse. "Damn."

179

It was no good. When she looked back again, there were tears in Mirror Jordan's eyes and the pupils were expanding.

She cut off the light and, blinded, felt her way back to the bedroom, guided by the even sound of Murphy's breathing. She felt for her jeans and jacket and snowboots.

She dressed in the living room. It was going to be cold with no undergarments, not even a sweater, but they were on the other side of the bed. She zipped the jacket up to her neck.

It was snowing lightly when she pulled the door shut behind her. Jock had come into the living room and she rubbed his muzzle before closing the door in his face. As she slogged to the Camaro, snowflakes caught in her hair.

What was the name? Manning. Ray Manning. Not the old man, the hype'd warned her. Get the son.

She glanced at her watch. Twenty minutes past two. There was probably no need to push the car down the sloping drive. With those pain pills in him, Murph wouldn't hear a bomb go off.

It wasn't as cold as she'd expected, but Jordan was shivering badly anyway, and it had nothing to do with the temperature.

"This is a surprise." Ray Manning was a small man. His face was stubbled with the beginnings of a beard. Beneath a heavy tan, his skin was sallow. "You too. You're a surprise."

"Were you asleep?" Jordan looked around the living room of the condominium. Neat. Not a trace of dust, with freshly vacuumed carpets and couches, but the place smelled musty. Empty.

"Me?" His grin was savage. A look she knew. "At two-thirty in the morning? Don't be absurd." His eyes hadn't shifted from hers. "Lon told me you might call, so I waited up. I waited a long time, Miss Adler."

She tried to remember. Lon was the hype. Big, but round and soft. Soft as snot. She put the name with the face.

"I . . . don't have much with me." She avoided his eyes. "I've been thinking about quitting."

His laugh was short and hard, a snapping sound. "Yeah, you have. I can see you have. Rationing, aren't you?"

"I . . ."

"I know about that." He grinned again. "What's worse is when someone else tries to do it for you. But Silvercat's a good town. You just gotta know who to talk to."

He was sitting in front of her on a glass coffee table. When he reached over and took her hand, she didn't resist. It lay, twitching slightly, in his grasp.

"But, hey. You're in no mood for this, huh? Small talk later. Let's get you fixed first. You do any rock?"

"No." She shook her head emphatically. When was he going to quit stalling? "No way. That stuff'll kill you."

Manning laughed, high-pitched, nearly a giggle. "Right. Right, my love. Whereas this"—he pulled an ebony cigarette box across the coffee table—"is just like mother's milk, isn't it?"

Just do it, she thought. But she made herself sit still. When he released her hand, she withdrew it into her lap.

"Okay." He opened the top of the box. A built-in spring released the music. It was an old song.

"Recognize that?" Manning thrust a small blade into the white mound and tapped it carefully onto the glass. "It's a golden oldie. 'Smoke Gets in Your Eyes.' Cute, huh?"

Hurry up, damn you! She didn't reply.

With the blade's edge he shaped a square on the glass. "Of course, I guess we could bring the lyrics more up to date. How about 'Snow Blows in Your Eyes'?" He giggled again, dividing the square into four thick lines, each about an inch long. He looked up. "You don't talk much, do you, love?"

The alkaline, chalky odor rose up to her, and Jordan felt her trembling worsen.

Manning handed her a small glass tube. "We go first-class here," he said. "No dollar bills. It's clean, by the way. I just—"

She took it without looking at him and blocked her left

nostril with a fingertip. She leaned forward, inserted the glass tube in her right nostril, and inhaled one of the lines.

When it hit her, she was never prepared. When her nostril and sinuses seemed to explode, then the very top of her head. She shifted the tube to her left nostril and drew another line.

"Hoo, baby!" said Manning. "You suck it up like a *biggg* girl."

"Screw you," she whispered. She felt herself lean back into the cushions of the couch, the back of her throat already raw with bitter postnasal drip.

"Now, there's a thought." Manning nodded cheerfully. "But . . . first things first. Know what this is?"

Jordan watched without much interest as he produced a water pipe and a glass vial containing several pink-orange chunks. "I've seen it," she murmured. "I'm not impressed."

"No?" He put a piece about the size of his fingernail into the pipe and lit it. "No?" he repeated. "Then you don't know much, do you?" Gray smoke swirled inside the water pipe as the chunk cooked. He took a long drag and held it.

"I've seen it," she said again, and she had. Pat Calder had introduced her to it. He'd barbecued his goddamned brains on the stuff. Pat had been to Kathmandu in the seventies, just like that Bob Seger song.

Manning sat beside her as the cocaine started taking her off at the neck. When he unzipped her jacket, she hardly noticed.

Murphy lay on his side, facing the wall. He didn't move when he felt her slip back into bed.

She slid up behind him and laid her head against his back. Her face felt hot, almost feverish, although her legs and body were cold. She ran her hand around his ribs and onto his chest.

"Where've you been?" He asked it quietly, and felt her stiffen against him.

"Bathroom," she whispered after a moment. "I had to pee." She pressed the hard mound of her pubic bone into the cleft of his buttocks and began to move slowly, her thighs warming against the backs of his legs. "Want to wake up?"

"No," he lied. "Go to sleep."

She relaxed against him. "Okay, but you don't know what you're missing." She kissed his shoulder. "Then again, I guess you do."

She lay there for a long time before she went to sleep, and once he felt her tears, wet on his neck. He kept very still, inhaling the bitter smell of her breath against his ear. His eyes were open, and he waited for morning.

In morning light that filtered through clouds and then the kitchen curtains, Sara Nichols watched Neddie Cameron rehearse his speech.

"The only things in this world that sit completely still are dead," he began again, checking his time on the butcher-block clock above the dining-room door. "Think about that." He paused for his imaginary audience. "It's true, isn't it? Everything that's alive . . ."

She tuned him out. She'd heard it before.

Her tea tasted bitter, and she put it aside. Her mind drifted back, for a second, to the bedroom night table and the photograph.

Child bride. She saw the eyes and the confident smile. Then she was seeing other eyes. Not young or blue or so confident. Older, gray, and troubled. Hurting.

She had to try. And if it didn't work out, she'd have to try again.

"I'm going home, Neddie." She put down the cup. For no apparent reason, just saying it made her feel better.

". . . taking these new resources and . . . What?"

"I said I'm going home. I have to think about some things."

"But . . ." His expression was confused. "I thought we were going skiing. It's the first day, Sara. And you know Ed's counting on—"

"You go." She headed for the bathroom to collect her things. He trailed along behind her, the note cards for his speech held loosely in one hand. "Just tell Mr. Manning—"

"Ed. He wants you to call him Ed."

"Tell Mr. Manning I have to go into the paper today. Some background work on the Delaney story."

He leaned in the doorway, and she had to brush against him to pass. "And is that the truth?" he asked.

She looked up from packing her overnight bag. "What about Marilyn?" she countered. "How much of the truth have you told me?"

"So that's it." He walked toward her. "God, Sara, there's no need to be so jealous." He slipped an arm around her waist. "Just forget all about—"

"It's not that." She slipped free and moved toward the front hall. "That was a small part of it once, I guess. But there's more."

"What?" He stopped following her and stood in the hall. "What more? What other problem could there be?"

But she didn't answer that one even though she knew. Even though she was finally certain.

She went back and kissed him on the cheek. "I'll call you," she said. "Before Monday, I promise." And left his house. She knew it was for the last time.

The town was jammed along the turnoff to the Village. Cars were bumper to bumper on First, and Henry Light, herding traffic at the corner of Hammersmith, had run out of patience. So much for the "unannounced" opening a day early for the locals.

"Hold it!" He blew his whistle again. "You! Right there! Yeah, you! Wait your turn!"

The driver of the custom van shot him the finger and continued to inch forward off First into the flow of traffic backed up on Hammersmith.

"Hey, goddammit!" Light's hand instinctively slid toward his holster. Oh, that's real smart, he rebuked himself. What are you going to do? Shoot the silly bitch? Then how'd you get that van out of the traffic flow? Word was the Village had commissioned a private road for next summer so ski customers wouldn't even have to come through Silvercat—much to the indignation of the town's merchants—but what would he do *this* season?

"Hey!" Light yelled again. He walked toward the van. "Let those people go by! You'll get your turn!"

The driver, a large, florid-faced woman, rolled down her window.

"Yeah?" she yelled. "We been settin' right here ten minutes and the lifts are already started." She had a nasal southern accent. "An' I can jus' fasten all over the idea a' drivin' all night an' then settin' here on my ass while everybody else goes skiin'!"

Light tried tact. "Lady, I'll bet that van cost twenty thousand dollars."

"Twenny-eight. My hubby's an exec at Texas Instruments."

"And you don't want to get it scraped up. So just let me do my job, okay?"

"Up yours, pal." The van inched forward again. "You wanna take the time out to arrest me, go right ahead. You'll have a bottleneck from here halfway to goddamn New Mexico. If I see an openin', I'm goin'."

Light turned just as a northbound car on Hammersmith stopped and motioned the van forward in front of it.

"Hot damn!" he heard the woman say. "There's a hole. Outta the way, cop!"

He also saw, on the almost deserted west side of First, a rusty green Ford Pinto careening toward the intersection at a formidable rate of speed. Behind the wheel, Estrella DePriest was waving at someone out her side window.

"So go!" Henry Light yelled to the woman in the van. "It's on your head, lady!"

"Damn straight!" The woman roared into the intersection as the policeman leaped aside.

It was going to be one hell of a mess, he decided, diving for the safety of the curb, but worth it.

On the mountain, the first skiers of the season loaded at the new gondola. The lines weren't long yet, mainly because— someone said—of a big smashup down in the town involving one of those custom supervans and some local woman. Traffic was bottlenecked halfway to goddamned New Mexico.

Murphy sat on the edge of the huge redwood deck and watched Jordan Adler glide down Overkill, a beetling, black-diamond cliff at the west side of the basin. There hadn't been enough expert skiers on it yet to dig the hip-deep moguls it would wear later in the season, but it was still steep as hell, and she was making it look like a novice slope. Tight parallel turns in the fall line, upper body motionless except for her pole plants, hips and thighs in perfect angulation on each weight shift. Murphy had been fairly good before his knee made him a spectator, but he knew he'd never skied like Jordan.

She waved as she flashed by on the flat and into the short line for the Express, a double chair that serviced only the advanced trails.

Murphy saw Edward Manning and son getting the royal treatment at the gondola. The ski instructor was merely a convenience enabling them to cut the line. His job was to get lost at the top, then meet them down at the lift when they were ready to board again. A fairly common practice for those who could afford it.

Neddie Cameron was there, too, also cutting the line. Murphy wondered where Sara Nichols was.

He'd heard the rumors in the town, or course. About Sara and Cameron and Cameron's wife. He hadn't believed them at first, and then decided it was none of his business, anyway. Now, he wasn't certain what he thought.

He glanced at his watch and rose painfully to his feet. Hobie didn't give a damn what Jordan Adler did. As far as the sheriff was concerned, she'd done her bit and was no longer on the payroll. But he would expect his deputy to be on the job.

He'd blame it on the traffic, he decided. It was wall-to-wall tourists down there.

He limped across the deck toward the corner of the lodge. And when Doug Hutchins yelled at him from the lift line, he didn't hear because his mind was circulating an endless circle

of images. Sara Nichols and A.J. and a faceless shadow—
familiar, somehow—running into the blizzard. Hobie and
DeVane and the slim, nude body of Jordan Adler. And a
bogus bottle of 4-Way Nasal Spray.

The clouds continued through the weekend, with occasional light snow. Ski Silvercat had the earliest opening of any
"glitter" resort in the state, and reaped full rewards in a type
of publicity more pleasing to the corporation than what they'd
been seeing. Celebrity chasers from a dozen major newspapers and magazines descended on the town to chronicle every
parallel turn and speculate on every après-ski flirtation. Power
breakfasts were held and meetings were taken, and business
cards exchanged hands more often than currency. The
Aspenification of Silvercat had begun.

The rich and famous rode the gondola and skied the
mountain. Though it was only the beginning of ski season,
most were already deeply tanned, causing Sara Nichols to
recall a comment by a former companion—a campus radical—
that it was always considered chic to be brown so long as
one's natural skin color was white. When the lifts closed, the
celebrities partied at the Village, to the delight of the culture
vultures, and at the Dutchman, to the even greater delight of
the tourists. A young man from Phoenix spent the entire
weekend impersonating Derek Westphal—who was detained
in Los Angeles doing voice-overs on the cuts of his first
album—in the taverns of the town. Before he was finally
exposed, he enjoyed tremendous success in terms of compli-
mentary drinks, food, lodging, and illegal drugs, not to
mention equally impressive results with a series of starry-
eyed female tourists.

In the town—where Sara finally made her promised telephone call to Neddie Cameron on Sunday—the local busi-
nessmen bitched about the tourists and celebrities, reminisced
sadly about simpler times, and shoveled money into their cash
registers, too busy even to watch the Broncos clobber
Indianapolis. Fewer people mentioned the Slasher as the news
media's emphasis switched from murder to movie stars, and

the investigations of both the sheriff's and police departments bogged down. At *The Sentinel*, Marvin Lanier received an anonymous letter of confession to all the attacks from a person who said he'd acted on a command to destroy the harlots of the world by his pet gerbil, who was in fact the Messiah. As they had with Toya Jalecka, many local residents made a conscious effort to forget A. J. Delaney, who wasn't *really* one of their own, after all. It was their experience that bad things ignored sometimes just went away.

17

Monday, October 28

Murphy Davis slumped down in the Toyota Land Cruiser and watched the parking lot fill up. He flipped another capsule into his mouth and washed it down with a swig of Coor's.

The auditorium held five hundred people, which was one hundred more than the high school's enrollment. From the look of the parking lot, there'd be people standing up tonight.

Murphy's focus was a little fuzzy. The security lights outside the building had a soft nimbus about them, and he looked out to see if it was snowing again. It wasn't.

"Must be the pills," he said aloud, before remembering he was alone. Glorified Jock was at home, and Jordan Adler was already inside the auditorium.

"Don't take these with booze, Murph." Murphy tried without success to imitate Arthur Morse's peevish tone. But he had, or course. Taken them with booze, that is, ever since he'd received the prescription. And tonight it was beginning to feel like he'd taken about one too many.

Like Jordan, he thought in a moment of cold clarity. About one too many.

That's a great excuse, Davis. And great timing, too. The Debate of the Century ready to begin in—he looked at his watch, which was also a little fuzzy—less than twenty minutes, and one of the debaters was about two-thirds shit-faced.

You don't hurt that much, pal, he thought. Can't even feel it, as a matter of fact. Oh, no. The problem is you got

189

problems, boyo. And one of them is that you're scared of this debate.

But not anymore. He thought he laughed aloud. Not anymore. We took care of that problem, didn't we?

No more pills now. They'd taken off the edge of pain and fear just like they did in the old days, and sorrow, like they have to in these new days, so it was time to sit still and straighten up. Look over the notes on those three-by-five index cards for your opening statement. You don't have to win this thing, pal. Hobie was right about that. The town's behind you, and they'll outvote those Yuppie fuckers from the Village any day. Just get through it and don't make an ass of yourself. That's all it'll take.

He flipped through the cards and decided he had it down cold. One change occurred to him. He'd start off with a joke to get the locals even more firmly in his camp. Good old Murph.

His mouth felt cottony and dry, so he reached into the floorboard for the plastic ring tab of Coor's. Only one left? That didn't seem likely. The dented can had been lying upside down, and when he opened it, beer sprayed everywhere. Some went onto the windshield, but most of it went onto his suit. A wet, yeasty odor filled the Land Cruiser.

"Good shot!" He laughed. "Way to go, Davis. Never trust a wounded beer, you know that." He plucked a handful of tissues from a box between the seats and blotted himself as dry as possible. "Oh, well." He shrugged. "No harm, no foul."

It was nearly time, too late to go home and change, and he needed to get into the auditorium, anyway. Get set up, accustomed to the lights and the crowd before the thing began. He opened the door and stepped out onto the slick glaze of old snow. He was amazed that he'd been nervous before. The pills had kicked in, and he felt calm. Supremely in control.

"This is an excellent turnout." Charlotte Post looked around her. "I'd really never expected this many people."

"Polarity," Sara replied. They were sitting together near the center of the auditorium, despite Charlotte's joking remark that perhaps they should get on opposite sides of the room. Sara hadn't mentioned her telephone call to Neddie Cameron. She was too busy keeping her eyes off the slim redhead sitting several rows in front of them.

"Polarity?" Charlotte cocked an eyebrow in Sara's direction. "I thought that was a magnetic term. Please remember that I only had one year of college, Sara."

"You know exactly what I mean. I'm talking about people, and we've both had more than one year of them. This place is packed partly because of newcomers and Villagers who want to hear Neddie's views on the issues, and—"

"Issues!" Charlotte snorted. She cut her eyes back toward the upper-left area of the room. "They're here because they want to see Ed Manning and that bunch of TV types he imported for the weekend."

"—and the rest," Sara continued with a smile, "are the old-timers who've come to see Murphy Davis kick the city slicker's ass."

Charlotte laughed. "What an elegant way you have with words, my dear," she said. "But I imagine you're right, and that bothers me. A polarized community's not what Silvercat needs. Especially not now."

"It can't be helped, Char. It's inevitable. Anytime you have this much change occurring in an old town, it has to happen. The new group wants to alter the place into a copy of what they left behind, and the old group wants things the way they were before. Someone has to lose."

"Why? Why not combine the best of both progressive and traditional? They both have merit."

"Pretty words, boss lady." Sara nodded. "It'd make a hell of an editorial, but I'm not sure how realistic . . . Oh, look. Here comes Murphy—" Her voice suddenly stopped.

"My God!" Charlotte whispered.

Murphy Davis had come out from the side of the stage and was shaking hands with Neddie Cameron. Even from her distance, Sara clearly saw him stumble against a chair and Cameron's reaction, nostrils flaring as if he smelled something. There was some type of stain on the front of Murphy's brown suit, along the jacket, and all down his pants.

"Hey, check it out!" said a young man off to her left. "Neddie's already scared the piss out of him!"

"You better watch your mouth, boy!" a balding man near her snapped. There was a hearing aid in his ear. "Even a little faggot like you should be able to see Murphy Davis makes about two of your buddy Cameron, which equals three of you!"

"Hey, this isn't the Mr. Silvercat contest, Pop," answered the young man. "It's a debate. And your washed-up jock's about to fall off the stage." There was laughter and applause from around him.

"Pop?" The balding man stood, the seat of his chair flipping up behind him. "Pop? I'll pop you, you skinny little—"

"Ben!" Charlotte's voice stilled the laughter around her. "Ben Dubose, you calm down."

Dubose looked around, a blush on his ruddy features. "Oh . . . sorry about that, Ms. Post," he said. "I didn't see you." He turned back toward the stage. "Give 'im hell, Murph!" he yelled, then sat down.

"It's already starting." Charlotte leaned back in her seat. "And the debate isn't even going yet."

"But what *is* that on his suit?" Sara whispered. She controlled her voice, which was trying to break. "Char, he's not . . . drunk, is he?"

"Of course not!" But Charlotte's pale blue eyes were wide with concern.

On the stage, Murphy Davis stepped away from Cameron and went to sit on a folding chair at one side. It appeared to Sara that his gait was unsteady.

Marvin Lanier bustled out from behind the curtains, a last puff of cigarette smoke trailing behind his head, and went to the main podium at center stage. It was large and made of heavy-looking dark wood, with a crest on the front that read

"Presented to Granite County High School by the Class of 1973." There were two smaller, post-supported podiums on either side of the stage.

"Let's get started," said Lanier without preamble. "Anyone who isn't here can sneak in the back."

He looked out over the audience, which had gradually grown silent. "For those of you who don't know me—" Sara saw him glance meaningfully toward the large group from the Village. She recognized a couple of faces from network television. "—my name is Marvin Lanier, and I'm the editor of *The Silvercat Sentinel*."

"Way to go, Marv!" yelled a man sitting just down from Ben Dubose.

"Thanks, Cecil," said Lanier dryly. "But I'd advise you to behave, if you're planning to stay. *The Sentinel*'s sponsoring this debate, and I won't have anyone in the audience acting the fool. I expect the candidates'll do enough of that on their own."

There was laughter, and a ripple of applause. "Way to go, Marv," Sara heard Charlotte whisper.

"Okay, then. We'll begin with each man making a short opening statement he's prepared. After that, as moderator, I'll provide a series of questions for the debate. Now, who wants to go first?"

Neddie Cameron gave a polite "after you" gesture. Sara saw Murphy's face pale a little, then he rose. When he walked to the central podium, the stain on his suit glaring under the stage lights, there were a few titters from the audience. Ben Dubose glowered in their direction.

"Good evening." Murphy leaned too close to the microphone and got a screeching feedback. "Woops." He grinned.

"As you can see, I had a small accident on my way to this debate tonight," he said. "I'm afraid I got a little too intimate with a can of Coor's."

There was scattered laughter, only a small percentage of it sarcastic.

"To begin with, I'd like to thank Cecil Fielder for his encouragement to us all," said Murphy. The men around

Fielder applauded, and he responded by raising twin fingers in the victory signal. "Many of you know that Cecil's a lifelong bachelor, by the way, but that's not to say he never has any . . . fun. Of course, being the age he is, Cecil has to take pretty much what he can get." Murphy's lean features began to spread into a bleary grin. "Which probably explains why, anytime he goes to the city, the first thing Cecil does is start following the Meals-On-Wheels truck."

There was a moment of stunned silence, then a trickle of embarrassed laughter. A man sitting by Cecil Fielder nudged him broadly.

Oh, God, Murphy, Sara thought.

Through the auditorium, she heard an undercurrent of whispering. Hobie Jameison, sitting a few rows in front of her, bowed his head and appeared to be studying a fingernail.

Murphy stood quite still for a moment, staring at the podium top, then he removed some cards from his coat pocket. During his opening speech that followed, he rarely looked up.

It was completely predictable, and just as boring. There were spots he'd clearly including as opportunities for humor, but he skirted past them in the same monotone and bulled ahead. He closed with a vague statement about the town's need for a "transition and continuation of Hobie Jameison's type of stable leadership" and a pledge to support "sane, controllable growth in Granite County." To his credit, Sara noticed, he made no reference to his rescue of Alison Delaney.

He sat down to mild applause, eyes still downcast. Sara saw a number of people around her staring at him, Ben Dubose included, with troubled expressions.

Neddie Cameron used no note cards. He had memorized his opening statement.

"The only things in this world that sit completely still are dead," he began, his blue eyes riveting the audience from behind steel-rim glasses. "Think about that. It's true, isn't it? Anything that's alive has movement.

"Silvercat and Granite County, Colorado, are alive." He

pointed a finger out toward the audience. "Because you and your fellow citizens *are* Silvercat and Granite County. And being alive, you cannot remain motionless. This county cannot remain motionless, caught in a time warp, no matter how much some of us might wish it could. It has to move forward, people, or it will surely slide back.

"That's my platform, friends. Simple as that. I support growth. The growth offered by the Silvercat Ski Corporation, and by the other businesses it will engender in our town. I support new buildings, new jobs, the new money that will flow into this county. I favor taking these new resources and plowing them back into the county's future. Into improved schools"—there was a burst of applause—"into better water sanitation and landfill management—"more applause—"and certainly into creating our own state-of-the-art hospital district."

"Ned-die!" shouted the young man who'd argued earlier with Ben Dubose. A few others took up the chant. "Ned-die! Ned-die!"

He waved them to silence.

"My opponent seems to gear his campaign only to longtime residents of Granite County. I hope he doesn't imply, by that, that people who were not born and raised here don't have just as much concern for its future"—a roar of approval from the Silvercat Village section—"because statistics I've found indicate forty-one percent of our residents have lived here ten years or less.

"There's nothing wrong with being newcomers," Cameron continued, "and there's nothing wrong with tourism, either. It's not a dirty word. The outside world's discovering the awesome beauty of this area. Those people want to come here, to share just a little of that beauty we sometimes take for granted. And in exchange for a small amount of inconvenience to us, they spend enormous sums of money. Money that helps reduce sales and property taxes for those of us who live here. *They* put money in our pockets! *They* pay for the good things in this county that benefit us year round!"

Applause thundered in the auditorium, mostly from the Village group, but some of the townspeople were beginning to join in.

"Ned-die! Ned-die! Ned-die!"

"I thought he was running for sheriff," Charlotte muttered. "Not president."

Sara looked at Murphy Davis, sitting on his folding chair on one side of the stage. She felt a tightness welling up in her throat.

"My opponent says he favors 'sane, controllable growth,' " continued Cameron. "Which I take to mean growth without a trashy, boomtown atmosphere, and without the mushrooming crime and polluting problems we've seen cripple other beautiful mountain communities in this state. I completely agree. I suppose that means we've got the same platform. Hey, Murph!" He grinned across at Murphy. "Maybe we should just flip a coin for it. I sure as heck don't want to arm-wrestle you!"

Laughter and more applause. A clever ad-lib, Sara admitted. With that one line, he'd made a joke of Murphy's physical qualifications.

"Seriously, though," said Cameron. "If we both want the same good things for Granite County, and I believe we do, what you voters must decide is which candidate can best help achieve them. And that's what we're here to debate tonight."

He sat down to prolonged applause.

"Thanks for that...*short* opening statement, Mr. Cameron," said Marvin Lanier, returning to the central podium. "Now, let's get to the reason we're all here. We'll keep it simple. A list of questions was compiled by the members of *The Sentinel*'s staff, by the town council, and by the school board. Since many were repetitious, I've whittled on 'em a bit—" There was laughter. "Way to go, Marv!" came softly from the back. "—and ended up with these." He tapped a sheet of paper with his finger. "The candidates will take turns, which is fair, with one speaking first and the other able to rebut. And let's please keep the replies brief, gentlemen." He stared at Cameron. "I know I'd like to get to bed at a decent hour."

More applause.

"Okay, Mr. Cameron," he continued. "Since Mur—Deputy Davis spoke first, how about your having this question?"

The two men rose and stepped behind the small side podiums. Sara looked at Murphy Davis. He stood, shifting his weight at first, then he put both hands on the sloping wooden top. His brown suit, obviously rarely worn, was too tight, and the stain on the front was still visible. His dark blond hair was long and looked ragged compared to Cameron's, and his tie was crooked. She was certain he'd lean on the flimsy podium at some point and break the damned thing.

Neddie Cameron stood erect, one hand resting lightly on his podium, the other in his pants pocket. His blue pin-striped suit coat was unbuttoned, the vest making a V into his white shirt and navy blue tie. His hair and short beard, both neatly trimmed, reflected sprinkles of silver under the lights. He regarded Marvin Lanier with a friendly, mildly amused expression.

It began.

And to Sara's surprise, Murphy Davis held his own. His answers and rebuttals lacked Cameron's flair, but they were solid, often showing a substantial knowledge of the subject. Around her, as the minutes passed, she could feel his supporters beginning to rally.

The question, addressed to Murphy, concerned the fear that new money and a "faster, more sophisticated life-style" would bring additional drug problems. His answer had included plans for more extensive drug education programs in the schools and increased surveillance of known exchange points around the town and at the Village. There were some muffled boos and hisses, mostly good-natured, from the group sitting around the Mannings.

Cameron rose to rebut. For a long moment, he stared out over the audience's heads. His expression clearly said; This is distasteful to me, but I have no choice.

"Mr. Davis." His voice was low, and people toward the back leaned forward. "Tell me, what exactly is Blue Thunder?"

Sara saw Murphy recoil slightly at the same instant the realization of what Cameron was doing struck her.

Neddie. Oh, Jesus, Neddie.

"Blue . . ." Murphy hesitated.

"Blue Thunder. Correct me if I'm wrong, Deputy. Isn't that a slang term for a type of anabolic steroid more commonly known as Dianabol? Are you familiar with the term?"

Murphy's face went stone hard. "Yes," he said finally. "I am."

"What about greenies? Isn't that also a slang term? For amphetamines, also commonly referred to as 'speed' or 'uppers'?"

"Yes."

"Deputy Davis." Cameron's expression was a picture of broad disgust, like a man peering into a septic tank. "If you will, please tell me and the people assembled here how it is that you're familiar with these terms."

Lie, dammit! she thought. He can't prove a thing. Lie!

"I . . ." Murphy began, then coughed. He began again. "I'm familiar with them from my career in sports." His eyes on Cameron had gone direct and unwavering. "At one time or another, I made use of them."

There was the buzz of low voices through the auditorium. Behind her, Sara heard a snicker, like a hard bark, short and cruel. A few rows below, Jorden Adler had placed a trembling hand over her eyes.

Damn you, Neddie. Oh, damn you for this. You used me. Things I said without thinking. Idle remarks passed lazily . . .

Next to her, Charlotte Post was swearing softly, fluently, under her breath. From the seats behind a smiling Ed Manning came a loud voice. "All *right*, bro! Hey, turn it on and tune it in!"

"I believe those are prescription *drugs*, aren't they?" On stage, Cameron was pursuing. "Illegal without a doctor's prescription? Did you have prescriptions for the use of those *drugs?*''

"Sometimes," said Murphy. "Usually not."

"And are you still obtaining and abusing prescriptions illegally, Deputy? Are you under the influence of drugs right now?"

The buzz rose to a roar.

"Quiet!" Marvin Lanier snapped down a gavel on the podium. "Let's have—"

"Are you aware that a . . . houseguest of yours, one Jordan Adler, is known to be in possession of controlled substances, even as we speak here."

"All *right!*" came the voice from the audience. "Hey, Dep-u-tee! Maybe you can help me. I'm trying to score some—"

"I said shut up!" Lanier pointed a nicotine-stained finger. "You! Right there! If I hear one more word from you, the only thing you'll score is an arrest for disorderly conduct! Do you understand me?"

"On the night of Monday, October twenty-first," Cameron shouted above the din in the huge room, "when you arrived too late to save Alison Delaney from the trauma that's rendered her a helpless catatonic, were you also under the influence—"

Sara saw Hobie Jameison shake off his wife's arm and leap to his feet. "You goddamned sack of shit!" she heard him yell, breaking free into the aisle and starting toward the stage. "You lying, trash-mouth son of a bitch!"

That was what she was hearing, along with the roar of the audience, as she ran from the auditorium. At the door, blinded by her own tears, she blundered into a well-dressed man, standing and watching the chaos with a tight, mocking smile.

He's an Indian. The manic thought slid through her mind. An Indian in a three-piece suit. Then she pushed by him with a muttered apology and out into the lobby.

Murphy drove down the canyon, skidding the banked turns at sixty miles an hour. Sometime, probably at the liquor annex next to the Stop-N-Go at the edge of town, he'd picked up a bottle of Cutty Sark.

"Bitch," he whispered. He took another drink from the bottle. "Just handed it to you, didn't I? Just handed it to you, so you could hand it to him." His eyes blurred, and he wiped the back of one hand across them.

The Land Crusier crossed the double yellow stripe, and he pulled it back. Outside the tunnel of his headlights, the silhouettes of trees flashed by. And a signpost.

Eighteen more miles. He'd see her at the hospital, along with the doctor and the parents who'd praised him for saving her life. They knew the truth, not those laughing, yelling people at the school. More than anything else at that moment, he needed to see A.J. and have her open her soft brown eyes and look at him. And talk to him.

Murphy Davis, the man with two last names . . .

But the face he saw reflecting back through the windshield was Sara Nichols's.

Two kinds of people in this world. The words of a song were in his head. Winners, losers . . . He took a long drink from the bottle.

Two kinds of trouble in this world . . .

His lights took the curve ahead of him and picked up the deer herd by the side of the road. A doe panicked and ran in front of him, and he hit the brakes in a slow-motion dream. In slow motion his right front fender collided with the animal, throwing her up into the windshield and killing her instantly, and twisting the vehicle into a spin that ended in impact with the snow piled at the side of the road.

After a time—he didn't know how long—he crawled out, head bleeding, and walking in a staggering shamble to the deer. He was sitting in the road in his ruined brown suit, crying and stroking the animal's stiffening flank, when the Highway Patrol arrived.

Later, handcuffed, he was taken on into the hospital. The nurse's aide on duty in the emergency room was Ellen Bailey, who at first refused to believe he was Deputy Murphy Davis from Silvercat. Finally, while cleaning the cuts on his face and forehead, she told him that Alison Delaney had been transported to the airport by ambulance earlier that day for flight home to Gadsden, Alabama. At the time she was checked out, Alison was still unresponsive to treatment.

After that, Murphy was taken to police headquarters to be booked. He made his telephone call to Hobie Jameison.

The Third Week
October 29–31

A BEAST IN THE HEART

"They call it Paradise,
 I don't know why.
 You call someplace Paradise,
 Kiss it goodbye..."
—The Eagles, "The Last Resort"

"Two kinds of trouble in this world,
Livin'... dyin'..."
—Lindsay Buckingham, "Go Insane"

18

Tuesday, October 29

The residents of Silvercat, Colorado, were arising to a windy, partly sunny day. But on the "Little Buddy and Big Harv Show" on KCAT, meteorologist Kermit (High Pressure Dome) Dudley, a syndicated weatherman who'd never set foot within a thousand miles of Silvercat, issued a warning about the approach of a powerful storm system off Baja and predicted snow for Halloween. He was alternately cursed by the town's children and praised by the stockholders of the SSC. Then Little Buddy took his listeners back to K-Kat Kountry Klassics with Pagosa Springs' very own J. B. Killacommie doing his latest single, "Lurlene's Back in a Pink Cadillac (From Sellin' Mary Kay)."

Debra Martindale was awakening at the Mountain Brook Motel and staring at the blond wig hanging from a coatrack by the door. She shifted onto her back and cataloged her various ailments, starting with a head cold and sore throat and working her way down to aching legs and a possible yeast infection. At a hundred dollars a night she'd pocketed four hundred already, but she was no closer to becoming a celebrity than she'd been Friday night. As of Tuesday morning, it had been eight days since the attack on Alison Delaney, and it appeared the Silvercat Slasher had taken early retirement. She listened to muffled, adenoidal snoring beside her and tried to recall, without peeking, if it was Killian or Morlan this time. It was getting really tough for a girl to make a buck.

DeVane Belleau, who hadn't spoken to his old friend Hobie Jameison for nearly a week, was placing and receiving telephone calls in his private office at the police station. He was unusually pale and seemed preoccupied, a cup of coffee getting cold next to his hand. He finished the last call, long-distance collect from Albuquerque, shortly before noon, then locked his office and left. He didn't return that day.

In an emergency session at the courthouse, the county commissioners were giving their decision to Sheriff Jameison. His deputy, Murphy Pless Davis, was suspended indefinitely, without pay, as of that moment. If Deputy Davis was foolish enough to continue his campaign for sheriff—a venture surely doomed to failure in light of the disclosures at the previous night's debate—that was none of their concern. But his arrest for driving under the influence and reckless endangerment, on the heels of the drug allegations, showed them all they needed to see. Jameison argued and swore and blamed the lady psychiatrist from California, but he left the room without a deputy.

In a snow-laden cabin several miles from the town, Merrill the Feral was eating his first full meal in a week. The numbness in his frostbitten fingers and toes had turned first to itching and then to pain, but he mostly ignored it. He knew she was gone, taken home to Mississippi or Texas or some-where, and that he'd never see her again. But he'd stopped crying about it because that served no purpose, and he had a definite purpose now. He held the hand ax between powerful knees, blade up, and honed its edge with a file. It was an Indian tomahawk, handle of hardened ash, that he'd always carried to the Mountain Rendezvous—where they knew him as Merrill LeBouf—for the amusement of his friends there. It wouldn't bring her back to the Dutchman, but it was the best he could do. The blade's edge was already sharp enough to slice his gray-blotched thumb when he tested it, but he continued with the file.

Sara Nichols was proofreading copy from Melissa Carter—who wrote "Up at the Village," a gossipy column for the paper—for the third time, having just replaced her phone on the hook. As usual, Melissa was having hell with syntax as well as merrily shifting tenses within the same sentence. Each time Sara read it, the blue marks increased, but her concentration was so poor she kept missing all but the most obvious errors.

Where was he? She started to call again on the chance he simply wasn't answering his phone. There were things she had to say, to explain. About Neddie Cameron and the accusations at the debate. She had to make him see how it really was.

And other things, too, if she could find the courage.

Hell, yes, she thought. Why not? Got to keep up the Nichols women's family tradition, right? Always fall for the losers. She lifted the phone and dialed again.

"At times like this, I almost believe it's a blessing Alva's dead." Walter Davis's voice was a petulant, high-pitched whine. "When I think of the shame . . ."

The phone began ringing again. Don't touch the damned thing, Hobie had warned, but Murphy was tempted. Anything, even a request for an in-depth with photos by Paul Killian, would surely beat sitting in his own house being browbeaten by his uncle. He let the phone ring.

"You're lucky they let you out at all, Murphy." Uncle Walt nodded toward the telephone. There was a hard smile on his face and a ring of buttermilk on his upper lip. "Released on recognizance, wasn't it?"

"Hobie came after me." Murphy closed his eyes and let the fatigue wash over him. Every joint in his body ached, the cuts on his face were beginning to hurt, and the skin on his forearms was itching. Nothing unusual about that, because Uncle Walt always made him itchy. "You want to give it a rest, Uncle Walt? I'm real tired."

"As well you might be." Walter Davis drained the glass of buttermilk and cast covetous eyes on Murphy's refrigerator. Like all the Davis men, he was large. Well over six feet and big-boned. But unlike his two brothers and their combined four sons, Uncle Walt had gone to fat. Layers of soft, quivering flesh below a chest-length reddish gray beard cut in the square, no-mustache fashion often seen on Mennonites.

"Tight-ass Walt," Murphy had once heard his uncle Evan comment. "Poor bastard hasn't been worth shooting since he saw Sister Le-Etta Browner cure some guy of shingles at a tent revival back in '69. Old Walt's just been a pimple on the ass of reality ever since."

"Don't wonder you're tired." Uncle Walt had risen and was taking a circuitous route around Glorified Jock toward the kitchen. "That's the weight of sin on your shoulders, Murphy. You're in a bad way. Where's that young . . . woman who supplies you with drugs?"

"She's not here, and she doesn't—"

"Of course she does. They impounded your car—"

"I can drive Dad's old Willys."

"—for evidence, I hear. May lose your license, too. You're in a tight spot, Murphy. An iron box forged of drugs and alcohol and fornication." He rummaged the bread hamper. "Don't you think it's time you allowed Jesus to . . . Why are you scratching, boy?"

Because you make me nervous, you old fart, thought Murphy. He shrugged.

"Praise Jesus! The plagues of Exodus, chapters eight through twelve! You have the Itch, Murphy. Sent upon the heathen by God."

"The . . . what?"

"But I can cure it, Murphy. Through the power of prayer and the use of God's natural medicines."

"I don't have the Itch, Uncle Walt. I've never even heard of the—"

"Of course you do." Uncle Walt was smearing thick layers of butter onto two slices of wheat bread. "It's the outward manifestation of your inner sin. Let's see, I'll need blueing. They still make that, don't they?" He folded an entire piece of bread into his mouth. "Mix it with water and sulfur and baking grease into a poultice—you got any cheese, boy? —and then you pray—"

The phone began to ring again. "Jesus," Murphy groaned, then he had to smile. It must already be working, he decided, 'cause Uncle Evan sure as hell had him praying.

* * *

Arthur Morse turned east on Fifth and hurried along a snow-covered sidewalk. The sun was a pale disk at his back, dropping below the level of the trees lining the street. He felt the warmth of the day go with it.

Slow down, you old fool. You don't have the lungs for this anymore. He slid one hand inside his coat and pressed it against his thin chest. His heart pounded, slightly arrhythmic, and he counted for what he estimated as ten seconds.

Eighteen. Multiplied by six is one hundred and eight. Way too fast, so just take it slower. The heart's okay if you give it enough oxygen to work with. It's these goddamned lungs.

And so thinking, he reached into his coat pocket for another cigarette.

It's not fair, he decided peevishly. Old Marv Lanier's past my age and he smokes like cheap motor oil, and he'll probably live to be two hundred and two. Morse took a deep drag off the unfiltered Camel. And here I am, the goddamned doctor, goddammit, and I'm the one on the edge of emphysema.

He walked more slowly, the pavement getting slick again as the melt began to refreeze. He was thinking of Charlotte Post or, more accurately, Charlotte Post's mother. Of course, there was nothing extraordinary about that.

He was approaching the intersection at San Miguel, deep in memory, when the car passed in front of him. At first, he thought it was just a part of his reverie. Then he looked again, and fingers of ice closed around his throat.

"Wha . . . !" The jolt struck him like a physical blow, and his first thought was a coronary (O God not here not now not where all these people will see). He grabbed for the iron railing of the corner house. Cold tore like needles through his gloves to his fingers and, no, it wasn't a heart attack at all. Just terrible, incredible shock.

"Oh, my God!" he whispered, holding on to the fence for support while first the fact then its inescapable conclusion roared through his brain. "Oh, no! Oh, you bastard! You . . ."

He stood and watched the huge old model Buick plow along the slushy street, turning west on Sixth.

* * *

Three miles beyond Silvercat Village, the logging road passes a cutoff. At a few minutes past sundown, just when the color leaves the landscape and mutes it to whites and grays and blacks, there's a set of tracks where a large vehicle has bulled its way through onto the side trail. A few hundred feet on, hidden from the logging road by a stand of bare-limbed aspen, a Buick sits cooling down.

Heading away are two sets of footprints, one human and one animal. They pass through the trees toward the northwest and lead to a rounded knoll overlooking a small beaver pond, its edges already half-frozen out toward its center. The figure that stands there absently rubs the head of a little curly-haired dog leaning against his leg.

The mounds at their feet, two small and one somewhat longer, are covered by snow that hasn't melted between storms and would hardly be visible to someone not looking for them. After a while, as gray fades into twilight, the tall figure pushes the dog gently aside and kneels next to the largest mound. A gloved hand, placed on the slope, is black against the purity of the snow.

He watched her from the motel-room couch. She was standing at the window, her back toward him, and her shoulders had stopped quivering. She was no longer crying.

"So I smoked a little stuff in college," she said. Her voice sounded hoarse. "No big deal. My roommate and me, the Doobie sisters." Her laugh was short, like a cough.

"Jordan . . ."

"No, listen." She turned back from the window. Mascara had streaked her cheeks, and she passed a hand across it. "This is expensive mascara." She looked at her fingers. "It's not supposed to run."

"Jordan, I'm not blaming you." Murphy half rose, but she retreated a step, so he sat back down. "What happened was my fault. It was booze and pills, and just plain being scared. That and my big mouth. What Cameron said about you—"

"Was true." She sat on the bed across from him. "He must have a helluva pipeline into this town."

"Lon, you said. That'd be Lon Everell. That's his pipeline. Right through the Mannings, I'd guess."

"Manning?" He saw her mouth tighten. "The SSC people? I don't believe I've had the pleasure."

"You haven't missed much. Jordan . . ."

"Wait." She raised her hand. A fingertip touch toward his lips. "Please. Don't say anything else, Murphy. Okay? Not now. Just let me say this."

Murphy's insides were churning. Don't, he thought. Don't say it. I don't want . . . "Okay," he said.

"It was the kids," she said. "Like the one I told you about. After that, I began to get them all." She rose and started pacing the small room. "All the children. Because I was good, and I was young. 'Talk to Jordie,' they'd say. 'Refer it to Adler. It's her specialty.'" Jordan squeezed her hands together, and Murphy saw the tendons tighten in her wrists.

"They weren't all like Joseph," she said. "He survived. Some of them . . . I started to see their faces, Murphy. All the little Josephs."

"You helped him, Jordan. And I'll bet there were others."

"Did I?" Tears were standing in her eyes again. "And where's he going to be in ten years, Murphy? Standing on some corner with his own knife in his pocket? Looking for small blonde women with China blue eyes? Don't you see, that's why I had to come here. I thought, if I can do this right, help this poor bastard before he kills again . . ."

"He's not your Joseph, Jordan."

"I know. I know that." She wiped at her eyes. "And it hasn't helped, anyway. The faces, they're still there, behind my eyes whenever I close them. There was only one thing that made them go away. Until I met you."

Murphy shook his head. "It's going to take more than me, Jordan. It's going to take—"

"No! Don't you see? You can do it, Murphy. You can give me everything I need. At first I had Pat—Pat Calder, the guy

I mentioned—but he was strung out worse than me. He's the one who got me on cocaine.''

"What happened to him?"

She laughed. "He kicked it, can you believe that? He married some born-again type and she moved them off to Kentucky. Isn't that a good one? He went off and left me like this, and now he's a goddamned halfway-house counselor in Louisville. Probably teaches a Sunday-school class.''

"I'm not some born-again type, Jordan. And I can't move you off to Kentucky.''

"You don't have to. Just let me stay here with you. You like me, Murphy. I can tell you do. And I don't need the kind of help he did, anyway. I just get a little high sometimes. So would you, if you'd seen the things I have.''

"Those things happen, Jordan. I know they're not pretty. . . .''

"Yeah?'' She stopped pacing, and anger snapped into her voice. "What do you know about it? Until this Slasher thing, I'll bet the worst you ever saw was some drunk puking on your shoes. What the hell do you know about my life?'' She took a plastic spray bottle from her pocket.

"Don't do that!'' He sprang from the couch and slapped the bottle from her hand. "Dammit, Jordan! Do you think I don't know what's in that thing? You tell me that I can help you, then you stand there and feed your Jones right in front of me and think I'm too much of a hick to know what you're doing!''

"I . . .'' She looked at the plastic bottle on the floor. "You *can* help me. I swear to God you can.''

"I can't, Jordan. I'm sorry, but I can't. You need help, but the last person you need it from is me.'' Murphy took her into his arms. She tried to pull away at first, her face twisting with anger, then she seemed to collapse, laying her head on his chest. "We're a pair of cripples, Jordan. Maybe we can help ourselves alone, and maybe it'll take someone else. But the one thing I know is that we can't help each other.''

He stroked her hair. She cried, the sound muffled against his body.

* * *

I can fix it, she thought later, driving out of town in the rented Camaro. He'll see that I can. I'm strong, especially if I want something—or somebody—badly enough.

She'd get into a rehab back in Los Angeles. Her associates would cover her caseload, no problem. She was one of the best, a rising star, and they wouldn't want to lose her. Besides, one of them—Llewelyn—had been in rehab himself.

And when she was straight, she wouldn't handle the child-abuse things anymore. Not for a while, anyway. She'd specialize in paranoid matrons who were sure their husbands were unfaithful. Or in performance anxiety, maybe. With the pressures in L.A., half the town had gone flaccid.

Then, when she was clean as a baby, pumped on Nautilus and health food and looking purely bitchin', she'd come back and he'd love her then. And he'd forget this town and the sheriff's job he wasn't going to win, anyway, and they'd leave. Off to Oregon, maybe, or Alaska.

It was going to be perfect.

In Durango, she stopped at the mall to phone a number Manning had given her. Just a little something to get her home, nothing more.

After the cold, sunny Tuesday, the night was clear. As was common on such nights at that altitude, the day's warmth fled upward and temperatures plummeted thirty degrees from the afternoon high.

Clinton Golden Sun cut off the radio after hearing it was nineteen degrees outside at thirty-five minutes before midnight. The snow tires of his Jeep Wagoneer followed another set of tracks as he checked his odometer again.

Then he saw a sign at the end of the cone of his headlights. It was on the right, snow encrusted, with icicles hanging from its base.

DRIPPING SPRINGS CAMPGROUND

SILVERCAT, COLORADO

ELEVATION 9,536 FT.

And below that, another sign suspended by two chains that read CLOSED FOR THE WINTER.

It was still nearly a half mile off the road up to the alpine meadow Lupita Diaz had described over the telephone. He shifted into the low range of four-wheel drive and turned in to follow a single set of tire tracks.

Lupita. In English, Little Wolf. Gold's thin face set in a bitter smile. Apropos, as it had turned out, wasn't it? Little Wolf.

Whenever he thought of her, it was always in odors. The dry, dusty smell of her old sweat mixing with the hotness of the new, dripping with salt fire into the cuts on his shoulders and buttocks. The sweet smell of oiled leather and the bright, coppery scent of his own blood. And finally, after she'd rolled him onto his burning back and mounted him, dark and silent, the pewter smell of his semen that she let gush down onto his belly and thighs when she pulled free. She was Llano Comanche, and her female ancestors had giggled and gossiped while they carved the genitals off dying enemy warriors on the battle-field. Lupita. Little Wolf.

The Wagoneer bounced through a rut hidden by snow, and Gold pulled directly into the tracks of the other vehicle. For perhaps the fifth time since he'd checked into the Village Inn the night before, he considered a trap. And dismissed it again. For one thing, they knew he'd made copies. For another, they no longer had the need. They had Lupita, which meant his information was useless, so why bother? Better luck next time, redskin.

It had been stupid to press it after he found out about Belleau. Cops have connections. They can find out your secrets. Never go up against a rich white man with a cop on the payroll.

Manning. That *cabrón*. Give the little bastard credit for thoroughness, then duck and cover your own ass, Golden Sun. Better luck next time.

He followed the tracks up through heavy spruce, tires spinning on ice beneath the snow. Finally he pulled through an opening onto the edge of a broad meadow, cutting off his lights. The reflection of the waning moon off snow created a twilight nearly bright enough to read by.

They wanted isolation, they sure as hell got it. His car door crackled as he opened it to icy air. He pulled on a leather and fleece coat before stepping outside, a thick accordion-file folder tucked under his arm.

God, it was cold! The kind of high mountain cold that never reached Albuquerque. He thought for a moment of childhood winters in North Dakota. Freeze your cock to your fly, his father used to say.

He looked around for tire tracks and saw only his own. Across the meadow, in the moon shadow of some trees, was a small campfire.

A nice touch. They must have angled their vehicle off on that last steep pitch. He locked the Wagoneer and put the keys into his coat pocket, then he rolled the cuffs of his slacks above his Wellington boots and carried the documents across.

The campfire was low, beginning to break down into coals. There were several large stones encircling it, and he bent forward, removing a glove, to warm his hand.

"Golden Sun."

It wasn't a question. The voice, soft and faintly mocking, came from somewhere to his right.

"Manning?" He straightened and replaced the glove. The voice hadn't sounded like Edward Manning. "Lupita? Is she with you?"

"You don't mind if I call you Golden Sun?" It wasn't Manning. "I like the sound of it. A real Indian name."

He squinted toward the trees, but his night vision was gone from looking into the campfire. "I don't care." He took a careful step backward. "Whatever you call me, I've been called worse."

There was a light chuckle. "I'll bet that's true." The voice had shifted locations. "And probably by your own people, huh? You're not much of a credit to your race, are you? Selling them out..."

"That's not your concern." Gold fought down a surge of

anger. "Shall we get on with it? I brought the papers. All of them, just like I—"

"I wonder." The voice had moved again, to Gold's left. "Is it guilt? Is that why you can only get it off with someone like that Indian whore? And then only if she whips you bloody? Kinky stuff."

"Shut up, goddamn you!"

"Kinky stuff, counselor. Perverted, some might say. Definitely not the thing to get you elected to Congress next fall, is it? You know what they say. Blackmail's a poor line of work for an ambitious man."

Gold took a deep breath. Control. Don't let this errand boy break through to you again. "Look," he said with exaggerated patience. "We went through all this on the phone, and I thought we had an agreement. I turn these over to Manning, and he forgets about me. I don't even see why I had to come up here tonight—"

"Don't you?"

Gold felt a trace of uneasiness. "No, I don't. It's a standoff."

"But then, things are rarely that simple, are they?"

He saw a shadow move near a tree, and he slipped one hand inside his coat. Through leather gloves, the butt of the pistol was cold. "Listen," he said. "I don't like the way this conversation's going. Here are the papers. You just tell Manning we're quits."

"Sorry. That's not how it's going to be."

Gold pulled the gun, a short-nosed .38 Police Special, from its inside holster. "Hey, don't be a jerk, *pendejo!* You were right a minute ago. I am an ambitious man. Which means I'm no problem for your boss anymore."

"Not now, maybe, but what about later?" The shadow moved again. "Things happen, don't they? Whores die."

"Stay back! You see this gun?" Gold shuffled away from the firelight. "Use your head, dammit! You'd never make it rhyme. Besides, I lied. I made other copies."

"Of course you did." There was the soft chuckle again. "We'd have been disappointed in you otherwise. They won't mean anything before long. And as for any loose ends, this is Silvercat. Haven't you heard? We have an insane murderer running loose."

Gold pointed his gun at the moving shadow. "Why?" His voice felt bottled up in his throat. "Why are you doing this?"

"Why not?" the voice whispered. "Since we can."

Gold dropped to one knee and fired the pistol once, then again at the shadow. Then the campfire exploded in front of his face.

The shriek he heard was his own. Blazing embers peppered his coat as he flung himself to the snow. Searing pain as they hit his face and neck.

He rolled over and over, beating at the smoking fleece with gloved hands. Then instinct brought him to his feet running, tripping over a buried log, and running again until he slammed into the trunk of a tree and fell at its base.

He was blinded, seeing only bright flashes, red and yellow, in the total blackness. He crawled around the side of the tree and lay on his stomach behind it.

There was no sound at all. Not even the normal night sounds of a forest. He peered over a large exposed root, night vision slowly returning, and realized he had run into the trees to the left of the campfire. He had held on to the pistol, but he was completely across the meadow from the Wagoneer. It sat in vague outline fifty yards away, chrome faintly reflecting moonlight.

I can't cross it, he thought. Which left two choices. Circle around through the woods or wait here for daylight.

Forget that. It was too cold, and getting colder by the minute. His legs in the thin slacks were going numb. He felt frozen to the ground.

He could still get out of this if he kept his head. Where was the man behind the voice? Down from the two shots? Be still and listen.

There was the thudding of his heart. There was his labored breathing that he tried to quieten. And there was the creaking of the big trees settling under their own weight, but that was all.

Move it. Get to the car. He rose to his knees and then to his feet, the front of his pants wet from the snow. His vision was continuing to improve, and he could see each tree clearly against the ghostly white beneath them. He began to move, concentrating on every step and keeping the meadow on his left. Each time he came to a tree, he stopped to stand completely still and listen.

He was sweating under the heavy coat and down his forehead. A bead of perspiration trickled into a burn on his cheek, and the sting brought tears to his eyes and made him think of Lupita Diaz.

Had she known about this part of it? Probably not, he decided. Just a goddamned moon-faced Indian whore who would as soon spend Manning's money as his. Her dark eyes were flat and empty. Empty when she whipped him and empty while she serviced him. Blank and empty when she took the honky's money and sold Clinton Golden Sun out.

Another tree. A dip where a creek ran in summertime and a deadfall of lightning-blasted spruce he picked his way across. Beyond it, he saw the outline and the glint of the Wagoneer.

Stop here. Squat down and wait. Listen.

The man could hide behind the car, or on the roof. Maybe even crawl underneath. Or he could be somewhere back behind, lying in the snow where Gold had fired, bleeding from a pair of .38 slugs.

The son of a bitch was probably dead, and wouldn't that be a dose? Crawling around in the woods, freezing his ass off to get away from a stiff.

Holding the pistol low and forward, Gold advanced out of the trees. He ducked and saw torn snow beneath the Wagoneer's frame. Nothing there. He circled swiftly, moving crablike around the vehicle with weapon outthrust. He stretched on tiptoes. Nothing on top.

He moved into a crouch to the driver's side. He was certain now he'd nailed the bastard with the two shots, but he was still taking no chances. He'd relax when he got back to Albuquerque, not before. And Ed Manning was going to pay. The voice had been right about one thing. Whores die.

He had reached into the coat pocket a second time before he realized his car keys were gone, but he checked again. All his pockets. They must have fallen out when he dove into the snow.

"Damn!" he muttered aloud. The car was locked, and it was a long walk back to the road. He'd freeze his...

Then he noticed, for the first time, an odd shape on the otherwise smooth hood of the Wagoneer. In starlit twilight he looked more closely at the small clump with its bristling shape.

His car keys were on the hood.

His breath came out in a low hiss. Holding the gun high, his heart pounding against his chest, he backed in a staggering shuffle into the trees again. And when a powerful arm dropped around his throat, he was hardly surprised.

19

Wednesday, October 30

Henry Light was by the police car blocking the campground's entrance. When he saw Murphy turn in, he stepped forward and held up his hand, palm outward.

"Murph," he said. "What in hell are you doing here? You're not even supposed to be operating a vehicle on public road, are you?"

"Come on, Hank." Murphy half opened his door and hung one arm out. A cold wind riffled his jacket sleeve. "You're not going to get technical on me, are you? Is Hobie up at the meadow?"

"Yep." Light put his freckled hands back into the pockets of his leather coat. "But DeVane left me down here to see no lookie-loos get in. That's you, Murph. You ain't official no more."

"Hank, I need to talk to Hobie. It must be important or he wouldn't have called me. Look, I've helped you out once or—"

"Aw, hell. You're not gonna start in on those friggin' tickets again. Every time you need something, Davis, it's always—" He stopped. "Well, shit," he said, after a pause. A slight grin stretched his brush mustache. "Go ahead on, but—"

"Thanks, Hank." Murphy stuck the old Willy's jeep into low gear.

"Whoa! Wait a minute and hear me out. You park that damned relic below the meadow and walk in, you understand

220

me? And stay away from Belleau. I don't intend to end up like Dimwit Dimmit.''

Murphy nodded. "If he spots me, I'll say I cut in by Cox's place and you never saw me. I'll go up that way now. I owe you, Hank.''

"No, you don't. But we're square on those damned tickets, once and for all.''

Murphy shifted into reverse and backed out onto the road, then drove a hundred yards farther up to the campground's north entrance. Across the way, Gabriel Cox was standing by his mailbox in the early-morning sunlight.

"Murph.'' He nodded. He was a small man with a short, graying beard who was always immaculately groomed. Murphy couldn't recall ever having seen him without a tie.

"Hi, Mr. Cox.'' He idled the Willys into neutral as Cox ambled across the road. "Pretty morning.''

"A little cool.'' Cox put one hand on the jeep's dingy door, then pulled it back. "Hear we may have some weather for Halloween.'' He removed a tightly folded handkerchief and rubbed his fingers. "What's going on up there?''

"Hard to say. I guess I'll know more when I get there.''

Cox nodded. "You still a deputy, Murph?'' He looked embarrassed. "I thought . . .'' He shrugged thin shoulders. "You know.''

"Yeah.'' Murphy adjusted the outside mirror. "Hobie phoned me, Mr. Cox. I'm going up to see him.''

"Oh, sure.'' Cox nodded more vigorously. "Someone get killed up there? Another girl?''

"I don't know,'' said Murphy. "That's what I hope to find out.''

Cox stepped back from the vehicle. "Then you go to it. Listen, Claire and I were at that damned debate, Murph. It was a real hatchet job, and we're still behind you.'' The man fidgeted with what appeared to be indecision. "Oh . . . and something else.''

"Sir?'' Murphy resisted the impulse to slip the Willys into gear.

"If you have time, give me a call later on. You or Hobie.

There's something I want to...something I'd better tell you.''

Then he was hurrying away, across the road with quick, military strides. Past his mailbox without stopping or looking back.

Murphy shook his head. What in hell was that? He locked into four-by-four and broke through the crust of the roadside. There were two sets of tracks going ahead of him. One set looked fresh.

The north trail was steeper than the main road through the campground, and Alva Davis's 1954 Willys jeep rode like a bucking horse with virtually no padding in the seat, but the old vehicle had lost none of its power. Murphy climbed into heavy forest, following the twin set of tracks. Just before the north trail cut over in a half circle to join the main road, he saw a glint of metal off to his left. He depressed the pressure clutch and rolled his window down again.

A red Jeep CJ-5 was parked off to the side, partly concealed by the trees. On its door was a plastic stick-on sign: "Leaverson's Rent-A-Jeep, Silvercat, Colorado." There were footprints in the snow beside it.

Eagle-Eye Light, thought Murphy. Why bother to ask permission? Just drive on in.

He left the Willys about fifty yards below the meadow opening and cut through the underbrush, his knee protesting mildly against the pull of the snow despite the high-top Sorels he was wearing. At the edge of the clearing he saw a Jeep Wagoneer, overnight frost still thick on its windows, and two of DeVane Belleau's cops. They were busy trying to unscrew the top of a thermos bottle and didn't look in his direction. Murphy stepped behind a tree to check things out.

There were three other vehicles behind the Wagoneer, including Hobie Jameison's Blazer. Murphy saw movement at the edge of the meadow to his left, and then Jameison appeared, talking to Belleau. A part-time writer for *The Sentinel*, Dorey Buckner, followed a few steps behind. His gait was a dazed lurch, and his face was bone white.

Belleau also looked awful. Even at a distance of a hundred

feet, his pale jowls were puffy, eyes sunken. He and Jameison were talking in whispers, but Murphy could see the anger on the sheriff's face.

". . . you, then, DeVane!" he heard Jameison snap. *The Sentinel* writer never looked up as Hobie stormed toward the Blazer. "You wanta wave goddamned jurisdiction at me, you can just—" He looked up and saw Murphy in the trees, but he never broke stride. "I've gotta go take a leak," he snarled back over his shoulder. "Probably 'cause you got me so pissed off."

He swerved in Murphy's direction. The two policemen, who'd stopped to watch the argument, went back to wrestling the thermos. The writer was shuffling in uneven circles around the meadow.

Jameison cut through the trees, grabbing Murphy's arm as he passed, and pulled him along. He stopped when they were several yards farther back.

"Good," he said in a low voice. "I was afraid they wouldn't let you in."

"Hank did. Remember those Super Bowl tickets I got him in '78? Broncos and—"

"And the Cowboys. How many times have you cashed in that favor?"

"This is the last, I imagine. What's up? I heard you and DeVane arguing."

Jameison pulled off a cloth cap and scratched his white crew cut. "The guy's gone weird on me, Murph." His voice was puzzled. "I've known him for. . . what, twenty years at least? And I've never seen him like this. Open and shut, he says. The lunatic slasher strikes again, he says. And, oh yeah, Dripping Springs is in the town limits, so it's his jurisdiction. So, thanks, Hobie, but no thanks!" Jameison took his pipe from his coat pocket. He bit down on it so hard Murphy heard his teeth crack.

"Slow down, Hobie." He put a hand on the older man's arm. "What's the story, anyway?"

"Okay." Jameison fumbled for his matches. "First of all, this time the victim's a man."

"A . . . Wait a minute. That can't be right."

"But it is. Here's the pitch. Early this morning I got a call from Gabe Cox. You know him, lives across the road from the campground."

"Yeah. I just talked to him. He was acting kind of strange."

Jameison snorted. "He's always strange. He washes his hands *before* he takes a leak. Anyway, he said he'd heard what sounded like gunshots up here last night. He was worried about it, so he phoned me."

"Why'd he wait until morning?"

"He didn't say. So I called DeVane and came on up. Only, when I got here, the cops were all over the place like a Chinese fire drill, stomping evidence flat, and Belleau was on his high horse. Maybe 'cause Gabe phoned me instead of him, I don't know. That's when I drove down to the pay phone and called you."

Jameison pulled Murphy over to a clearer view of the meadow. "That Wagoneer was sitting there, all frosted up, and there were several sets of tracks over to those trees and a burned-out campfire. Most've the tracks belonged to the cops." He spat in disgust.

"Warm ashes?"

"Only in the center, down about four inches. The outside was cool. I figure there was a fire there about, oh, six to eight hours ago."

"What time did Cox hear the shots?"

"About the same. A little past midnight. Also, there's black ash all over the area. Looks like an unopened beer can exploded in the fire, and you know what kind of hell that can raise."

"Maybe that's what Cox heard."

"Nope. Bear with me. There's these two sets of tracks making their way through the woods from the campfire over to there." Jameison pointed to where he and Belleau had emerged earlier. Murphy saw a pair of emergency medical technicians working back in the brush. "DeVane says his men didn't make them, for a change. Oh, and the body.

Male. Indian, I'd say. His wallet was in his pocket—lots of cash in it—with the name Clinton Gold on the driver's license. Forty-three years old, five-nine, a hundred forty. New Mexico license, Albuquerque address. Also a gun, a .38 Police Special, with two rounds fired."

"Gold doesn't sound like an Indian name."

"Nope. Also some business and credit cards. The guy was a lawyer. Now, here's the kicker, Murph. The poor bastard bled to death, looks like, unless he died of shock first. His pants were cut open and his, uh, genitals were hacked off. And he was disemboweled."

"Jesus! Just like . . ."

"As near as you could get with a man, Belleau said. Though I don't see how he could tell."

"Where's Art? Shouldn't he be here?"

"Yeah, but he's took sick. I called him late yesterday but he wouldn't say much, except that he took sick yesterday evening. So the EMTs are handling it until that new kid from the Village—Wyckerson?—gets here."

"This guy. What about his—"

"Gone, Murph. His eyelids are gone, just like the women. It's a real mess over there. Cat Creek all over again."

"It doesn't make sense, Hobie. Why would the killer turn to men? After all these years?"

"Who knows? That psychiatrist pal of yours speculated once about him possibly being gay, remember? Maybe he's finally out of the closet."

Murphy bent over and pretended to scrape mud from his boot. He'd wondered if it would hurt when she was mentioned again. Now he no longer had to wonder.

Jameison studied him as he straightened back up. "Hey, Murph, I'm sorry if . . ."

"Forget it, Hobie." Murphy slipped on a pair of reflectorized sunglasses against the snow's glare. "Ancient history. Anything else?"

"Not much. I figure this Gold drove the Wagoneer up here for some reason and walked over to the campfire."

"You're sure it's his car?"

"Rented to him. The keys were in his inside coat pocket, and we found the rental papers when we opened it up. Anyway, he was at the campfire when it blew. There's ash and fresh burn marks on his chin and neck, and his coat was scorched."

"You think he knew the killer?"

Jameison shrugged. "I think he came up here with a gun to meet *someone*. It looks like, after the can exploded, he circled back to his car through the woods and was killed where the cops found him. I think the other tracks were made by whoever he met at the campfire. Followed him and killed him. But it's hard to tell much about the murder scene itself now everything's been trampled by Silvercat's finest."

"Damn. It's going to be the same media circus all over again, isn't it?"

"Can't be avoided." Jameison spent a few seconds relighting his pipe. "Some of 'em never left, like that ignorant turd Killian. Did you know he's spending every night following some hooker in a blond wig around town? Thinks he's goddamn whatzizname . . . Bernhardt?"

"Bernstein." Murphy grinned. "Killian Black."

"Yeah. Anyway, that's what gave me the idea to call you. Where were you yesterday evening?"

"Not answering the phone, like you ordered. And I spent part of it with my uncle Walt, learning the error of my ways while he cleaned out my refrigerator."

"Oh, lord." Jameison rolled his eyes. "Tight-ass Walt. That had to be a comfort. Did he persuade you to sign over all your earthlies to Oral Roberts?"

"Jimmy Swaggart, actually."

"Hallelujah. Well, listen, here's what I came up with. You saved A.J. Everyone knows that, including those newsies who'll be coming back into town. So I'm seeing Bruce Douglas and the other county commissioners after I leave here. With this new killing and the national press behind every bush, I'll have you reinstated by tomorrow. You just lay low until then. Keep a low profile, as they say, and I'll—"

"I'll be out of town," said Murphy. "All day."

"Yeah?" Jameison appeared to be waiting for something further. "Well, okay. That's probably a good idea. Call me at home tonight. I'll know more by then."

After the sheriff cut off toward the meadow, Murphy went back to his father's jeep. He was only a short distance back down the north trail when he came upon the rental floundering through a drift at the edge of the road. He saw a head with coal black hair on the passenger side.

"Sea Warrior." Paul Killian scrambled from the CJ-5. He looked nervously in both directions. "Fancy running into you up here."

Murphy stood on the Willys running board and leaned on the top of the door. "Killian Black," he said. "I was just talking about you. Out for some bird-watching?" He saw Hacker Morlan behind the Jeep's steering wheel. "I figured you two . . . journalists'd be off covering the Miss Nude Nebraska Pageant by now."

"That was in August," said Morlan, spiky head thrust out the window. "Miss Nude America, that is."

"Marvelous. And what are you two doing—"

"You shoulda seen this one chick, Murph," said Morlan, opening his door. He was talking fast. "She invites me up to her room for some, y'know, pictures?" He winked broadly. "So I knock—"

"I'm happy for you, Morlan, but that doesn't answer—"

"I knock on the door, and she throws it open wearing nothing but black gloves and a pair of black high heels. She goes 'Da-dum!' and spreads her hands and feet like a cheerleader. She looked just like—"

"The five of spades." Murphy got out of the Willys. "I've heard it before, Morlan. So has most of the civilized world." He walked over to the rental. "Which still doesn't explain what you two are doing roaming the woods around a crime scene."

He stopped before he reached the Jeep and stared up at the rocky hillside behind it. There had been movement up there in the trees. He was sure of it. Near a snow-glazed, shattered boulder.

"Didn't you get suspended, Sea Warrior?" Killian was

saying. "That's the story I hear." He followed Murphy's gaze. "See something?"

"No. I thought I did, just for a second. Something big."

"Probably a moose. You have mooses here?" Killian leaned back against the rental. "Or maybe Bigfoot. Anyway, I'm not sure you have any legal business questioning us. Do you?"

"Not a bit. Just unofficial curiosity."

"Oh." Killian noticeably relaxed. "In that case, we're simply following the news where it leads us. 'The Silvercat Slasher Strikes Again.' " He made a framing gesture with his hands. "A man this time, huh?"

"It's a little early—"

"To tell a man from a woman? Officially, maybe it is. But off the record, this"—Killian consulted a notepad—"this Clinton Gold, an Albuquerque attorney, is the first male victim. Correct?"

"Killian, I imagine they'd like a little time on this thing."

"No doubt. And I'd like a Pulitzer, which isn't too likely, either. In any case, it's already on the wire."

"It's . . . You're bluffing."

Killian shrugged. "Notice how wet Hacker's jeans are? That's from galloping through the snow to that pay phone down at the campground. We're only hanging around for possible follow-ups. Any comments you'd like recorded for posterity?"

Murphy shook his head in disbelief. "You two assholes are nuts. Record that. Did they see you up there?"

"Are you kidding?" Morlan grinned. "Hack of the High Country's what they call me, when they're not calling me the Python of Love. That Gold looked like an Indian to me, except he's pretty pale-faced right now."

"Jesus," muttered Murphy. "Why don't you two just get lost?"

"Glad to." Killian climbed back into the CJ-5. "We have some film to develop, anyway. By the way, ex-Deputy Davis, what were *you* doing at the scene of the crime?"

Morlan shifted into first, stripping the gear, and the rental lurched down the trail.

Granite County EMTs Jerry Meyers and Darla Esquibel pulled a plastic body bag around Clinton Golden Sun. It wasn't easy. The corpse had stiffened into a coiled position, legs splayed apart, and the zipper was being stubborn.

Meyers leaned his beefy shoulder against cold, unyielding flesh. "Try it now," he grunted. "Better?"

"Yeah." Esquibel straightened up, fingers kneading her lower back. "Let's move him."

Meyers was careful to disturb as little of the terrain as possible. "First man, huh?" he said, reaching under the knees. "Think he got tired of blondes?"

"I don't think that's it at all." Esquibel slipped back on her gloves. "I bet he's a religious nut. One a' those right-wing Holy Rollers. ChainSaws for Christ, y'know? You read about stuff like this all the time."

They packed their burden across a spiky layer of exposed rock and then past a deadfall of trees where a huge, bearded man stood hidden, watching them go. Between hauling and cursing and trying to preserve the integrity of the crime scene, they were so busy they never looked in his direction.

Sara was in Marvin Lanier's office when the call came in. At the time, she was mulling over two other telephone calls. One of them, a continuation of the empty, ringing sounds at Murphy Davis's number, she was keeping to herself.

"Bisbee, Arizona," she said, regarding the other one. "That's where he lives, isn't it?"

"And what am I supposed to say to him?" Lanier worried the blotch on his forehead with a stained fingernail. "Sara, I haven't seen or talked to Daniel Post since he left here. Not even a Christmas card. And that was twenty-five years ago."

"Just say . . . hell, I don't know." Sara waved her hands in the air. "Say his only child needs him. Say she's depressed and worried about something, and she won't confide in us."

"Sara, listen." Lanier took a cigarette from a crumpled

pack. "Daniel Post took off right after his wife died. He signed the paper over to Charlotte and left me as editor. She wasn't yet twenty-one, only a year of college, and he just dumped it on her. Does that sound like someone who would suddenly care about her now?"

"She mentions him at least once a day, Marv," said Sara. "And there's that big painting in her office. You know she worships the old bastard . . . excuse me. And you can't tell me that kind of love was never returned."

Lanier shrugged. "I don't know. The Daniel Post I knew was an odd bird in some ways. Listen, maybe you should talk to Art Morse before you go getting personally involved. He knows Char far better than you or I, and he was devoted to her mother. Talk to him later, and let's get back to this Dripping Springs mess."

"Fair enough." Sara nodded. "But sooner or later one of us is going to contact Daniel Post. If you won't call Bisbee, then—"

Which was when the telephone call came in, routed back by Andrea Lymner at the front desk.

"*Sentinel*." Sara picked up Lanier's phone, not noticing his wry smile. "This is Sara Nichols."

"You got a dead man there," said a voice. It was a woman's voice, low, with a faint accent.

"What? This is *The Silvercat Sentinel*. The newspaper—"

"I know that." The voice was impatient. "You got a dead man there, in your town. Clinton Golden Sun."

Sara felt her pulse quicken. "Yes," she said, signaling Lanier to another phone. "There was a . . . death reported this morning, but we don't have many of the details yet. Who is this?"

"It was Clinton Golden Sun. I know. I know why he died. And I may know who killed him."

"You . . ." Sara kept her voice even. "Could you give me your name, please?"

"Don't matter. What I want to know is how much you'll pay."

"Pay?"

"Jesus, don't you listen, lady? I said I know why he was killed, and who did it, too. They're after me now, and I got some papers you'll want. Explains everything. Now, what'll you pay?"

"I . . . I'm not sure what to tell you. Our publisher's out of the office right—"

"Okay, I'll tell you then. I want five thousand, no, ten thousand dollars. And no cops. This is big, lady, and my time's running out. If you don't want it, I'll take it somewhere else."

"No, wait!" Sara looked over at Lanier, who shrugged helplessly. "Can I call you back? In an hour? I'm sure we can work out something that'll satisfy—"

"Shit. You think I'm real stupid, huh? Maybe I'll be around. Or maybe I'll take it to someone else. You talk to your boss about money."

"Listen, you can call me back—"

The phone went dead.

By noon almost everyone in Silvercat knew about the Dripping Springs murder, and by afternoon news-station helicopters were once again landing in the snow on the high-school parking lot. The national media, drawn away to other stories when the Silvercat Slasher went cold, were back.

Early-season skiers continued to roll into the town. Those who left because of the killer's reemergence were more than replaced by others who wanted desperately to be *somewhere* when *something* was happening. Motels and lodges filled and put out NO VACANCY signs, and the town took on a frenetic, carnival atmosphere. At the Dutchman Lon Everell announced the end of his literary problems with orifices. His next book would be nonfiction, written under his own name, about the Slasher.

Charlotte Post contacted Hobie Jameison about the call Sara had received. The sheriff suggested she verbally agree to any demands and set up a meeting. He stayed with them, dressed in civilian clothes, until the afternoon, when a mes-

sage came that Gabriel Cox was waiting at his office on some
unexplained matter. At that time, the call still hadn't come.

During the vigil, under the pretext of a bathroom break,
Sara slipped into her own office. The sight of Char, pale and
listless, had finalized her decision not to bother with Arthur
Morse. And if Daniel Post wanted to tell her to go to hell,
that was fine, too. Let him.

Bisbee, Arizona, information had no number listed for
Daniel Post. After brandishing the newspaper's name, she
was placed in contact with a supervisor at the city government
office. Mrs. Edna Earle Close, who had lived there all her
life, informed Sara that as far as she could recall, no one
named Daniel Post had ever lived in Bisbee.

She was starting back up the hall when a hand closed on
her shoulder.

The woman was almost as tall as Sara. She was wearing a
purple dress cinched at the waist with a wide belt, and her
dark, bare arms were pimpled with gooseflesh. Her hair was
black and shoulder length, and her eyes—the same color—
had a flat emptiness that curled Sara's stomach. In one hand
she held a large manila envelope.

"You the one I talked to on the phone?" she asked, and
Sara instantly recognized the voice. "You got the money?"

"I—"

"Bastards thought I was just another stupid whore," the
woman hissed. "Pay me off, then shut me up permanent,
huh? Well, I'm not stupid, lady. They'll find that out. C'mon,
we'll talk outside. You got the money?"

He rages about the house. Alistair Three creeps into the
kitchen and lies beneath the table, whining softly, while the
shadows lengthen into darkness outside.

He turns on the TV, sees the same news report, and snaps it
off. Then he sits at the piano, fingers picking out a complex,
counterbalanced version of "Penny Lane," and stops when
he realizes he's pounding the keys.

They're blaming him. Saying he killed some man. That

he's a murderer. He picks up the phone and starts to dial the sheriff's office, then puts it down.

She's to blame, somehow. She's done it to hurt him, to embarrass him. It's not the first time she tried to hurt him, even to kill him. But he's still alive.

She does it from hiding. Always. Hiding while those two fools follow the woman in the wig around the streets at night. Trying to trap him.

That's why he can't find her. But he will, and soon now, because he's being very smart and careful now. And he's known about hiding for years.

20

Wednesday, October 30

On July 6, 1925, the Denver and Rio Grande's Silver Special passed through a mountain tunnel northeast of Durango. As always on that incline, the engine slowed to a crawl.

Four men were scattered along outcroppings of rock above the tracks and jumped on board the train just before it entered the tunnel. One of them, the oldest, was behind a tree a few feet from the edge and had to run down a shattered boulder to leap onto a flatcar loaded with railroad ties. He caught his foot in the rock and fell ten feet onto the stacked wood, breaking his hip. Then he slid off the flatcar and onto the tracks where his arm was severed by the train's wheels. The booming echo of the engine entering the tunnel drowned out his screams, and the train passed on. His body was found by his younger brother an hour later.

The other three were more successful. On another flatcar, a boxcar, and the top of the mail car they rode through the tunnel, gasping for air and coughing the poisonous smoke that compressed and billowed around them. When the Silver Special emerged at the other end, they drew pistols and crawled forward.

The larger of the twin brothers reached the engine and struck the fireman in the head as he turned, knocking him senseless. Then he pressed the nine-inch barrel of his Colt .44 against the engineer's bulging midsection and ordered him to stop the train.

While this was happening, the smaller twin and his young cousin had moved into position. The twin climbed down the running ladder of the mail car and the cousin made his way to the caboose.

When the train stopped, along a sheer cliff's edge eighty feet above the river, the cousin braced the conductor. The mail car remained closed and locked.

The larger twin came back with the engineer, both walking gingerly and glancing down at the rapids in the canyon below, and the cousin came forward with the conductor. When the man inside the mail car refused to unlock the door, even at the threat of death to his comrades, the robbers began to shoot. The .44, which used slugs nearly the size of an adult's index finger, tore gaping holes in the wood. Within minutes a section of the door near its handle was blown to shreds. The men entered to find the mail clerk huddled in a corner, holding his coat to his bleeding face where a fragment of metal had struck him in the eye.

The robbers demanded he open the safe—a huge Bannister-Stratton with its top, bottom, and two sides formed from a single plate of sheet iron—but he refused, even when the .44 was cocked next to his ear. The robbers had half expected that and, having no intention of shooting anyone, had brought along dynamite stolen by the twins' father from a mine site where he worked. The explosion they set off blew out both sides of the mail car, brought down a landslide of trees and rock onto the roof, and tilted the roadbed toward the cliff, but the Bannister-Stratton sat smoking and scarred. And unopened.

The robbers were leaderless without the cousin's older brother, so they cursed awhile and then debated their next step. The twins favored throwing the railroad employees, who could identify them, into the canyon, but the cousin disagreed. He took the four captives and began walking down the tracks toward the tunnel. When the larger twin swore at him and whistled a .44 slug past his ear, he turned and fired intentionally high with his .22 single-action. The twins ran the other way.

Just above the tunnel was a climbing trail down to the river. The cousin sent the railroaders down with a warning not to stop, then he crossed the tracks and clambered up into the trees, ran back to where the horses were hobbled, and rode away to search for his brother.

When the train reached Durango, descriptions of the robbers were given to the police. But by the time faces and identities were connected, the twins had fled into Mexico. The larger one was last seen in Culiacán, near the Pacific coast, then vanished altogether. His brother returned to New Mexico with three new friends in 1928 and tried to rob a man, who turned out to be a vacationing Texas Ranger, in his Model-T outside Roswell. The Ranger ended the abortive robbery by the persuasive process of shooting the entire bunch.

When the police arrived at the cousin's house, they found him waiting on the porch with his brother's body. Despite the railroaders' testimony that he had saved their lives, he was sentenced to twenty years at hard labor in Canon City. In keeping with the times, Jesse DePriest served fifteen years before being released on Labor Day, 1942, two weeks before his thirty-second birthday.

"The Silver Special." Jesse's grin was toothless again, the store teeth back at Estrella's house in town, where her ruined Ford Pinto was sitting on blocks. "Did you know how much money was in that damn safe, Murph?"

Murphy had heard the story before. "How much?" he asked.

"Maybe fifty bucks." Jesse laughed and slapped Murphy's arm. "That and some checks we couldn't have cashed anyway. Those damn miners, they always got paid just before the Fourth of July. Everybody knew that but us. We were just dumb-ass redskins. It was Lorenzo's fault. He was older than the rest of us, and it was his idea. But I guess he paid for it, all right."

The day had brightened as they climbed, but the wind continued, and it grew colder with the elevation. When they'd left his house, Jesse had predicted it would be their last chance for the trip.

"Storm tomorrow," he'd said. "Maybe tomorrow night at

the latest. And it'll be a good one, like the night your friend got hurt.''

"Then maybe we should put this off until later.''

"No.'' Jesse had shook his head. "This one's not going to melt off, Murph. Winter's coming early this year. If we wait, we'd have to go up there on snowshoes.''

They crossed a sunny, sheltered area with exposed meadow grass brown and dead at their feet, then entered forest again. When they emerged, it was onto snow-covered tundra at the timberline.

"Are you sure this is okay, Jesse?'' Murphy stopped to look at the towering cliff above them.

"Why not?'' said Jesse. "I'm not offended, and you don't believe in it, anyway.''

"Maybe not. But you do.''

"Let's climb up to those rocks and take a rest, Murph.'' Jesse started up the steep slope. "I'm not as young as I once was.''

Murphy followed in the older man's steps. In spite of himself, he felt a subtle change in the atmosphere. A stillness. Then he realized that a rocky ridge to their left was blocking part of the wind's force.

Stupid, he thought to himself.

Jesse sat on a broad slab of granite at the edge of the talus and removed his navy-surplus pea jacket. He was wearing a maroon T-shirt beneath it with a logo that read "Half-foolish and Dangerous.'' He began to roll a cigarette.

Murphy braced one foot and leaned back. It was the first time since his childhood that he'd been this close to the Place of Power.

The cliff rose in jagged spires, crisscrossed by diagonal scars holding pockets of snow. Toward its summit, nearly a thousand feet of gray rock above his head, it grew so steep it seemed to overhang, and he felt his spine contract as he strained to see the top.

"Don't fall over backward, Murph.'' Jesse's voice was amused. "First time you came up here, you leaned back so far you fell flat on your ass. Remember?''

"I remember how you laughed. I was ten years old. That was . . . what? Twenty-eight years ago?"

"Twenty-eight years," Jessé mused. "You're getting old, Murph."

"Don't I know it." Murphy gave up looking for the top, and when he relaxed his neck, a needle of pain shot through his shoulder. "And some parts of me are older than others."

He walked over to sit by Jesse on the rock. The old man was removing a leather thong from around his neck. He opened a pouch hanging from it and brought out a peyote button. It was a dusty bluish green in color and slightly smaller than a radish.

"Are you starting on those already?" Murphy looked away as Jesse bit into one side. "I thought that was for after we got there."

"Just a little traveling music, Murph." Jesse shifted the small bite to the one side of his jaw where he still had some teeth. "You know what Quanah Parker said? He said that white men go into their church and talk about Jesus. Indian goes into the peyote ceremony and talks *to* Jesus." He chuckled a little, inclining his head and closing his eyes. "Talks *to* Jesus," he said again.

To the west and below them was the dome of the Gray Lady. In places it still showed bare rock, but all the trails were glistening white, with skiers microscopic in the distance. Lester Nelson's Snow Gods had done their work well.

"Talking about churches." Jesse had opened his eyes and was also watching the skiers. "You remember what I told you about that preacher in New Mexico?"

"The Navajo preacher? Sure."

"His church. That's what he called it. 'My church.' "

"I doubt he meant it that way, Jesse."

"Maybe not, but look down there. Look at those *vatos* on the Gray Woman. What if *it* was a church?" A small grin twitched at the corners of his mouth.

"I don't follow."

"A big, white man's church. As big as one of those cath—whaddayacallit?"

"Cathedrals?"

"Yeah. Do you think they'd sink poles into it and slide down the sides then?"

Murphy got the point. "No, I guess we wouldn't, Jesse." For a moment, looking at the old man's smile, he thought of his uncle Walt.

"Didn't think so. We prayed to the mountains in the old days, Murph. Some of us still do." He shrugged thin shoulders and looked upward. Back to the east, the moon hung in the sky above the Continental Divide, nearly invisible in the day's brightness.

"The moon too." He nodded. "Then white men got in a rocket and flew there. Walked around on it. It's not much of a god anymore."

Gods of neon, gods of light. Murphy thought of the town below the moon. He didn't know what to say to Jesse, so he watched the tiny figures of the skiers. At the Gray Lady's summit there was a building going up near the unload ramp of the top lift. He saw figures moving around it, and a puff of diesel smoke from a Caterpillar. Maybe a restaurant, he thought. Sure is big, though.

Jesse spat the chewed-up bite of cactus onto the snow and put the remainder back into his pouch. "Ready?" He stood up and pulled on the pea jacket. "It's not much farther."

"Hobie." Gabriel Cox rose from the leather chair by the wood stove when the sheriff entered. He was wearing a tight gray suit with wide lapels, and Jameison noticed he'd been sitting on a white handkerchief he'd spread over the cracked and peeling surface. "Didn't mean to get your seat."

"No problem, Gabe. Sit. You want some coffee?"

"Depends. Is it decaf?"

"God, no." Jameison poured a cup. "I'd sooner drink horse piss."

"I'll pass, then." Cox looked more uncomfortable than usual. "Did Murph give you my message?"

"Message? No. He did say that he spoke with you this morning. It was pretty hectic up there, Gabe."

"Oh, understood. Understood." Cox fidgeted in the chair. "That's why I decided to come on in. This is something . . . I think I will take some of that coffee."

Jameison poured another cup, then sat in the wooden chair across from Cox. "This is something what?" he prompted.

"Important. Something important." Cox accepted the cup. "Last night, like I told you on the phone, I heard what sounded like shots." He sipped the coffee and grimaced. "I don't sleep well, anyway. That's way I drink decaf. So it woke me up and I went out onto my porch. It was cold, but I had on my coat, so I took a turn around the front yard. I'd finally gone inside and had just turned out the light when I heard a car engine, going real slow."

Hobie Jameison had been sitting lethargically, his mind on the anonymous call to the newspaper, when Cox's last statement registered.

"What?" He leaned forward and the front legs of his chair hit the floor. "What? You saw someone?"

Cox didn't meet his eyes. He nodded.

"Gabe . . ." Jameison scooted himself closer. "Why in hell didn't you mention this before now?" He tried to keep from shouting at the little man.

Cox swallowed more coffee, no longer fighting the taste. His Adam's apple crawled into the gray whiskers beneath his chin. "For the same reason I didn't call you till morning." His jaw set stubbornly. "I had to think about it."

"Okay." The sheriff leaned back again. He lowered his voice. "So you thought about it, and you're here. Now, what happened?"

"I went back onto the porch, but I left off the light," said Cox. "And I saw a truck turn onto the road from the north entrance. Back toward town. He didn't see me, and he was trying to be quiet. Real slow through each gear."

Jameison held his patience in an iron grip. "And?" he said.

"I had to think about it," said Cox. "At first I figured he probably had police business up there. None of my—"

"Police?" Jameison felt the color drain from his face. "Police? You don't mean DeVane—"

"Of course I mean DeVane!" snapped Cox. "Why'd you think I called you instead of him?"

"You saw DeVane Belleau pulling out of that campground."

"In his red and silver Ford Ranger pickup. Damned right. Then when I heard today there'd been another killing up there . . ." He hesitated, wide eyes searching Jameison's face. "I like DeVane, Hobie. I didn't know what to do."

Jameison set his cup carefully on a small round table by the chair. He heard Cox's voice vaguely, as if from a distance.

"I did the right thing, didn't I, Hobie? I always try to do the right thing. . . ."

Cox noticed that his hand on the cup was rock steady.

They crossed a wide snowfield below the cliff, moving toward the east and away from the Gray Lady. When they reached a deep ravine at the edge, Murphy looked up and saw the true summit of Silvercat Peak, two thousand feet above them.

"This is where we go down," said Jesse, moving along the lip.

"Down there?" Murphy peered over the side. "Forget it, Jesse. That's a sheer drop."

"It's not as bad as it looks." Jesse kicked snow away from the edge and vaulted lightly onto some rocks about four feet below. "C'mon, Murph. Just follow me."

When Murphy climbed down, consciously protecting his knee, he saw for the first time a narrow trail slanting along that side of the ravine, back in the direction of the peak. It was snow-covered for the first thirty feet, then turned to a granite and marble mix.

"You didn't show me this when I was here before," he said, following behind Jesse.

"You were a child then. It's not a place for children."

The trail was no more than a three-foot-wide ledge, and Murphy, with his greater size, had to navigate parts of it by turning his back to the wall. Jesse continued to amble along, discount-store sneakers clinging to the rock. They dropped about fifty feet into the ravine, its bottom yawning below them, then the ledge leveled out. After a short distance toward a boxed end, Murphy heard the sound of running water, and the air turned warmer and more humid.

The trail's surface softened, and just before the ravine dead-ended into a sheer wall, it turned left through an opening of wind-sharpened pinnacles like boar's teeth. There was steamy air in Murphy's face, and an odor like rotten eggs.

"I'll be damned." Murphy stopped just inside the pinnacles and stared at the hot springs. "Jesse, I never knew..."

"Of course you didn't." Jesse took off his coat. "This is a secret place. The Place of Power."

"I thought that was the cliff."

"It is. And so is this."

The trail had widened into a bowl-shaped crevasse in the rock perhaps thirty feet across. It was open to the sky, light filtering down from its upper edges far above. Murphy realized that without the narrow trail, the spot where he stood could only have been reached with technical climbing gear.

Water trickled out of cracked rock at the back, mineral deposits forming on both sides into rose-colored stalagmites. It pooled up in the base of the crevasse, then poured down through another gash in the stone and disappeared. Rock moss and ferns, a brilliant green, grew around the pool in the billows of sulfury mist.

On the far side of the pool was a rounded hut made from aspen branches bent and then overlaid with badly stained rawhide. Before it on the ground was a crescent-shaped clay structure, about three inches high and two feet across.

"We're here, Murph." Jesse pulled his T-shirt over his head. "Let's get wet."

At first he thought the hot water would peel his skin right off. But after Murphy edged into the pool an inch at a time, he decided he'd stay right there and await the millennium. The rest of the world could go fish.

"You like it, huh?" Jesse was lying back in a few inches of water at the edge. His penis floated, surprisingly strong and ruddy, in a cloud of black-and-gray public hair.

"I love it!" Murphy laughed. "This is the best my shoulder's felt in years. Have you always known about this place?"

Jesse nodded. "I was born in 1910," he said. "And I remember coming here when my brother Lorenzo said I was old enough. I was thirteen."

"God. Sixty-five years ago."

"Yeah, but look, Murph. I still have a young pecker. And I have a young belly, too."

Murphy glanced downward with a grin. From years of holding in his own stomach, the skin over his abdominal muscles was a network of creases. Jesse, on the other hand, had obviously allowed his belly to hang free all his life. In the steamy water, it lay smooth and round like a brown bean pot.

"Okay, I admit it," said Murphy. "I have an ancient belly to match my ancient joints. But no cracks about my pecker."

"No cracks." Jesse nodded. "Lay back and let the water soak you, Murph. We're almost ready to begin."

The heat in the sweat lodge had been intense, held in and magnified by its rawhide cover, and it seemed to Murphy they had stayed inside for hours. But when they sat on either side of the clay altar, the sunlight was still streaming down from the opening high above. He felt light-headed. Dizzy.

Jesse placed his leather pouch at the closed end of the crescent. "Down on the plains," he said, unfastening its end, "the people there—Sioux, Cheyenne, Arapaho—they used the sweat lodge to get ready for the sun dance. Danced themselves nuts in the old days. Sometimes they even sliced off a finger or cut holes in their skin. Crazy bastards." He removed a handful of peyote buttons.

"I've heard of that." Murphy eyed the cactus buds. He felt his heartbeat slowly accelerating. "Saw it in a movie once."

"This way's better." Jesse leaned forward and placed one of the buttons next to Murphy's bare foot. "First, the journey, then a soak in the water for tired bones. Then the sweat lodge for purification." He looked up at Murphy. "Then this."

Murphy stared at the button.

"Pick it up," said Jesse. "It's no big deal. You pick up a bottle, don't you? You swallow pills. That's what they're saying now in the town."

"To hell with the town." Murphy's voice was hoarse. Against his will, he was thinking of Jordan Adler.

"Pick it up. And don't let the ghosts scare you, Murph. Whenever you have people dying unhappy, you're gonna get ghosts. They don't mean any harm."

The cactus bud was light, nearly weightless, and dry against his fingers.

"Take a small bite and put it in your jaw. Then chew it a little at a time."

Murphy closed his eyes and bit into the bud. It was bitter, alkaline, and his mouth filled with saliva.

"God," he breathed. "This is awful, Jesse." His teeth ground together as though tasting a lemon. "I think I'll stick to Coor's."

"Chew it slowly." Jesse took a smaller pouch from the pocket of the corduroy pants that lay beside him. "And don't swallow it. I know some who do, but they're old and don't give a shit if they die." He opened the smaller pouch and removed four smooth stones. "Why'd you decide to come up with me, Murph?"

Murphy shifted the bite against his back teeth. His mouth was awash in saliva, and he couldn't swallow fast enough. "Nothing else is working." He shrugged. "It can't hurt, can it?"

"Not unless the truth hurts you. Chew it."

After several minutes Murphy's teeth began to make a squeaking sound that seemed abnormally loud in his ears. He wasn't certain how long he'd been chewing the piece. "Hobie thinks you're bad off as some junkie kited on coke," he heard himself saying. "He thinks you've burned out your brain."

"Hobie's a good man," Jesse replied. He turned his head to spit before taking another bite from the bud in his hand. It was a polite, almost effeminate gesture. "When I was in Canon City, there were about fifteen Indians where I was. We were divided up. Mexicans over there, gypsies back there, the gringos—no offense, Murph—up there."

"None taken. Not honkies?"

"We didn't know that word then. Keep chewing." Jesse's voice was taking on a cadence, Murphy thought. He decided to measure its rhythm. "There was this little guy from down near the Mexican border. He was an Apache, and he was mean as cat shit. He called the guards White-Eyes, but then he was always reading Zane Grey. The rest of us, we just said gringos. Spit that out and take another bite."

When Murphy leaned over to spit, he lost his balance and held himself upright with a hand against the patterned blanket beneath him. He noticed without much surprise that he was getting an erection.

"Good. Another bite," said Jesse. "Anyway, we asked the warden for a sweat lodge. That's what reminded me of this story. That, and what you said about Hobie." Jesse's voice *was* in a cadence. Murphy was sure of it. The old man was beginning to weave back and forth on the other side of the crescent altar. His hairless chest hung down over the round belly like a pair of ancient tits. "We said it was for religious ceremonies. The warden got a real laugh out of that."

"Laugh?" Murphy shifted the bite, still rancid but less so, to the other side of his jaw.

"That was before civil rights, Murph. He said if we wanted religion, go to church and stop burning out our brains on peyote." Jesse spat and took another bite. "Always church. He wanted us to get baptized, just like that damn Navajo. Damn Navajos, always trying to point us the way. We're eagles led by rabbits, Murph."

"Goddamn rabbits . . ." Murphy bit into a new button. He thought he'd spat out the other piece, but he wasn't sure.

"Why'd you decide to come with me, Murph?"

"Toldya. Nothing else is working. Can't hurt, right?" Oh, God, thought Murphy in a moment of clarity. Oh, God, I am so damned stoned.

Jesse didn't reply.

"I mean, the Slasher's slashing, isn't he? Doing what he does best?" Murphy put his hand down again to steady himself. "And the rest of us, we're doing what we do best, too. Fucking up. Fucking up the investigation. And the election. And our lives..."

Shit, Murphy thought. It's too hot in here. Shit.

"A.J.'s gone," he said. "Gone way off, Jesse. So far she may never get back. And Jordan, in a different way. I liked her. And I'm not going to be sheriff because I fucked that up, too."

Do you want to be? He wasn't sure who said that. Or if anyone did.

"I don't know." It popped out before he could close his hand over his mouth. "Maybe not without Hobie. But I wanted to win."

The old man didn't answer. He was moving slowly, side to side. There was a soft sound coming from him.

"I wanted to win." Murphy remembered to spit before taking another bite. "I wanted to show them...her. Sara. But you know what, Jesse? *Sabes qué?* A loser's afraid to win, so he always looks for a way to fuck it up."

He giggled. Jesus. Locker-room Philosophy 101. Jesus, Jesse, I'm so damned stoned.

Jesse's voice had grown louder, had become a low background monotone. It was a chant, the cadence slow at first, then speeded to a resolution. Then repeated.

"That's why I came with you, Jesse." Murphy knew the old man wasn't listening. "That's the real reason. Because it doesn't matter if I do or I don't. I'm finished, Jesse. I've made all the difference I'm going to."

His legs were numb. When he uncrossed them, he tumbled sideways onto his bad shoulder, but there was no pain.

Jesus, I'm crying. I'm crying on this dirty blanket. Jesus, Davis, why can't you act like a man...?

There were colors exploding around him. Brown and white in the blanket next to his face, and the bleached wood of the hut's aspen branches. Tan rawhide reflecting gold and silver through his hair that was in his eyes. *Jesus, I have gray hair. My hair's turning gray.*

Deep, glowing pink around the pool, shades of rose and crimson on green. Jesse's arm was orange, then bronzed gold as he flipped out the stones next to the altar.

I know why you came, Murph. He heard the voice, but Jesse's lips were still moving in the chant. *Forget your lies. The real reason you came was because you know I'm telling the truth about the Beast. You came to find it.* Jesse cast the stones again. *It's here, Murph.*

It was.

Like a black cloud unfolding, it rose from behind the old man. Taller and taller, larger and larger, spreading like a dark flower before the moon. It was huge. Monstrous.

Its massive shoulders were covered with thick, black fur like the pelt of a wolf. The fur lay across its chest where female breasts jutted forth, the nipples black, and down a sinewy, corded belly to hang on either side of a gigantic, erect phallus.

Its head was square, with an elongated jaw and pointed ears. Its mouth was open, gleaming fangs and a black tongue, and its eyes were silver.

Jesse cast the stones.

Its long arms, black fur hanging from shoulder to waist, reached out over the old man's head. *Jesse, look out!* Murphy screamed, but his friend smiled, showing toothless gums.

Four casts of four, he heard the voice say. *For the four levels.*

The arms reached forward, and Murphy shrank back on the blanket. The hands were wide and thick, each finger tipped with a black claw.

Then its hands withdrew to behind Jesse's head, and they were no longer empty. They were clenched around the waist of a naked woman.

She was long and slim. Her blond hair fell in her face, hiding it, as her head lolled unconscious to the side. It held her, suspended in the air, behind Jesse's head.

Tell the truth, Murph. This is what you came to find, isn't it?

It held her with one hand, her feet dangling inches above the rock. Its other hand touched her breasts, and where it touched, lines of bright red appeared and blood began to flow down onto her nipples. Hanging there before dripping onto Jesse's head and shoulders.

It reached down and parted her legs, placing each one on the outside of its huge, fur-covered thighs, then it put its hand on her buttocks and tilted her pelvis forward. It looked at Murphy and grinned.

Then, as it entered her, he saw for the first time that its penis was as silver as its eyes. And razor-edged . . .

Her head shot up, eyes opened green and wide, mouth a silent O of terror and pain. Her blond hair fell back from her face.

She was Sara Nichols.

Sara! he screamed, and tried to rise. His arm gave way and he fell again, still without pain. The side of his head hit the altar, and that didn't hurt either.

When he looked up, Jesse sat alone across from him. His lips were still moving in the chant, but Murphy heard music instead. It was familiar.

What did you think, Murph? The voice was amused, the music still there as a background for the words. Did you think the Beast had long fangs and fur, like in some Abbott and Costello movie? The Beast is here, in the heart. And the heart's more deadly than any damn monster you ever dreamed of. Now sit up and let's go get some food.

It went away in flashes. When he climbed back into the hot water, it helped. But when he lay there looking at the far wall, shadows began to form and move and he had to look away.

"C'mon, Murph. Get out of the water." Jesse was dressed again and standing over him. "I'm so hungry I could eat the crotch out of a dead horse. Jump out of there."

"Jump? After you pumped me full of the rankest shit I ever touched?"

"Crawl, then. You can take me to the Colonel's. I'll have the nine-piece bucket, all dark meat extra crispy. Aren't you hungry? Peyote always makes me hungry."

Murphy gave an involuntary shudder. "No," he said, climbing to his feet. Hot, smelly water dripped off him. "No, I don't think I could eat."

"Well, I could. And we need to get down the mountain. It's going to be cold tonight." He stopped, his faded black eyes keen on Murphy's face. "You learned something." He nodded. There was no room for doubt in his voice. "What was it?"

Murphy shook his head. "I don't know," he said.

21

Wednesday, October 30

Murphy's telephone was ringing when he opened the door with Glorified Jock dancing around his legs. The sound was a surreal echo against his mind, and he flinched at the shadows gathering in the corner of the room.

"Murph? Goddammit, Davis, where've you been?" Hobie Jameison's voice was harsh, but there was something else there, too. Something infinitely sad.

"You wouldn't believe it," he replied. "I'm not sure I—"

"Never mind. I'm at the office. Get down here now."

The sun was setting on Halloween eve. It was cold, and the wind from the high peaks and the Place of Power was finding its way into the town.

He *is* sad. Murphy looked at Jameison, sprawled in his cracked leather chair by the wood stove. Sad and old. Jesus, we've all gotten so damned old this fall.

"Sit down." The sheriff nodded toward a wooden chair. "And just shut up and listen. We have a few minutes before Hank gets back."

"Hank? Hobie, I'm sorry if—"

"I don't wanna hear it. Shut up and listen. Get some coffee if you like."

"Not now. My stomach . . ."

"DeVane Belleau killed that guy up at Dripping Springs." Jameison's face was gray. Set in frozen lines. "Butchered the poor son of a bitch to make it look like the others."

250

"DeVane? Oh, bullshit, Hobie."

"Shut up. That's why Cox wanted to see us. You forgot to tell me, didn't you? Cox heard gunshots, and then he saw Belleau come sneaking out of there a little later. Alone."

"DeVane?" The word blended in Murphy's head. With the mescaline and the voices and the music and the— "You're saying DeVane's the killer? All those girls . . ."

"No!" Jameison snapped. "Pay attention, dammit! Have you been drinking again? I said he tried to make it look that way." He lifted some papers from a side table. "See all this? These are my copies, xeroxed from other copies."

"What is it?"

"You can read it later. There's no time now, so I'll give you a quick capsule." He held the papers on his lap and began to flip through. "DeVane's in Manning's pocket," he said. "I better start with that so the rest will make sense. Have you seen that building that's going up on the summit of the Gray Lady?"

"The restaurant?"

"Casino. It's not going to be a restaurant, Murph. It's going to be a gambling casino, right off some postcard of the Vegas strip. Up there on top of that damned mountain, with floor shows and big-name entertainers that'll make Ski Silvercat the hottest resort between Tahoe and Atlantic City. We're talking millions of dollars here. Maybe billions, in time."

"Come on," said Murphy patiently. "Casino gambling's illegal in Colorado, Hobie. Even Manning knows that."

Jameison nodded. "At the moment it is. But it keeps popping up in the state legislature every year, doesn't it? We have the lottery, right? And now half the bozos in the state are playing the numbers, legal as hell, on that new electronic Lotto, so don't be too sure of anything. Besides, gambling laws don't apply to Indian land."

"The Gray Lady isn't Indian land anymore. SSC bought it out three or four years ago."

"You bet they did. Like I said, Murph, shut up and listen." Jameison poured himself some more coffee.

Murphy leaned back in the chair and held the arms for balance. He couldn't stop the room from spinning, and there were shadows there, in the corner. . . .

"Okay," said Jameison. "Here's how it plays. Manning and this guy in the Forest Service, a character named Morrison, work out the papers for a land swap. Morrison gets title to a private parcel Manning owns down on the San Juan, valuable stuff if he leases out the grazing rights. In return, Manning gets just a little piece of land. Just a cliff area of national forest up on Silvercat Peak. Follow me?"

Murphy felt his mouth fall open. It was a drunken reaction, and he clapped it shut. "You're talking about the Place of Power."

"Exactly. Maybe you're smarter than you look. So, Manning and this Morrison draw up some papers, then Manning sends a flunky named Turley to the old tribal guys. Shows 'em the papers and tells 'em his boss is going to run a ski lift up there, right on their sacred mountain."

"He couldn't do that, Hobie. The gentleman's agreement..."

"Is worthless in a court of law," said Jameison. "So, this Turley has the old guys in a panic. But before they talk to someone else, he offers them a deal. Manning won't build on their mountain. He won't even go near it provided they go along and keep quiet. Instead, he'll donate an area at the top of the Gray Lady back to the tribes, and they'll all get rich."

Murphy finally nodded. "Which makes it Indian land again."

"Yep. And according to a Supreme Court decision involving the Florida Seminoles, Indian land's not bound by state civil regulations. So, the tribes operate the casino with SSC as a silent partner for a percentage. A big percentage, 'cause Manning's holding paper on their sacred mountain."

"That's straight-out extortion. Could he make it work?"

Jameison chuckled. It was the first time he'd smiled since Murphy had entered the office. "Not a chance," he said.

"It's all a scam built on ignorance and fear. And greed, 'cause those old guys stand to make a bundle too. Anyway, that's the beauty of it. It doesn't have to work, at least not for very long."

"I don't follow."

Jameison began to pack his pipe. "It's a holding action," he said. "For six months or so. One ski season. And if it's done right, it'll get SSC the first bite of casino money in the state. To begin with, there'd never be a land swap with the Forest Service. Those things require public hearings and environmental-impact studies. Manning and Morrison knew that. Morrison took a bribe, cash and that grazing land, just to fill out the bogus papers."

"Then all that about building on the big peak was just a bluff?"

"Of course. And that's where timing comes in. Get the secret agreement, then move in a hurry. Evidently, Manning's associates have some serious juice in Denver. Lobbyists with the means to make some interesting promises. By the time the Colorado Bureau of Investigation fights its way past a maze of Indian-rights litigation and restraining orders, the ski season'd be over and there'd be the chance of legalized casino gambling, at least in the big resorts. And if it passed, SSC would've jumped the gun on Aspen and Vail by a full year. Think of the money they'd make this winter. Even if it eventually fell through, the short-term profits before they got shut down'd be in the millions. And that money would be long gone, Murph. Count on it."

"You're serious." Murphy exhaled loudly. "Jesus, I don't believe it. How could they pull that off right under our noses?"

"That's where DeVane came in." Jameison's face hardened again. "Also Neddie Cameron. It's a fragile setup. Requires *all* the law around here in their pocket, at least till they got it off the ground."

"Neddie?"

"Him too. Which is what made this election so important to them. With these papers . . ." Jameison tossed the stack onto Murphy's lap. "The job's yours, if you still want it. And, incidentally, you've also been reinstated as my deputy, effective now."

Murphy held the xeroxed pages. He felt them hot in his grasp, though he knew that was only his imagination. Like the shadows in the room . . .

"Come on in, Hank." Jameison turned toward the opening door. "You're letting out all the warm air."

Henry Light shifted uneasily in the doorway. "I got the warrant, Hobie," he said. His expression was mournful, and he wouldn't look at either of them.

"I don't know where she is, Mr. Manning." DeVane Belleau moved the telephone to his other ear. "No, I called that number already. My guess would be that she's heard about Gold and figured out she's next. Probably hauled ass for Mexico. No. She wouldn't be that smart, even if he did leave her with copies. I'll guarantee you if she tried to squeeze anyone, it'd be us, and then we'd have her."

Belleau walked over to a portable bar by the wall, pulling the phone's long cord behind him. He carefully avoided looking at a framed photograph of himself and Hobie Jameison taken several years before on an elk hunt. In it, his arm was slung over Hobie's shoulder and they were exchanging caps. He stopped for a moment, listening to a faint sound outside the back window of the dining room.

"Look," he said, uncapping a bottle of Johnny Walker, "that's the problem. You're accustomed to those five-hundred-bucks-a-date sharpies. This is just a stupid Indian whore who's too dumb and too scared to do anything but run. Yeah. Gold? I sure wouldn't worry about him anymore. He's still dead, and I predict no change in his condition. Maybe that stuff will surface eventually. It probably will. But by that time . . ." He heard the sound again.

"Hey, gotta call you back," he said, and hung up the phone. He walked through the dining room and into his kitchen. Outside, twilight was settling into purple.

Why so damned jumpy? Probably the wind. Or trick-or-treaters. No, that was tomorrow night, and they'd come to the front. . . .

He heard it again.

He reached instinctively for the pistol. It was in the study.

"Hey!" he shouted through the closed kitchen door, out to the screened back porch. "Hey, cut it out, whoever you are! I'm the police chief, and I'm armed!"

There was a ripping sound. The tearing of screen.

"Hey, dammit!" He slid the dead-bolt lock on the kitchen door. "Get out of here! I'm warning you!"

He backed into the dining room and considered the front door. He headed instead for the gun.

A crashing sound came from the back of the house. A splintering of glass.

He ducked into the study. He closed the door and turned the key in a heavy, old-fashioned lock, then stepped away.

Good move, Belleau. No phone in the study, and no window either, since it was an inside room. But that didn't matter, because the gun was there.

There was silence in the house. He heard the wind through the old brick fireplace behind him. And he heard, or felt, something flapping monotonously against an outside wall.

Then there was breathing, hoarse and labored, in the hallway outside the door.

He took his revolver from the top drawer of an antique desk. "You'd better get out of here, shithead!" he yelled. He spun the cylinder. All five chambers full. "I have a gun in here!"

The door buckled under the impact of a body against the other side. There was a ripping sound as wood and metal tore.

Belleau sighted in on the center of the door.

It exploded inward.

He fired a shot, then two more before a body smashed into his. Another slug went into the ceiling as they hurtled over the desktop and crashed into a bookcase.

There was a burning pain in his chest. A heavy impact

against his head. He tried to raise the gun again, but he was blinded by something splashing into his eyes.

But not before he saw his own ribs. White of bone, pink of tendon and cartilage.

And, oh, the blood . . .

"The problem was Gold." Hobie Jameison cut to the inside on the curve, the Blazer riding its momentum into a slingshot effect at seventy miles an hour. "One of the old guys didn't buy Turley's bullshit. So he got in touch with Gold, who was associated in a peripheral sort of way with DNA, the Navajo legal service."

Murphy glanced into the backseat at Henry Light. He'd never seen Light use a seat belt before. Behind them, the headlights of another car were keeping pace.

"So Gold was going to the Forest Service?" he asked.

The sheriff's laugh was mirthless. "Not a chance. Gold was one smart guy, especially when it came to money. No, he told the old men the papers were perfectly legitimate, then he put the bite on Manning to keep quiet about it. Only, as it turned out, Manning . . . and DeVane found something on him, too. It's in that report I added at the end"—he gave a gesture of disgust—"if you think you need to see it.

"So it should have been a standoff, but I guess Manning wasn't taking any chances." Hobie turned off the highway onto a snowy side road. His headlights illuminated tire tracks and a single set of footprints headed toward a lighted house halfway up the sloping hillside. " 'Cause it looks like Belleau set up the meeting, then killed Gold and tried to lay it off with the other attacks. What they didn't figure on was Gabriel Cox having had insomnia for the past hundred years—DeVane should've remembered that—and just how smart an Albuquerque hooker named Lupita Diaz turned out to be."

They stopped in front of a long front porch. Snow had been neatly shoveled off to create a pyramid at one end.

"I don't like this." Jameison's face was like granite. "DeVane was my friend for a lot of years." Murphy and

Henry Light followed him onto the porch. Back down at the highway, headlights were turning up the road.

That better not be Killian, Murphy thought. If there's one thing we don't need right now...

Hobie knocked for a second time.

"Maybe he's gone, Hobie," said Murphy. "If he knows we're onto him, he might've taken off."

"Nope. Porch light's on. Living-room light's on. DeVane's too cheap to go off and leave lights on." Jameison gave the door another rap. "Check around back, wouldya, Hank? And take it slow."

Henry Light's face was a mask of indecision. Finally, he shrugged and went down the porch steps.

"There's no way for him to know about Gabe." Jameison stepped away from the door. "Or about the Diaz woman showing up at *The Sentinel* ... speaking of which." He nodded toward the turquoise Volvo pulling in behind the Blazer. "Friend of yours invited herself along."

Murphy felt his chest tighten as Sara Nichols stepped from the car. She was wearing faded jeans and a black leather jacket over a sweatshirt, and her long, dark hair hung free. The wind blew it across her face.

"Hobie." She pulled her hair back as she mounted the steps into the light of the porch. She looked at Murphy. "There you are," she said. "I've been trying to call you for two days."

Her green eyes held his, unreadable. He started to reply, but then the wind swept her hair across her face again. . . .

She was long and slim. Blond hair fell in her face, hiding it as her head lolled, unconscious, to the side. . . .

"Hobie!" The sound was a scream borne on the wind. "Hobie! Get around here!"

It was Henry Light's voice.

They ran through snow, drifted deep on the north side, to the back.

"Hank, what in hell . . ."

They stopped short, and Murphy felt Sara slam into his shoulder. Then she went down hard into the snow.

The back door hung crazily on one hinge. A torn piece of screen and wood thumped against the house in the wind.

Without thought, they drew their guns. Murphy intended to tell Sara to stay outside, but his throat had gone dry, tongue cloven to the roof of his mouth. She followed them onto the porch, and he felt her hand against his back.

The kitchen door had a glass inset that was shattered inward. Shards of glass reflected an overhead light.

"Go slow," the sheriff muttered. "Go real slow."

More glass in the hallway. Then the study door.

"God," Sara whispered.

The door was splintered and sagging to one side. Jameison stepped over dangling shreds.

"Go slow. Go . . . ah, shit!" he gasped. "Ah, shit!"

The study was like a slaughterhouse. Blood on the floor, gore-spattered walls.

There was a sound. Murphy whirled, gun held low and away. He saw a leg extending from behind a desk. Leather pants, he thought in that moment.

Jameison was on the other side of the desk, and Murphy heard a sharp intake of breath. "DeVane? Ah, shit, DeVane . . ."

The two men lay nearly side by side. Murphy glanced briefly at what remained of DeVane Belleau, then dropped to one knee.

"Be still, Merrill," he said. "Don't move a muscle."

The huge man's eyes opened. "Ain't gonna." He grinned. "Ain't never gonna again. But I fixed him."

He shifted, coughed, and the bloodstained hand ax slid from his grip.

"He hurt her." The voice was a bass rumble. "But I made it right."

Murphy heard Sara's voice from the hallway, low and urgent. After a moment he realized she was using the telephone.

A gigantic hand, blood-smeared, closed over his arm.

"You tell her, Murph. Tell her old Merrill made it right."

His eyes, fierce and black, were beginning to soften. To glaze. "I fixed him, didn't I, Murph? Didn't I?"

"Yeah, Merrill," Murphy whispered. "You fixed him."

"He never knew the difference." Murphy took a drink from the can of Diet Coke, then held it down for Glorified Jock to sniff. "I guess he found out somehow about Belleau and Gold and figured he was getting the one who hurt A.J."

"Which was exactly what Belleau wanted people to believe. Ironic, isn't it?" Since they'd entered the house, he hadn't been able to meet her eyes, or to stop talking.

"Ironic. Yeah. I guess it's good he never knew. Only now, we've got no real connection between Manning and Gold's murder—"

"Murphy," she said. "Would you please just shut up for a minute?"

"—without DeVane's testimony." He stopped. "Okay," he said with a faint grin. "This seems to be my night for being told to shut up."

"I'm sorry, but I followed you over here to say something." Sara's fingers were white, gripping the couch's wooden arm. "And I want to say it before...I lose my nerve."

Murphy sat back and studied her, with the firelight playing across her face. Her eyes were shadowed, nearly invisible. He wondered if he was right about what she was going to say. And about how much he wanted to hear it.

In the background, Uncle Evan's clock belched again.

"The other night," she said. "At the debate..." She seemed to be waiting for him to interrupt. "I...guess we both know where Neddie got his information."

"I guess." His voice sounded thick to him, lodged in his throat.

"But I promise you I never dreamed...I never imagined he'd use it against you. Murphy, it was just an offhand remark that I made."

"Why would you be making offhand remarks to your boyfriend about me?"

"Dammit, he's not . . ." she flared, then stopped. Even in the dim light, he could see her blush. "It's not like that. At least, not anymore. Murphy, it was already over between Neddie and me before the debate."

It was getting harder to speak. "Uh-huh," he mumbled. "Why tell me?"

"Because." She rose, long and lean in the firelight, and walked around the coffee table. "Move, Jock," she said, and lowered herself next to him in the big chair. "I just thought you might want to know."

"Oh." Great, he thought. Just great, Davis. The master of romantic repartee, aren't you?

"Yeah." She was beside him, her body touching his, shoulder to knee, and he smelled her. Clean, with only a touch of fragrance. "You know something else?"

"What?" Oh, outstanding. But he did put his arm around her.

"You hurt me tonight."

"I . . . what?"

"When I ran into you." There was a gleam of humor in her eyes. "And you knocked me flat. I'm all sore." Her face was only inches from his.

"Oh. Uh . . . where does it hurt? Here?" He began to massage her back, slim-muscled through the sweatshirt. She wasn't wearing a bra.

"Yeah." She lay her head against his chest and they stayed like that for a while. He wasn't sure how long.

He slid his hand along her shoulder. "Anywhere else?"

She took his hand in hers and brought it to her lips. Then she placed it on her breast. Through the fleecy material he felt her nipple harden between his fingers.

"Right there," she whispered. "Right on the end."

Then she raised her head and kissed him. Very thoroughly and for a long time.

He continued to stroke her throughout the kiss, and became aware she was moving against him in a slow, gentle rhythm. After a while he found the rhythm, too.

"Is that better?" His voice was hoarse as they broke the

kiss. And up an octave, too, he noticed. "Does it . . . uh, hurt
anywhere else?"

Her grin was wicked in the firelight. "I think I may have a
pulled groin muscle," she said.

Glorified Jock shared the bed until things got especially
athletic. When the humans were still again, he came back.

Murphy felt Sara move against him and murmur in her
sleep. She lay on her side, one leg across his, and her long
hair tickled his chest and ribs. He didn't move, though.

Outside, the wind was increasing, and it looked, for once,
like Kermit (High Pressure Dome) Dudley was on the money.
A major storm for Halloween. Murphy glanced at the illuminated clock face by his bed. And it was nearly Halloween
now. Another few minutes.

From the foot of the bed, Glorified Jock raised his head for
a moment, then rolled onto his side.

You've shared space with a few, haven't you, pal? Is it
different this time? She hadn't said much. He'd been afraid to
say much. Who could know what her ghosts were?

Don't let the ghosts scare you, Murph. . . .

A.J. was home in Alabama, taking her small, faltering
steps back to who she was before. Maybe, someday, someone
would tell her how Merrill the Feral had killed and died for
her.

And Jordan, who had lain where Sara was now. Whose
heartbeat he'd listened to in sleeping rhythm against his own.
Her ghosts were dark and vicious, and sometimes they wore
the face of a tortured child. . . .

When I was young, he thought, sex was for a turn-on, for
the heat. It was just a game, and I never conceived of it as a
comfort, or solace from pain. That idea would've really
turned me off in those days.

He pulled Sara closer to him.

Tonight was solace as much as passion. Warmth as much
as heat. God, I must really be getting old.

We've all gotten so damned old this fall. .

He kissed the top of her head, and her hair spreading across her face brought back a memory. Cold . . .

Don't let the ghosts scare you, Murph. . . .

But the memory, half-formed, half-remembered, wouldn't let go. It was the Beast, and he held her tighter still. In her sleep, she stretched and whispered and kissed his neck. He hoped she'd whispered I love you, but he wasn't sure.

Toward morning a light snow began to fall.

22

Thursday, October 31

The wind nipped at Halloween decorations along the street. Paper skeletons peered out snow-clouded windows in the uncertain light, and jack-o'-lanterns grinned from covered porches.

Sara maneuvered the Volvo carefully over deepening snow. Larimer Street was long and narrow, and the plows hadn't scraped it yet. She saw a tree on her right, a small snow-laden pine, covered in wet toilet paper that extended up to the window shutters of a house. Someone had gotten an early start, she decided, and made a private wager that the place belonged to some not-too-popular teacher. She remembered for a moment going with friends—Belinda and Sam and Larry—to TP Old Man Woodsen's house. Only that had been a long time ago, in a place where Halloween was celebrated in a tank top and shorts, not long underwear. And Larry Bowlin had been more than a friend, even then.

Which brought her back to Murphy Davis.

There it had always been, she conceded. Nothing mysterious. Murphy was bigger than Larry and not as handsome, but she'd seen her ex-husband every time she looked at him. Same attitude too. A star, who expected everything in life to be handed to him because he was Larry Bowlin (Murphy Davis?) and he was a star.

Many of the house numbers were partly covered by snow. She slowed to five miles an hour and pushed a button to lower her window.

So she'd been frightened by what she suspected. And she'd

263

held him away with hostility and sarcasm, and she'd used him—in a way—just as she'd once used Larry Bowlin. Only Larry was a predator. He'd used her, too, and she was tired of all that. Using and being used. That was something that Murphy would never...

Part of the number was 59. Simple mathematical progression made it 1659. Then she saw the sign, and that was that.

It was an old rock and masonry house with a narrow front porch. The sign, made of carved, varnished aspen, had been suspended by two chains above the railing.

> ARTHUR J. MORSE, M.D.
> 1659 LARIMER ST.
> 9:00 A.M. TO 6:00 P.M.

She saw a dim light burning behind thin curtains downstairs and what looked like a single figure passing by the window inside. She pulled her car to the curb across the street.

Of course, things *hadn't* been handed to him lately, had they? Not with his friend A.J. and the pain she'd seen in his eyes after that night at the school. And not with the debate, and the DUI and suspension that had followed.

Which brought her back to Neddie Cameron.

Her jaw tightened. Neddie at the debate. Neddie and Manning. Neddie's bed.

She and Neddie had used each other, too. But she'd known her private truth all along. She'd suspected it and feared it, so she'd fought it until that morning in Char's office. Some people grew smaller when things began to stack up against them. She'd sure as hell known her share of those people. But some got bigger and stronger because they had to. Murphy was no Larry Bowlin, and she'd know then....

They weren't easy words for her. They rolled like sugar drops off the tongues of some people, but not Sara Nichols. But tonight—when they were at the costume party and her courage was bolstered by a couple of strong drinks—tonight she'd find a way to say them.

Snow dusted her hair as she got out of the car. She zipped the leather jacket up around her neck and crossed the street.

Morse's front door was the clinic entrance, and it was locked. She looked through the glass and saw a reception desk and an empty chair behind it. Eleanor Loomis, who'd been Morse's receptionist, secretary, and nurse for years was nowhere in sight.

She knocked again, glass rattling slightly, then stepped back. After waiting another minute, she went down the steps and around the side of the house. The driveway was empty, and the old garage that sat at the back of the property was closed.

At the rear of the building was a screened, covered porch that reminded her, for an uneasy moment, of DeVane Belleau's house. The screen door was unlatched, and so was the kitchen door.

"Dr. Morse?" She stood on patterned linoleum. "Art? Are you here? It's Sara Nichols."

The place stank. It smelled like a cheap bar—cigarettes and booze—and it was cold.

"Dr. Morse? Are you—"

"Don't have to yell, do you?"

She jumped back at the sound and hit the door frame. A spark of pain shot through the shoulder she'd fallen on the night before.

"God!" she gasped. "You—"

"Glad you recognize me," he said dryly, walking barefoot into the kitchen. "That's an old joke Lyndon Johnson used to use. Arrogant bastard, he was."

Morse was wearing a pair of wrinkled, baggy blue trousers and a T-shirt that made his frail torso look even thinner. He apparently hadn't shaved that day, and a cigarette, mostly droopy ash, trembled between stained fingers.

"Like the look?" he asked. "Stubble's very in now, y'know? Except I don't think it's supposed to be gray. When it's gray, you don't look much like an undercover cop. You look like some half-dead wino."

"Dr. Morse?" Sara edged into the room. "Are you all right? Can I make you some coffee?"

"Got some." He pointed toward the stove. "And why wouldn't I be all right, young woman?"

"I . . . I'd heard you were ill. And you didn't . . . the three deaths. The Indian man and Belleau . . ."

"And Merrill and Feral." Morse nodded. "Dropping like flies, aren't they? What is that, four violently dead in less than three weeks? And another nearly? I'd imagine that's clear off the statistical curve for a town the size of Silvercat." He stumbled over to sit at a Formica-covered kitchen table. "So they sent you around to spy me out, huh?"

"No, I—"

"See why good ole Doc Morse isn't in there, hacking and slicing. They'll get by. That young doctor up at the Village— Wyckerson, is that him?—may just have to take a little time off from putting splints on Yuppies and get his hands dirty. They're . . . what's that word I just saw? Pygalgiacs." He laughed suddenly. "You, too, newspaper lady."

"Pyg . . . I beg your pardon?"

"Pygalgia." He rose and went to the cupboard. "By definition, a nonspecific spasm in the large muscles of the derriere. In other words—"

"A pain in the ass," said Sara.

"Couldn't have put it better." Morse took a fifth of Jim Beam from a shelf and poured into a Flintstones glass. "I really enjoy talking to you young, liberated females. Don't have to watch my language."

"Dr. Morse, are you drunk?"

He took the bottle and returned to the table. "I sincerely hope so," he said.

"And I sincerely hope not." Sara sat across from him. "Because I need to talk to you about something really important."

"Too late." He grimaced as he took a drink. "The doctor's not in. Not for autopsies. Not for medical consultations—"

"It's about Char, Dr. Morse."

He stopped. He slowly looked up at Sara, and the cold

clarity in his eyes forced her to slide back involuntarily in the chair. He's not drunk at all, she thought.

"Charlotte?" he said. "What about her?"

The sitting room gradually warmed, heat radiating from the wood stove as Sara stoked the fire and talked. Across from her on an old-fashioned davenport with floral-decorated slip-covers, Arthur Morse huddled in a flannel and corduroy robe, holding a cup of hot coffee between his hands. He hadn't spoken since she began.

"So, can you help me?" Sara backed up to the stove and let its warmth soak up to her aching shoulder. "Marv said—"

"Marv's an idiot," Morse replied. "A lovable one, granted, and he'll dance on my tombstone if he'll ever get those skin tumors looked after. But an idiot, nonetheless."

"He speaks well of you, too." Sara smiled. "And he's right when he says how much you care for Char, isn't he?"

Morse stared at her for a moment before he replied. "I like it when you smile like that," he said. "A pretty woman like you should do it more often." He placed the cup on the end table. "Marv's right, but he's also wrong."

"How do you mean?"

"Come here and sit by me, Sara, and I'll tell you a story. You're very privileged, because I've never told it to anyone and I swore to carry it to my grave. But when you smile at me like that, you look so much like someone I once knew, you see, so I'll tell you. It's a sad story, and an ugly one. And with what I know now"—he swallowed, and she saw the look come back into his eyes—"I have to tell someone."

It was on the radio before it was in the newspaper. The announcer at the radio station in Window Rock was reading from the documents verbatim, unaware that Lupita Diaz had sold them to *The Silvercat Sentinel* the day after mailing copies to KTNN.

She heard it on her car radio, heading southwest through clearing weather toward Flagstaff and eventually San Diego. If Clinton Golden Sun had been alive to see her smile, he might have thought again of Comanche women kneeling in bloody sand, knives busy amid the moans of the dying, and of the blank eyes and red smile of his Little Wolf. And how, in its own peculiar way, a trust was indeed a trust.

The telephone rang while Ed Manning was loading his briefcase.

"Edward." There was a pause and a gulp for air. "Happy Halloween, Edward."

"I . . ." Manning felt the cold hit him in the stomach. It was like his veins were flooding with ice. "I . . . was just about to call you."

"No doubt." The Whispering Man never wasted precious air on laughter, but it was there in the undertones of his voice. "I've been . . . hearing things . . . about your project." Five years before, the Whispering Man had lost his larynx to cancer and had been fitted with a mechanism that enabled him to speak by belching air. Listening to him was unnerving under the best of circumstances. "I've always . . . favored innovation, Edward. Though it can . . . get out of hand."

"Look, this is just a temporary problem." Sweat dripped onto Manning's glasses and into his eyes. "Belleau's dead. No one can prove any laws were broken."

"My own . . . father, for instance . . . once became overly . . . creative with . . . *his* employer's resources. There was . . . a valuable lesson . . . in it for me."

"Listen to me. Things are very complicated around here right now. My son—"

"Let's . . . uncomplicate. Will you . . . open the casino . . . on schedule?"

"I can't! Not with the whole thing going public. I'm going to have the CBI up here on my ass!"

"Did the tribal . . . leaders confirm . . . the agreement?" The voice was soft. Implacable.

Manning took a deep breath. "No," he said finally.

"Do you have . . . my money?"

"No."

"Not so . . . complicated, after all. I'm in mind . . . of a well-known Asian . . . curse. You were in . . . Japan, weren't you? It says . . . 'May you live in . . . interesting times.' Perhaps it has . . . an equivalent in . . . tribal dialect. I expect you'll . . . soon come to know . . . Edward.''

''Listen! Please! It'll still work out! They can't prove—'' The line went dead.

''What's up, Pop?'' He flinched at the voice behind him. Slurred, high-pitched.

''Ray!'' Manning spun around. ''My God, Ray, where have you been? You look awful.''

''You don't look so hot yourself.'' Ray came into the office and closed the door. ''Who was that on the phone? Or do I need to ask?''

He was wearing a white knit LaCoste shirt, the front splashed with what Manning at first took to be a wine stain. His new beard was gradually filling in, darkening his cheeks below hollow eyes.

''That's blood on your shirt,'' Manning said.

Ray grinned. ''Just a nosebleed. I get 'em sometimes. Usually when it's snowing.'' He laughed suddenly. ''Snowing,'' he said again.

''Ray . . .''

''Better worry about your own ass, Poppy.'' Ray took a bottle from the drink caddy. He glanced up at the faded Japanese banner. ''That was him on the phone, wasn't it? Ol' Plastic Tonsils, huh?''

''Yes.''

''Thought so.'' Ray tried for another laugh and began to cough. He drank directly from the bottle, and Manning watched his Adam's apple jerk.

''It's all going south,'' said Ray. His smile was a death's head. ''First Belleau and Neddie. Then the casino deal.'' He wiped his nose, and Manning saw that his fingers were bloody. ''So what'd you expect from the Whispering Man anyway? 'Hey, that's . . . all right, Ed.' '' He tried to imitate the voice and the cadence. '' 'Better luck . . . next time.' Shit, it's his money, Pop.''

''I know.''

Ray slid the bottle back onto the caddy. "Well, I hate to miss the big party tonight, but I'm not hanging around. I'd advise you to follow my lead."

Manning looked down at his briefcase. "They'd only find me," he said, then he stared at his son. "You too."

Ray's sallow features sagged for a moment and Manning thought, That stuff's killing him. Even if they let him off, he's finished. He'll be dead in a year.

"Maybe they won't bother with me." Ray started for the door. "I'm the next best thing to snail food already. But you, Ed . . ."

"Shut up."

"Ol' DeVane finally got to host 'The Twilight Zone,' didn't he? Right from his own house. When you get there, tell him I said to save me a chair."

Manning turned away from the closing door and continued to load his briefcase. He stared at the bushido knife on the desk and thought of the tall, scarred man in Hiroshima.

No question about what he'd have done. Quick and honorable, huh?

Only it wasn't quick. He'd talked to people who'd seen Seppuka in that autumn forty years before. Once right on the street. And there was nothing quick about it. And honor? Screw honor and give me the change.

He wasn't finished yet. Not like some crooked cop or half-dead junkie. He continued to pack.

"I'm the one who found her." Arthur Morse ran a shaking hand along his lips. "Danielle, I mean. I wasn't even surprised."

"Danielle?" Sara pressed closer, her knees touching his. "Was that Char's mother? She died from a stroke, didn't she?"

"It was 1960. In the fall, about this time of year. Kennedy and Nixon." Morse didn't seem to hear her question. "Danielle'd been to me, so I knew what was coming. And I knew what it meant."

"Dr. Morse? Was Danielle Char's mother?"

"Huh?" He looked at her with cloudy eyes. "Yes, of

course she was. Daniel and Danielle. Dan and Danni. He loved it. Alliteration, you see. Daniel and Danielle Post.

"I went to her house . . . their house, and it was like now. Late October, snow on the ground. I knew she was alone. Charlotte was at college and he . . . well, he wasn't there, either.

"It was so quiet without that damned little dog. All curtained shadows. But not windy like today. It was so quiet I heard a drip, drip. Just like it was in the next room.

" 'Danielle,' I called. I never called her Danni, 'cause I knew she didn't like it. 'Danielle, where are you?' Nothing. Just the shadows and drip, drip.

"So I knew right then, and I didn't hurry anymore. Up the stairs, past Charlotte's bedroom all filled with her doll collections, past . . . their bedroom. And into the bathroom.

"The door was closed, but it wasn't locked. It was so warm in there. The mirror was all fogged over. So was the window. The water . . . the water in the tub wasn't hot anymore—I put my finger in it—but it was still warm."

"Art?" Sara slipped her arm around his thin shoulders. He didn't seem to notice.

"She'd filled up the tub." His voice began to go ragged, and he stopped, then began more slowly. "Filled it with hot water and got in and slit her wrists." It came out in a flat monotone. "She used his special razor, the one he shaved with. Double-edged, with a silver handle.

"She was lying back, and she'd pinned up her hair so it wouldn't get wet. Her eyes were closed, and there was this little smile on her face, like when she'd tease or when she'd won at rummy. And the faucet was dripping into the water. Not red water like you'd expect. More of a rose color. I put my finger—"

"Charlotte's mother killed herself? But I thought . . ."

"She had to." Morse smiled patiently, as if explaining it to a backward child. "She was pregnant."

"She committed suicide because she was pregnant? A married woman? What kind of reason was that?"

"Could I have some more coffee?" Morse pulled his robe tighter around him. "It's cold in here."

She was hurrying back with the pot when he looked up at her.

"Do you know what pedophilia is?" he asked.

"I . . . isn't it when someone wants to . . . have sexual relations with a child?"

"Daniel Post started in on Charlotte before she was ten years old. Steady, dammit!" Morse held up his cup. "These carpets are older than you are."

"What?" Sara put the pot onto the coffee table. "What are you saying?"

"Put it on the doily." Morse shifted the pot. "And sit down. I told you it was both sad and ugly. You've heard the sad part."

Sara was on the davenport, unsure of how she got there.

"I didn't know about it." Morse brought the cup to his lips. "Neither did anyone else at first, including Danielle.

"I was in love with her. Danielle, I mean. I always have been. Funny, people around here think it's Charlotte. I let 'em. It's flattering, I guess.

"I found out about it . . . the incest . . . when Charlotte was sixteen or so. Danielle and I were friends—she didn't know how I felt then—and she came to me with the story. Post had started threatening Charlotte. Threatening her with violence, accusing her of 'changing' and of corrupting him, Danielle said. Started calling *her* Danni."

"Char?"

"Her name's Charlotte Danielle Post. After her mother and grandmother. Danielle wasn't stupid, and she finally got the truth out of Charlotte.

"I figure he was a classic pedophile. So, naturally, when Charlotte entered puberty, it all went sour for him. But the incest continued. Danielle even believed Charlotte wanted it to, that she was in love with the filthy bastard by that time. But she wasn't a prepubescent anymore. I believe that when he saw her as a woman and she still wanted him, it suddenly all became her fault in his eyes."

"God," murmured Sara. "Oh, Char . . ."

"From the time she found out, Danielle tried to keep her

daughter away from him, but it was a small town and it was a long time ago. You didn't reveal things like that, especially about the town's leading citizen. To this day, Charlotte isn't aware I know anything about it.''

"She loved him.'' In her mind's eye, Sara saw the huge painting in Char's office. The handsome face with its thin mustache and brooding blue eyes. ''That's why she couldn't stay away from him.''

"And he'd begun to hate her,'' Morse replied. ''Danielle could see it, even it Charlotte wouldn't. Even if she ignored the danger. And the older and more beautiful she became, the more she'd changed from what he wanted her to be.'' Morse pointed at an old desk in the corner. ''Look in that second drawer over there. Bring me what's wrapped in the scarf.''

The scarf was burgundy silk, with a faint fragrance. Sara felt a wooden frame wrapped inside it.

Morse undid the folds slowly, his hands trembling. ''Look,'' he said. There was reverence in his voice. ''Look at this.''

It was a photograph of two women. Or rather a woman and a girl. They'd smiled at the camera.

"Danielle and Charlotte,'' said Morse. ''Charlotte was nineteen. Home for a visit.''

"My God!'' gasped Sara.

The older woman looked to be in her middle years. Her long, dark hair showed traces of gray under the photo studio's lights and there were shadows beneath her eyes, but neither detracted from her quiet beauty. Only the brilliance of her daughter could do that.

Charlotte Post had a slim face, oval-shaped beneath blue eyes and high cheekbones. A full lower lip, nearly in a pout, with long blond hair cascading around a pale throat and shoulders. She was beautiful. Spectacular.

"You see?'' Morse's fingers tenderly brushed the glass above Danielle Post's hair. ''He couldn't deal with it. Not when his little girl changed into someone like that. Danielle was afraid for Charlotte's safety, so she packed her off, kicking and screaming, to a private school in Wisconsin. And then she was alone . . . with him.''

"And with you," Sara said quietly. "You became lovers, didn't you?"

Morse smiled. "Of course we did," he said.

"And the baby. It was yours, wasn't it?"

"Yes." Arthur Morse's eyes filled for a moment. "Yes, it was. Post didn't know. All he knew or cared about was that his Charlotte had changed. He started pressing Danielle to have another baby. Another little girl . . ."

Sara felt her breath catch in her throat.

"He didn't know she was pregnant. She hadn't willingly let him touch her in years, not since she found out about Charlotte. So he attacked her in their own house. Dragged her into Charlotte's room and raped her. She told me. Up there with all the dolls watching them . . ." Tears slid down his cheeks.

"I begged her to leave him. With me. And she might have, except she was pregnant."

"But it was your baby."

"It was also adultery, and she was sure he'd claim the baby. I tried to convince her he'd never get custody if she told about Charlotte, but she wouldn't do that to her daughter. So what she did finally, in that bathtub, she did for both her children. Born and unborn."

He rubbed his stubbly jaw, and the tears made dirty streaks on the back of his hand. "I fixed up the death certificate, with Post's cooperation, of course. It said a stroke, and made no mention of the pregnancy. The town never knew. Charlotte never knew. And I threatened that son of a bitch, because I had him. He could never have stood the scandal.

"Oh, yeah, he was big, handsome Daniel Post, and I was just a runty little GP who'd loved his wife, but I told him to get out of Silvercat. And I warned him if he ever tried to hurt Charlotte, I'd tell everything he'd done. And so he left, right after she came home for the funeral. Turned over the paper to his daughter, cleaned out his bank account, and left town." Morse looked up at Sara. His eyes were red-streaked and wide.

"Only, now he's back."

"Daniel Post? Here?"

Morse gestured impatiently. "Use your brain, Ms. Nichols. You're supposed to have a reporter's logic, aren't you? Then use it! It's Daniel Post. He's the one who's been killing these girls, the ones we know of and God knows how many more. Can't you see? He's been killing Charlotte for twenty years because she betrayed him by growing up."

Sara's mind was reeling, trying to keep pace. "Char's father? And you knew?"

"Shit, woman! Of course I didn't know. Do you think I'd have kept quiet all these years for a piece of garbage like Daniel Post? I didn't connect it until I saw his car. And not for certain until you told me about Bisbee, Arizona."

"What—"

"Because he was never there, except to send mail. He lied to Charlotte. She showed me a few cards he sent from there at first. A Christmas card, maybe her birthday. Terse and to the point. 'Your father, Daniel Post.' And none of them in the past twenty years or so. So where's he been all this time, newspaper lady, and what's he been doing? I could make a guess."

"And now... he's here?" Sara felt the hairs prickle along her arm.

"Ever since I saw that car, I've been thinking. Drinking, too, I admit it. And what you've told me today completes the picture. See it? Only two things have kept Charlotte alive. The fact she doesn't look like she did then, and the fact that Daniel Post's crazy as a poisoned dog. He's not a human anymore, Sara. He's a monster, a beast, and we have to find him before he really finds Char. My God, what'll it do to her when she knows he's back?"

Sara saw Char's face again. She thought of the past few days.

"I think she already knows, Dr. Morse," she said.

He was almost at the intersection when the old Buick passed him. He'd been driving slowly, woolgathering, and then it was past and turning west on Sixth.

"You son of a bitch!" Arthur Morse whispered. He hesitated. Turn right and follow Fifth to Charlotte's street, or left and follow the Buick? Morse turned left on Sixth.

The old car, apparently as well maintained as it had been in the early sixties, moved solidly through slush and falling snow. The wind gusts that shook Morse's Chevette—Eleanor'd been on him for years to get a new car—didn't seem to faze it. About a block ahead of him, it turned again, north on Hammersmith.

He's headed out of town, Morse thought. Up to the Village. He maintained the same distance on the winding switchbacks. Traffic was heavy both ways as they approached the Ski Silvercat exit. It was nearly three P.M.

The Buick passed the exit and slowed through the main loop of Silvercat Village. Morse cut his speed accordingly.

"What the hell?" he muttered. "Where are you going, you bastard?"

On through the Village, and afterward heavy forest bordered both sides of the road. The traffic was thinner, and Morse dropped back again.

Then, after several more miles, the big car ahead slowed and turned left off the road. Morse followed at ten miles an hour until he reached the cutoff, a snowed-in logging trail.

Okay, he thought. You don't drive up that trail. It only goes back in the trees, and there's a homicidal lunatic at the end of it. What you do is head for a phone in the Village and call the sheriff's office. Sara's been there by now, and she has Hobie and Murph filled in. This is where the marines take over.

He saw her smile, and it was sad and a little tired. . . .

He cut off the Chevette's engine and stepped out into the snow.

There go the tracks, and there's something up there ahead. Chrome reflecting light? Good. When Hobie and Murph get here, he'll be stuck like a goddamned bug in a jar.

He knew she was dead, even before he spoke to her. There in the rose-colored water . . .

He reached behind the seat and took out a sawed-off baseball bat before he began following the tire tracks.

Looks like the car's pulled off into some bushes. Footprints are headed through the trees over that way. All right. He'll never get away from them on foot.

And the more she suffered at his hands, the more beautiful she became. So much warmth. So much love. He removed his hand from the water. He gently touched her face . . .

He stepped into the tracks of the longer strides, the bat held cocked in his right hand, and ascended through the trees.

He no longer fantasized about making a telephone call.

At the top of a knoll a tall figure stood, back toward him, the wind-whipped snow blurring it from his vision. His attention was caught for a moment by the symmetrical mounds near the figure's feet.

"It's been a long time, Arthur," came the familiar voice. "But then, you never could learn to mind your own business, could you?"

Then the figure spun toward him, down the hill and toward him, and he recognized the blade, the silver handled razor, at once.

And so many things became clear.

23

Thursday, October 31

Halloween dusk came a little before six. The snow picked up, driven ahead of a northwesterly wind.

It had been three hours since Hobie Jameison and Acting Police Chief Henry Light had put out an alert for a black 1958 Buick Roadmaster.

It had been two hours since Paul Killian's man at the police station had again exchanged information for money, sending Killian and Hacker Morlan to the telephone.

And it had been two hours since Sara Nichols found Charlotte Post alone at her office desk, beneath the huge oil painting on the wall.

"Char?" Sara spoke after standing in the doorway for a full minute. Charlotte was writing something, her concentration absolute. "Tell me what you think."

"What I think about what?" Charlotte glanced up briefly. "You have to give me . . ." Her voice trailed off. Her blue eyes widened, completely rimmed in white.

"It's part of my costume." Sara touched the long blond wig she was wearing. "You know, Marie Antoinette. For the party tonight?"

She'd tried. God knows she'd tried to think of a way to tell Char about Daniel Post. About the manhunt that had already started on the streets of the town. But she couldn't. She simply couldn't, and neither could Marv, so she'd put on the wig from her costume to make Char laugh.

Only Charlotte wasn't laughing.

She was frozen, half out of her chair, and her eyes just kept getting wider. Bewildered . . .

"Party?" she said, her voice a gravelly whisper.

It's too late, Sara thought. She already knows. Someone's already told her. "Yeah, you remember," she forged ahead. "Up at the Village with the culture vultures. 'Local rabble will meet and converse with nobility.'" She put on a snooty accent, pretending to read from an invitation. "Are you . . . still going?"

"Yes." Charlotte settled back in her chair. She smiled suddenly. "Oh, yes, I'll be there. I wouldn't miss it."

My God, she doesn't know yet. Tell her. Tell her right now, before she hears it somewhere else. Before someone besides Hobie or Hank, someone who doesn't care for her the way we do, comes bursting in here with videocams and prying questions to destroy her present with her past. Tell her.

But Sara still couldn't do it.

"Tonight," she said instead, "at the party, there's something Murphy and I need to talk to you about. Would that be okay?"

"Fine." Sara had expected Charlotte to react quickly and probably humorously to the reference to her and Murphy Davis. But she didn't seem to even notice. "That'll be fine." She was still smiling, and her eyes hadn't left Sara's face.

"Well . . . all right, then." Sara reached back for the door frame. "I . . . I guess we'll see you there. We'll be on the lookout for the prettiest cat burglar in the place."

"Yes."

Charlotte was still smiling as the door closed.

She can't know, Sara thought, walking back to her own office. She's too . . . relaxed, is that the word? Serene. Char had looked more at peace just then than she had all week.

Murphy knows her, she decided. He'll help me talk to her. They'd been apart only hours, but she was already aching to see him again.

Charlotte sat looking at the closed door for a minute, then she removed the tailored jacket she'd been wearing. She picked up the piece of paper she'd been writing on and studied it. Her expression was puzzled.

"Char?" Marvin Lanier tapped on the door while opening it. That was his usual way. "Got a minute?"

For a few seconds her eyes were perfectly blank, then she smiled. "Of course," she said. She turned the paper face-down on her desk.

"There's a rumor," he said, shifting his feet nervously. "Real strong one, that Hobie's found out who the Slasher is." He avoided her eyes.

"Then pursue it, Marvin." Charlotte's voice was soft, detached. "Get the story, of course. Use anyone . . . but Sara. She and I are going to a costume party tonight."

"A costume . . ."

"It's Halloween, Marvin. Time for all the monsters to come out. Isn't that right?"

"I guess so." He took a step back, his creased face slack with confusion, and looked for an exit line. "I, uh, I see that cut's finally healing up. Still say you should've taken it to a doctor. Art Morse—"

"Would've just made a fuss." Charlotte glanced down at her left forearm, neatly bandaged with gauze over cotton. "I'm used to taking care of little cuts and bruises myself, Marvin. Now, shouldn't you be getting on that story?"

When she was alone, she took the paper from her desk and swiveled her chair around. She sat looking up at the oil painting and tearing the page into tiny shreds, humming to herself.

Dark came and brought Halloween with it. Also trick-or-treaters being transported by car rather than walking through the building storm. Mothers and fathers bundled up little ones, ruining the effect of their costumes, and many wished they could spend just one more Halloween where it was still warm. . . .

It was the locusts chirping in the old willow outside her bedroom window that awakened A.J. in the muggy darkness.

That, and not the dreams, because the dreams no longer came every night.

"Jimmie?" she called, and patted the pillow beside her. There was a shifting sound by the night light, and a long-legged German shepherd pup hopped lightly onto the bed.

"Oh, Jimmie," she whispered, and drew the dog to her. He was nervous, still new to the house and the girl, but he settled onto the pillow with his nose next to her ear.

A.J. was thinner than she'd been in Silvercat, and there was a sallow tinge to her skin. But with the vitality of a nineteen-year-old, she was coming back. Except for the dreams.

It was odd. In most ways she wanted the dreams to stop—she was tired of the bed and being treated like a goddamned child—but in one way she didn't. Because it was in the dreams that she could almost remember, and she knew she *would* remember if they continued. She pictured herself calling Murphy Davis and telling him. Solving the mystery. Then arriving back in Silvercat a heroine and seeing him standing there. . . .

There was a thudding sound outside the window.

"What . . . ?" She bolted upright in bed. Jimmie was up beside her, a high-pitched growl in his throat.

There were movements outside her window in the warm darkness. And it wasn't the willow tree.

"Wait . . ." She murmured it without thought, her body stiffening against the big pup. "Just wait. Just . . ."

And when the jack-o'-lantern's fiery grin pressed against the screen, she began to scream.

There were footsteps in the hall. There was a muffled curse from outside the window, mixed with smothered giggling, and the jack-o'-lantern disappeared. Then the door of her room was thrown open and a tall figure stood there, slim and blond-haired. . . .

And A.J. recoiled in terror from her mother.

"Alison? Alison, my God!"

"Carlene, get away!" Riley Delaney pushed through the door. He hurried to the bed and pulled his daughter, clinging to her dog, into his arms. "Goddamned kids! Goddamned heartless little bastards! Don't cry, baby. Please don't . . ."

But A.J. went on crying. Because, finally, she remembered.

The culture vultures were looking for Edward Manning, but without any luck. Ditto Neddie Cameron.

Not that they'd have been easy to recognize amid all the costumes and masks. There were Satans and gypsies, vampires and princesses, Conans and punk rockers. And the rumors persisted, even more pervasive than the one claiming Manning's body had been found in a Utah ditch, that Daniel Post himself was present, disguised and watching. The culture vultures had never been so titillated, even to the point of forgiving rivals who were wearing the same costume.

Murphy was thinking about A.J. and her mother. He was holding Sara close as they danced, her blond-wigged head against his neck, and trying to remember if he'd ever been this happy and sad at the same time. But he was thinking about A.J. and her mother and had been—in a perfunctory sort of way—ever since Sara had told Art Morse's story. And he couldn't decide why. Mothers and daughters, he thought. That must be it.

"Yo, there, Deppity."

The voice roused him, and he stepped on Sara's foot . . . again. "Sorry," he muttered, and looked down at her but saw she was as distracted as he.

"It's okay." She smiled faintly. "Hi, Lon."

Lon Everell was being John Wayne, and he had the height for it, if nothing else. He wore a blue western bib-shirt and a huge hat, with a holstered plastic pistol on his right hip.

"Love your outfit." He grinned. "But it's kinda typecasting, isn't it?"

Murphy blushed slightly. The high-school football uniform that Doug Hutchins had commandeered for him was somewhat small, especially with the pads. He tried very hard to look at Everell without thinking of Jordan Adler. It would serve no purpose now.

"I got it on short notice," he said without smiling.

"You look great, too, Marie." Everell turned to Sara. "Though I do notice two basic flaws."

Sara glanced down ruefully. "I know." She smiled. "But I'm not to blame. My mother's flat-chested, too."

"No, no!" Everell cackled. "I meant your earrings. I once wrote an historical romance called *The Flaming Fleur-de-Lis* and found that Marie Antoinette rarely wore earrings."

"That's real interesting, Lon," said Murphy, then, seeing the writer had no intention of leaving, he said, "So, how's the new book coming?"

Everell beamed. "Great. Couldn't be better. And how about this socko real-life ending? After all these years, the Slasher turns out to be—"

"Lon." Sara's voice was harsh. "Do you mind? Char's here somewhere."

Everell held up huge, soft-looking hands in mock surrender. "Okay there, pilgrim," he said, affecting his John Wayne imitation. "But it's gonna be a sockdollager. Probably earn me at least—"

"Hello, love."

The voice was low, barely audible above the music.

Charlotte was wearing a pair of black corduroy pants, softened and faintly stained with age, above black, low-heeled boots. Her sweatshirt, also black, was new, as were her gloves. Her hair was pinned close to her head, and she had drawn in a thin brown mustache on her upper lip.

"I've been looking for you," she said to Sara. "I didn't think I'd ever find you."

"Aha, the famous cat burglar." Sara glared at Everell, who blandly returned her stare. "Murphy, do you mind if Char and I go somewhere to talk?"

"Not at all." That hadn't been the plan, but Murphy was as embarrassed as Sara *something* wondering how much *something familiar* Char had overheard. "Lon and I were going to get a drink, anyway. That's a nice costume, Char."

But she was already following Sara toward the door onto the enclosed deck *moving away from him something familiar* and didn't look back. Damn! He was sure she'd overheard Everell. That loudmouth.

She walks ahead of him, blond hair gleaming in the light, and his heart is pounding, pounding.

He's found her, finally and without doubt. After all the years and all her tricks, it's nearly over.

"Let's go over by the stairs," she's saying. Smiling back at him as she walks, that smile he knows. Teasing him. But not for much longer now.

Come on, Danni . . .

The phone woke Hobie Jameison from a nodding stupor.

"Well, hell," he mumbled, and his chin jerked upward off his massive chest. "Murph? Wouldya get . . ."

No. Eighty-six that. Murph wasn't there. He was up at the Village with Sara Nichols. Jameison had insisted he go.

"Okay. Okay, dammit!" He rose too quickly from his big leather chair by the wood stove, and his forehead went hot with sudden dizziness. His right leg had cramped up in his sleep. God, was it really past eight o'clock?

Gotta go home, he thought as he lifted the phone. It was like he'd told Murph when he sent him off. Post hadn't made a move in nearly two weeks. It'd keep till morning.

"Yeah. Jameison."

The voice on the other end was tinny, shrill with controlled excitement. It was Riley Delaney calling from Gadsden, Alabama. A.J.'s father. It seemed his daughter had just solved Hobie's case for him.

"Dammit, Murph. Lighten up." Everell gulped a glassful of punch. "She didn't hear me. I saw her coming across the floor while I was talking, and she wasn't looking at anyone but Sara. Besides, it's all over town by now. She's bound to know. Hey, are you listening to me?"

"Huh?" *Something. What was it?* "Oh, sorry, Lon. You're probably right. She couldn't have heard you, not with the music."

Poor Char. It was incredible, but it fit, except for being in love with him. Abused by him, threatened, but loving him in spite of it all, if Art was right. Jordan would've said *she* was the one who was fixated. . . .

"Helluva deal," Everell was saying. "That old loony hiding out all these years. Y'know, that part of it doesn't make much—"

Poor A.J., too. His mind went back to her again. Back to the crazy-quilt *something* cycle of thought that had revolved around her all night. At the hospital, listless at first, then terrified and screaming because . . .

"—sense to me. I mean, how'dya hide out for twenty years? Someone's bound to see you. Of course, it'll make a better story for me if he's caught soon. People love the gory stuff, but only—"

. . . because her mother touched her.

"—if the ending leaves 'em feeling safe, y'know?"

Her mother . . . Stage makeup, Ellen Bailey said. Beards, mustaches. Mustaches . . . and so familiar, moving away . . . with Sara.

He remembered.

"Hey, Murph! Where're you going? Jeez, run over me next time! Murph?"

She turns to face him by the stairs, and she smiles again. She's so near he can reach out and touch her. The sounds from inside the ballroom are fading to a background haze. . . .

"Char," she's saying, "I'm so sorry I couldn't say anything earlier at the paper. God, I'm such a coward." She reaches out and touches his arm. And it burns right through him.

"I found you," he says, the joy bubbling up inside him. At last. At last. "I have something for you, Danni."

"I know when you first heard it, you must have—" She stops in midsentence. "Char? What did you . . . call me?"

In one fluid motion, he bends and pulls the razor from his boot. "Danni," he whispers. "Oh, my love . . ."

* * *

No way. It was ridiculous.

Murphy elbowed through the crowd near the door. A long-haired young woman dressed as Cleopatra grabbed his arm.

"Mr. Touchdowns," she said. Her eyes were as glazed as the gray smoke smoldering from the pipe in her manicured hand. "I know you. Are you Somebody?"

"Not a soul." Murphy pulled away from her. Over her head he could see out onto the enclosed deck. It was empty.

"Shit," he heard her say, and giggle as he surged ahead. "I thought he was Somebody."

He didn't see them anywhere.

No way. His mind tried to push it away from him. No way in hell.

But he remembered the figure at the school. Distant in the hallway, moving away but familiar. And there was the dream— vision? drug hallucination?—of Sara with blond hair. Sara held in the grasp of the Beast, with its silver, razorlike phallus. And its breasts . . .

Cold air was gusting from somewhere. It rippled the SSC insignia that hung, white and green, from a center wall support.

Near the left corner of the deck was a staircase. The cold air hit him in the face when the reached the rail above it. On the second step down, he saw Sara's purse.

Jesus. Jesus, Joseph, and Mary.

Then he saw the figures through the glass. Outside, below, crossing toward the corner of the building. Both tall, both blond, but one in a light-colored gown. And the other pursuing.

She runs ahead of him, her gown billowing in the wind. Snow blows in his eyes and blinds him, but the joy . . . surging, surging, because this time it will be different.

The fresh powder on the outside deck keeps tripping him, and he fights to maintain his balance. Once he could run forever, but something's wrong tonight. He can't catch her.

"Char!" A voice from behind him. "Goddammit, Char! Don't."

He doesn't look back.

Then she trips rounding the corner of the lodge. He sees her tumbling down the embankment toward the parking lot. He gathers himself and leaps after her.

They roll down, down, toward a snow-covered retaining wall. She hits it first, and above the scream of the wind, he hears the bone snap.

Then he's on her, flipping her onto her back. The blade is out, its silver reflecting off car lights coming up the lot below. The snow rips across him, but he doesn't feel it or the wind or the cold.

"Danni," he whispers through his tears, and his gloved hand finds her legs through the gown, but . . .

But something's wrong. He looks up at her face, her eyes dazed with pain and shock, and . . .

And at her dark brown hair braided close to her head. And at the blond wig lying in the snow.

"Dan . . . Danielle?" he whispers *she whispers they whisper*. "Mother?"

They look at the double-edged razor held in their hand.

"Hold it right there!" The roar of a pistol shot and a shrill whine past *his* upraised hand. Then he vaults off the girl and over the retaining wall to the road. And he runs for the old Buick parked near the end of the lot.

Murphy was rolling down the embankment, both hands supporting his knee, as Hobie Jameison came floundering up from below. Murphy slid to a stop next to Sara and scooped her into his arms. Her bare shoulders above the costume gown were bone white.

"Careful," he heard Jameison say. The older man was wheezing for air. "That elbow's broken for sure."

Murphy folded Sara's other arm across her waist and staggered upright with her. "I heard a shot," he gasped. "Did you hit her?"

"Nope." The sheriff's eyes were slitted against the driving snow. "Didn't try to. Let's get Sara inside."

She was regaining consciousness by the time they carried her into the lobby. A parking attendant had been sent for Dr. Noel Wyckerson, who was attending the party upstairs, and he met them at the door to the Ski Patrol's first-aid station.

"Cute outfit," said Jameison to the young black doctor, who was dressed as Michael Jackson, even to the sequined glove. "Real cunning."

"Yo Momma," replied Wyckerson equably. "Put her over here."

"Take care of her, please." Murphy placed Sara gently on a padded examining table. "We have to go."

"Murphy." She tried to push up against Wyckerson's softly restraining hand, her eyes glassy and vacant. "There was something I wanted to say to you."

But he was already out the door.

He turns into the alley, tires sliding on ice, and follows his own set of tracks. Along a corridor of wooden fences through the cone of his headlights until he reaches the old garage.

He jumps out and unfastens a heavy Yale lock, then swings the wooden door open. It's dark inside until he pulls in, lights reflecting off the brilliant blue sheen of a late-model Chrysler sitting to one side.

He gets out of the Buick and locks it, then pulls a heavy tarp over it, carefully avoiding the radio aerial as always. Then he leaves the garage, refastening the lock, and hurries through a backyard almost knee-deep in snow.

In the house he pushes the small dog aside and, pulling the sweatshirt over his head, climbs the stairs. Despair weights his steps, and the stairs seem endless.

He'd been so sure this time. So certain. But he'd been wrong. It was Danielle . . . no, that was wrong, too. Danielle was dead. Danielle had . . . a stroke. Yes, a stroke.

At the top of the stairs he hesitates. Then he goes into *her* room and closes the door.

"Danni," he whispers, and he feels his eyes begin to burn. "Where are you, Danni?"

But there's no answer in her room. There never is. Just the pink-and-white canopied bed with its ripped mattress. And the photos lying faceup on the covers. And the dolls that sit on the pillow and all along the quilted window seat and bureau top, dusty and cobwebbed, staring at him. Accusing him with their wide, blank eyes.

He's very tired, the wound from the dog bite throbbing again beneath its bandage. He thinks he may have reopened it digging the grave out at the knoll, but there's no blood showing. Then something about that makes him cry again, so he stops thinking of it. Tears track through the makeup mustache and are dark, bitter on his lips. He hears Alistair Three scratching at the door, and he rises wearily from the bed.

He passes her makeup table, which he fought against so vehemently—*She doesn't need makeup, for God's sake! She's just a little girl!*—and he stops. He sits down on the pink-and-white bench and looks into the mirror.

Danni? A face looks back at him. Blue eyes, clouded, nearly drugged in appearance. Frosted hair held tight against his head with bobby pins. The first beginnings of a sag in the firm jawline.

Then he *she they* raise their hand to the face. They unpin the hair.

He was going to leave me, they think. He said he didn't love me anymore. That he wished I was dead. Because I changed . . .

I'm sorry, Daddy. It's my fault. I deserve to be punished.

They brush out the hair, framing the face. They put cold cream on a tissue and wipe away the heavy eyebrows and the mustache, all the things that are getting harder to do each time. Their hand touches an old photo lying there, cut in half down the center. They glance at it.

But he didn't leave me. They smile faintly. And he won't. Not ever.

But Danni . . . Charlotte Danielle . . . Where is *she?*

Then they stare down at the photo, then into the mirror with dabs of cold cream at the corners of the mouth. They stare and stare, back and forth.

The photo, the mirror.

The photo, the mirror.

The photo . . .

Their *her his* eyes widen in recognition.

All the years he couldn't find her. All the miles and all the years. Because he'd been looking in the wrong place. His tears are tears of joy, of gratitude.

"Danni," he whispers, and he sees her smiling back at him. "Oh, my love . . ."

"Art was so sure," said Murphy as the Blazer turned off Fifth. "He was so damned sure it was Daniel Post."

"Maybe it was," said Jameison. "You saw her costume. Think about it."

"I can't. All I know is she's our friend, and she needs our help."

The Blazer slid to a stop outside an old Victorian house.

"Go slow," said Jameison. "Friend or not. Slow and careful."

Murphy's eyes blurred. Jesus, Char. Aloud, he asked, "Do you really think she's in there?"

"I don't know." Jameison looked up at the house. "She could be. She could be watching us right now."

"Shut up, Hobie." Murphy came around the vehicle. "Just shut up, okay?"

They opened the iron gate and walked up the steep steps to the porch. Murphy thought of standing on that porch as a teenager. Of her limitless patience during his awkward, embarrassed attempts at conversation. Teenage dreams of Charlotte Post.

"Do we knock?" Murphy wasn't surprised when Hobie Jameison turned to him for confirmation. It had been that kind of night. "Might be smarter not to."

"No." Murphy stepped ahead of him to the door. "We knock."

There was no answer, and after another knock, Murphy pushed on the door. It wasn't locked, of course. Charlotte had always said the day she needed to lock her door, she'd leave Silvercat.

"Expecting us?" Jameison whispered, and he drew his pistol.

"Put that away." Murphy's hand was on the sheriff's arm. "This is Char's house. Put it away." And he bent down to remove his cleated shoes before stepping onto the polished hardwood in the hallway.

"That wasn't Charlotte I saw up there in the snow, Murph. At least not the Charlotte I know," said Jameison. But he holstered the gun.

Murphy looked into the living room, elegantly decorated in tones of blue. Light from the hall reflected back from the polished top of the piano.

Char and her piano. He remembered how well she played, and how she loved the old Beatles tunes.

And how the music, half-forgotten, half-remembered, from his dream at the Place of Power had been piano music.

"Char?" His voice was loud in the stillness, echoing. "Char? It's me, Murph. Hobie's with me."

Then he heard a sound, and he realized he'd been hearing it since they'd entered the house. Faint subsound. It came from upstairs.

"Char?" The stairs were carpeted, creaking beneath his weight. At the top the sound was clearer. It was a clicking sound, softly repeated.

There was a dimly lit hallway with framed pictures at regular intervals. It was dusty, close-smelling up there, the sheen and furniture polish that had characterized the downstairs completely missing.

It's a different world up here, Murphy thought. Who lives up here?

"Char?"

The sound stopped.

There was a door partly ajar. At its base, the dry, peeling wood bore long scratches.

Murphy pushed open the door and walked into the room with Jameison behind him. He saw Charlotte lying on a canopied bed with dolls piled all around her. She was wearing a pink-and-white nightgown.

The dolls and Charlotte stared at Murphy. Their eyes were wide and lidless and so were hers. Long swaths of blood painted both her cheeks down onto her neck.

Like the dark stain that had spread across the torn, quilted coverlet and onto the floor, heavy and clotting on the pink-and-white nightgown that was bunched up above her thighs. Where the silver-handled razor was.

"Jesus God!" Hobie Jameison moaned. "Oh, Jesus, Charlotte!"

At the sound of his voice, the little terrier looked up curiously at the men, then it went back to licking the hardwood floor. Its tongue made a regular, clicking sound against its teeth.

EPILOGUE

It was a new month, and the town began its recovery in bright sunshine under cobalt blue skies. Its wounds from the three weeks of a dark October were numerous, as were the means by which it healed itself. Gossip and long silences, paranoia and opportunistic grasping, jokes in incredibly poor taste and tears.

The town would go on, growing more rapidly than the old-timers would like, but more slowly than the entrepreneurs had dreamed. The former cursed the October horror because it had brought the eyes of the outside world, and the latter cursed it because it scared away much of the development they'd sought. And all those touched by it personally were changed in ways both trivial and fundamental.

Hobie Jameison retired as sheriff at age fifty-nine after twenty years of continuous service to Granite County. He and his wife Maribeth took their first real vacation in all that time and were present at the birth of their second grandchild in Sterling, Colorado.

Henry Light was passed over by the city council in their selection of a new police chief. He left Silvercat for a job in Wyoming.

Doug Hutchins, who'd spent the second half of the football season with his Mountaineers jeered at and labeled the Silvercat Slashers, had the satisfaction of an Alpine League championship and a team that reached the state AA quarterfinals.

The body of Edward Manning was discovered by the Utah State Highway Patrol under a culvert on U.S. 163 a few miles south of Blanding. He had been shot once behind the right ear with a small-caliber pistol.

The Silvercat Ski Corporation disbanded briefly, then reorganized with fresh leadership and financial backing. The new building at the summit of the Gray Lady opened as a luxury restaurant reachable year round by gondola.

Neddie Cameron and his wife Marilyn left Colorado for Los Angeles, where he applied before the California Bar Association and she filed for divorce.

Ray Manning had already reached Dallas when he received word of his father's death. His whereabouts from that point forward remain unknown.

Marvin Lanier, through the provisions of Charlotte Post's will, became majority owner of *The Silvercat Sentinel*. He remains on staff as an editorialist and the newspaper's publisher.

Paul Killian received a six-figure fee from a Florida-based tabloid for his lurid, detailed account of the Silvercat Slasher. Shortly thereafter, he and Hacker Morlan were arrested in Key West when a South American investment went sour. They have made bail and are currently filming an exposé on Caribbean drug trafficking.

Lon Everell's book, *The Silvercat Slasher,* was purchased at auction by a major New York publishing house for the largest fee of his writing career. He has since moved to Aspen.

Jesse DePriest disappeared from Silvercat during the night of October 31. After two days he returned, apparently none the worse, speaking of prayers offered and answered.

Dr. Jordan Adler died of hypoxemia from an apparent drug overdose during the night of November 16 in her Hermosa Beach, California, apartment.

A. J. Delaney, after a long period of recuperation and emotional therapy, returned to Mississippi State University, where she was selected a member of the homecoming queen's court the following autumn.

Lupita Diaz sold her car in San Diego and disappeared.

Dr. Arthur Morse's Chevette was discovered November 2 on a logging trail north of Silvercat Village. A subsequent search uncovered a series of shallow graves on a nearby knoll. Two of them contained the bones of small dogs. A third held Dr. Morse's body. In the fourth was found decomposed remains identified by a 1961 Colorado driver's license as Daniel Post. Examiners were unable to determine the cause of death definitely, but estimated the body had been in the ground for over twenty years.

Murphy Davis was elected sheriff of Granite County on November 5 and, shortly afterward, underwent knee surgery at Mercy Medical Center in Durango. He was informed by doctors that he'd probably never again play professional football.

Sara Nichols underwent elbow surgery on November 1, also at Mercy Medical, and was informed by doctors that she'd probably never play the violin. She became editor in chief of *The Silvercat Sentinel* the following week and celebrated by taking newly elected Sheriff Murphy Davis, accompanied by various casts and crutches and Glorified Jock, out to dinner, where she finally told him what she had wanted to say to him.

His reply came as no surprise.

DON'T MISS
THESE CURRENT
Bantam Bestsellers

Now there are two great ways to catch up with your favorite thrillers